From the reviews of *Cocaine Nights*:

'It is a rare experience to glance at the publisher's hype on a book sleeve and agree with its claims for the author. But when his publishers describe J.G. Ballard as being "at the forefront of modern British fiction writing for over three decades", whatever your literary taste, this is an incontestable fact. It is also a triumph for the queasy beauty of Ballard's unnerving vision of worlds gone wrong. *Cocaine Nights*, with its seamlessly plotted narrative and heightened naturalism shot with abrupt poetry, offers us a chilling version of the Good Life'

DEBORAH LEVY, *The Times*

'J.G. Ballard is a novelist who is always full of surprises and *Cocaine Nights*, a Goldingesque story of murder on the Costa del Sol, is guaranteed to keep you reading into the early hours'

GEORDIE GREIG, *Sunday Times*

'This is classic Ballard territory, with all the usual stylistic tics and obsessions' NICHOLAS ROYLE, *Guardian*

'Ballard is as thrillingly wired as ever . . . still conjuring up the most dazzlingly original and unsettling images . . . also some stunningly prescient new snapshots from the uniquely wired Ballard mindscape. The future is leisure plus technology and it's not for the squeamish. *Cocaine Nights* is built on a terrific premise and is pitted with stylish detail' NICHOLAS WROE, *Independent*

'One of the most blackly visionary of writers . . . For all their extremes and decadence, his novels are cautionary fables - weird, improbable and sensational, and invariably original. This crazed thriller-turned-parable is yet another instalment in Ballard's apocalyptic race towards a future which has become the present'
EILEEN BATTERSBY, *Irish Times*

'A curious fable . . . It is no exaggeration to describe him as one of Britain's greatest imaginative writers, but he has always occupied his own peculiar niche, just beyond the margins of the literary world' MICK BROWN, *Daily Telegraph*

'On one level this book is a whodunit but, behind the taut, unnerving fiction, Ballard asks worrying and pertinent questions. Are kicks and kinks the only antidote to vegetal channel-zapping?' GEORGE MELLY, *Daily Express*

'That brittle, deviant atmosphere, the sense of morality turned on its head, those casual acts of brutality - long-time J.G. Ballard admirers will be reassured to learn that all the familiar elements of his fiction are clearly in place at the start of *Cocaine Nights* . . . the swiftness of characterisation is unbeatable'
JOHN PRESTON, *Sunday Telegraph*

'There is a lot of sex, violence and drugs and a lot of drugged, violent sex. A page-turner and an occasional stomach-turner . . . As *Cocaine Nights* progresses, it becomes that familiar Ballardian object, a vision of apocalypse'

JOHN SUTHERLAND, *Sunday Times*

'A true master . . . J.G. Ballard is an established maverick English writer - and on this evidence still one of the best we've got . . . a man who can turn a sentence like a Nijinsky pirouette. *Cocaine Nights* is a must for all his fans, most definitely, but also for anyone who wants an exciting, visually brilliant read that makes you think. Top class' BEN DOWELL, *Manchester Evening News*

'J.G. Ballard has always been out on a limb. With his uncompromising style and futuristic visions, he puts other writers in the past tense. *Cocaine Nights* is archetypal Ballard . . . he is as compulsive as ever, writing about the drives of humanity in his inimitable way, always seeing the world too clearly for our own good' ALICE THOMPSON, *Scotsman*

'This is the first book I have read by this prolific and popular author. I am therefore unable to say if this is "vintage" Ballard or a dazzling new departure for him, or indeed just how it fits into the massive and star-spangled Ballard oeuvre. I can only say that it is a wonderfully readable and self-confident book, soothingly written yet brimming over with frightening ideas'

ANDREW BARROW, *Spectator*

'If he has ever written a dud book it has not come my way. Quite aside from its intriguing storyline, *Cocaine Nights* is a brisk and delightful read, not only for its keen irony but also for that visual acuity that seems to set Ballard apart'

DAVID PROFUMO, *Literary Review*

J.G. BALLARD

Cocaine Nights

FOURTH ESTATE • London

Fourth Estate
An imprint of HarperCollins*Publishers*
77-85 Fulham Palace Road
Hammersmith
London W6 8JB

This edition published by Fourth Estate 2010
29

Previously published in paperback by Flamingo 1997 (reprinted 21 times)
and by Harper Perennial 2006 (reprinted 5 times)

First published in hardback in Great Britain by Flamingo 1996

A catalogue record for this book is available from the British Library

ISBN: 978-0-00-655064-8

Typeset in Bembo by
Palimpsest Book Production Limited, Falkirk, Stirlingshire

Printed and bound in Great Britain by Clays Ltd, St Ives plc

Contents

COCAINE NIGHTS

1

Frontiers and Fatalities

CROSSING FRONTIERS is my profession. Those strips of no-man's land between the checkpoints always seem such zones of promise, rich with the possibilities of new lives, new scents and affections. At the same time they set off a reflex of unease that I have never been able to repress. As the customs officials rummage through my suitcases I sense them trying to unpack my mind and reveal a contraband of forbidden dreams and memories. And even then there are the special pleasures of being exposed, which may well have made me a professional tourist. I earn my living as a travel writer, but I accept that this is little more than a masquerade. My real luggage is rarely locked, its catches eager to be sprung.

Gibraltar was no exception, though this time there was a real basis for my feelings of guilt. I had arrived on the morning flight from Heathrow, making my first landing on the military runway that served this last outpost of the British Empire. I had always avoided Gibraltar, with its vague air of a provincial England left out too long in the sun. But my reporter's ears and eyes soon took over, and for an hour I explored the narrow streets with their quaint tea-rooms, camera shops and policemen disguised as London bobbies.

Gilbratar, like the Costa del Sol, was off my beat. I prefer the long-haul flights to Jakarta and Papeete, those hours of club-class air-time that still give me the sense of having a real destination, the great undying illusion of air travel. In fact we sit in a small cinema, watching films as blurred as our hopes of discovering somewhere new. We arrive at an airport identical to the one we left, with the same car-rental agencies and hotel rooms with their adult movie channels and deodorized bathrooms, side-chapels of that lay religion, mass tourism. There are the same bored bar-girls waiting in the restaurant vestibules who later giggle as they play solitaire with our credit cards, tolerant eyes exploring those lines of fatigue in our faces that have nothing to do with age or tiredness.

Gibraltar, though, soon surprised me. The sometime garrison post and naval base was a frontier town, a Macao or Juarez that had decided to make the most of the late twentieth century. At first sight it resembled a seaside resort transported from a stony bay in Cornwall and erected beside the gatepost of the Mediterranean, but its real business clearly had nothing to do with peace, order and the regulation of Her Majesty's waves.

Like any frontier town Gibraltar's main activity, I suspected, was smuggling. As I counted the stores crammed with cut-price video-recorders, and scanned the nameplates of the fringe banks that gleamed in the darkened doorways, I guessed that the economy and civic pride of this geo-political relic were devoted to rooking the Spanish state, to money-laundering and the smuggling of untaxed perfumes and pharmaceuticals.

The Rock was far larger than I expected, sticking up like a thumb, the local sign of the cuckold, in the face of Spain. The raunchy bars had a potent charm, like the speedboats in the harbour, their powerful engines cooling after the latest high-speed run from Morocco. As they rode at anchor I thought of my brother Frank and the family crisis that had brought me to Spain. If the magistrates in Marbella failed to acquit Frank, but released him on bail, one of these sea-skimming craft might rescue him from the medieval constraints of the Spanish legal system.

Later that afternoon I would meet Frank and his lawyer in Marbella, a forty-minute drive up the coast. But when I collected my car from the rental office near the airport I found that an immense traffic jam had closed the border crossing. Hundreds of cars and buses waited in a gritty haze of engine exhaust, while teenaged girls grizzled and their grandmothers shouted at the Spanish soldiers. Ignoring the impatient horns, the Guardia Civil were checking every screw and rivet, officiously searching suitcases and supermarket cartons, peering under bonnets and spare wheels.

'I need to be in Marbella by five,' I told the rental office manager, who was gazing at the stalled vehicles with the serenity of a man about to lease his last car before collecting his pension. 'This traffic jam has a permanent look about it.'

'Calm yourself, Mr Prentice. It can clear at any time, when the Guardia realize how bored they are.'

'All these regulations . . .' I shook my head over the rental agreement. 'Spare bulbs, first-aid kit, fire extinguisher? This Renault is better equipped than the plane that flew me here.'

'You should blame Cadiz. The new Civil Governor is obsessed with La Linea. His workfare schemes are unpopular with the people there.'

'Too bad. So there's a lot of unemployment?'

'Not exactly. Rather too much employment, but of the wrong kind.'

'The smuggling kind? A few cigarettes and camcorders?'

'Not so few. Everyone at La Linea is very happy – they hope that Gibraltar will remain British for ever.'

I had begun to think about Frank, who remained British but in a Spanish cell. As I joined the line of waiting cars I remembered our childhood in Saudi Arabia twenty years earlier, and the arbitrary traffic checks carried out by the religious police in the weeks before Christmas. Not only was the smallest drop of festive alcohol the target of their silky hands, but even a single sheet of seasonal wrapping paper with its sinister emblems of Yule logs, holly and ivy. Frank and I would sit in the back of our father's Chevrolet, clutching the train sets that would be wrapped only minutes before we opened them, while he argued with the police in his sarcastic professorial Arabic, unsettling our nervous mother.

Smuggling was one activity we had practised from an early age. The older boys at the English school in Riyadh talked among themselves about an intriguing netherworld of boot-leg videos, drugs and illicit sex. Later, when we returned to England after our mother's death, I realized that these small conspiracies had kept the British expats together and given them their sense of community. Without the liaisons and con-traband runs our mother would have lost her slipping hold on the world long before the tragic afternoon when she climbed to the roof of the British Institute and made her brief flight to the only safety she could find.

At last the traffic had begun to move, lurching forward in a noisy rush. But the mud-stained van in front of me was still detained by the Guardia Civil. A soldier opened the rear doors and hunted through cardboard cartons filled with plastic dolls. His heavy hands fumbled among the pinkly naked bodies, watched by hundreds of rocking blue eyes.

Irritated by the delay, I was tempted to drive around the van. Behind me a handsome Spanish woman sat at the wheel of an open-topped Mercedes, remaking her lipstick over a strong mouth designed for any activity other than eating. Intrigued by her lazy sexual confidence, I smiled as she fingered her mascara and lightly brushed the undersides of her eyelashes like an indolent lover. Who was she – a nightclub cashier, a property tycoon's mistress, or a local prostitute returning to La Linea with a fresh stock of condoms and sex aids?

She noticed me watching her in my rear-view mirror and snapped down her sun vizor, waking both of us from this dream of herself. She swung the steering wheel and pulled out to pass me, baring her strong teeth as she slipped below a no-entry sign.

I started my engine and was about to follow her, but the soldier fumbling among the plastic dolls turned to bellow at me.

'*Acceso prohibido . . .*!'

He leaned against my windshield, a greasy hand smearing the glass, and saluted the young woman, who was turning into the police car park beside the checkpoint. He glared down at me, nodding to himself and clearly convinced that he had caught a lecherous tourist in the act of visually molesting the wife of his commanding officer. He moodily flicked through the pages of my passport, unimpressed by the gallery of customs stamps and visas from the remotest corners of the globe. Each frontier crossing was a unique transaction that defused the magic of any other.

I waited for him to order me from the car and carry out an aggressive body-search, before settling down to dismantle the entire Renault until it lay beside the road like a manufacturer's display kit. But he had lost interest in me, his spare eye noticing a coach filled with migrant Moroccan workers who had taken the ferry from Tangier. Abandoning his search of the van and its cargo of dolls, he advanced upon the stoical Arabs with all the menace and dignity of Rodrigo Diaz out-staring the Moors at the Battle of Valencia.

I followed the van as it sped towards La Linea, rear doors swinging and the dolls dancing together with their feet in the air. Even the briefest confrontation with police at a border crossing had the same disorienting effect on me. I imagined Frank in the interrogation cells in Marbella at that very moment, faced with the same accusing eyes and the same

13

assumption of guilt. I was a virtually innocent traveller, carrying no contraband other than a daydream of smuggling my brother across the Spanish frontier, yet I felt as uneasy as a prisoner breaking his parole, and I knew how Frank would have responded to the trumped-up charges that had led to his arrest at the Club Nautico in Estrella de Mar. I was certain of his innocence and guessed that he had been framed on the orders of some corrupt police chief who had tried to extort a bribe.

I left the eastern outskirts of La Linea and set off along the coast road towards Sotogrande, impatient to see Frank and reassure him that all would be well. The call from David Hennessy, the retired Lloyd's underwriter who was now the treasurer of the Club Nautico, had reached me in my Barbican flat the previous evening. Hennessy had been disturbingly vague, as if rambling to himself after too much sun and sangria, the last person to inspire confidence.

'It does look rather bad . . . Frank told me not to worry you, but I felt I had to call.'

'Thank God you did. Is he actually under arrest? Have you told the British Consul in Marbella?'

'Malaga, yes. The Consul's closely involved. It's an important case, I'm surprised you didn't read about it.'

'I've been abroad. I haven't seen an English paper for weeks. In Lhasa there's not much demand for news about the Costa del Sol.'

'I dare say. The Fleet Street reporters were all over the club. We had to close the bar, you know.'

'Never mind the bar!' I tried to get a grip on the conversation. 'Is Frank all right? Where are they holding him?'

'He's fine. On the whole he's taking it well. He's very quiet, though that's understandable. He has a lot to think over.'

'But what are the charges? Mr Hennessy . . . ?'

'Charges?' There was a pause as ice-cubes rattled. 'There seem to be a number. The Spanish prosecutor is drawing up the articles of accusation. We'll have to wait for them to be translated. I'm afraid the police aren't being very helpful.'

'Do you expect them to be? It sounds like a frame-up.'

'It's not as simple as that . . . one has to see it in context. I think you should come down here as soon as you can.'

Hennessy had been professionally vague, presumably to protect the Club Nautico, one of the more exclusive sports complexes on the Costa del Sol, which no doubt depended for its security on regular cash disbursements to the local constabulary. I could well imagine Frank, in his quizzical way, forgetting to slip the padded manila envelope into the right hands, curious to see what might result, or omitting to offer his best suite to a visiting commandant of police.

Parking fines, building-code infringements, an illegally-sited swimming pool, perhaps the innocent purchase from a dodgy dealer of a stolen Range Rover – any of these could have led to his arrest. I sped along the open road towards Sotogrande, as a sluggish sea lapped at the chocolate sand of the deserted beaches. The coastal strip was a nondescript plain of market gardens, tractor depots and villa projects. I passed a half-completed Aquapark, its excavated lakes like lunar craters, and a disused nightclub on an artificial hill, the domed roof resembling a small observatory.

The mountains had withdrawn from the sea, keeping their distance a mile inland. Near Sotogrande the golf courses began to multiply like the symptoms of a hypertrophied grassland cancer. White-walled Andalucian pueblos presided over the greens and fairways, fortified villages guarding their pastures, but in fact these miniature townships were purpose-built villa complexes financed by Swiss and German property speculators, the winter homes not of local shepherds but of Düsseldorf ad-men and Zürich television executives.

Along most of the Mediterranean's resort coasts the mountains came down to the sea, as at the Côte d'Azur or the Ligurian Riviera near Genoa, and the tourist towns nestled in sheltered bays. But the Costa del Sol lacked even the rudiments of scenic or architectural charm. Sotogrande, I discovered, was a town without either centre or suburbs, and seemed to be little more than a dispersal ground for golf courses and swimming pools. Three miles to its east I passed an elegant apartment building standing on a scrubby bend of the coastal road, the mock-Roman columns and white porticos apparently imported from Las Vegas after a hotel clearance sale, reversing the export to Florida and California in the 1920s of dismantled Spanish monasteries and Sardinian abbeys.

The Estepona road skirted a private airstrip beside an imposing villa with gilded finials like a castellated fairy battlement. Their shadows curved around a white onion-bulb roof, an invasion of a new Arab architecture that owed nothing to the Maghreb across the Strait of Gibraltar. The brassy glimmer belonged to the desert kingdoms of the Persian Gulf, reflected through the garish mirrors of Hollywood design studios, and I thought of the oil company atrium in Dubai that I had walked through a month earlier, pursuing my courtship of an attractive French geologist I was profiling for *L'Express*.

'The architecture of brothels?' she commented when I told her of my longstanding plans for a book during our rooftop lunch. 'It's a good idea. Rather close to your heart, I should think.' She pointed to the retina-stunning panorama around us. 'It's all here for you, Charles. Filling-stations disguised as cathedrals . . .'

Could Frank, with his scruples and finicky honesty, have chosen to break the law on the Costa del Sol, a zone as depthless as a property developer's brochure? I approached the outskirts of Marbella, past King Saud's larger-than-life replica of the White House and the Aladdin's cave apartments of Puerto Banus. Unreality thrived on every side, a magnet to the unwary. But Frank was too fastidious, too amused by his own weaknesses, to commit himself to any serious misdemeanour. I remembered his compulsive stealing after we returned to England, slipping corkscrews and cans of anchovies into his pockets as we trailed after our aunt through the Brighton supermarkets. Our grieving father, taking up his professorial chair at Sussex University, was too distracted to think of Frank, and the petty thefts forced me to adopt him as my little son, the sole person concerned enough to care for this numbed nine-year-old, even if only to scold him.

Luckily, Frank soon outgrew this childhood tic. At school he became a wristy and effective tennis player, and sidestepped the academic career his father wanted for him, taking a course in hotel management. After three years as assistant manager of a renovated art deco hotel in South Miami Beach he returned to Europe to run the Club Nautico at Estrella de Mar, a peninsular resort twenty miles to the east of Marbella. Whenever we met in London I liked to tease him about his exile to this curious world of Arab princes, retired gangsters and Eurotrash.

'Frank, of all the places to pick you choose the Costa del Sol!' I would exclaim. 'Estrella de Mar? I can't even imagine it . . .'

Amiably, Frank always replied: 'Exactly, Charles. It doesn't really exist. That's why I like the coast. I've been looking for it all my life. Estrella de Mar isn't anywhere.'

But now nowhere had at last caught up with him.

When I reached the Los Monteros Hotel, a ten-minute drive down the coast from Marbella, there was a message waiting for me. Señor Danvila, Frank's lawyer, had called from the magistrates' court with news of 'unexpected developments', and asked me to join him as soon as possible. The over-polite manners of the hotel manager and the averted eyes of the concierge and porters suggested that whatever these developments might be, they were fully expected. Even the players returning from the tennis courts and the couples in towelling robes on their way to the swimming pools paused to let me pass, as if sensing that I had come to share my brother's fate.

When I returned to the lobby after a shower and change of clothes the concierge had already called a taxi.

'Mr Prentice, it will be simpler than taking your own car. Parking is difficult in Marbella. You have enough problems to consider.'

'You've heard about the case?' I asked. 'Did you speak to my brother's lawyer?'

'Of course not, sir. There were some accounts in the local press . . . a few television reports.'

He seemed anxious to steer me to the waiting taxi. I scanned the headlines in the display of newspapers beside the desk.

'What exactly happened? No one seems to know.'

'It's not certain, Mr Prentice.' The concierge straightened his magazines, trying to hide from me any edition that might reveal the full story of Frank's involvement. 'It's best that you take your taxi. All will be clear to you in Marbella . . .'

Señor Danvila was waiting for me in the entrance hall of the magistrates' court. A tall, slightly stooped man in his late fifties, he carried two briefcases which he shuffled from hand to hand, and resembled a distracted schoolmaster who had lost control of his class. He greeted me with evident relief, holding on to my arm as if to reassure himself that I too was now part of the confused world into which Frank had drawn him. I liked his concerned manner, but his real attention seemed elsewhere, and already I wondered why David Hennessy had hired him.

'Mr Prentice, I'm most grateful that you came. Unfortunately, events are now more . . . ambiguous. If I can explain –'

'Where is Frank? I'd like to see him. I want you to arrange bail – I can provide whatever guarantees the court requires. Señor Danvila . . . ?'

With an effort the lawyer uncoupled his eyes from some feature of my face that seemed to distract him, an echo perhaps of one of Frank's more cryptic expressions. Seeing a group of Spanish photographers on the steps of the court, he beckoned me towards an alcove. 'Your brother is here, until they return him to Zarzuella jail in Malaga this evening. The police investigation is proceeding. I am afraid that in the circumstances bail is out of the question.'

'What circumstances? I want to see Frank now. Surely the Spanish magistrates release people on bail?'

'Not in a case such as this.' Señor Danvila hummed to himself, switching his briefcases in an unending attempt to decide which was the heavier. 'You will see your brother in an hour, perhaps less. I have spoken to Inspector Cabrera. Afterwards he will want to question you about certain details possibly known to you, but there is nothing to fear.'

'I'm glad to hear it. Now, what will they charge Frank with?'

'He has already been charged.' Señor Danvila was staring fixedly at me. 'It's a tragic affair, Mr Prentice, the very worst.'

'But charged with what? Currency violations, tax problems . . . ?'

'More serious than that. There were fatalities.'

Señor Danvila's face had come into sudden focus, his eyes swimming forwards through the thick pools of his lenses. I noticed that he had shaved carelessly that morning, too preoccupied to trim his straggling moustache.

'Fatalities?' It occurred to me that a cruel accident had taken place on the notorious coastal road, and perhaps had involved Frank in the deaths of Spanish children. 'Was there a traffic accident? How many people were killed?'

'Five.' Señor Danvila's lips moved as he counted the number, a total that exceeded all the possibilities of a humane mathematics. 'It was not a traffic accident.'

'Then what? How did they die?'

'They were murdered, Mr Prentice.' The lawyer spoke matter-of-factly, detaching himself from the significance of his own words. 'Five people were deliberately killed. Your brother has been charged with their deaths.'

'I can't believe it . . .' I turned to stare at the photographers arguing with each other on the steps of the courthouse. Despite Señor Danvila's solemn expression, I felt a sudden rush of relief. I realized that a preposterous error had been made, an investigative and judicial bungle that involved this nervous lawyer, the heavy-footed local police and the incompetent magistrates of the Costa del Sol, their reflexes confused by years of coping with drunken British tourists. 'Señor Danvila, you say Frank murdered five people. How, for heaven's sake?'

'He set fire to their house. Two weeks ago – it was clearly an act of premeditation. The magistrates and police have no doubt.'

'Well, they should have.' I laughed to myself, confident now that this absurd error would soon be rectified. 'Where did these murders take place?'

'At Estrella de Mar. In the villa of the Hollinger family.'

'And who were the victims?'

'Mr Hollinger, his wife, and their niece. As well, a young maid and the male secretary.'

'It's madness.' I held Danvila's briefcases before he could weigh them again. 'Why would Frank want to murder them? Let me see him. He'll deny it.'

'No, Mr Prentice.' Señor Danvila stepped back from me, the verdict already clear in his mind. 'Your brother has not denied the accusations. In fact, he has pleaded guilty to five charges of murder. I repeat, Mr Prentice – guilty.'

2

The Fire at the Hollinger House

'CHARLES? DANVILA TOLD ME you'd arrived. It's good of
you. I knew you'd come.'

Frank rose from his chair as I entered the interview room.
He seemed slimmer and older than I remembered, and the
strong fluorescent light gave his skin a pallid sheen. He peered
over my shoulder, as if expecting to see someone else, and
then lowered his eyes to avoid my gaze.

'Frank – you're all right?' I leaned across the table, hoping
to shake his hand, but the policeman standing between us
raised his arm with the stiff motion of a turnstile bar. 'Danvila's
explained the whole thing to me; it's obviously some sort of
crazy mistake. I'm sorry I wasn't in court.'

'You're here now. That's all that matters.' Frank rested his
elbows on the table, trying to hide his fatigue. 'How was the
flight?'

'Late – airlines run on their own time, two hours behind
everyone else's. I rented a car in Gibraltar. Frank, you look . . .'

'I'm fine.' With an effort he composed himself, and managed a brief but troubled smile. 'So, what did you think of
Gib?'

'I was only there for a few minutes. Odd little place – not
as strange as this coast.'

'You should have come here years ago. You'll find a lot to
write about.'

'I already have. Frank –'

'It's interesting, Charles . . .' Frank sat forward, talking too quickly to listen to himself, keen to sidetrack our conversation. 'You've got to spend more time here. It's Europe's future. Everywhere will be like this soon.'

'I hope not. Listen, I've talked to Danvila. He's trying to get the court hearing annulled. I didn't grasp all the legal ins and outs, but there's a chance of a new hearing when you change your plea. You'll claim some sort of mitigating factor. You were distraught with grief, and didn't catch what the translator was saying. At the least it puts down a marker.'

'Danvila, yes . . .' Frank played with his cigarette packet. 'Sweet man, I think I've rather shocked him. And you, too, I dare say.'

The friendly but knowing smile had reappeared, and he leaned back with his hands behind his head, confident now that he could cope with my visit. Already we were assuming our familiar roles first set out in childhood. He was the imaginative and wayward spirit, and I was the stolid older brother who had yet to get the joke. In Frank's eyes I had always been the source of a certain fond amusement.

He was dressed in a grey suit and white shirt open at the neck. Seeing that I had noticed his bare throat, he covered his chin with a hand.

'They took my tie away from me – I'm only allowed to wear it in court. A bit noose-like, when you think about it – could put ideas into the judge's mind. They fear I might try to kill myself.'

'But, Frank, isn't that what you're doing? Why on earth did you plead guilty?'

'Charles . . .' He gestured a little wearily. 'I had to, there wasn't anything else I could say.'

'That's absurd. You had nothing to do with those deaths.'

'But I did. Charles, I did.'

23

'You started the fire? Tell me, no one can hear this – you actually set the Hollinger house ablaze?'

'Yes . . . in effect.' He took a cigarette from the packet and waited as the policeman stepped forward to light it. The flame flared under the worn hood of the brass lighter, and Frank stared at the burning vapour before drawing on the cigarette. In the brief glow his face seemed calm and resigned.

'Frank, look at me.' I waved the smoke aside, a swirling wraith released from his lungs. 'I want to hear you say it – you, yourself, personally set fire to the Hollinger house?'

'I've said so.'

'Using a bomb filled with ether and petrol?'

'Yes. Don't ever try it. The mixture's surprisingly flammable.'

'I don't believe it. Why, for God's sake? Frank . . . !'

He blew a smoke ring towards the ceiling, and then spoke in a quiet and almost flat voice. 'You'd have to live for a while at Estrella de Mar even to begin to understand. Take it from me, if I explained what happened it would mean nothing to you. It's a different world, Charles. This isn't Bangkok or some atoll in the Maldives.'

'Try me. Are you covering up for someone?'

'Why should I?'

'And you knew the Hollingers?'

'I knew them well.'

'Danvila says he was some sort of film tycoon in the 1960s.'

'In a small way. Property dealing and office development in the City. His wife was one of the last of the Rank Charm School starlets. They retired here about twenty years ago.'

'They were regulars at the Club Nautico?'

'They weren't regulars, strictly speaking. They dropped in now and then.'

'And you were there on the evening of the fire? You were in the house?'

'Yes! You're starting to sound like Cabrera. The last thing an interrogator wants is the truth.' Frank crushed his cigarette in the ashtray, briefly burning his fingers. 'Look, I'm sorry they died. It was a tragic business.'

His closing words were spoken without emphasis, in the tone he had used one day as a ten-year-old when he had come in from the garden and told me that his pet turtle had died. I knew that he was now telling the truth.

'They're taking you back to Malaga tonight,' I said. 'I'll visit you there as soon as I can.'

'It's always good to see you, Charles.' He managed to clasp my hand before the policeman stepped forward. 'You looked after me when Mother died and in a way you're still looking after me. How long are you staying?'

'A week. I should be in Helsinki for some TV documentary. But I'll be back.'

'Always roaming the world. All that endless travelling, all those departure lounges. Do you ever actually arrive anywhere?'

'It's hard to tell – sometimes I think I've made jet-lag into a new philosophy. It's the nearest we can get to penitence.'

'And what about your book on the great brothels of the world? Have you started it yet?'

'I'm still doing the research.'

'I remember you talking about that at school. You used to say your only interests in life were opium and brothels. Pure Graham Greene, but there was always something heroic there. Do you smoke a few pipes?'

'Now and then.'

'Don't worry, I won't tell Father. How is the old chap?'

'We've moved him to a smaller nursing home. He doesn't recognize me now. When you get out of here you must see him. I think he'd remember you.'

'I never liked him, you know.'

'He's a child, Frank. He's forgotten everything. All he does is dribble and doze.'

Frank leaned back, smiling at the ceiling as his memories played across the grey distemper. 'We used to steal – do you remember? Strange that – it all started in Riyadh when Mother fell ill. I was snatching anything I could lay my hands on. You joined in to make me feel better.'

'Frank, it was a phase. Everyone understood.'

'Except Father. He couldn't cope when Mother lost control. He started that weird affair with his middle-aged secretary.'

'The poor man was desperate.'

'He blamed you for my stealing. He'd find my pockets full of candy I'd pinched from the Riyadh Hilton and then accuse you.'

'I was older. He thought I could have stopped you. He knew I envied you.'

'Mother was drinking herself to death and no one was doing anything about it. Stealing was the only way I could make sense of how guilty I felt. Then she started those long walks in the middle of the night and you'd go with her. Where exactly? I always wondered.'

'Nowhere. We just walked around the tennis court. Rather like my life now.'

'Probably gave you a taste for it. That's why you're nervous of putting down roots. You know, Estrella de Mar is as close to Saudi as you can get. Maybe that's why I came here . . .'

He stared bleakly at the table, for the moment depressed by all these memories. Ignoring the policeman, I reached across the table and held his shoulders, trying to calm the trembling collarbones. He met my eyes, glad to see me, his smile stripped of irony.

'Frank . . . ?'

'It's all right.' He sat up, brightening himself. 'How is Esther, by the way? I should have asked.'

'She's fine. We split up three months ago.'

'I'm sorry. I always liked her. Rather high-minded in an unusual way. She once asked me a lot of strange questions about pornography. Nothing to do with you.'

'She took up gliding last summer, spent her weekends soaring over the South Downs. A sign, I guess, that she wanted to leave me. Now she and her women friends fly to competitions in Australia and New Mexico. I think of her up there, alone with all that silence.'

'You'll meet someone else.'

'Maybe . . .'

The policeman opened the door and stood with his back to us, calling across the corridor to an officer sitting at a desk. I leaned over the table, speaking quickly. 'Frank, listen. If Danvila can get you out on bail there's a chance I can arrange something.'

'What exactly? Charles?'

'I'm thinking of Gibraltar . . .' The policeman had resumed his watch over us. 'You know the special skills there. This whole business is preposterous. It's obvious you didn't kill the Hollingers.'

'That's not quite true.' Frank drew away from me, the defensive smile on his lips again. 'It's hard to believe, but I am guilty.'

'Don't talk like that!' Impatient with him, I knocked his cigarettes to the floor, where they lay beside the policeman's feet. 'Say nothing to Danvila about the Gibraltar thing. Once we get you back to England you'll be able to clear yourself.'

'Charles . . . I can only clear myself here.'

'But at least you'll be out of jail and safe somewhere.'

'Somewhere with no extradition treaty for murder?' Frank stood up and pushed his chair against the table. 'You'll have to take me with you on your trips. We'll travel the world together. I'd like that . . .'

The policeman waited for me to leave, carrying my chair to the wall. Frank embraced me and stood back, still smiling his quirky smile. He picked up his cigarettes and nodded to me.

'Believe me, Charles, I belong here.'

3

The Tennis Machine

BUT FRANK DID NOT belong there. As I left the driveway of the Los Monteros Hotel, joining the coast road to Malaga, I drummed the steering wheel so fiercely that I drew blood from a thumbnail. Neon signs lined the verge, advertising the beach bars, fish restaurants and nightclubs under the pine trees, a barrage of signals that almost drowned the shrill tocsin sounding from the magistrates' court in Marbella.

Frank was innocent, as virtually everyone involved in the murder investigation accepted. His plea of guilty was a charade, part of some bizarre game he was playing against himself, in which even the police were reluctant to join. They had held Frank for a week before bringing their charges, a sure sign that they were suspicious of the confession, as Inspector Cabrera revealed after my meeting with Frank.

If Señor Danvila was the old Spain – measured, courtly and reflective – Cabrera was the new. A product of the Madrid police academy, he seemed more like a young college professor than a detective, a hundred seminars on the psychology of crime still fresh in his mind. At ease with himself in his business suit, he contrived to be tough and likeable, without ever lowering his guard. He welcomed me to his office and then came straight to the point. He asked me about Frank's childhood, and whether he had shown an overlit imagination as a boy.

'Perhaps a special talent for fantasy? Often a troubled

childhood can lead to the creation of imaginary worlds. Was your brother a lonely child, Mr Prentice, left by himself while you played with the older boys?'

'No, he was never lonely. In fact, he had more friends than I did. He was always good at games, very practical and down-to-earth. I was the one with the imagination.'

'A useful gift for a travel writer,' Cabrera commented as he flicked through my passport. 'Perhaps as a boy your brother displayed a strain of would-be sainthood, taking the blame for you and his friends?'

'No, there was nothing saintly about him, not remotely. When he played tennis he was fast on his feet and always wanted to win.' Sensing that Cabrera was more thoughtful than most of the policemen I had met, I decided to speak my mind. 'Inspector, can we be open with each other? Frank is innocent, you and I both know that he never committed these murders. I've no idea why he confessed, but he must be under some secret pressure. Or be covering up for someone. If we don't find the truth the Spanish courts will be responsible for a tragic miscarriage of justice.'

Cabrera watched me, waiting silently for my moral indignation to disperse with the rising smoke of his cigarette. He waved one hand, clearing the air between us.

'Mr Prentice, the Spanish judges, like their English colleagues, are not concerned with truth – they leave that to a far higher court. They deal with the balance of probabilities on the basis of available evidence. The case will be investigated most carefully, and in due course your brother will be brought to trial. All you can do is wait for the verdict.'

'Inspector . . .' I made an effort to restrain myself. 'Frank may have pleaded guilty, but that doesn't mean he actually committed these appalling crimes. This whole thing is a farce, of a very sinister kind.'

'Mr Prentice . . .' Cabrera stood up and moved away from his desk, gesturing at the wall as if outlining a proposition on a blackboard before a slow-witted class. 'Let me remind you that five people were burned to death, killed by the most cruel means. Your brother insists he is responsible. Some, like yourself and the English newspapers, think that he insists too loudly, and must therefore be innocent. In fact, his plea of guilty may be a clever device, an attempt to unfoot us all, like a . . .'

'Drop-shot at the net?'

'Exactly. A clever stratagem. At first, I also had certain doubts, but I have to tell you that I'm now inclined to think of your brother and guilt in the same context.' Cabrera gazed wanly at my passport photograph, as if trying to read some guilt of my own into the garish photo-booth snapshot. 'Meanwhile, the investigation proceeds. You have been more helpful than you know.'

After leaving the magistrates' court Señor Danvila and I walked down the hill towards the old town. This small enclave behind the beachfront hotels was a lavishly restored theme village with mock-Andalucian streets, antique shops and café tables set out under the orange trees. Surrounded by a stage set, we silently sipped our iced coffees and watched the proprietor scatter a kettle of boiling water over the feral cats that plagued his customers.

This scalding douche, another stroke of cruel injustice, promptly set me off again. Señor Danvila heard me out, nodding mournfully at the oranges above my head as I repeated my arguments. I sensed that he wanted to take my hand, concerned as much for me as he was for Frank, aware that my brother's plea of guilty also involved me in some obscure way.

He agreed, almost casually, that Frank was innocent, as the police's delay in charging him tacitly admitted.

'But now the momentum for conviction will increase,' he warned me. 'The courts and police have good reason not to challenge a guilty plea – it saves them work.'

'Even though they know they have the wrong man?'

Señor Danvila raised his eyes to the sky. 'They may know it now, but in three or four months, when your brother comes to trial? Self-admitted guilt is a concept they find very easy to live with. Files can be closed, men reassigned. I extend my sympathies to you, Mr Prentice.'

'But Frank may go to prison for the next twenty years. Surely the police will go on looking for the real culprit?'

'What could they find? Remember, the conviction of a British expatriate avoids the possibility of a Spaniard being accused. Tourism is vital for Andalucia – this is one of Spain's poorest regions. Inward investors are less concerned by crimes among tourists.'

I pushed away my coffee glass. 'Frank is still your client, Señor Danvila. Who did kill those five people? We know Frank wasn't responsible. Someone must have started the fire.'

But Danvila made no reply. With his gentle hands he broke his tapas and threw the pieces to the waiting cats.

If not Frank, then who? Given that the police had ended their investigation, it fell to me to recruit a more aggressive Spanish lawyer than the depressed and ineffective Danvila, and perhaps hire a firm of British private detectives to root out the truth. I drove along the coast road to Malaga, past the white-walled retirement complexes marooned like icebergs among the golf courses, and reminded myself that I knew almost nothing about Estrella de Mar, the resort where the deaths had occurred. Frank had sent me a series of postcards from the

Club, which portrayed a familiar world of squash courts, jacuzzis and plunge-pools, but I had only the haziest notions of day-to-day life among the British who had settled the coast.

Five people had died in the catastrophic fire that had gutted the Hollinger house. The fierce blaze had erupted without warning about seven o'clock in the evening of 15 June, by coincidence the Queen's official birthday. Clutching at straws, I remembered the disagreeable Guardia Civil at Gibraltar and speculated that the fire had been started by a deranged Spanish policeman protesting at Britain's occupation of the Rock. I imagined a burning taper hurled over the high walls on to the tinder-dry roof of the villa . . .

But in fact the fire had been ignited by an arsonist who had entered the mansion and begun his murderous work on the staircase. Three empty bottles containing residues of ether and gasoline were found in the kitchen. A fourth, half-empty, was in my brother's hands while he waited to surrender to the police. A fifth, filled to the brim and plugged with one of Frank's tennis club ties, lay on the rear seat of his car in a side-street a hundred yards from the house.

The Hollingers' mansion, Cabrera told me, was one of the oldest properties at Estrella de Mar, its timbers and roof joists dried like biscuit by a hundred summers. I thought of the elderly couple who had retreated from London to the peace of this retirement coast. It was hard to imagine anyone finding the energy, let alone the necessary malice, to bring about their deaths. Steeped in sun and sundowners, wandering the golf greens by day and dozing in front of their satellite television in the evening, the residents of the Costa del Sol lived in an eventless world.

As I neared Estrella de Mar the residential complexes stood shoulder to shoulder along the beach. The future had come ashore here, lying down to rest among the pines. The white-walled pueblos remained me of my visit to Arcosanti, Paolo

Soleri's outpost of the day after tomorrow in the Arizona desert. The cubist apartments and terraced houses resembled Arcosanti's, their architecture dedicated to the abolition of time, as befitted the ageing population of the retirement havens and an even wider world waiting to be old.

Searching for the turn-off to Estrella de Mar, I left the Malaga highway and found myself in a maze of slip-roads that fed the pueblos. Trying to orientate myself, I pulled into the forecourt of a filling-station. While a young Frenchwoman topped up my tank I strolled past the supermarket that shared the forecourt, where elderly women in fluffy towelling suits drifted like clouds along the lines of ice-cold merchandise.

I climbed a pathway of blue tiles to a grass knoll and looked down on an endless terrain of picture windows, patios and miniature pools. Together they had a curiously calming effect, as if these residential compounds – British, Dutch and German – were a series of psychological pens that soothed and domesticated these émigré populations. I sensed that the Costa del Sol, like the retirement coasts of Florida, the Caribbean and the Hawaiian islands, had nothing to do with travel or recreation, but formed a special kind of willed limbo.

Although seemingly deserted, the pueblos contained more residents than I first assumed. A middle-aged couple sat on a balcony thirty feet from me, the woman holding an unread book in her hands as her husband stared at the surface of the swimming pool, whose reflection dressed the walls of a nearby apartment house with bands of gold light. Almost invisible at first glance, people sat on their terraces and patios, gazing at an unseen horizon like figures in the paintings of Edward Hopper.

Already thinking of a travel article, I noted the features of this silent world: the memory-erasing white architecture; the enforced leisure that fossilized the nervous system; the almost Africanized aspect, but a North Africa invented by someone who had never visited the Maghreb; the apparent absence of any social structure; the timelessness of a world beyond boredom, with no past, no future and a diminishing present. Perhaps this was what a leisure-dominated future would resemble? Nothing could ever happen in this affectless realm, where entropic drift calmed the surfaces of a thousand swimming pools.

I returned to my car, reassured by the distant sounds of the coastal highway. Following the Frenchwoman's instructions, I found my way back to the Malaga signpost and rejoined the motorway, which soon skirted an ochre beach and revealed a handsome peninsula of iron-rich rock.

This was Estrella de Mar, as generously wooded and landscaped as Cap d'Antibes. There was a harbour lined with bars and restaurants, a crescent of imported white sand, and a marina filled with racing yachts and cruisers. Comfortable villas stood behind the palms and eucalyptus trees, and above them was the liner-like prow of the Club Nautico, topped by its white satellite dish.

Then, as the motorway turned through the coastal pines, I saw the gutted eminence of the Hollinger mansion on its hill above the town, the charred roofing timbers like the remains of a funeral pyre on a Central American mesa. The smoke and intense heat had blackened the walls, as if this doomed house had tried to camouflage itself against the night to come.

Traffic overtook me, speeding towards the hotel towers of Fuengirola. I turned off on to the Estrella de Mar slip-road and entered a narrow gorge cut through the porphyry rock of the headland. Within four hundred yards I reached the wooded neck of the peninsula, where the first villas stood behind their lacquered gates.

Purpose-built in the 1970s by a consortium of Anglo-Dutch developers, Estrella de Mar was a residential retreat for the professional classes of northern Europe. The resort had turned its back on mass tourism, and there were none of the skyscraper blocks that rose from the water's edge at Benalmadena and Torremolinos. The old town by the harbour had been pleasantly bijouized, the fishermen's cottages converted to wine bars and antique shops

Taking the road that led to the Club Nautico, I passed an elegant tea salon, a bureau de change decorated with Tudor half-timbering, and a boutique whose demure window displayed a solitary but exquisite designer gown. I waited as a van emblazoned with *trompe-l'œil* traffic scenes reversed into the courtyard of a sculpture studio. A strong-shouldered woman with Germanic features, blonde hair pinned behind her neck, supervised two teenaged boys as they began to unload butts of modelling clay.

Within the open studio half a dozen artists worked at their sculpture tables, smocks protecting their beach clothes. A handsome Spanish youth, heavy genitals scarcely contained by his posing pouch, stood with sullen grace on a podium as the sculptors – every one an amateur, judging by their earnest manner – massaged their clay into a likeness of his thighs and torso. Their burly instructor, a ponytailed Vulcan at his forge, moved among them, tweaking a navel with a stubby forefinger or smoothing a furrowed brow.

Estrella de Mar, I soon discovered, had a thriving arts community. In the narrow streets above the harbour a parade of commercial galleries showed the latest work of the resort's painters and designers. A nearby arts and crafts centre displayed a selection of modernist costume jewellery, ceramic wares and textiles. The local artists – all, I assumed from their parked Mercedes and Range Rovers, residents of nearby villas – sat behind their trestle tables like Saturday vendors in the Portobello Road, their confident voices ringing with the accents of Holland Park and the Sixteenth Arrondissement.

Everyone in the town seemed alert and confident. Customers crowded the bookshops and music stores, or scrutinized the racks of foreign newspapers outside the *tabacs*. An adolescent girl in a white bikini crossed the street at the traffic lights, a violin case in one hand, a hamburger in the other.

Estrella de Mar, I decided, possessed far more attractions than I had guessed when Frank first arrived to manage the Club Nautico. The monoculture of sun and sangria that becalmed the pueblo residents had no place in this vibrant little enclave, which seemed to combine the best features of Bel Air and the Left Bank. Opposite the gates of the Club Nautico was an open-air cinema with an amphitheatre carved from the hillside. A placard by the ticket kiosk advertised a season of Katharine Hepburn and Spencer Tracy films, the very height of intellectual chic of a certain kind.

The Club Nautico was quiet and cool, its afternoon trade yet to appear. Sprinklers rotated over the crisp lawns, and beside the deserted restaurant terrace the surface of the pool was smooth enough to walk upon. A single player was practising on one of the hard courts with a tennis machine, and the clunk-clunk of the bounding balls was the only sound to disturb the air.

I crossed the terrace and entered the bar at the rear of the restaurant. A blond steward with a babyish face and a sail-rigger's shoulders was folding paper napkins into miniature yachts, origami decorations for the peanut saucers.

'Are you a guest, sir?' He grinned cheerfully. 'I'm afraid the club is closed to non-members.'

'I'm not a guest – or a non-member, whatever strange form of life that is.' I sat down on a stool and helped myself to a few nuts. 'I'm Frank Prentice's brother. I think he was the manager here.'

'Of course . . . Mr Prentice.' He hesitated, as if faced with an

apparition, and then eagerly shook my hand. 'Sonny Gardner –
I crew on Frank's thirty-footer. By the way, he still is the
manager.'

'Good. He'll be glad to hear that.'

'How is Frank? We're all thinking about him.'

'He's fine. I met him yesterday. We had a long and interesting talk together.'

'Everyone hopes you can help Frank. The Club Nautico
needs him.'

'That's fighting talk. Now, I'd like to see his apartment.
There are personal things I want to collect for him. I take it
someone has the keys?'

'You'll have to speak to Mr Hennessy, the club treasurer.
He'll be back in half an hour. I know he wants to help Frank.
We're all doing everything we can.'

I watched him delicately fold the paper yachts with his
calloused hands. His voice had sounded sincere but curiously
distant, lines from a previous week's play spoken by a distracted
actor. Turning on my stool, I gazed across the swimming pool.
In its glassy surface I could see the reflection of the Hollinger
house, a sunken fire-ship that seemed to rest on the tiled floor.

'You had a grandstand view,' I commented. 'It must have
been quite a spectacle.'

'View, Mr Prentice?' Lines creased Sonny Gardner's baby-
smooth forehead. 'What of, sir?'

'The fire at the big house. Did you watch it from here?'

'No one did. The club was closed.'

'On the Queen's birthday? I would have thought you'd be
open all night.' I reached out and took the paper yacht from
his fingers, examining its intricate folds. 'One thing puzzles
me – I was at the magistrates' court in Marbella yesterday. No
one from Estrella de Mar turned up. None of Frank's friends,
no character witnesses, no one who worked for him. Just an
elderly Spanish lawyer who's given up hope.'

'Mr Prentice . . .' Gardner tried to fold the paper triangle when I returned it to him, then crushed it between his hands. 'Frank didn't expect us there. In fact, he told Mr Hennessy that he wanted us to stay away. Besides, he pleaded guilty.'

'But you don't believe that?'

'Nobody does. But . . . a guilty plea. It's hard to argue with.'

'Too true. Then tell me – if Frank didn't set fire to the Hollinger house, who did?'

'Who knows?' Gardner glanced over my shoulder, eager for Hennessy to appear. 'Maybe nobody did.'

'That's hard to believe. It was a clear case of arson.'

I waited for Gardner to reply, but he merely smiled at me, the reassuring smile of professional sympathy reserved for the bereaved at funeral chapels. He seemed unaware that his fingers were no longer folding the paper napkins into his miniature flotilla, but had started to unwrap and smooth the triangular sails. As I walked away he leaned over his little fleet like an infant Cyclops, and called out to me in a hopeful voice: 'Mr Prentice . . . perhaps it was spontaneous combustion?'

Rainbows rode the rotating sprinklers, slipping in and out of the spray like wraiths leaping a skipping-rope. I strolled around the pool, whose untidy water swilled below the diving board, disturbed by a long-legged young woman swimming a crisply efficient backstroke.

I sat down at a pool-side table, admiring her graceful arms as they cleft the surface. Her wide hips rolled snugly in the water, and she might have been lying in the lap of a trusted lover. When she passed me I noticed a crescent-shaped bruise that ran from her left cheekbone to the bridge of her strong nose, and the apparently swollen gums of her upper jaw. Seeing me, she swiftly turned into a fast crawl, hands ransacking the waves, a pigtail of long black hair following her like a faithful water-snake. She hoisted herself up the ladder at the shallow end, snatched a towelling robe from a nearby chair and set off without a backward glance for the changing rooms.

The clunk-clunk of the tennis machine had resumed, sounding across the empty courts. A fair-skinned man in a turquoise Club Nautico tracksuit was playing against the machine as it fired balls across the net, barrel set to swing at random. Despite the screens of wire netting I could see that an intense duel was taking place between player and machine. The man leapt across the court on his long legs, feet raking the clay as he raced to return every ball. Cross-court volley, lob and backhand flip followed one another at breakneck pace. A misfire brought him skidding to the net to cut a drop-shot into the tramlines, but he ran back to reach a baseline serve with his outstretched racket.

Watching him, I realized that he was urging on the machine, willing it to beat him, beaming with pleasure when an ace knocked the racket from his hand. Yet I felt that the real duel taking place was not between man and machine, but between rival factions within his own head. He seemed to be provoking himself, testing his own temper, curious to know how he would respond. Even when exhausted, he drove himself on, as if encouraging a less skilful partner. Once, surprised by his own speed and strength, he waited for the next ball with a dazed schoolboy grin. Although in his late twenties, he had the pale hair and youthful looks of a subaltern barely out of his teens.

Deciding to introduce myself, I made my way through the courts. A skied ball sailed over my head and bounced across the empty clay. I heard him slam heavily into the side netting and, a moment later, the sound of a racket slashed against a metal post.

He was leaving when I reached the practice court, stepping through the wire door by the opposite baseline. Surrounded by dozens of balls, the machine stood on its rubber wheels, timer ticking, the last three balls in its hopper. I crossed the court and stood among the skidmarks, the choreography of a violent duel, of which the machine had been little more than a spectator. Tossed aside, the broken racket lay on a linesman's chair, its shaft a mass of splinters.

I held the racket in my hand, and heard the whipcrack of the tennis machine. A heavy top-spin serve swung across the net and bit the clay a few inches inside the baseline, swerving past my legs to rebound against the fencing. A second ball, faster than the first, clipped the top of the net and stung the ground at my feet. The last ball bounced high at my chest. I flailed at it with the damaged racket and sent it over the netting into the next court.

Beyond the tennis machine the wire door opened briefly. A raised hand saluted me, and above the towel around the player's neck I saw a wry but cheerful grin. Then he strode away, slapping the netting with the vizor of his cap.

Nursing the torn skin on my hand, I left the court and strode back to the club, in time to see him disappear through the rainbows that swayed across the lawn. Perhaps the tennis machine had malfunctioned, but I guessed that he had reset the mechanism when he saw me approach, intrigued to know how I would react to the vicious serves. Already I was thinking of the testing games that this high-strung man would almost certainly have played with Frank, and of the luckless machine now summoned to take my brother's place.

4

An Incident in the Car Park

ESTRELLA DE MAR was coming out to play. From the balcony
of Frank's apartment, three floors above the swimming pool,
I watched the members of the Club Nautico take their places
in the sun. Tennis players swung their rackets as they set off for
the courts, warming up for three hard-fought sets. Sunbathers
loosened the tops of their swimsuits and oiled themselves
beside the pool, pressing their lip-gloss to the icy, salty rims
of the day's first margaritas. An open-cast gold mine of jewellery lay among the burnished breasts. The hubbub of gossip
seemed to dent the surface of the pool, and indiscretion ruled
as the members happily debriefed each other on the silky
misdemeanours of the night.

To David Hennessy, who hovered behind me among the
clutter of Frank's possessions, I commented: 'What handsome
women . . . the *jeunesse dorée* of the Club Nautico. Here that
means anyone under sixty.'

'Absolutely, dear chap. Come to Estrella de Mar and throw
away the calendar.' He joined me at the rail, sighing audibly.
'Aren't they a magnificent sight? Never fail to make the balls
tingle.'

'Sad, though, in a way. While they're showing their nipples
to the waiters their host is sitting in a cell in Zarzuella jail.'

Hennessy laid a feather-light hand on my shoulder. 'Dear
boy, I know. But Frank would be happy to see them here.
He created the Club Nautico – it owes everything to him.

Believe me, we've all been hoisting our piña coladas to him.'

I waited for Hennessy to remove his hand, so soft against my shirt that it might have belonged to the gentlest of importuning panders. Bland and sleek, with an openly ingratiating smile, he had cultivated a pleasant but vague manner that concealed, I suspected, a sophisticated kind of shiftiness. His eyes were always elsewhere when I tried to catch them. If the names in his Lloyd's syndicate had prospered, even that unlikely outcome would have had an ulterior motive. I was curious why this fastidious man had chosen the Costa del Sol, and found myself thinking of extradition treaties or, more exactly, their absence.

'I'm glad Frank was happy here. Estrella de Mar is the prettiest spot that I've seen on the coast. Still, I would have thought Palm Beach or Nassau more your style.'

Hennessy waved to a woman sunbathing in a pool-side lounger. 'Yes, friends at home used to say that to me. To be honest, I agreed with them when I first came here. But things have changed. This place isn't like anywhere else, you know. There's a very special atmosphere. Estrella de Mar is a real community. At times I think it's almost too lively.'

'Unlike the retirement complexes along the coast – Cala-honda and so on?'

'Absolutely. The people of the pueblos . . .' Hennessy averted his gaze from the poisoned coast. 'Brain-death disguised as a hundred miles of white cement. Estrella de Mar is more like Chelsea or Greenwich Village in the 1960s. There are theatre and film clubs, a choral society, cordon bleu classes. Sometimes I dream of pure idleness, but not a hope. Stand still for a moment and you find yourself roped into a revival of *Waiting for Godot*.'

'I'm impressed. But what's the secret?'

'Let's say . . .' Hennessy checked himself, and let his smile drift across the air. 'It's something rather elusive. You have to

43

find it for yourself. If you have time, do look around. I'm surprised you've never visited us before.'

'I should have done. But those tower blocks at Torremolinos throw long shadows. Without being snobbish, I assumed it was fish and chips, bingo and cheap sun-oil, all floating on a lake of lager. Not the sort of thing people want to read about in *The New Yorker*.'

'I dare say. Perhaps you'll write a friendly article about us?'

Hennessy was watching me in his affable way, but I sensed that a warning signal had sounded inside his head. He strolled into Frank's sitting room, shaking his head over the books pulled from the shelves during the police searches, as if enough rummaging had already taken place at Estrella de Mar.

'A friendly article?' I stepped over the scattered seat cushions. 'Perhaps . . . when Frank comes out. I need time to get my bearings.'

'Very sensible. You can't guess what you might find. Now, I'll drive you to the Hollingers'. I know you want to see the house. Be warned, though, you'll need to keep a strong grip on yourself.'

Hennessy waited as I made a last tour of the apartment. In Frank's bedroom the mattress stood against the wall, its seams slit by the police investigators searching for the smallest evidence that might corroborate his confession. Suits, shirts and sportswear lay strewn across the floor, and a lace shawl that had belonged to our mother hung over the dressing-table mirror. In the bathroom the hand-basin was filled with shaving gear, aerosols and vitamin packs swept from the shelves of the medicine cabinet. The bathtub was littered with broken glass, through which leaked a stream of blue shower gel.

On the sitting-room mantelpiece I recognized a childhood photograph of Frank and myself in Riyadh, standing with Mother outside our house in the residential compound. Frank's sly smile, and my owlish seriousness as the older brother, contrasted with our mother's troubled gaze as she strained to be cheerful for Father's camera. Curiously, the background of white villas, palms and apartment houses reminded me of Estrella de Mar.

Beside the row of tennis trophies was another framed photograph, taken by a professional cameraman in the dining room of the Club Nautico. Relaxed and pleasantly high, Frank was holding court in his white tuxedo among a group of his favourite members, the spirited blondes with deep *décolletages* and tolerant husbands.

Sitting beside Frank, hands clasped behind his head, was the fair-haired man I had seen on the tennis court. Frozen by the camera lens, he had the look of an intellectual athlete, his strong body offset by his fine-tuned features and sensitive gaze. He lounged back in his shirtsleeves, dinner jacket slung over a nearby chair, pleased with the happy scene around him but in some way above all this unthinking revelry. He struck me, as he must have done most people, as likeable but peculiarly driven.

'Your brother in jollier times,' Hennessy pointed to Frank. 'One of the theatre club dinners. Though photographs can be misleading – that was taken a week before the Hollinger fire.'

'And who's the brooding chap beside him? The club's leading Hamlet?'

'Far from it. Bobby Crawford, our tennis professional, though he's far more than that, I may say. You ought to meet him.'

'I did this afternoon.' I showed Hennessy the sticking-plaster which the concierge had pressed against my bleeding palm. 'I still have a piece of his tennis racket in my hand. I'm surprised he plays with a wooden one.'

'It slows down his game.' Hennessy seemed genuinely puzzled. 'How extraordinary. Were you on the courts with him? Bobby does play rather fiercely.'

45

'Not with me. Though he was up against someone he couldn't quite beat.'

'Really? He's awfully good. Remarkable fellow in all sorts of ways. He's actually our entertainments officer, and the absolute life and soul of the Club Nautico. It was a brilliant coup of Frank's to bring him here – young Crawford's totally transformed the place. To be honest, before he came the club was pretty well dead. Like Estrella de Mar in many ways – we were turning into another dozy pueblo. Bobby threw himself into everything: fencing, drama, squash. He opened the disco downstairs, and he and Frank set up the Admiral Drake regatta. Forty years ago he'd have been running the Festival of Britain.'

'Perhaps he still is – he's certainly preoccupied with something. Yet he looks so young.'

'Ex-army man. The best junior officers stay young for ever. Strange about that splinter of yours . . .'

I was still trying to prise the splinter from my hand as I stared at the charred timbers of the Hollinger house. While Hennessy spoke to the Spanish chauffeur on the intercom I sat in the passenger seat beside him, glad that the windshield and the wrought-iron gates lay between me and the gutted mansion. The heat of the conflagration still seemed to radiate from the bruised hulk, which sat atop its hill like an ark put to the torch by a latter-day Noah. The roof joists jutted from the upper walls, a death-ship's exposed ribs topped by the masts of the chimneys. Scorched awnings hung from the windows like the shreds of sails, black flags flapping a sinister semaphore.

'Right – Miguel will let us in. He looks after the place, or what's left of it. The housekeeper and her husband have gone. They simply couldn't cope.' Hennessy waited for the gates to open. 'It's quite a spectacle, I must say . . .'

'What about the chauffeur – do I tell him that I'm Frank's brother? He may . . .'

'No. He liked Frank, sometimes they went scuba-diving together. He was very upset when Frank pleaded guilty. As we all were, needless to say.'

We entered the gates and rolled on to the thick gravel. The drive rose past a series of terraced gardens filled with miniature cycads, bougainvillea and frangipani. Sprinkler hoses ran across the hillside like the vessels of a dead blood system. Every leaf and flower was covered with white ash that bathed the derelict property in an almost sepulchral light. Footprints marked the ashy surface of the tennis court, as if a solitary player had waited after a brief snowfall for an absent opponent.

A marble terrace ran along the seaward frontage of the house, scattered with roof-tiles and charred sections of wooden gabling. Potted plants still bloomed among the overturned chairs and trestle tables. A large rectangular swimming pool sat like an ornamental reservoir beside the terrace, constructed in the 1920s, so Hennessy told me, to suit the tastes of the Andalucian tycoon who had bought the mansion. Marble pilasters supported the podium of the diving board, and each of the gargoyle spouts was a pair of carved stone hands that clasped an openmouthed fish. The filter system was silent, and the surface of the pool was covered with waterlogged timbers, floating wine bottles and paper cups, and a single empty ice-bucket.

Hennessy parked the car under a canopy of eucalyptus trees whose upper branches had been burned to blackened brooms. A young Spaniard with a sombre face climbed the steps from the pool, gazing at the devastation around him as if seeing it for the first time. I expected him to approach us, but he remained thirty feet away, staring at me stonily.

'Miguel, the Hollingers' chauffeur,' Hennessy murmured. 'He lives in the flat below the pool. A little tact might be in order if you ask any questions. The police gave him a hell of a time.'

'Was he a suspect?'

'Who wasn't? Poor chap, his whole world literally fell in on him.'

Hennessy took off his hat and fanned himself as he gazed at the house. He seemed impressed by the scale of the disaster but otherwise unmoved, like an insurance assessor surveying a burned-out factory. He pointed to the yellow police tapes that sealed the embossed oak doors.

'Inspector Cabrera doesn't want anyone sifting through the evidence, though God only knows what's left. There's a side door off the terrace we can look through. It's too dangerous to go inside the place.'

I stepped over the shattered tiles and wine glasses at my feet. The intense heat had driven a jagged fissure through the stone walls, the scar of a lightning bolt that had condemned the property to the flames. Hennessy led the way towards a loose French door levered off its hinges by the firemen. Wind gusted across the terrace, and a cloud of white ash swirled around us like milled bone, restlessly hunting the air.

Hennessy pushed back the door and beckoned me towards him, smiling in a thin way like a guide at a black museum. A high-ceilinged drawing room looked out over the sea on either side of the peninsula. In the dim light I found myself standing in a marine world, the silt-covered state-room of a sunken liner. The Empire furniture and brocaded curtains, the tapestries and Chinese carpets were the decor of a drowned realm, drenched by the water that had poured through the collapsed ceiling. The dining room lay beyond the interior doors, where an oak table carried a pile of laths and plaster and the crystal debris of a chandelier.

I stepped from the parquet flooring on to the carpet, and found my shoes sinking as the water welled from the sodden fabric. Giving up, I returned to the terrace, where Hennessy was gazing at the sunlit peninsula.

'It's hard to believe one man started this fire,' I told him. 'Frank or anyone else. The place is completely gutted.'

'I agree.' Hennessy glanced at his watch, already keen to leave. 'Of course, this is a very old house. A single match would have set it going.'

The sounds of a tennis game echoed from a nearby court. A mile away I could make out the players at the Club Nautico, a glimmer of whites through the haze.

'Where were the Hollingers found? I'm surprised they didn't run on to the terrace when the fire started.'

'Sadly, they were upstairs at the time.' Hennessy pointed to the blackened windows below the roof. 'He was in the bathroom next to his study. She was in another of the bedrooms.'

'This was when? About seven o'clock in the evening? What were they doing there?'

'Who can say? He was probably working on his memoirs. She might have been dressing for dinner. I'm sure they tried to escape, but the intense blaze and the ether fumes must have driven them back.'

I sniffed at the damp air, trying to catch a scent of the hospital corridors of my childhood, when I had visited my mother in the American clinic at Riyadh. The air in the drawing room carried the mould-like odours of a herb garden after a rain shower.

'Ether . . . ? There's something curious about that. Hospitals don't use ether any more. Where was Frank supposed to have bought all this bottled ether?'

Hennessy had moved away, watching me from a distance as if he had realized for the first time that I was a murderer's brother. Behind him Miguel stood among the overturned tables. Together they seemed like figures in a dream-play, trying to remind me of memories I could never recover.

'Ether?' Hennessy pondered this, moving aside a broken glass with one shoe. 'Yes. I suppose it does have industrial uses. Isn't it a good solvent? It must be available at specialist laboratories.'

'But why not use pure petrol? Or lighter fuel for that matter? No one would ever trace the stuff. I take it Cabrera tracked down the lab that's supposed to have sold this ether to Frank?'

'Perhaps, but I somehow doubt it. After all, your brother pleaded guilty.' Hennessy searched for his car keys. 'Charles, I think we ought to leave. You must find this a dreadful strain.'

'I'm fine. I'm glad you brought me here.' I pressed my hands against the stone balustrade, trying to feel the heat of the fire. 'Tell me about the others – the maid and the niece. There was a male secretary?'

'Roger Sansom, yes. Decent fellow, he'd been with them for years – almost a son.'

'Where were they found?'

'On the first floor. They were all in their bedrooms.'

'Isn't that a little odd? The fire started on the ground floor. You'd expect them to climb out through the windows. It's not that long a jump.'

'The windows would have been closed. The entire house was air-conditioned.' Hennessy tried to steer me across the terrace, a curator at closing time ushering a last visitor to the exit. 'We're all concerned for Frank, and absolutely mystified by the whole tragic business. But try to use a little imagination.'

'I'm probably using too much ... I assume they were all identified?'

'With some difficulty. Dental records, I suppose, though I don't think either of the Hollingers had any teeth. Perhaps there are clues in the jawbone.'

'What were the Hollingers like? They were both in their seventies?'

'He was seventy-five. She was quite a bit younger. Late sixties, I imagine.' Hennessy smiled to himself, as if fondly remembering a choice wine. 'Good-looking woman, in an actressy way, though a little too ladylike for me.'

'And they came here twenty years ago? Estrella de Mar must have been very different then.'

'There was nothing to see, just bare hillsides and a few old vines. A collection of fishermen's shacks and a small bar. Hollinger bought the house from a Spanish property developer he worked with. Believe me, it was a beautiful place.'

'And I can imagine how the Hollingers felt as all this cement crawled up the hill towards them. Were they popular here? Hollinger was rich enough to put a spoke into a lot of wheels.'

'They were fairly popular. We didn't see too much of them at the club, though Hollinger was a major investor. I suspect they assumed it was going to be for their exclusive use.'

'But then the gold medallions started to arrive?'

'I don't think they worried about gold medallions. Gold was one of Hollinger's favourite colours. Estrella de Mar had begun to change. He and Alice were more put off by the art galleries and the Tom Stoppard revivals. They kept to themselves. In fact, I believe he was trying to sell his interest in the club.'

Hennessy reluctantly followed me along the terrace. A narrow balcony circled the house and led to a stone staircase that climbed the hillside fifty feet away. A grove of lemon trees had once filled the bedroom windows with their oily scent, but the fire-storm had driven through them, and now only the charred stumps rose from the ground like a forest of black umbrellas.

'Good God, there's a fire escape . . .' I pointed to the cast-iron steps that descended from a doorway on the first floor. The massive structure had been warped by the heat, but still clung to the stone walls. 'Why didn't they use this? They would have been safe in seconds.'

Hennessy removed his hat in a gesture of respect for the victims. He stood with his head bowed before speaking. 'Charles, they never left their bedrooms. The fire was too intense. The whole house was a furnace.'

'I can see that. Your local fire brigade didn't even begin to get it under control. Who alerted them, by the way?'

Hennessy seemed hardly to have heard me. He turned his back on the house, and gazed at the sea. I sensed that he was telling me only what he knew I would learn elsewhere.

'As a matter of fact, the alarm was raised by a passing motorist. No one called the fire services from here.'

'And the police?'

'They didn't arrive until an hour later. You have to understand that the Spanish police leave us very much to ourselves. Few crimes are ever reported in Estrella de Mar. We have our own security patrols and they keep an eye on things.'

'The police and fire services were called only later . . .' I repeated this to myself, visualizing the arsonist making his escape across the deserted terrace and then climbing the outer wall as the flames roared through the great roof. 'So, apart from the housekeeper and her husband there was no one here?'

'Not exactly.' Hennessy replaced his hat, lowering the brim over his eyes. 'As it happens, everyone was here.'

'Everyone? Do you mean the staff?'

'No, I mean . . .' Hennessy gestured with his pale hands at the town below. '*Le tout* Estrella de Mar. It was the Queen's birthday. The Hollingers always threw a party for the club members. It was their contribution to community life – a touch of noblesse oblige about it, I have to admit, but they were rather nice shows. Champagne and excellent canapés . . .'

I cupped my hands and stared at the Club Nautico, visualizing the entire membership decamping to the Hollinger mansion for the loyal toast. 'The fire took place on the night of the party . . . that was why the club had closed. How many people were actually here when it started?'

'Everyone. I think all the guests had arrived. I suppose there were about . . . two hundred of us.'

'Two hundred people?' I walked back to the south face of the house, where the balcony overlooked the swimming pool and terrace. I imagined the trestle tables decked in white cloths, the ice-buckets gleaming in the evening lights, and the guests chattering beside the unruffled water. 'There were all these people here, at least two hundred of them, and no one entered the house and tried to save the Hollingers?'

'Dear boy, the doors were locked.'

'At a party? I don't get it. You could have broken in.'

'Security glass. The house was filled with paintings and *objects d'art*, not to mention Alice's jewellery. In previous years there'd been pilfering and cigarette burns on the carpets.'

'Even so. Besides, what were the Hollingers doing indoors? Why weren't they out here mingling with their guests?'

'The Hollingers weren't the mingling type.' Hennessy gestured patiently. 'They'd greet a few old friends, but I don't think they ever joined the other guests. It was all rather regal. They kept an eye on things from the first-floor veranda. Hollinger proposed the Queen's toast from there, and Alice would wave and acknowledge the cheers.'

We had reached the swimming pool, where Miguel was raking the floating debris from the water at the shallow end. Piles of wet charcoal lay on the marble verge. The ice-bucket floated past us, an unravelled cigar inside it.

'David, I can't understand all this. The whole thing seems . . .' I waited until Hennessy was forced to meet my eyes. 'Two hundred people are standing by a swimming pool when a fire starts. There are ice-buckets, punchbowls, bottles of champagne and mineral water, enough to dowse a volcano.

But no one seems to have moved a finger. That's the eerie thing. No one called the police or fire brigade. What did you do – just stand here?'

Hennessy had begun to tire of me, his gaze fixed on his car. 'What else was there to do? There was tremendous panic, people were falling into the pool and running off in all directions. No one had time to think of the police.'

'And what about Frank? Was he here?'

'Very much so. We stood together during the Queen's toast. After that he started circulating, as he always does. I can't be sure I saw him again.'

'But in the minutes before the fire started? Tell me, did anyone see Frank light the fire?'

'Of course not. It's unthinkable.' Hennessy turned to stare at me. 'For heaven's sake, old chap, Frank is your brother.'

'But he was found with a bottle of ether in his hands. Didn't it strike you as a little odd?'

'That was three or four hours later, when the police arrived at the club. It may have been planted in his apartment, who knows?' Hennessy patted my shoulders, as if reassuring a disappointed member of his Lloyd's syndicate. 'Look, Charles, give yourself time to take it all in. Talk to as many people as you want – they'll all tell you the same story, appalling as it is. No one thinks Frank was responsible, but at the same time it's not clear who else could have started the fire.'

I waited for him as he walked around the pool and spoke to Miguel. A few banknotes changed hands, which the Spaniard slipped into his pocket with a grimace of distaste. Rarely taking his eyes from me, he followed us on foot as we drove past the ash-covered tennis court. I sensed that he wanted to speak to me, but he operated the gate controls without a word, a faint tic jumping across his scarred cheek.

'Unnerving fellow,' I commented as we rolled away. 'Tell

me, was Bobby Crawford at the party? The tennis professional?'

For once Hennessy answered promptly. 'No, he wasn't. He stayed behind at the club, playing tennis with that machine of his. I don't think he cared overmuch for the Hollingers. Nor they for him . . .'

Hennessy returned us to the Club Nautico, and left me with the keys to Frank's apartment. When we parted at the door of his office he was clearly glad to be rid of me, and I guessed that I was already becoming a mild embarrassment to the club and its members. Yet he knew that Frank could not have started the fire or taken even the smallest role in the conspiracy to kill the Hollingers. The confession, however preposterous, had stopped the clock, and no one seemed able to think beyond his guilty plea to the far larger question mark that presided over the gutted mansion.

I spent the afternoon tidying Frank's apartment. I replaced the books on the shelves, remade the bed and straightened the dented lampshades. The grooves in the sitting-room rugs indicated where the sofa, easy chairs and desk had stood before the police search. Pushing them back into place, I felt like a props man on a darkened stage, preparing the scene for the next day's performance.

The castors settled into their familiar ruts, but little else in Frank's world fitted together. I hung his scattered shirts in the wardrobe, and carefully folded the antique lace shawl in which we had both been wrapped as babies. After our mother's death Frank had retrieved the shawl from the bundle of clothes that Father had consigned to a Riyadh charity. The ancient fabric, inherited from his grandmother, was as grey and delicate as a folded cobweb.

I sat at Frank's desk, flicking through his cheque-book stubs and credit-card receipts, hoping for a pointer to his involvement with the Hollingers. The drawers were filled with a clutter of old wedding invitations, insurance renewal notices, holiday postcards from friends, French and English coins, and a health passport with its out-of-date tetanus and typhoid vaccinations, the trivia of everyday life that we shed like our skins.

Surprisingly, Inspector Cabrera's men had missed a small sachet of cocaine tucked into an envelope filled with foreign stamps that Frank had torn from his overseas mail and was evidently collecting for a colleague's child. I fingered the plastic sachet, tempted to help myself to this forgotten cache, but I was too unsettled by the visit to the Hollinger house.

In the centre drawer was an old photographic album that Mother had kept as a girl in Bognor Regis. Its chocolate-box covers and marbled pages with their art nouveau frames seemed as remote as the Charleston and the Hispano-Suiza. The black and white snaps showed an over-eager little girl trying hopelessly to build a pebble castle on a shingle beach, beaming shyly by her father's side and pinning the tail on a donkey at a birthday party. The flat sunless world was an ominous start for a child so clearly straining to be happy, and scant preparation for her marriage to an ambitious young historian and Arabist. Prophetically, the collection came to a sudden end a year after her arrival at Riyadh, as if the blank pages said everything about her growing depression.

After a quiet dinner in the deserted restaurant I fell asleep on the sofa, the album across my chest, and woke after midnight as a boisterous party spilled from the disco on to the terrace of the swimming pool. Two men in white dinner jackets were splashing across the pool, wine glasses raised to toast their wives, who were stripping to their underwear beside the diving board. A drunken young woman in a gold sheath dress tottered along the verge, snatched off her stiletto shoes and hurled them into the water.

Frank's absence had liberated his members, transforming the Club Nautico into an intriguing mix of casino and bordello. When I left the apartment to return to Los Monteros an amorous couple were testing the locked doors in the corridor. Almost all the staff had left for home, and the restaurant and bridge rooms were in darkness, but strobe lights from the disco veered across the entrance. Three young women stood on the steps, dressed like amateur whores in micro-skirts, fishnet tights and scarlet bustiers. I guessed that they were members of the club on the way to a costume party, and was tempted to offer them a lift, but they were busily checking a list of telephone numbers.

The car park was unlit, and I blundered among the lines of vehicles, feeling for the door latch of the rented Renault. Sitting behind the wheel, I listened to the boom of the disco drumming at the night. In a Porsche parked nearby a large white dog was jumping across the seats, unsettled by the noise and eager to see its owner.

I searched the shroud of the steering column for the ignition switch. When my eyes sharpened I realized that the dog was a man in a cream tuxedo, struggling with someone he had pinned against the passenger seat. In the brief pause between the disco numbers I heard a woman's shout, little more than an exhausted gasp. Her hands reached to the roof above the man's head and tore at the fabric.

Twenty feet away from me a rape was taking place. I switched on the headlamps and sounded three long blasts on the horn. As I stepped on to the gravel the Porsche's door sprang open, striking the vehicle beside it. The would-be rapist leapt from the car, the tuxedo almost stripped from his back by the frantic victim. He swerved away through the darkness, leaping between the Renault's headlamps. I ran after him, but he raced across the knoll beside the gates, straightened the tuxedo with a careless shrug, and vanished into the night.

The woman sat in the passenger seat of the Porsche, her bare feet protruding through the door, skirt around her waist. Her blonde hair gleamed with the attacker's saliva, and her blurred lipstick gave her a child's jamjar face. She pulled her torn underwear up her thighs and retched on to the gravel, then reached into the back seat and retrieved her shoes, brushing the torn roof liner from her face.

A few steps away was the booth from which the parking attendant kept watch on his charges during the day and evening. I leaned across the counter and snapped down the master switch of the lighting system, flooding the car park with a harsh fluorescence.

The woman frowned at the sudden glare, hid her eyes behind a silver purse and hobbled on a broken heel towards the entrance of the club, creased skirt over her ripped tights.

'Wait!' I shouted to her. 'I'll call the police for you . . .'

I was about to follow her when I noticed the row of parked cars that faced the Porsche across the access lane. Several of the front seats were occupied by the drivers and their passengers, all in evening dress, faces concealed by the lowered sun vizors. They had watched the rape attempt without intervening, like a gallery audience at an exclusive private view.

'What are you people playing at?' I shouted. 'For God's sake . . .'

I walked towards them, angry that they had failed to save the bruised woman, and drummed my bandaged fist on the windshields. But the drivers had started their engines. Following each other, they swerved past me towards the gates, the women shielding their eyes behind their hands.

I returned to the club, trying to find the victim of the assault. The fancy-dress whores stood in the lobby, phone lists in hand, but turned towards me as I strode up the steps.

'Where is she?' I called to them. 'She was damn nearly raped out there. Did you see her come in?'

The three gazed wide-eyed at each other, and then began to giggle together, minds slewing across some crazed amphetamine space. One of them touched my cheek, as if calming a child.

I searched the women's rest-room, kicking back the doors of the cubicles, and then blundered through the tables of the darkened restaurant, trying to catch the scent of heliotrope that the woman had left on the night air. At last I saw her beside the pool, dancing shoeless on the flooded grass, the backs of her hands smeared with lipstick, smiling at me in a knowing way when I walked towards her and tried to take her arm.

5

A Gathering of the Clan

FUNERALS CELEBRATE ANOTHER frontier crossing, in many ways the most formal and protracted of all. As the mourners waited in the Protestant cemetery, dressed in their darkest clothes, it struck me that they resembled a party of well-to-do emigrants, standing patiently at a hostile customs post and aware that however long they waited only one of them would be admitted that day.

In front of me were Blanche and Marion Keswick, two jaunty Englishwomen who ran the Restaurant du Cap, an elegant brasserie by the harbour. Their black silk suits shone in the fierce sun, a sheen of melting tar, but both were cool and self-composed, as if still keeping a proprietary eye on their Spanish cashiers. Despite the large tip I had left the previous evening, they had scarcely smiled when I complimented them on their cuisine.

Yet for some reason they now seemed more friendly. When I stepped past them, hoping to photograph the ceremony, Marion held my arm with a gloved hand.

'Mr Prentice? You're not leaving so soon? Nothing has happened.'

'I think everything has happened,' I rejoined. 'Don't worry, I'll stay to the end.'

'You look so anxious.' Blanche straightened my tie. 'I know the grave yawns, but there's no room for you there, even though she's the merest slip of a thing. In fact, they could almost use a child's casket. I wish your brother were here, Mr Prentice. He was very fond of Bibi.'

'I'm glad to hear it. Still, it's a fine send-off.' I gestured at the fifty or so mourners waiting by the open grave. 'So many people have turned up.'

'Of course,' Blanche affirmed. 'Bibi Jansen was immensely popular, and not only with the younger set. In some ways it's a pity she ever went to live with the Hollingers. I know they meant well but . . .'

'It was a terrible tragedy,' I told her. 'David Hennessy drove me to the house a few days ago.'

'So I heard.' Marion glanced at my dusty shoes. 'David's setting himself up as some sort of tour guide, I fear. He can't resist putting a finger in every pie. I think he has a taste for the macabre.'

'It *was* a tragedy.' Blanche's eyes were sealed within the dark wells of her sunglasses, a lightless world. 'But let's say the sort that brings people together. Estrella de Mar is far closer after all this.'

Other mourners were arriving, a remarkable turn-out for a junior domestic. The bodies of Hollinger, his wife and their niece Anne, together with the secretary, Roger Sansom, had been flown to England, and I assumed that those attending the burial of the Swedish maid were paying their respects to all five victims of the fire.

Immediately beyond the high wall was the Catholic cemetery, a cheerful township of gilded statues and family vaults like holiday villas. I had walked around the graves for fifteen minutes, preparing myself for the bleak Protestant service. Flowers decked even the simplest headstones, and each bore a vitrified photograph of the deceased – smiling wives, cheerful teenage girls, elderly burghers and sturdy soldiers in uniform. By contrast the Cementerio Protestante was a boneyard of coarse soil bleached white by the sun, locked away from the world (as if a Protestant death were somehow illicit), entered by a small gate whose key could be rented at the lodge for a hundred pesetas. Forty graves, few with a headstone, lay under the rear wall, mostly those of British retirees whose relatives could not afford to repatriate them.

If the cemetery was a gloomy place, there were few signs of gloom among the mourners. Only Gunnar Andersson, a young Swede who tuned speedboat engines at the marina, seemed grief-stricken. He stood alone by the waiting grave, thin and stooped in his borrowed suit and tie, a wisp of beard on his gaunt cheeks. He squatted down and touched the damp soil, clearly reluctant to consign the girl's remains to its stony embrace.

The remaining mourners waited comfortably in the sun, talking to each other like members of a recreational society. Together they formed a cross-section of the expatriate business community – hoteliers and restaurateurs, a taxi company proprietor, two satellite-dish agents, a cancer specialist from the Princess Margaret Clinic, property developers, bar-owners and investment counsellors. Looking at their sleek and suntanned faces, it struck me as curious that there was no one present of Bibi Jansen's age, for all the talk of her popularity.

Nodding my respects to the Keswick sisters, I left the main party of mourners and walked towards the graves below the rear wall. Here, as if deliberately holding herself apart from the others, stood a tall, strong-shouldered woman in her late fifties, platinum hair tightly crowned by a wide-brimmed black straw hat. No one seemed willing to approach her, and I sensed that a formal invitation was needed merely to bow. Behind her, serving as her baby-faced bodyguard, was the bar steward from the Club Nautico, Sonny Gardner, his yacht-rigger's shoulders constrained by a smart grey jacket.

I knew this was Elizabeth Shand, Estrella de Mar's most successful businesswoman. A former partner of Hollinger's, she now controlled a web of companies in the property and service sectors. Her eyes surveyed the mourners with the ever-watchful but tolerant gaze of a governor at a light-regime prison for executive criminals. As if keeping up a private commentary on her charges, her lips murmured to themselves in an almost louche way, and I saw her as part martinet, part bawdy-house keeper, the most intriguing of all combinations.

I knew that she was a major shareholder in the Club Nautico and a close colleague of Frank's, and was about to introduce myself when her eyes moved sharply from the grieving Swede and fixed themselves on a late arrival at the cemetery. Her mouth opened with a rictus of such distaste that I expected the mauve lipstick to peel from the irritated skin.

'Sanger? Good God, the man's got a nerve . . .'

Sonny Gardner stepped forward, buttoning his jacket. 'Do you want me to see him off, Mrs Shand?'

'No, let him know what we think of him. The sheer neck of it . . .'

A slim, silver-haired man in a tailored tropical suit was making his way over the rough ground, his slender hands parting the air. He moved with light but deliberate steps, his eyes searching the diagram of stones around him. His handsome face was smooth and feminine, and he had the easy manner of a stage hypnotist, but he was clearly conscious of the hostile mourners stirring around him. His faint smile seemed almost wistful, and he now and then lowered his head, like a sensitive man aware that because of some minor quirk of character he had never been liked.

Clasping his hands behind his back, he positioned himself at the graveside, the soil breaking under his patent-leather shoes. I assumed that he was the Swedish pastor of some obscure Lutheran sect to which Bibi Jansen had belonged, and that he was about to officiate at her interment.

'Is this the pastor?' I asked Gardner, whose flexing arms

threatened to split the seams of his jacket. 'He's rather curiously dressed. Is he going to bury her?'

'Some say he already has.' Gardner cleared his throat, looking for somewhere to spit. 'Dr Irwin Sanger, Bibi's "psychiatrist", the one mad person in the whole of Estrella de Mar.'

I listened to the cicadas rasping while the mourners stared with varying degrees of hostility at the silver-haired newcomer, and reminded myself that there were far more tensions below the surface of this charming beach resort than first seemed apparent. Elizabeth Shand was still staring at the psychiatrist, clearly disputing his right to be present. Protected by her baleful presence, I raised my camera and began to photograph the mourners.

No one spoke as the sounds of the motor-drive echoed off the walls. I knew they disapproved of the camera, as they did of my continued presence at Estrella de Mar. Watching the mourners through the viewfinder, it occurred to me that almost all of them would have attended the Hollingers' party on the evening of the fire. Most were members of the Club Nautico and knew Frank well. None, I had been relieved to find, accepted that he was guilty.

Every morning, since my first visit to Estrella de Mar, I had driven from the Los Monteros Hotel, carrying out my detective investigation. I cancelled my TV assignment in Helsinki and telephoned my agent in London, Rodney Lewis, asking him to put all other commitments on hold.

'Does that mean you've found something?' he asked. 'Charles . . . ?'

'No. I've found absolutely nothing.'

'But you think it's worth staying out there? The trial won't start for several months.'

'Even so. It's an unusual place.'

'So is Torquay. You must have some idea what happened?'

'No . . . to tell the truth, I haven't. I'll stay here, though.'

Nothing I had found gave me the slightest hint of why my brother, at home and at ease for the first time in his life, should have turned into an arsonist and murderer. But if Frank had not set fire to the Hollinger mansion, who had? I asked David Hennessy for a list of his fellow-guests at the party, but he refused point-blank, claiming that Inspector Cabrera might charge other guests with the crime if Frank withdrew his confession, and perhaps incriminate the entire community.

The Keswick sisters told me that they had attended the Queen's birthday parties for years. They had been standing by the pool when the flames erupted through the bedroom windows, and left with the first stampede of guests to their cars. Anthony Bevis, owner of the Cabo D'Ora Gallery and a close friend of Roger Sansom, claimed that he had tried to force the French window but had been driven back by the exploding tiles that were leaping from the roof. Colin Dewhurst, manager of a bookshop in the Plaza Iglesias, had helped the Hollingers' chauffeur to carry a ladder from the garage, only to watch the upper rungs catch fire in the intense blaze.

None of them had seen Frank slip into the house with his lethal flagons of ether and petrol, or could conceive of any reason why he might want to kill the Hollingers. I noticed, however, that of the thirty people I questioned not one suggested any other suspect. Something told me that if his friends really believed in Frank's innocence they would have hinted at the identity of the true assassin.

Estrella de Mar seemed a place without shadows, its charms worn as openly as the bare breasts of the women of all ages who sunbathed at the Club Nautico. Secure on their handsome peninsula, the people of the resort were an example of the liberation that follows when continuous sunlight is shone on the British. I could understand why the residents were less than keen for me to write about their private paradise, and already I was beginning to see the town through their eyes. Once I had freed Frank from prison I would buy an apartment of my own and make it my winter base.

In many ways Estrella de Mar was the halcyon county-town England of the mythical 1930s, brought back to life and moved south into the sun. Here there were no gangs of bored teenagers, no deracinated suburbs where neighbours scarcely knew each other and their only civic loyalties were to the nearest hypermarket and DIY store. As everyone never tired of saying, Estrella de Mar was a true community, with schools for the French and British children, a thriving Anglican church and a local council of elected members which met at the Club Nautico. However modestly, a happier twentieth century had rediscovered itself in this corner of the Costa del Sol.

The only shadow cast across its plazas and avenues was the fire at the Hollinger house. In the late afternoon, when the sun moved behind the peninsula and set off towards Gibraltar, the silhouette of the gutted mansion crept along the palm-lined streets, darkening the pavements and the walls of the villas below, silently wrapping the town in its sombre shroud.

As I stood among the graves beside Elizabeth Shand, and waited for the casket of the young Swedish woman, it occurred to me that Frank might have pleaded guilty in order to save Estrella de Mar from being overrun by British and Spanish police, or by private detectives hired by relations of the Hollinger family. This innocence of crime might even explain the voyeuristic gaze of the people I had caught in the floodlights of the Club Nautico car park. Never having seen a rape, they had watched the assault as if it were some folkloric or pagan rite from a more primitive world.

One of the couples, I suspected, was present among the mourning party, a retired Bournemouth accountant and his sharp-eyed wife who ran a video-rental store in the Avenida Ortega. Both tried to avoid my camera lens and only relaxed when a black Cadillac hearse drew up outside the cemetery.

In Estrella de Mar death alone had been franchised to the Spanish. The pallbearers of the funeral firm in Benalmadena eased the polished casket from the hearse and transferred it to a cart manned by the cemetery staff. Preceded by the Reverend Davis, the pale and earnest vicar of the Anglican church, the cart rumbled towards the waiting grave. The clergyman's eyes were fixed on the grating wheels, teeth gritted against the painful sounds. He seemed embarrassed and uneasy, as if in some way holding the mourners responsible for the Swedish girl's death.

Stiletto heels teetered on the stony ground as everyone stepped forward. Heads were lowered, eyes avoiding the coffin and the hungry vault that would soon embrace it. Only Gunnar Andersson watched as it sank jerkily from sight, fed into the ground by the gravediggers' tapes. Tears gleamed through the faint beard on his sallow cheeks. His long legs straddled the heap of damp soil when the men reached for their spades, delaying the interment to the last moment.

A few feet from him Dr Sanger was staring at the coffin. His slim chest inflated at ten-second intervals, as if he were unconsciously starving himself of air. He smiled in a tender but almost remote way, like the owner of a dead pet briefly remembering their happier days together. He picked a handful of soil from the ground and threw it on to the coffin, then ran his hand through his shock of blow-dried hair, leaving a few grains of sand in the silvery waves.

The Reverend Davis was about to speak, but waited for a group of late arrivals who had entered the cemetery. David Hennessy led the way, nodding to the mourners as he carried out a quick head-count and confirmed that everyone he had notified was present, glad to lend his special skills to that even larger club than the Nautico, with its unlimited membership and no waiting list.

Behind him, face hidden by a silk scarf, was Dr Paula Hamilton, the dark-haired swimmer I had seen soon after my arrival. A resident physician at the Princess Margaret Clinic, she was one of the few people who had declined to talk to me. She had failed to return my telephone calls, and refused to see me at her office in the Clinic. Now she seemed as reluctant to attend the burial service, standing behind Hennessy with her eyes fixed on his heels.

Bobby Crawford, the Club Nautico's tennis professional, followed her from the gate. Dressed in a black silk suit and tie, sunglasses over his eyes, he resembled a handsome and affable gangster. He greeted the mourners with a reassuring wave, his outstretched hands touching a shoulder here and patting an arm there. Everyone seemed to revive in his presence, and even Elizabeth Shand raised the brim of her new straw hat to beam at him maternally, lips fleshing as she murmured sleekly to herself.

The Reverend Davis completed his perfunctory address, never once meeting the mourners' eyes and clearly eager to be back with his parish. Stones rattled on the coffin lid as the gravediggers spaded the heavy soil into the grave, shoulders bent in the sunlight. Unable to control himself, Andersson seized the spade from the older of the men and flailed at the loose soil, shovelling sand and grit on to the casket as if determined to shield the dead girl from any sight of the world that had failed her.

The mourners began to disperse, led by the uneasy clergyman. They stopped to look back when a spade rang against an old marker stone. There was a high and almost strangled shout, which Mrs Shand involuntarily echoed.

'Dr Sanger . . . !' Andersson stood astride the grave, spade held across his chest like a jousting pole, glaring in a deranged way at the psychiatrist. 'Doctor, why did you come? Bibi didn't invite you.'

Sanger raised his hands, as much to calm the watching mourners as to restrain the young Swede. His melancholy smile seemed to float free of his lips. Eyes lowered, he turned from the grave for the last time, but Andersson refused to let him pass.

'Sanger! Doctor Professor . . . don't go away . . .' Andersson pointed mockingly to the grave. 'Dear Doctor, Bibi's here. Have you come to lie with her? I can make you comfortable . . .'

A brief but ugly brawl followed. The two men grappled like clumsy schoolboys, panting and heaving until Bobby Crawford wrenched the spade from Andersson's hands and sent him sprawling to the ground. He helped Sanger to his feet, steadied the shaken psychiatrist and dusted his lapels. Ashen-faced, his silver hair breaking around his ears, Sanger limped away, guarded by Crawford as he held the spade in a two-handed racket grip.

'Let's try to calm things . . .' Crawford raised his arms to the mourners. 'This isn't a bull-ring. Think of Bibi now.' When the Reverend Davis stepped quickly through the gate with an embarrassed flurry, Crawford shouted: 'Goodbye, Vicar. Our thanks go to you.'

Handing the spade to the impassive gravediggers, he waited for the mourners to move away. He pulled off his black crêpe tie and shrugged his crumpled jacket on to his shoulders, the same gesture that I had seen at the Club Nautico when the would-be rapist made his escape.

The cemetery was almost empty. Paula Hamilton slipped away with Hennessy, denying me another chance of speaking to her. Mrs Shand was helped by Sonny Gardner into the rear seat of her white Mercedes, where she sat grim-mouthed. Andersson stared at the grave for a last time. He smiled gamely at Crawford, who waited amiably beside him, saluted the settling earth and walked stiffly to the gate.

The gravediggers nodded without comment as they accepted Crawford's tip, resigned to any behaviour by the foreigners in their midst. Crawford patted their shoulders and stood beside the grave, head lowered as he mused to himself. Almost alone now in the cemetery, he had switched off his ready grin, and a more thoughtful face settled itself over his fine bones. An emotion close to regret seemed to touch his eyes, but he gestured in a resigned way and set off for the gate.

When I left a few minutes later he was staring over the wall at the gilded statues of the Catholic cemetery.

'Cheerful, aren't they?' he commented as I walked past him. 'One good reason for being a Catholic.'

'You're right.' I stopped to size him up. 'Still, I imagine she's happy where she is.'

'Let's hope so. She was very sweet, and that's cold ground in there. Can I give you a lift?' He pointed to a Porsche parked under the cypresses. 'It's a long way back to town.'

'Thanks, but I have a car.'

'Charles Prentice? You're Frank's brother.' He shook my hand with unfeigned warmth. 'Bobby Crawford, tennis pro and dogsbody at the Club Nautico. It's a pity we had to meet here. I've been away a few days, looking at property along the coast. Betty Shand's itching to open a new sports club.'

While he spoke I was struck by his intense but refreshing manner, and by the guileless way he held my arm as we walked towards our cars. He was attentive and eager to please, and I found it hard to believe that he was the man who had carried out the attempted rape. I could only assume that he had lent the car to a friend with far rougher tastes.

'I wanted to talk to you,' I said. 'Hennessy tells me you're an old colleague of Frank's.'

'Absolutely. He brought me into the club – until then I was just a glorified tennis bum.' He grinned, showing his expensively-capped teeth. 'Frank never stops talking about you. In a way I think you're his real father.'

'I'm his brother. The boring, older brother who always got him out of scrapes. This time I've lost my touch.'

Crawford stopped in the middle of the road, ignoring a car that swerved around him. He stared at the air with his arms raised to the sky, as if waiting for a sympathetic genie to materialize out of the spiralling dust. 'Charles, I know. What's going on? This is Kafka re-shot in the style of *Psycho*. You've talked to him?'

'Of course. He insists he's guilty. Why?'

'No one knows. We're all racking our brains. I think it's Frank playing his strange games again, like those peculiar chess problems he's always making up. King to move and mate in one, though this time there are no other pieces on the board and he has to mate himself.'

Crawford leaned against his Porsche, one hand playing with the tattered roof liner that hung over the passenger seat. Behind the reassuring smile his eyes were taking in every detail of my face and posture, my choice of shirt and shoes, as if searching for some clue to Frank's predicament. I realized that he was more intelligent that his obsessive tennis playing and over-friendly manner suggested.

'Did Frank have it in for the Hollingers?' I asked him. 'Was there any reason at all why he might have set fire to the house?'

'No – Hollinger was a harmless old buffer. I won't say I cared for him myself. He and Alice were two of the reasons why Britain doesn't have a film industry any longer. They were rich, likeable amateurs – no one would have wanted to hurt them.'

'Someone did. Why?'

'Charles . . . it may have been an accident. Perhaps they microwaved one too many of their god-awful canapés, there was a sudden spark and the whole place went up like a haystack. Then Frank, for some weird reason of his own, begins to play Joseph K.' Crawford lowered his voice, as if concerned that the dead in the cemetery might overhear him. 'When I first knew Frank he talked about your mother a lot. He was afraid he'd helped to kill her.'

'No – we were far too young. We didn't even begin to grasp why she wanted to kill herself.'

Crawford brushed the dust from his hands, glad to acquit us of any conceivable complicity. 'I know, Charles. Still, there's nothing more satisfying than confessing to a crime you haven't committed . . .'

A car emerged from the Catholic cemetery and turned to cruise past us. Paula Hamilton was at the wheel, David Hennessy beside her. He waved to us, but Dr Hamilton stared ahead, dabbing her eyes with a tissue.

'She looks upset.' I winced at a clumsy gear change. 'Why the Catholic cemetery?'

'She's seeing an old boyfriend. Another doctor at the Clinic.'

'Really? A strange rendezvous. Rather macabre, in a way.'

'Paula doesn't have much choice – he's lying under a headstone. He died a year ago from one of these new malarias he picked up in Java.'

'That's hard . . . Was she close to the Hollingers?'

'Only to their niece and Bibi Jansen.' Crawford stared through the gate into the Protestant cemetery, where the gravediggers were loading their spades on to the cart. 'A pity

72

about Bibi. Still . . . You'll like Paula. Typical woman doctor – a calm and efficient front, but inside rather shaky.'

'What about the psychiatrist, Dr Sanger? No one wanted him here.'

'He's something of a shady character . . . interesting in his way. He's one of those psychiatrists with a knack of forming little ménages around themselves.'

'Ménages of vulnerable young women?'

'Exactly. He enjoys playing Svengali to them. He has a house in Estrella de Mar, and owns some bungalows in the Costasol complex.' Crawford pointed to a large settlement of villas and apartment houses a mile to the west of the peninsula. 'No one's sure what goes on there, but I hope they have fun.'

I waited as the gravediggers pushed their cart through the cemetery gate. A wheel lodged in a stony rut, and one of the spades fell to the ground. Crawford stepped forward, ready to help the men, then watched wistfully as the cart moved along the pavement, its wheel-rims grating. In his black suit and sunglasses he seemed a fretful figure, faced for once with a fast service he had no hope of returning. I guessed that he, Andersson and Dr Sanger were the only ones to mourn the dead girl.

'I'm sorry about Bibi Jansen,' I said when he returned to the car. 'I can see you miss her.'

'A little. But these things are never fair.'

'Why did the others bother to attend? Mrs Shand, Hennessy, the Keswick sisters – for a Swedish housemaid?'

'Charles, you didn't know her. Bibi was more than that.'

'Even so. Could the fire have been a suicide attempt?'

'By the Hollingers? On the Queen's birthday?' Crawford began to laugh, glad to free himself from his sombre mood. 'They'd have been posthumously stripped of their CBEs.'

'What about Bibi? I take it she was once involved with Sanger. She might have been unhappy at the Hollingers.'

Crawford shook his head, admiring my ingenuity. 'I don't think so. She liked it up there. Paula had weaned her off all the drugs she was taking.'

'Who knows, though? Some sort of hysterical outburst?'

'Charles, come on.' His spirits lightening, Crawford took my arm. 'Be honest with yourself. Women are never that hysterical. In my experience, they're intensely realistic. We men are far more emotional.'

'Then what can I do?' I unlocked the driver's door of the Renault and fiddled with the keys, reluctant to take my seat. 'I need all the help I can get. We can't just leave Frank to rot. The lawyer estimates he'll get at least thirty years.'

'The lawyer? Señor Danvila? He's thinking of his fees. All those appeals . . .' Crawford opened the door and beckoned me into the driver's seat. He took off his sunglasses and stared at me with his friendly but distant eyes. 'Charles, there's nothing you can do. Frank will solve this one himself. He may be playing his end-game, but it's only just begun, and there are sixty-three other squares on the board . . .'

6

Fraternal Refusals

THE RETIREMENT PUEBLOS lay by the motorway, embalmed in a dream of the sun from which they would never awake. As always, when I drove along the coast to Marbella, I seemed to be moving through a zone that was fully accessible only to a neuroscientist, and scarcely at all to a travel writer. The white façades of the villas and apartment houses were like blocks of time that had crystallized beside the road. Here on the Costa del Sol nothing would ever happen again, and the people of the pueblos were already the ghosts of themselves.

This glacier-like slowness had affected my attempts to free Frank from Zarzuella jail. Three days after Bibi Jansen's funeral I left the Los Monteros Hotel, carrying a suitcase filled with fresh clothes for Frank's court appearance in Marbella that morning. I had packed the case in his apartment at the Club Nautico after a careful search through his wardrobe. There were striped shirts, dark shoes and a formal suit, but as they lay on the bed they resembled the elements of a costume that Frank had decided to discard. I hunted the drawers and tie-rack, unable to make up my mind. The real and far more elusive Frank seemed to have turned his back on the apartment and its dusty past.

At the last moment I threw in some pens and a block of writing paper – the latter suggested by Señor Danvila in the vain hope of persuading Frank to withdraw his confession. Frank would be brought from Malaga to attend the hearing in the magistrates' court, a formal identification of the five victims by Inspector Cabrera and the autopsy pathologists. Afterwards, Señor Danvila told me, I would be able to speak to Frank.

As I parked in a narrow street behind the courthouse I weighed what I would say to him. More than a week of amateur sleuthing had yielded nothing. Naively, I had assumed that the unanimous belief in Frank's innocence held by his friends and colleagues would somehow force out the truth, but in fact that unanimity had only wrapped another layer of mystery around the Hollinger murders. Far from springing the lock of Frank's prison cell it had given the key another turn.

Nevertheless, five people had been killed, by someone almost certainly still walking the streets of Estrella de Mar, still eating sushi and reading *Le Monde*, still singing in a church choir or modelling clay at a sculpture class.

As if unaware of this, the hearing at the magistrates' court unfolded in its interminable way, a Möbius strip of arcane procedures that unwound, inverted themselves and returned to their departure points. Lawyers and journalists each embrace a rival physics where motion and inertia reverse themselves. I sat behind Señor Danvila, only a few yards from Frank and his translator, as the pathologists testified, stood down and testified again, body by body, death by death.

Eager to talk to Frank, I was surprised by how little he had changed. I expected him to be thin and drained by the grey hours of sitting alone in his cell, forehead harrowed by the stress of maintaining his absurd bluff. He was paler, as the sunlight of Estrella de Mar faded from his face, but he seemed composed and at ease with himself, offering me a ready smile and a handshake quickly cut off by his police escort. He took no part in the proceedings, but listened intently to his translator, emphasizing for the magistrate's benefit his central role in the events described.

76

When he left the court he gave me a wave of encouragement as if I were about to follow him into the headmaster's study. I waited on a hard seat in the public corridor, deciding to avoid a direct confrontation. Bobby Crawford had been right to say that the initiative lay with Frank, and by sticking to pleasantries I might force him to show his hand.

'Mr Prentice, I must apologize . . .' Señor Danvila hurried towards me, mournful face agitated by yet another setback. His hands fumbled at the air as if searching for an exit from this ever-more-confusing case. 'I'm sorry for making you wait, but a small problem has arisen . . .'

'Señor Danvila . . . ?' I tried to calm him. 'When can I see Frank?'

'There's a difficulty for us.' Señor Danvila searched for his absent briefcases, eager to shuffle them. 'It's hard for me to say. Your brother does not wish to see you.'

'Why not? I don't believe it. This whole thing's becoming absurd.'

'My sentiments too. I was with him a moment ago. He spoke very clearly.'

'But why? For heaven's sake . . . you told me yesterday that he'd agreed.'

Danvila gestured to a statue in a nearby alcove, calling on this alabaster knight to be his witness. 'I spoke to your brother both yesterday and the day before. He did not refuse until now. My sympathies, Mr Prentice. Your brother has his own reasons for making up his mind. I can only advise him.'

'It's ridiculous . . .' I sat wearily on the bench. 'He's determined to convict himself. What about bail? Is there anything we can do?'

'Impossible, Mr Prentice. There are five murders and a confession of guilt.'

'Can we get him declared insane? Mentally incompetent to plead?'

77

'It's too late. Last week I contacted Professor Xavier of the Juan Carlos Institute in Malaga – a distinguished forensic psychiatrist. With the court's permission he was willing to examine your brother. But Frank refused to see him. He insists he is entirely sane. Mr Prentice, I have to agree with him . . .'

Dazed by all this, I waited outside the courthouse, hoping to see Frank taken to one of the police vans for his return journey to Malaga. But after ten minutes I gave up and returned to my car. The snub hurt. Frank's refusal was not only a rejection of my traditional role as protective older brother, but a clear signal that he wanted me away from Marbella and Estrella de Mar. A deviant logic was at work, driving him towards decades of confinement in a provincial Spanish prison, an ordeal he seemed so calmly to welcome.

I drove back to Los Monteros and walked along the beach, a forlorn shelf of ochre sand littered with driftwood and water-logged crates, like the debris of a ransacked mind. After lunch I slept through the afternoon in my room, waking at six to the sounds of serve and volley from the hotel's tennis courts. I sat up and began to write one of my longest letters to Frank, reaffirming my faith in his innocence, and asking him for the last time to withdraw his confession to an atrocious crime that not even the police believed he had committed. If I had no reply from him I would leave for London and return only for the trial.

It was dusk when I sealed the letter, and the lights of Estrella de Mar trembled across the dark water. My senses sharpened as I gazed at this private peninsula with its theatre clubs and fencing classes, its louche psychiatrist and handsome doctor with her bruised face, its tennis professional obsessed by his serving machine, and its deaths in high places. I was sure that the solution to the Hollinger murders lay not in Frank's involvement with the retired film producer but in the unique nature of the resort where he had died.

I needed to become part of Estrella de Mar, sit in its bars and restaurants, join its clubs and societies, and feel the shadow of the gutted mansion fall across my shoulders in the evening. I needed to live in Frank's apartment, sleep in his bed and shower in his bathroom, insinuate myself into his dreams as they hovered on the night air above his pillow, faithfully waiting for him to return.

An hour later I had packed my suitcases and settled my account. As I drove from the Los Monteros Hotel for the last time I decided that I would stay on in Spain for at least another month, cancel my future assignments and transfer enough funds from my London bank to keep me going. Already I felt a curious complicity in the crime I was trying to solve, as if not only Frank's claims to guilt were being questioned but my own. Twenty minutes later, when I turned off the Malaga highway and took the slip-road to Estrella de Mar I sensed that I was going back to my true home.

Across the Avenida Santa Monica, a hundred yards from the gates of the Club Nautico, was a small late-night bar that drew its clientele from off-duty chauffeurs and the engine-fitters and deckhands who worked at the marina boatyard. Above it was a billboard advertising Toro cigarettes, a coarse, high-nicotine brand. I drew up at the kerb and gazed at the proud black bull lowering his horns at any would-be smoker.

For years I had tried to start smoking again, but without any success. In my twenties a cigarette had always calmed the nerves or filled a conversational pause, but I had given up smoking after a bout of pneumonia, and the social taboos were now so strong that I could never even bring myself to place an unlit cigarette in my mouth. Yet in Estrella de Mar the constraints of the new puritanism seemed less intense. I left the engine running and opened the door, deciding to buy a packet of Toros and test the powers of my will against a narrow-minded social convention.

Two young women in familiar micro-skirts and satin bustiers emerged from an alley beside the bar. Their high heels tapped the pavement, and they moved towards me with an easy swagger, assuming that I was waiting for them to accost me. I sat at the steering wheel, admiring their tough but relaxed charm. The prostitutes of Estrella de Mar had a confidence all their own, and were unconcerned by the possible presence of the vice police, so unlike the streetwalkers elsewhere in the world, with their illiterate, edgy minds, their pocked skins and weak ankles.

Tempted by these two young women, who might conceivably know something about the Hollinger fire, I waited for them to reach me. But as they stepped into the light I recognized their faces, and realized that their naked bodies would offer nothing in the way of surprise. I had already watched them from the balcony of Frank's apartment, lying on the chairs beside the pool as they gossiped over their fashion magazines and waited for their husbands, partners in a travel agency in the Paseo Miramar.

I closed my door and rolled along the kerb towards the women, who thrust out their thighs and breasts like department store demonstrators offering a free tasting of a new delicacy. When I drove past them they waved to my rear lights and retreated to a dark doorway beside the bar.

I sat in the car park at the Club Nautico, and listened to the unending beat of music from the disco. Were the two women game-playing, trying to excite their husbands, like latter-day versions of Marie Antoinette and her ladies in waiting, though posing as prostitutes rather than milkmaids? Or were they the real thing? It struck me that the residents of

Estrella de Mar might not be as prosperous as they seemed.

On the hill-slopes below the club a security alarm sounded, drilling like a metal cicada at the night. The answering siren of the volunteer security patrol wailed among the palms, a banshee floating above the darkened villas. The sleep of Estrella de Mar was quickened by anonymous crimes. I thought of the *favelas* in Rio, the violent shanty communities on the heights above the city. They reminded the sleeping rich in their luxury apartments of an even more elemental world than money. Yet I had slept my deepest sleep of all in Rio.

The disco doors opened and strobe music poured into the night. Two men, at first sight off-duty Spanish waiters, backed away from the glare when a young couple ran to their car. The men hovered by an ornamental flower-bed, as if ready to relieve themselves on the cannas, hands deep in the pockets of their reefer jackets, feet moving in the restless quick-step of dealers waiting for their clients.

The pool terrace was deserted, the choppy water settling itself for the night. I carried my suitcases to the doors of the elevator, which was stationary on the third floor. The corridor led to Frank's apartment, two locked administration offices and the club's library. No one, not even in Estrella de Mar, borrowed a book after midnight. I waited for the elevator, stepped out on to the third-floor landing and gazed through the glass doors at the shelves of forgotten best-sellers and the racked copies of the *Wall Street Journal* and the *Financial Times*.

Outside Frank's apartment the deep pile of the carpet, raked by a maid's vacuum-cleaner that morning, was bruised by heel marks. As I opened the door a light seemed to dim somewhere beyond the bedroom, the faint afterglow of a dying bulb. The beam of the Marbella lighthouse swept the peninsula, flaring over the rooftops of Estrella de Mar. Carrying my cases, I quietly closed the door behind me and set the security catch. Cloaks of moonlight lay over the furniture like dust-sheets. A faint scent hung on the air, an effeminate aftershave of the kind favoured by David Hennessy.

I walked into the dining room, listening to my footsteps as they dogged me across the parquet flooring. The whisky decanters stood on the blackwood sideboard, a favourite of my mother's that Frank had shipped to Spain. In the darkness I felt the crystal necks of the decanters. One stopper was loose, the glass bung still damp. I tasted the sweet Orkney malt, trying to tune my ears to the silent apartment.

The maid had tidied the bedroom, turning down the bed as if in preparation for Frank's arrival. Carried away by her thoughts of Frank, she had rested on his bed, pressing her head into the pillow as she allowed her memories to play across the ceiling.

I lowered my cases to the floor and smoothed the pillow before stepping into the bathroom. I searched the wall for the light-switch and by mistake opened the medicine cabinet. In the mirror I saw someone emerge from the balcony and enter the bedroom behind me, pausing on the way to the sitting room.

'Hennessy . . . ?' Tired of this charade, I left the bathroom and moved through the shadows towards the bed. 'Switch on a light, old chap. We'll be able to see ourselves playing the fool.'

The intruder collided with a suitcase, stumbled and fell across the bed. A skirt flared and a woman's thighs flashed in the moonlight. A coil of thick black hair scattered itself over the pillow, and a scent of sweat and panic filled the room. I bent down and held the woman's shoulders, trying to lift her on to her feet, but a hard fist punched me below the breast-bone. Winded, I slumped on to the bed as she thrust herself away from me. I reached out and seized her hips, pulled her on to the pillows and pinned her hands to the headboard, but she wrenched herself from me and knocked the bedside lamp to the floor.

'Leave me alone!' She struck my hands away, and I saw a strong chin and fierce teeth in the sweeping beam of the lighthouse. 'I told you – I won't play that game any more!'

I released her and sat on the bed, rubbing the bruised pit of my stomach. Setting the lamp on the bedside table, I straightened the shade and switched on the bulb.

7

An Attack on the Balcony

'DR HAMILTON?'

Kneeling in front of me, her hair in a dishevelled mane around her torn blouse, was the young physician who had arrived at the funeral with Hennessy and Bobby Crawford. She seemed startled to see me, eyes in a slight divergent squint as she tried to take in all four walls of the room and my presence on the bed. She quickly recovered, setting her lips firmly across her teeth, glaring up at me like a cornered puma.

'Doctor, I'm sorry . . .' I reached out to help her. 'I think I hurt you.'

'Leave me alone. Just keep away from me and stop that heavy breathing. You'll hyperventilate.'

She raised her hands to fend me off, then stood up and smoothed her skirt around her thighs. She winced over her bruised knees, and in a show of temper kicked the suitcase that had tripped her. 'Bloody thing . . .'

'Dr Hamilton . . . I thought you were –'

'David Hennessy? Good God, how much time do you spend rolling about on a bed with him?' She rubbed her flushed wrists, spitting on the skin. 'For a clumsy man, you're certainly strong. Frank must have had his work cut out with you bumping around him.'

'Paula, I didn't realize who you were. All the lights were off.'

'It's all right – when you grabbed me I was expecting someone else.' She managed a quick smile and began to examine my face and chest, sweeping her hair over her shoulders so that she could see me. 'It looks as if you'll live – I apologize for the uppercut. I'd forgotten how strong a frightened woman can be.'

'Just don't take up kick-boxing – I'm sure there are classes here.' Her scent clung to my hands, and without thinking I wiped them on the pillow. 'Your perfume – I thought it was David's aftershave.'

'Are you staying here? You'll smell me all night. What a dreadful thought . . .' She buttoned her blouse, watching me with some curiosity and perhaps matching me against Frank. She stepped back and bumped into the other suitcase. 'Good God, how many of these things are there? You must be a menace at airports. How on earth did you become a travel writer?'

Her handbag lay on the floor, contents scattered around the bedside table. She knelt and replaced her car keys, passport and prescription pad. Between my feet lay a postcard addressed to the staff at the Club Nautico. As I handed it to her I saw that it carried a reproduction of a tourist photographer's snapshot of Frank and Paula Hamilton outside Florian's bar in the Piazza San Marco. Muffled in heavy coats against a misty Venetian winter, they were grinning like honeymooners. I had seen the postcard in Frank's desk, but scarcely glanced at it.

'Is this yours?' I handed the postcard to her. 'You look as if you had fun.'

'We did.' She stared at the photograph and tried to straighten a creased corner. 'That was two years ago. Happier days for Frank. I dropped by to look for it. We sent it together, so it's partly mine.'

'Keep it – Frank won't mind. I didn't know you were . . .'

'We're not. Don't excite yourself thinking about it. We're good friends now.'

She helped me to straighten the bed, plumping the pillows and tucking in the sheets with crisp hospital corners. It was easy to imagine her lying in the darkness before I arrived, postcard in hand, thinking of her holiday with Frank. As Bobby Crawford had said, behind the professional poise she presented to the world she seemed distracted and vulnerable, like an intelligent teenaged girl unable to decide who she really was, perhaps suspecting that the role of efficient and capable doctor was something of a pose.

When she slipped the postcard into her bag she smiled sweetly to herself, and then checked this little display of affection, pursing her lips over her strong teeth. I sensed that she wanted to give in to her feelings for Frank, but was held back by a fear of exposing her emotions, even to herself. The testy humour, and the edgy manner of someone unsettled by standing more than a few seconds in front of a mirror, would have appealed to Frank, as it did to me. I guessed that Paula Hamilton had always moved through life at an oblique angle, detached from her emotions and sexuality.

'Thanks for the help,' I told her when we had rearranged the furniture. 'I wouldn't want to shock the maid. Tell me, how did you get in here?'

'I have a key.' She opened her handbag and showed a set of door keys to me. 'I meant to give them back to Frank but never quite got around to it. Too final, I suppose. So you're moving into the apartment?'

'For a week or so.' We left the bedroom and stepped on to the balcony, breathing the cool night air with its hints of jasmine and honeysuckle. 'I'm trying to play the older brother, without any success. I need to be closer to things if I'm going to get Frank out of this nightmare. I tried to talk to him this morning at the court in Marbella, but no luck. To be honest, he refused to see me.'

'I know. David Hennessy spoke to Frank's lawyer.' She touched my shoulder in a sudden show of sympathy. 'Frank needs time to think. Something terrible happened to the Hollingers. It's upsetting for you, but try to see things from his point of view.'

'I do. But what is Frank's point of view? That's one window I can't open. I take it you don't think he's guilty?'

She leaned against the rail, hands drumming the cold steel in time to the distant disco beat. I wondered what had brought her to the apartment – the postcard seemed a trivial pretext for a midnight visit – and why she had previously refused to see me. She kept turning to look at my face, as if unsure whether she could confide in someone who resembled Frank, but was nonetheless a larger and clumsier version of her former lover.

'Guilty? No, I don't . . . though I'm not all that sure what guilty means.'

'Paula – we know exactly what it means. Did Frank set fire to the Hollingers' house? Yes or no?'

'No.' The reply was less than prompt, but I suspected that she was deliberately drawing me on. 'Poor Frank. You saw him on the day you arrived. How was he? Is he sleeping properly?'

'I didn't ask. I assume there's not much else to do except sleep.'

'Did he tell you anything? About the fire, and how it started?'

'How could he? He can't have any more idea than you and I.'

'I don't suppose he has.' She strolled along the balcony, past the giant ferns and succulent plants, to the far end where three chairs were drawn up around a low table. A white sailboard leaned against the wall, its mast and rigging beside it. She pressed her hands against the smooth hull, as if laying them against a man's chest. The lighthouse beam moved across her face, and I saw that she was biting her injured lip, reminding herself of whatever accident had bruised her mouth.

Standing beside her, I looked down at the silent pool, a black mirror that reflected nothing.

'Paula, you don't sound certain about Frank. Everyone else in Estrella de Mar is convinced he's innocent.'

'Estrella de Mar?' She seemed curious about the name, the title of a mythical realm as remote as Camelot. 'People here are convinced of all sorts of things.'

'So? Are you saying that Frank might have been involved? What do you know about the fire?'

'Nothing. A vent of hell suddenly opened. By the time it closed five people were dead.'

'Were you there?'

'Of course. Everyone was there. Wasn't that the point?'

'In what sense? Look –'

Before I could remonstrate with her she turned to face me, and touched my forehead with a calming hand. 'Charles, I'm sure Frank didn't start the fire. At the same time he may feel responsible in some way.'

'Why?' I waited for her to reply, but she was looking at the dark ruin of the Hollinger house on its unlit eminence above the town. She touched the fading bruise on her cheek, and I wondered if she had been injured during the stampede from the fire. Deciding to change tack, I asked: 'Let's suppose that Frank *was* involved. Why would he have wanted to kill the Hollingers?'

'There's no conceivable reason. The Hollingers were the last people he'd have tried to harm. Frank's so gentle, far more

88

innocent than you, I'd guess. Or me. If I had the nerve I'd light a dozen bonfires here.'

'You don't sound too keen on Estrella de Mar?'

'Let's say I know more about the place than you do.'

'Then why stay?'

'Why indeed . . .' She leaned back against the sailboard, one hand holding its keel, her black hair silhouetted against the white plastic, the pose of a fashion model. Already I sensed that she was looking on me with more favour, for whatever reasons of her own, and revealing an almost flirtatious side of herself. 'There's my work at the clinic. It's a cooperative practice, and I'd have to sell my investment. Besides, my patients need me. Someone has to wean them off the Valium and Mogadon, teach them how to face the day without a bottle and a half of vodka.'

'So what Joan of Arc was to the English soldiery you are to the pharmaceutical industry?'

'Something like that. I've never thought of myself as Joan. Not enough voices.'

'And the Hollingers? Did you treat them?'

'No, but I was great friends with Anne, their niece, and helped her through a bad overdose. Same thing with Bibi Jansen. She was in a coma for four days, very nearly snuffed it. Heroin overdoses shut down the respiratory system, and that isn't good news for the brain. Still, we saved her – until the fire.'

'Why was Bibi working at the Hollingers?'

'They saw her in the intensive care unit, lying next to Anne, and promised to look after her if she pulled through.'

I leaned over the rail, listening to the dull beat of the disco music, and noticed the dealers hanging about near the entrance. 'They're still there. So a lot of drugs are moving around Estrella de Mar?'

'What do you think? Be honest, what else is there to do in

paradise? You catch the psychoactive fruit that falls from the tree. Believe me, everyone here is trying to lie down with the serpent.'

'Paula, isn't that a little too cynical?' I took her arm and turned her to face me. I thought of her strong, swimmer's body as we wrestled on Frank's bed. In a real sense it was I who was the interloper. During their nights together she and Frank had made his bed their own, and I was now intruding among the pillows and their ghosts. 'You can't hate the people here that much. After all, Frank liked them.'

'Of course he did.' She checked herself and bit her lip, abashed by her sharp tongue. 'He loved the Club Nautico, and made a big success of it. It's practically the nerve centre of Estrella de Mar. Have you seen the pueblos along the coast? Zombieland. Fifty thousand Brits, one huge liver perfused by vodka and tonic. Embalming fluid piped door to door . . .'

'I dropped by – ten minutes was all I could take. The sun doesn't shine there, only satellite TV. But why is Estrella de Mar so different? Someone here winds up the clocks.'

'That was Frank. Before he came the place was pretty drowsy.'

'Art galleries, theatre clubs, choral societies. Its own elected council and volunteer police force. Maybe there are a few drug-pushers and wives who like to practise their streetwalking, but the place feels as if it's a real community.'

'So they say. Frank always claimed that Estrella de Mar is what the future will be like. Take a good look while it lasts.'

'He's probably right. How did he do all this on his own?'

'Easy.' Paula grinned to herself. 'He had one or two important friends who helped him.'

'You, Paula?'

'Not me. Don't worry, I keep the medicine cabinets locked. I love Frank but the last place I want to be is in the next cell at Zarzuella prison.'

'What about Bobby Crawford? He and Frank were very close.'

'They were close.' Her hands tightened around the rail. 'Too close, really. They should never have met.'

'Why not? Crawford seems very likeable. A little too manic sometimes but enough boyish charm for an entire chorus line. Did he have too much power over Frank?'

'Never. Frank used Bobby. That's the key to everything.' She stared at the Hollinger house, and with an effort turned her back on the dark ruin. 'Listen, I have to call in at the Clinic. Sleep well, if you can stand that disco music. The night before the fire Frank and I hardly got a wink between us.'

'I thought you said that your affair was over?'

'It was.' She stared boldly at me. 'But we still had sex together . . .'

I followed her to the door, eager to see her again but unsure how best to raise the subject. During our conversation she had deliberately left a number of doors ajar for me, but I assumed that most of them would lead to dead-ends.

'Paula, one last point. When we were struggling on the bed you said something about not wanting to play a game any more.'

'Did I?'

'What game did you mean?'

'I don't know. Adolescent horse-play? I never was keen on debaggings and that sort of thing.'

'But that wasn't horse-play. You thought you were being raped.'

She gazed at me patiently and held my hand, noticing the infected splinter wound that still contained part of Crawford's racket. 'Nasty. If you come to the Clinic I'll see to it. Raped? No. I mistook you for someone else . . .'

*   *   *

After closing the door I returned to the balcony and looked down at the swimming pool. The disco had closed, and the dark water seemed to draw all the silences of the night into itself. Paula emerged from the restaurant, taking the long route to the car park, handbag bouncing jauntily against her hip. She twice waved to me, clearly keen to hold my attention. Already I envied Frank for having touched the affections of this quirky young doctor. After grappling with her on Frank's bed it was all too easy to imagine us making love. I thought of her in the intensive care unit, among the comatose stock-brokers and cardiac widows, and the special intimacy of catheters and drips.

When her headlamps set off into the night I pushed myself from the rail, more than ready for sleep. But before I could step back there was a sudden flurry of foliage behind me as someone lunged through the giant ferns. A pair of violent hands seized my shoulders and hurled me against the rail. Stunned by the assault, I sank to my knees as a leather strap tightened around my throat. A hard breath, damp with the smell of malt whisky, filled my face. I gripped the strap and tried to free my neck, but felt myself swung to the tiled floor like a steer roped and decked by a skilled rodeo rider.

A foot kicked the balcony table against the chairs. The strap fell away, and the man's hands gripped my throat. Powerful but sensitive, they controlled the air I was able to gasp during the brief moments when the fingers eased their pressure. They searched the muscles and vessels of my neck, almost playing a melody with my death.

Barely breathing, I clung to the rail as the lighthouse beacon faded and the night closed inside my head.

8

The Scent of Death

'FIVE MURDERS ARE more than enough, Mr Prentice. We have no wish for a sixth. I make the point officially.'

Inspector Cabrera raised his stocky arms to the ceiling, ready to bear any weight rather than the problems I posed for him. Already I represented one seminar too many to this thoughtful young detective, as if I had personally decided to test to destruction all the lessons in the psychology of victimhood given to him by his instructors at the police academy.

'I understand, Inspector. But perhaps you'd speak to the man who attacked me. I appreciate your coming here.'

'Good.' Cabrera turned to Paula Hamilton as she fretted with the orthopaedic collar around my neck, asking her to witness his formal warning. He spoke tersely to me. 'Your brother's trial is in three months' time. For the present go back to England, go to Antarctica. If you stay, you may provoke another death — this time your own.'

I sat in Frank's leather armchair, my fingers kneading the soft, clubman's leather. I nodded my agreement to Cabrera, but I was thinking of the strip of far tougher hide that had driven the blood from my brain. Paula hovered beside me, one hand on my shoulder and the other on her medical valise, unsure of my state of mind. Any resemblance between Frank and myself had been erased by the attempt on my life and my lighthearted refusal to accept that someone had tried to kill me.

'You say "officially" – does that mean that I'm being formally expelled from Spain?'

'Of course not.' Cabrera scoffed at this, refusing to play my verbal games. 'Expulsion is a matter for the Minister and the Spanish courts. You can stay as and when you wish. I'm advising you, Mr Prentice, as a friend. What good can you do here? It's regrettable, but your brother refuses to see you.'

'Inspector, he may change his mind now.'

'Even so, his trial will not be affected. Think of your safety – a man tried to kill you last night.'

I adjusted the collar and beckoned Cabrera to a chair, wondering how to reassure him. 'As a matter of fact, I don't think he did want to kill me. If he had, I wouldn't be sitting here.'

'That's nonsense, Mr Prentice . . .' Cabrera patiently dismissed this amateurish notion, and gestured at the balcony. 'He may have been disturbed or seen from below in the lighthouse beam. You were lucky once, but twice is too much to expect. Dr Hamilton, speak to him. Convince him that his life is in danger. There are people in Estrella de Mar who guard their privacy at any cost.'

'Charles, think about that. You have been asking an awful lot of questions.' Paula sat on the arm of the chair, her hand trembling slightly against my shoulder. 'You can't help Frank, and you nearly had yourself killed.'

'No . . .' I tried to ease the collar away from the bruised muscles of my neck. 'That was a warning – a kind of free air-ticket back to London.'

Cabrera pulled up a straight-backed chair and straddled the seat, resting his arms on the back as if examining a large and obtuse mammal. 'If it was a warning, Mr Prentice, you should listen to it. You can turn over one stone too many.'

'Exactly, Inspector. In a way it's the breakthrough I've been waiting for. It's clear I provoked someone, almost certainly the Hollingers' killer.'

'You didn't see the man's face? Or recognize his shoes or his clothes? His aftershave . . . ?'

'No. He seized me from behind. There was a strange smell on his hands, perhaps some sort of special oil that professional stranglers use. He must have carried out similar attacks before.'

'A professional killer? It's remarkable that you can talk at all. Dr Hamilton says your throat isn't damaged.'

'It's hard to explain, Inspector.' Lips pursed, Paula pointed to the bruises on my neck left by the assailant's fingertips. The attack had shocked her. Usually so quick-witted, and never at a loss for a word, she was almost silent. By leaving me alone in the apartment she had made herself partly responsible for my injuries. Yet she seemed unsurprised by the assault, as if expecting it to take place. Speaking in her flat, lecture-room voice, she said: 'In cases of strangulation the voice-box is almost always crushed. In fact, it's difficult to strangle someone to the point of unconsciousness without doing serious structural damage to the nerves and blood vessels. You were lucky, Charles. If you blacked out that was probably because you hit your head on the floor.'

'Actually, I didn't. He lowered me there quite gently. My throat's very sore – I can barely swallow. He used a peculiar grip on my neck, like a skilled masseur. The strange thing is that I feel slightly high.'

'Post-traumatic euphoria,' Cabrera commented, at last slotting one of his psychology seminars into place. 'People who walk from plane crashes are often laughing. They call taxis and go home.'

When Cabrera first arrived at the apartment and found me sitting on the balcony, reassuring Paula that I was well, he obviously suspected that I had imagined the assault. Only when

Paula showed him the bruises to my jaw and neck, the clotted blood in the swollen veins, did he accept my account.

I had regained consciousness in the small hours of the morning, and found myself lying on the balcony among the overturned plants, my wrists tied to the table frame by the belt of my slacks. Barely able to breathe, I lay on the cold tiles as the lighthouse beam swept the grey dawn. When my head cleared I tried to recall any detail of my attacker. He had moved with the swiftness of a specialist in unarmed combat, like the Thai commandos I had seen in action at a passing-out parade in Bangkok, demonstrating how to seize and kill an enemy sentry. I remembered his heavy knees and strong thighs clad in some kind of black cord, and the cleated soles that sucked at the stone floor, the only sound apart from my strangled gasps. I was certain that he had been careful not to injure me, avoiding the large vessels and my larynx, and applying only enough pressure to suffocate me. Beyond this there was little to identify him. There was a waxy but astringent smell on his hands, and I guessed that he might have ritually bathed himself.

At six, when I freed my wrists, I limped to the telephone. Croaking to the startled night porter, I insisted that he call the Spanish police and report the assault. Two hours later a veteran detective arrived from the robbery squad at Benalmadena. As the concierge translated, I pointed to the scattered furniture and the violent scuff-marks on the tiled floor. The detective was unconvinced, and I heard him murmur '*domestica*' into his mobile phone. However, when he was told my surname his manner changed.

Inspector Cabrera arrived as Paula Hamilton was treating me. The concierge had telephoned her while I rested on the balcony, and she had driven immediately from the Princess Margaret Clinic. Shocked by the attack, and all too easily imagining Frank in my place, she was as puzzled as Cabrera by my calm manner. I watched her take my blood pressure and test my pupils, and noticed how confused she seemed, twice dropping her stethoscope on to the floor.

Despite her concern, I felt stronger than I expected. The attack had revived my flagging confidence. For a few desperate moments I had grappled with a man who might well be responsible for the Hollingers' deaths. My neck bore the imprint of the hands that had carried the ether bottles into the mansion.

Tired of the orthopaedic collar and the soft leather armchair, I stood up and stepped on to the balcony, hoping to work off my restlessness. Cabrera watched me from the door, restraining Paula when she tried to calm me.

He pointed to the overhanging *brise-soleil*. 'Entry from the roof is impossible, and the balcony is too high for a ladder. It's curious, Mr Prentice – there is only one way into the apartment – the front door. Yet you insist that you locked the door behind you.'

'Of course. I intended to spend the night here. In fact I'd decided to check out of my hotel and move into the apartment. I need a closer eye on everything.'

'Then how did your attacker gain access to the balcony?'

'Inspector, he must have been waiting for me.' I thought of the loose decanter stopper. Paula had entered the apartment, unaware that the assailant was hiding in its shadows and calmly helping himself to the Orkney malt. He had listened to us struggling in the bedroom, recognized my voice and then seized his chance once Paula left.

'Who else has the key?' Cabrera asked. 'The maids, the concierge?'

'That's all. No, wait a minute . . .'

I caught Paula looking at me in the mirror over the sitting-room mantelpiece. With her bruised mouth and untidy hair she resembled a guilty child, a startled Alice who had suddenly grown to adulthood and found herself trapped on the wrong side of the glass. I had said nothing to Cabrera about her visit to the apartment the previous evening.

'Mr Prentice?' Cabrera was watching me with interest. 'You've remembered something . . . ?'

'No. The keys weren't locked away, Inspector. Once you finished searching the apartment after Frank's arrest you handed them to Mr Hennessy. They were lying in his desk drawer. Anyone could have stepped in and had a copy made.'

'Of course. But how did your attacker know you were here? You decided only late in the evening to leave Los Monteros.'

'Inspector . . .' This pleasant but over-shrewd young policeman seemed determined to make me his chief suspect. 'I was the victim. I can't speak for the man who tried to strangle me. He may have been in the club when I arrived, and seen me unloading my suitcases in the car park. Perhaps he telephoned the Los Monteros Hotel after I left, and they told him that I was moving here. You might follow those leads up, Inspector.'

'Naturally . . . I happily take your advice, Mr Prentice. As a journalist you've seen so many police forces at work.' Cabrera spoke dryly, but his eyes were scanning the scuff-marks on the tiled floor, as if trying to calculate the assailant's height. 'You obviously have a feeling for the profession . . .'

'Does it matter, Inspector?' Paula stepped between us, irritated by Cabrera's questioning. Her face was calm now, and she took my arm, steadying me against her shoulder. 'Mr Prentice could hardly have attacked himself. What conceivable motive would he have had?"

Cabrera stared dreamily at the sky. 'Motives? Yes, how they complicate police work. There are so many of them, and they mean anything you wish to make them. Without motives our investigations would be so much easier. Tell me, Mr Prentice, have you visited the Hollingers' house?'

'A few days ago. Mr Hennessy took me there, but we couldn't get inside. It's a grim sight.'

'Very grim. I suggest another visit. This morning I had the autopsy reports. Tomorrow, when you have rested, I will take you there with Dr Hamilton. Her opinion will be valuable . . .'

I passed the afternoon on the balcony, my neck chafing inside the orthopaedic collar, my feet resting on the scuffed floor. In the soil scattered from the plant tubs a demented geometer had set out the diagram of a bizarre dance of death. I could still feel my assailant's hands on my throat, and hear his harsh breath in my ears, reeking of malt whisky.

Despite all I had said to Cabrera, I too was curious how my attacker had entered the apartment and why he had chosen the very evening that I left the Los Monteros Hotel. Already I sensed that I was being kept under surveillance by people who saw me as something more dangerous to them than Frank's concerned brother. Another murder would not have suited their purposes, but a near-strangulation might well send me to Malaga airport and a speedy return to the safety of London.

At six, shortly before Paula returned, I took a shower to clear my head. As I soaped myself with Frank's bath gel I recognized the scent, an odd blend of patchouli and orris oil, the same odour that had clung to my attacker's hands and which now covered my body.

As I rinsed away the offensive fragrance I guessed that he had been hiding in the shower stall when I arrived, and that his hand had touched the gel container in the dark. I assumed that he was searching the apartment as Paula let herself through the door with her spare key, and that she had not realized he was present while she hunted for the postcard.

Yet far from warning me off, the attack had turned up the

ratchet of my involvement with the Hollingers' deaths, and made certain that I would remain in Estrella de Mar.

I dressed and returned to the balcony, listening to the divers plunge into the pool below and the tennis machine serve its aces to the practice players on the courts. The faint scent of bath gel still clung to my skin, the perfume of my own strangulation that embraced me like a forbidden memory.

9

The Inferno

AN ASHY DUST cloaked the hill slopes as the nearside wheels of Cabrera's car raced through the verge, a chalky pall that swirled between the palms and floated up the drives of the handsome villas beside the road. When it cleared we could see the Hollinger house on its fire mountain, a vast grate choked with dead embers. Teeth clenched, Paula worked the gear lever, chasing the policeman's car around the bends and only slowing out of respect for my injured throat.

'We shouldn't be here,' she told me, clearly still shocked by my assault and the thought that such violence existed in Estrella de Mar. 'You aren't resting enough. I want you to come to the Clinic tomorrow for another X-ray. How do you feel?'

'Physically? I dare say, a complete wreck. Mentally, fine. That attack released something. Whoever seized me had a light touch – I once watched professional stranglers doing their stuff in northern Borneo, executing so-called bandits. Extremely nasty, but in a way I . . .'

'Know how it feels? Not quite.' She slowed down to give herself time to look me over. 'Cabrera was right – you're slightly euphoric. Are you strong enough to go round the Hollingers' house?'

'Paula, stop playing the head girl. This case is about to break, I sense it. And I think Cabrera senses it too.'

'He senses you're going to get yourself killed. You and

Frank – I thought you were so different, but you're even more mad than he is.'

I leaned my orthopaedic collar against the head-rest and watched her as she crouched over the steering wheel. Determined not to be left behind by Cabrera, she peered fiercely at the road, putting her foot down at the smallest opportunity. Despite her sharp tongue and brisk manner, below the surface lay a strain of insecurity that I found pleasantly attractive. She affected to look down at the expat communities along the coast, but had a curiously low estimate of herself, bridling whenever I tried to tease her. I knew that she was annoyed with herself for having concealed from Cabrera her presence at the apartment, presumably for fear that he might assume some personal involvement between us.

Miguel, the Hollingers' morose chauffeur, was opening the gates when we caught up with Cabrera. The wind had disturbed the ash that lay over the gardens and tennis court, but the estate was still bathed in a marble light, a world of glooms glimpsed in a morbid dream. Death had arrived at the Hollingers and decided to stay, settling her skirts over the shadowy pathways.

Cabrera greeted us when we parked, and walked with us to the front steps of the house.

'Dr Hamilton, thank you for giving up your time. Are you ready, Mr Prentice? You are not too tired?'

'Not at all, Inspector. If I feel faint I'll wait out here. Dr Hamilton can describe it to me later.'

'Good. In fact, your first sensible idea.' He was watching me closely, eager to see my reactions, as if I were a tethered goat whose bleats might draw a tiger from its lair. I was sure that by now he had no wish to see me return to London.

'Now . . .' Cabrera turned his back on the heavy oak doors,

still sealed by their police tapes, and pointed to the gravel path that led around the south-west corner of the mansion to the kitchen and garages. 'The hall and the downstairs rooms are too dangerous for anyone to enter. I suggest therefore that we follow the path taken by the assassin. This way we will see events in the order they took place. It will help us to understand what happened on that evening and, perhaps, read the psychology of the victims and their murderer . . .'

Enjoying his new role as stately home tour guide, Cabrera led us around the house. The Hollingers' blue vintage Bentley stood outside the garage, the only clean and polished entity in the estate. Miguel had washed and waxed the limousine, buffing the huge wings that flared above its wheels. He had followed us up the drive and now stood patiently beside the car. Still staring at me, he took up his leather and began to rub the high radiator grille.

'Poor man . . .' Paula held my arm, eyes avoiding the debris of charred timbers around us, and tried to smile at the chauffeur. 'Do you think he's all right here?'

'I hope so. It looks as if he's waiting for the Hollingers to return. Inspector, what do you know about the psychology of chauffeurs . . . ?'

But Cabrera was pointing to the flight of steps that led to the housekeeper's quarters above the garage. A wrought-iron gate beside the entry door opened on to the blighted hillside where the lemon orchard had once flourished. Cabrera sprinted up the steps and stood by the gate.

'Dr Hamilton, Mr Prentice . . . you will notice the gate from the orchard. We can now imagine the situation on the evening of 15 June. By seven o'clock the party is well in progress, with all the guests on the terrace beside the pool. As Dr Hamilton will remember, the Hollingers appear on the top-floor veranda and propose the toast to your Queen. Everyone is looking up at the Hollingers, glasses raised to Her

Majesty, and no one notices the arsonist when he opens the orchard gate.'

Cabrera skipped down the staircase and stepped past us to the kitchen entrance. He took a set of keys from his pocket and unlocked the door. I appreciated his tactful use of the term 'arsonist', though I suspected that the tour was designed to rid me of my faith in Frank's innocence.

'Inspector, Frank was mingling with the other guests on the terrace. Why would he leave the party and hide in the orchard? Dozens of people talked to him by the pool.'

Cabrera nodded his sympathy at this. 'Exactly, Mr Prentice. But no one remembers speaking to him after six-forty-five. Did you, Dr Hamilton?'

'No – I was with David Hennessy and some friends. I didn't really see Frank at all.' She turned away and stared at the gleaming Bentley, pressing the faded bruise on her mouth as if willing it to return. 'Perhaps he didn't go to the party?'

Cabrera firmly dismissed this. 'Many witnesses spoke to him, but none after six-forty-five. Remember, the arsonist needed to park his incendiary materials close at hand. No one would notice a guest walking up the steps to the orchard. Once there, he collects his bombs – three bottles filled with ether and gasoline that he buried the previous day in a shallow excavation twenty metres from the gate. As the Queen's toast begins he sets off to enter the house. The nearest and most convenient door is this one into the kitchen.'

I nodded at all this, but asked: 'What about the housekeeper? Surely she would have seen him?'

'No. The housekeeper and her husband were by the terrace, helping the temporary staff to serve the canapés and champagne. They were raising their glasses to Her Majesty and saw nothing.'

Cabrera pushed back the door and beckoned us into the

kitchen. A brick-built annexe to the main house, it was the only part of the structure undamaged. Saucepans hung from the walls, and the shelves were crowded with spices, herbs and bottles of olive oil. But the yeasty stench of sodden carpets and the acrid odour of charred fabrics filled the room. Pools of water lay on the floor, soaking a walkway of wooden boards laid down by the police investigators.

Cabrera waited until we found our footing and then continued. 'So: the arsonist enters the empty kitchen and seals the door. The house is now closed off from the outside world. The Hollingers preferred their guests not to enter their home, and all the doors on to the terrace were locked. In fact, the guests were completely segregated from their hosts – an English tradition, I assume. Now, let us follow the arsonist when he leaves the kitchen . . .'

Cabrera led the way into the pantry, a large room that occupied a section of the annexe. A refrigerator, washing-machine and spin-drier stood on the concrete floor, surrounded by pools of water. Beside a deep-freezer cabinet an inspection door opened into a head-high chamber that contained the central heating and air-conditioning system. Cabrera stepped through the inspection door and pointed to the partly dismantled unit, a furnace-sized structure that resembled a large turbine.

'The intake manifold draws air from a pipe on the kitchen roof. The air is filtered and humidified, then either cooled during the summer or heated during the winter, and finally pumped to the rooms around the house. The arsonist switches off the system – for the few minutes he needs no one will notice. He removes the cowling of the humidifier, drains off the water and refills the reservoir with his gasoline and ether mixture. All is now set for a huge and cruel explosion . . .'

Cabrera ushered us through the service corridor that led into the mansion. We stood in the spacious hall, looking at ourselves in the foam-smeared mirrors, visitors to a marine grotto. The staircase rose a dozen steps, then divided beneath a large baronial fireplace that dominated the hall. Tags of scorched cloth lay in the iron grate, and the ashes had been carefully sifted by the police investigators.

Watching me closely, Cabrera continued: 'Everything is ready. The guests are busy with their party outside, eager to drink the last of the champagne. The Hollingers, their niece Anne, the Swedish maid and the secretary, Mr Sansom, have retired to their rooms to escape the noise. The arsonist takes his remaining bottle of gasoline and ether and soaks a small carpet he has laid in the fireplace. The flames leap swiftly from his match or lighter. He then returns to the pantry. As the fire on the staircase begins to rage he switches on the air-conditioning system . . .'

Cabrera paused, waiting as Paula gripped my arm to steady herself, knuckles between her teeth.

'It's terrible to imagine. Within seconds the gasoline mixture is driven through the ventilation ducts. Ignited by the flames on the staircase, the rooms of the upper floor turn into an inferno. No one escapes, even though there are emergency steps that lead down to the terrace from a door on the landing. Mr Hollinger's film library, in a room next to his study, adds to the blaze. The house is a furnace, and everyone inside it perishes in a matter of minutes.'

I felt Paula stumble against me, and put an arm around her trembling shoulders. She had begun to cry to herself, and her tears stained the lapel of my cotton jacket. She seemed about to collapse, but rallied herself and murmured: 'Good God, who could do such a thing?'

'Certainly not Frank, Inspector.' Still supporting Paula, I spoke as calmly as I could to Cabrera. 'This dismantling of the air-conditioning system and turning it into an incendiary weapon – Frank could barely change a light-bulb. Whoever carried out this attack had the skills you find only in people trained as military saboteurs.'

'Perhaps, Mr Prentice . . .' Cabrera watched Paula with obvious concern, and offered her his handkerchief. 'But skills can be learned, especially dangerous ones. Let us continue our tour.'

The staircase was strewn with charred timbers and ceiling plaster, but the police investigators had cleared a narrow ascent. Cabrera climbed the steps, hands holding the scorched banisters, feet sinking in the sodden carpet. The oak panelling around the fireplace had turned to charcoal, but here and there the outlines of a heraldic shield had been preserved.

We paused on the landing, surrounded by blackened walls, the open sky above our heads. The bedroom doors had burned down to their locks and hinges, and through the empty frames we could see into the gutted rooms with their incinerated furniture. The forensic team had laid a catwalk of planks along the exposed joists, and Cabrera stepped warily towards the first of the bedrooms.

I helped Paula along the rocking timber and steadied her against the doorway. In the centre of the room were the remains of a four-poster bed. Around it stood the carbonized ghosts of a desk, dressing-table and a large oak wardrobe in the Spanish style. A line of framed photographs stood on the stone mantelpiece. Some of the glass had melted in the heat, but one frame, surprisingly intact, showed a florid-faced man in a dinner jacket, standing at a lectern inscribed with the legend: 'Beverly Wilshire Hotel'.

'Is that Hollinger?' I asked Cabrera. 'Speaking in Los Angeles to some film industry audience?'

'Many years ago,' Cabrera confirmed. 'He was much older when he came to Estrella de Mar. This was his bedroom. According to the housekeeper he slept for an hour before dinner.'

'What an end . . .' I stared at the mattress springs, like the coils of a huge electric grill. 'I only hope the poor man never awoke.'

'In fact, Mr Hollinger was not in the bed.' Cabrera pointed to the bathroom. 'He had taken refuge in the jacuzzi, probably to spare himself from the flames.'

We stepped into the bathroom, and gazed down at the semi-circular tub filled with tarry water. Roof-tiles lay on the floor, and the blue ceramic walls were streaked with smoke, but the room was almost intact, a tiled execution chamber. I imagined the elderly Hollinger, roused from sleep as the flames leapt from the masts of his four-poster, unable to warn his wife in her nearby bedroom, and driven into the jacuzzi as a fireball erupted from the air-conditioning vents.

'Poor devil,' I commented. 'Dying by himself in a jacuzzi. There's a warning there . . .'

'Possibly.' Cabrera moistened his hands in the water. 'Actually, he was not alone.'

'Really? So Mrs Hollinger was with him?' I thought of the elderly couple reclining in the jacuzzi before dressing for dinner. 'In a way it's rather touching.'

Cabrera smiled faintly. 'Mrs Hollinger was not here. She was in another bedroom.'

'Then who was with Hollinger?'

'The Swedish maid, Bibi Jansen. You went to her funeral.'

'I did . . .' I was trying to visualize the old millionaire and the young Swede in the water together. 'Are you sure it was Hollinger?'

'Of course.' Cabrera turned the pages of his notebook. 'His surgeon in London identified a special type of steel pin in his right hip.'

'Dear Jesus . . .' Paula released my arm and stepped past Cabrera to the wash-basin. She stared at herself in the cloudy mirror, as if trying to identify her reflection, and then leaned on the ash-strewn porcelain, her head lowered. Already I could see that the visit to the house was a far greater ordeal for her than it was for me.

'I didn't know Hollinger or Bibi Jansen,' I said to Cabrera. 'But it's hard to imagine the two of them together in a jacuzzi.'

'Technically, that's correct.' Cabrera was still noting my responses to everything. 'It would be more accurate to say there were three of them.'

'Three people in the jacuzzi? Who was the third?'

'Miss Jansen's child.' Cabrera helped Paula to the door. 'Dr Hamilton will confirm that she was pregnant.'

As Cabrera surveyed the bathroom, measuring the walls with a steel tape, I followed Paula out of Hollinger's bedroom. Crossing the catwalk of planks, we entered a small room along the corridor. Here the fire had raged even more fiercely. The blackened remains of a large doll lay on the floor like a charred baby, but the torrent of water hosed on to the roof had obliterated all other traces of the room's occupant. In one corner the fire had spared a small dressing-table, which still supported a CD player.

'This was Bibi's room,' Paula told me flatly. 'That heat must have been ... I don't know why she was here at all. She should have been by the pool with everyone else.'

She picked up the doll and placed it on the remains of the bed, then dusted the black ash from her hands. Pain and anger seemed to compete within her face, as if she had lost a valued patient as a result of a colleague's incompetence. I put my arm around her, glad when she leaned against me.

'Did you know she was pregnant, Paula?'

'Yes. Four or five weeks.'

'Who was the father?'

'I've no idea. She wouldn't tell me.'

'Gunnar Andersson? Dr Sanger?'

'Sanger?' Paula's fist clenched against my chest. 'For heaven's sake, he was her father-figure.'

'Even so. When were you last here?'

'Six weeks ago. She'd been swimming at night and caught a kidney chill. Charles, who would start a fire like this?'

'Not Frank, that's for sure. God knows why he confessed. But I'm glad we came. Someone obviously hated the Hollingers.'

'Perhaps they didn't realize how fast the fire would burn. It might have been a prank that went wrong?'

'It's too deliberate for that. The re-jigged air-conditioning system . . . this was a serious business.'

We rejoined Cabrera in a room across the landing. Its door had vanished, sucked into the night air by the vortex of flame and gas.

'This was the room of the niece, Anne Hollinger,' Cabrera explained, staring bleakly at the gutted shell. He spoke more quietly, no longer the police academy lecturer, as drained as Paula and I by the experience of visiting the death-rooms. 'The heat was so intense, she had no way of escape. Since the air-conditioning had been supplying cool air, all the windows were tightly closed.'

The forensic team had dismantled the bed, presumably to detach the niece's carbonized remains from the debris of mattress.

'Where was she found?' I asked. 'Lying on the bed?'

'No – she too died in the bathroom. Not in the jacuzzi, however. She was sitting on the toilet – a macabre posture, like Rodin's "Thinker".' As Paula shuddered against my arm Cabrera added: 'At least she was happy when she died. We found a hypodermic syringe . . .'

'What was inside it – heroin?'

'Who can say? The fire was too fierce for analysis.'

Below the window, perhaps cooled by the inrush of cold air through the shattered glass, a television set and video-recorder had survived intact. The remote-control unit lay on the bedside table, melted like black chocolate, blurred numerals still visible in the plastic.

Despite myself, I said: 'I wonder what programme she was watching? I'm sorry – that sounds callous.'

'It is.' Paula wearily shook her head as I tried to turn on the TV set. 'Charles, we've seen the news. Anyway, the current isn't on.'

'I know. What was Anne like? I take it she was a heavy drug-user.'

'She definitely wasn't. Not after her overdose. I don't know what she was injecting.' Paula stared across the sunlit rooftops of Estrella de Mar. 'She was great fun. Once she rode a camel around the Plaza Iglesias, swearing at the taxi-drivers like a haughty *torera*. One evening at the Club Nautico she picked a live lobster from the restaurant tank and had it brought to our table.'

'She ate it raw?'

'No. She took pity on the thing, waving its claws at her, and released it into the salt-water plunge pool. It took them days to catch the beast. Bobby Crawford was feeding it at night. And then she died here . . .'

'Paula, you didn't start the fire.'

'And nor did Frank.' She wiped her tears from my jacket. 'Cabrera knows that.'

'I'm not sure if he does.'

The Inspector was waiting for us outside the largest bed-room in the west wing of the house. The windows looked out over an open veranda to the sea, veiled by awnings that hung like black sails. It was from here that the Hollingers had proposed the Queen's birthday toast before retiring. Shreds of burnt chintz clung to the walls, and the dressing room resembled a coal scuttle in a rage.

'Mrs Hollinger's bedroom.' Cabrera held my arm when I stumbled on the catwalk. 'Are you all right, Mr Prentice? I think you have seen enough?'

'I'm fine – let's complete the tour, Inspector. Mrs Hollinger was found here?'

'No.' Cabrera pointed along the corridor. 'She had taken refuge at the rear of the house. Perhaps the flames there were less intense.'

We made our way down the corridor, to a small room with a single window overlooking the lemon orchard. Despite the destructive effects of the fire, it was clear that a sophisticated sensibility had devised a refined if faintly precious private world. A lacquered Chinese screen separated the bed from the living area, and what had once been a pair of handsome Empire chairs faced each other across the fireplace. Two of the walls were lined with books, whose spines peeled from the charred shelves. Above the bed was a small dormer window that contained the only intact glass I had seen on the upper floor of the mansion.

'Was this Hollinger's study?' I asked Cabrera. 'Or Mrs Hollinger's sitting room?'

'No – this was Mr Sansom's bedroom. He was the male secretary.'

'And Mrs Hollinger was found here?'

'She was on the bed.'

'And Sansom?' I searched the floor, almost expecting to find a body against the skirting-board.

'He was also on the bed.'

'So they were lying together?'

'In death, certainly. Her shoes were still in his hands, clenched very fiercely . . .'

Surprised by this, I turned to speak to Paula, but she had

left to make a last circuit of the other rooms. I knew almost nothing about Roger Sansom, a bachelor in his fifties who had worked for Hollinger's property company and then accompanied him to Spain as his general factotum. But to die in bed with his employer's wife showed an excessive sense of duty. It was too easy to visualize their last moments together as the lacquered screen burst into a fiery shield.

'Mr Prentice . . .' Cabrera beckoned me to the door. 'I suggest you find Dr Hamilton. She is very upset, it's a big strain for her. Meanwhile, you will have seen enough – perhaps you'll speak to your brother. I can oblige him to meet you.'

'Frank? What is there to talk about? I assume you've described all this to him?'

'He too has seen everything. On the day after the fire he asked me to take him around the house. He was already under arrest, charged with possessing an incendiary device. When he reached this room he decided to confess.'

Cabrera was watching me in his thoughtful way, as if expecting that I, in turn, would admit my role in the crime.

'Inspector, when I meet Frank I'll say that I've seen the house. If he knows I've been here he'll realize how absurd his confession is. The idea that he's guilty is preposterous.'

Cabrera seemed disappointed in me. 'It's possible, Mr Prentice. Guilt is so flexible, it's a currency that changes hands . . . each time losing a little value.'

I left him poking into the drawers of the bedside table, and made my way along the catwalk in search of Paula. Mrs Hollinger's bedroom was empty, but as I passed the niece's room I heard Paula's voice on the terrace below.

She was waiting for me by her car, talking to Miguel as he tried to clear the blocked vents of the swimming pool. I walked to the window and leaned out between the shreds of charred awning.

'We're through now, Paula. I'll be down in a minute.'

'Good. I want to go. I thought you were watching television.'

She had recovered her self-control, and smoked a miniature cigar as she leaned against the BMW, but her eyes avoided the house. She strolled towards the pool and wandered among the chairs on the terrace. I guessed that she was searching for the exact spot where she had stood at the moment the fire erupted.

Admiring her, I rested against the sill, and tried to loosen the orthopaedic collar around my neck. Looking down at the TV set, I noticed that a cassette protruded from the mouth of the video-recorder, ejected by the mechanism when the intense heat confused the circuitry. Dismayed by the destruction around them, and the grim task of removing bodies, the police team had missed one of the few objects to survive both the blaze and the deluge of water that followed.

I held the cassette and drew it carefully from the recorder. Its casing was intact, and I raised the shroud to find the tape still held tightly between the spools. The TV set was visible from the bathroom, and I imagined Anne Hollinger staring at the screen as she sat on the toilet and injected herself with heroin. Curious to see this last programme she had watched before the fire seized her life from her, I slipped the cassette into my pocket and followed Cabrera down the stairs.

10

The Pornographic Film

THE CHAUFFEUR'S SCOOP roamed across the surface of the pool, its ladle filled with debris, relics of a drowned realm salvaged from the deep: wine bottles, straw hats, a cummerbund, patent-leather shoes, gleaming together in the sunlight as the water streamed away. Miguel decanted each netful on to the marble verge, respectfully laying out the residues of a vanished evening.

His eyes scarcely left me as I rested beside Paula in the car. I listened to Cabrera's noisy Seat hunting the palm-lined avenues below the Hollinger estate. His departure seemed to expose us again to the full horrors of the burned mansion. Paula's hands gripped the upper quadrant of the steering wheel, fingers tightening and relaxing. The house was behind us, but I knew that her mind was roving through its gutted rooms as she carried out her own autopsies on the victims.

Trying to reassure her, I put my arm around her shoulders. She turned to face me, smiling in a distracted way like a doctor only half-aware of the attentions of an amorous patient.

'Paula, you're tired. Shall I drive? I'll leave you at the Clinic and take a taxi from there.'

'I can't face the Clinic.' She leaned her forehead against the wheel. 'Those desperate rooms . . . I'd like everyone in Estrella de Mar to walk around them. I keep thinking of all those people who drank Hollinger's champagne and thought he was just another old blimp with an actressy wife. I was one of them.'

'But you didn't start the fire. Remind yourself of that.'

'I do.' She sounded unconvinced.

We drove down to Estrella de Mar, as the sea trembled beyond the palms, and passed the Anglican church, whose members were arriving for choir practice. At the sculpture studio another young Spaniard in a posing pouch flexed his pectorals for the earnest students in their artists' smocks. The open-air cinema was alternating Renoir's *Le Règle du Jeu* with Gene Kelly's *Singing in the Rain*, and one of the dozen theatre clubs announced a forthcoming season of plays by Harold Pinter. Despite the Hollinger murders, Estrella de Mar was as serious in its pleasures as a seventeenth-century New England settlement.

From the balcony of Frank's apartment I looked down at the swimming pool, where Bobby Crawford, megaphone in hand, was training a team of women butterfly swimmers. He raced along the verge, cheerfully bellowing instructions to the thirty-year-olds who wallowed in the chaotic water. His commitment was touching, as if he genuinely believed that every one of his pupils had the ability to become an Olympic champion.

'That sounds like Bobby Crawford.' Paula joined me at the rail. 'What's he up to now?'

'He's exhausting me. All this physical keenness and that thudding tennis machine. It's a metronome, setting our tempo – faster, faster, serve, volley, smash. There's something to be said for the retirement pueblos ... Paula, can we take off this collar? I can't think with the damned thing on.'

'Well ... if you have to. Try it for an hour and see how you feel.' She unclipped the collar, grimacing at the livid bruises. 'Cabrera could almost lift a set of fingerprints – who on earth would want to attack you?'

'As it happens, quite a few people. There's another side to Estrella de Mar. The Harold Pinter seasons, the choral societies and sculpture classes are an elaborate play-group. Meanwhile everyone else is getting on with the real business.'

'And that is?'

'Money, sex, drugs. What else is there these days? Outside Estrella de Mar no one gives a damn about the arts. The only real philosophers left are the police.'

Paula's hands rested on my shoulders. 'Cabrera may be right. If you're in danger you ought to leave.'

She had revived after the visit to the Hollinger house and watched me as I paced restlessly around the balcony. I had assumed, misguidedly, that her interest in me was partly sexual, perhaps because I prompted memories of happier days with Frank. I now realized that she needed my help in some scheme of her own, and was still deciding whether I was astute and determined enough for her.

She turned up the collar of my shirt, hiding the bruises. 'Charles, try to rest. I know you were shocked by that dreadful fire, but it doesn't change anything.'

'I'm not so sure. In fact, I think it changes everything. Think about it, Paula. This morning we were looking at a snapshot, taken a few minutes after seven o'clock on the Queen's birthday. It's an interesting picture. Where are the Hollingers? Saying goodbye to their guests, watching the satellite relay from the Mall? No, they've lost interest in their guests and are waiting for them to go home. Hollinger's in his jacuzzi, "relaxing" with Andersson's Swedish girlfriend. She is pregnant with someone's child. Hollinger's? Who knows, he may have been fertile. Mrs Hollinger is sharing a bed with the male secretary, playing some very weird games with a pair of her shoes. Their niece is shooting up in her

117

bathroom. It's quite a ménage. Putting it bluntly, the Hollinger household wasn't exactly a domain of spotless propriety.'

'Nor is Estrella de Mar, or anywhere else. I'd hate people to start rooting around in my laundry basket.'

'Paula, I wasn't making a moral judgement. All the same, it isn't too difficult to think of any number of people with a strong motive for starting the fire. Suppose Andersson discovered that his nineteen-year-old girlfriend was having an affair with Hollinger?'

'She wasn't. He was seventy-five and getting over a prostate job.'

'Perhaps he was getting over it in his own special way. Again, suppose Andersson wasn't the child's father?'

'It certainly wasn't Hollinger. It might have been anyone. This is Estrella de Mar. People here are having sex too, though half the time they don't realize it.'

'What if the father was the shady psychiatrist, Dr Sanger? He might have decided to teach Hollinger a lesson, and not realized that Bibi was lying in the jacuzzi with him.'

'Unbelievable.' Paula roamed around the sitting room, feet tapping to the sounds of the tennis machine. 'Besides, Sanger isn't shady. He was an influence for good over Bibi. She stayed with him in the dark days before her collapse. I sometimes meet him at the Clinic. He's a shy, rather sad man.'

'With a taste for playing the guru to young women. Then there are Mrs Hollinger and Roger Sansom, and their shared shoe-fetish. Perhaps Sansom had a hot-tempered Spanish girlfriend with a fiery taste in revenge, who resented his infatuation with this glamorous film star.'

'That was forty years ago. She was a glorified starlet with a posh voice. The Alice Hollinger who lived in Estrella de Mar was rather motherly.'

'Finally, there's the niece, watching her last TV programme

as she shoots up in the bathroom. Where there are drugs there are dealers. As a group they get paranoid over even a penny owed to them. You can see them outside the disco every night – I'm amazed at Frank putting up with them.'

Paula turned to frown at me, surprised by this first overt criticism of my brother.

'Frank was running a successful club. Besides, he was tremendously tolerant about everything.'

'So am I. Paula, I'm pointing out that there are any number of possible motives for the arson attack. When I first went to the Hollinger house there seemed no reason why anyone should set fire to it. Suddenly there are too many reasons.'

'Then why hasn't Cabrera acted?'

'He has Frank's confession. As far as the police are concerned the case is closed. Besides, he may assume that Frank had strong motives of his own – probably financial. Wasn't Hollinger a major shareholder in the Club Nautico?'

'Along with Elizabeth Shand. You stood next to her at the funeral. They say she's an old flame of Hollinger's.'

'That puts her in the frame. She may have resented his affair with Bibi. People do the strangest things for the most trivial reasons. Perhaps –'

'Too many perhapses.' Paula tried to calm me, sitting me in the leather armchair and putting a cushion behind my head. 'Be careful, Charles. The next attack on you could be far more serious.'

'I've thought about that. Why should anyone want to frighten me? It's conceivable that the attacker had just arrived in Estrella de Mar, and thought I was Frank. He may have been given a contract to kill Frank or severely injure him. He realized who I was and broke off . . .'

'Charles, please . . .'

Confused by all this speculation, Paula stepped on to the balcony. I stood up and followed her to the rail. Bobby

Crawford was still urging on his butterfly swimmers, who waited at the deep end, eager to hurl themselves once again into the exhausted water.

'Crawford's a popular man,' I commented. 'All that enthusiasm is almost endearing.'

'That's why he's dangerous.'

'Is he dangerous?'

'Like all naive people. No one can resist him.'

One of the swimmers had lost her bearings in the pool, its waters so churned by flailing arms that it resembled a rutted field. Giving up, she swayed in the shoulder-high waves, losing her balance as she tried to wipe the foam from her eyes. Seeing her in difficulty, Crawford kicked off his espadrilles and leapt into the water beside her. He comforted the swimmer, held her by the waist and let her rest against his chest. When she had recovered he placed her in the arms-forward position, and calmed the waves so that she could regain her stroke. As she set off he swam beside her, smiling when her rounded hips began to porpoise confidently.

'Impressive,' I commented. 'Who is he exactly?'

'Not even Bobby Crawford knows that. He's three different people before breakfast. Every morning he takes his personalities out of the wardrobe and decides which one he'll wear for the day.'

She spoke tartly, refusing to be taken in by Crawford's gallantries, but seemed unaware of the affectionate smile on her lips, like a lover remembering a past affair. She clearly resented Crawford's charm and confidence, and I wondered if she had once been taken in by them. Crawford would have found this moody and sharp-tongued doctor even more difficult to play than his tennis machine.

'Paula, aren't you a little hard on him? He seems rather engaging.'

'Of course he is. Actually, I like him. He's a big puppy

with a lot of strange ideas he doesn't quite know how to chew. The tennis bum who's taken an Open University course in Cultural Studies and thinks paperback sociology is the answer to everything. He's a lot of fun.'

'I want to talk to him about Frank. He must know all there is to know about Estrella de Mar.'

'You bet. We sing to Bobby's hymn-sheet now. He's changed our lives and practically put the Clinic out of business. Before he arrived it was one huge, money-churning de-tox unit. Alcoholism, ennui and benzo-diazepine filled our beds. Bobby Crawford pops his head around the door and everyone sits up and rushes out to the tennis courts. He's an amazing man.'

'I take it you know him well.'

'Too well.' She laughed at herself. 'I sound mean, don't I? You'll be glad to hear that he's not a good lover.'

'Why not?'

'He's not selfish enough. Selfish men make the best lovers. They're prepared to invest in the woman's pleasure so that they can collect an even bigger dividend for themselves. You look as if you might understand that.'

'I'm trying not to. You're very frank, Paula.'

'Ah . . . but that's the artful way of hiding things.'

Warming to her, I placed my hand around her waist. She hesitated, and then leaned against me. Despite the show of self-control she lacked confidence in herself, a trait I admired. At the same time she was teasing me with her body, trying to spur me on and remind me that Estrella de Mar was a cabinet of mysteries to which she might hold the key. Already I suspected that she knew far more about the fire and Frank's confession than she had told me.

Leaving the balcony, I drew her into the shaded bedroom. As we stood together I placed my hand on her breast, my index finger following the blue vein that rose to the surface of her sunburnt skin before descending into the warm deeps below her nipple.

She watched me uncritically, curious to see what I would do next. Without moving my hand from her breast, she said: 'Charles, this is your doctor speaking. You've had enough stress for one day.'

'Would making love to you be very stressful?'

'Making love to me is always stressful. Quite a few men in Estrella de Mar would confirm that. I don't want to visit the cemetery again.'

'Next time I'm there I'll read the epitaphs. Is it full of your lovers, Paula?'

'One or two. As they say, doctors can bury their mistakes.'

I touched the shadow that lay across her cheek like a dark cloud on a photographic film. 'Who bruised your face? That was a hard slap.'

'It's nothing.' She covered the bruise with her hand. 'I was working out in the gym. Someone ran into me.'

'They play tough in Estrella de Mar. The other night in the car park . . .'

'What happened?'

'I'm not sure – if it was a game it was a rough one. A friend of Crawford's was trying to rape a girl. The odd thing is, she didn't seem to mind.'

'That sounds like Estrella de Mar.'

Leaving me, she sat on the bed and smoothed the coverlet, as if searching for the imprint of Frank's body. For a few moments she seeemed to forget that I was standing in the room beside her. She glanced at her watch, reminding herself who she was.

'I have to go. Amazingly, there still are a few patients at the Clinic.'

'Of course.' As we walked to the door I asked: 'What made you become a doctor?'

'Don't you think I'm a good one?'

'I'm sure you're the best. Is your father a physician?'

'He's a retired Qantas pilot. My mother left us when she met an Australian lawyer on a stand-by flight.'

'She walked out on you?'

'Just like that. I was six years old but I could see she'd forgotten us even before she packed her suitcases. I was brought up by my father's sister, a gynaecologist in Edinburgh. I was very happy, really for the first time.'

'I'm glad.'

'She was a remarkable woman – a lifelong spinster, not too keen on men but very keen on sex. She was amazingly realistic about everything, but especially sex. In many ways she lived like a man. Take a lover, fuck all the best sex out of him, then throw him out.'

'That's a hard philosophy – awfully close to a whore's.'

'Why not?' Paula watched me while I opened the door, pleasantly surprised to have shocked me. 'Whoring is something a good few women have tried, more probably than you realize. That's one education most men never get . . .'

I followed her to the lift, admiring her brazen cheek. Before the doors closed she leaned forward and kissed me on the mouth, her fingers lightly touching the bruises on my neck.

Soothing the tender skin, I sat in the armchair and tried to ignore the orthopaedic collar on the desk. I could taste Paula's kiss on my lips, the scent of lip-gloss and American perfume. But passion, I knew, was not the message conveyed. The fingers on my neck had been a reminder, cued into the keyboard of bruises, that I needed to find fresh spoors on the trail that led to the Hollingers' murderer.

I listened to the tennis machine firing its serves across the practice net, and to the splashing of the butterfly team.

Searching for a cigarette, the best antidote to all this health and exercise, I pulled my jacket from the desk and hunted through its pockets.

The cassette I had taken from Anne Hollinger's bedroom protruded from the inner pocket. I stood up and switched on the television set, inserting the cassette into the video-player. If the tape had recorded a live satellite programme while Anne sat in the bathroom with a needle in her arm, it would fix the exact moment when the fire engulfed the room.

The tape spooled forward, and the screen lit up to reveal an empty bedroom in an art deco apartment, with white-on-white decor, ice-pale furnishings and recessed lights in porthole windows. A queen-sized bed with a blue satin spread and a quilted headboard occupied the centre of the scene. A yellow teddy bear sat propped against the pillows, a sickly green tinge to his fur. Above the bed a narrow sill carried a collection of pottery animals that might have belonged to a teenaged girl.

The hand-held camera panned to the left as two women entered the room through an open, mirror-backed door. Both were in wedding regalia, the bride in a full-skirted gown of cream silk, a lace bodice giving way to a sunburnt neck and strong collarbones. Her face was hidden behind her veil, but I could see a pretty chin and strong mouth that reminded me of Alice Hollinger in her J. Arthur Rank days. The bridesmaid wore a calf-length gown, white gloves and toque hat, hair swept back from a deeply tanned face. They reminded me of the sunbathers at the Club Nautico: sleek, light-years beyond any concept of boredom, and happiest lying on their backs.

The camera followed them as they kicked off their shoes and began to loosen their clothing, eager to return to the sun-loungers. The bridesmaid unbuttoned her gown while helping to unzip the bride's wedding dress. Leaving them to share a joke and giggle into each other's ears, the camera focused on the teddy bear and began a heavy-handed zoom into its button-nose face.

The mirrored door opened again, reflecting a glimpse of a shaded balcony and the rooftops of Estrella de Mar. A second bridesmaid entered, a platinum-haired woman in her forties with a heavily-rouged face, barmaid's breasts straining through her jacket, neck and cleavage flushed by something more potent than sunshine. As she tottered about on one heel I guessed that she had made an early detour from the church to the nearest bar.

Stripped to their underwear, the women sat together on the bed, resting before they changed into their day clothes. Curiously, none of them looked at the friend shooting this amateur video record. They began to undress each other, fingers teasing at the bra straps, caressing their suntanned skins and smoothing away the pressure lines. The platinum-haired bridesmaid raised the bride's veil and kissed her mouth. She began to play with her breasts, smiling wide-eyed at the erect nipples as if witnessing a miracle of nature.

The camera waited passively while the women fondled each other. As I watched this parodic lesbian scene, I was sure that none of the women was a professional actress. They played their roles like members of an amateur theatrical group taking part in a bawdy Restoration farce.

Resting from their embraces, the women looked up with mock surprise as a man's torso and hips entered the frame. He stood by the bed, penis erect, thighs and chest muscles like oiled meat, the passive bull-shouldered stud of countless porno-films. For a moment the camera touched the lower half of his face, and I almost recognized the heavy neck and chubby chin.

The women sat forwards, displaying their breasts to him. Her face still veiled, the bride held his penis in her hands and began to suck its head in the distracted way of an eight-year-old with an over-large candy bar. When she lay back and parted her thighs I pressed the fast-forward, waiting as the manic, jerky spasms rushed to their climax, and returned to play-speed when the man withdrew and ejaculated, as custom demanded, across her breasts.

Sweat bathed the bride's shoulder and abdomen. She pulled back the veil and used a tissue to wipe away the semen. Again I saw an echo of the Rank Charm School in her refined features and perky gaze. She sat up and smiled at the bridesmaids, using the veil to dry her cheeks. Needle punctures marked her arms, but she seemed in ruddy health, laughing when the bridesmaids slipped her arms into the wedding dress.

The screen moved to the left, the camera jarred by the operator's confused hands. The lens steadied itself, and caught the bodies of two naked men who had broken into the bedroom from the balcony and hurled themselves across the floor. The bridesmaids seized their waists and pulled them on to the bed. The bride alone seemed startled, trying to hide her naked body behind the wedding dress. She wrestled helplessly with a thickset man with a hairy Arab back who seized her shoulders and threw her on to her face.

I watched the rape run its course, trying to avoid the desperate eyes crushed into the satin bedspread. The bride was no longer acting or colluding with the camera. The lesbian porno-film had been a set-up, designed to lure her to this anonymous apartment, the *mise-en-scène* for a real rape for which the bridesmaids, but not the heroine, had been prepared.

In turn the men assaulted the dishevelled bride, moving through a pre-arranged repertoire of sexual acts. Their faces never appeared on screen, but the dark-skinned man was of middle age, with the swarthy, fleshy arms of a nightclub bouncer. The younger of the two, with his tubular English body, seemed to be in his early thirties. He moved like a professional dancer, swiftly manipulating the victim's body as he found another posture, another forced entry point. Irritated by her frantic gasps, he seized the veil and stuffed it into her mouth.

The film ended in a mêlée of copulating bodies. In a bizarre attempt at an artistic finale, the camera moved around the bed, briefly pausing beside the mirrored door. The photographer, I realized, was a woman. She wore a black bikini, and a battery pack hung on a leather strap from her shoulder. A faint surgical scar ran from the small of her back and around her waist to her right hip.

The film came to its final moments. The men withdrew from the room, a blur of greasy thighs and sweating buttocks. The bridesmaids waved at the camera, and the large-breasted blonde lay back and sat the teddy bear astride her midriff, laughing as she jiggled the stuffed toy.

But I was looking at the bride. Set in her bruised features was a face still full of spirit. She wiped her eyes with a pillow, and rubbed the torn skin of her arms and knees. Mascara ran in black tears on to her cheeks, and the smudged lipstick slewed her mouth to one side. Yet she managed to smile at the camera, the plucky starlet facing the massed lenses of Fleet Street, or a brave child swallowing an unpleasant medicine for her own good. Sitting with the crushed wedding dress in her hands, she turned from the camera and grinned at the man whose shadow could be seen on the wall beside the door.

11

The Lady by the Pool

HER FACE SHADED by a wide-brimmed hat, Elizabeth Shand dozed at the lunch table beside the swimming pool, her unblemished white skin set off by an ivory swimsuit. Like a jewelled cobra half-asleep on an altar, she watched me walk across the lawn, and began to rub sun-oil into the backs of the two young men stretched out behind her. As she kneaded the oil into their heavily-muscled shoulders, ignoring the pained murmurs, she might have been grooming a pair of sleek racing hounds.

'Mrs Shand will see you now.' Sonny Gardner was waiting for me by the pool. He beckoned me towards the lunch table. 'Helmut and Wolfgang – two friends from Hamburg.'

'I'm surprised they aren't wearing dog-collars.' I scanned Gardner's watchful, babyish face. 'Sonny, we haven't seen you at the Club Nautico for a while.'

'Mrs Shand decided I should work here.' When a bird began to flutter in the rose pergola he raised his mobile phone to his lips. 'More security after the Hollinger fire . . .'

'Good idea.' I looked back at the handsome villa with its magnificent skyline views over Estrella de Mar and the Shand empire. 'We wouldn't want this place to burn down.'

'Mr Prentice, do join us . . .' Elizabeth Shand called to me across the pool. She wiped her hands on a towel and tapped the young Germans on the buttocks, dismissing them from her presence. They passed me as I circled the pool, but avoided my eyes, immersed in their own bodies and the play of muscle and oil. They sprinted across the lawn and stepped through a garden door into the courtyard of a two-storey annexe to the villa.

'Mr Prentice – Charles, come and sit next to me. We met at that dreadful funeral. In a way I feel I've known you as long as I've known Frank. I'm delighted to see you, though sadly I've nothing very useful to add to what you've already learned.' She crooked a finger at Gardner. 'Sonny, a tray of drinks . . .'

She gazed at me guilelessly when I sat beside her, running through an inventory that began with my thinning hair, moved to the fading bruises on my neck and ended with the dusty heels of my brogues.

'Mrs Shand, it's kind of you to see me. I'm worried that Frank's friends in Estrella de Mar have more or less closed the door on him. For three weeks now I've been looking for something that might help him. To be honest, I've got absolutely nowhere.'

'Perhaps there isn't anywhere to go?' Mrs Shand bared her over-large teeth in what passed for a concerned smile. 'Estrella de Mar may be a heavenly little place, but it's a very small heaven. There aren't that many hidden corners, more's the pity.'

'Of course. I assume you don't believe Frank set fire to the Hollinger house?'

'I don't know what to believe. It's all so horrific. No, he can't have done. Frank was much too gentle, too sceptical about everything. Whoever set fire to the house was a fanatic . . .'

I waited as Gardner set out the drinks and then resumed his patrol of the garden. On a balcony of the annexe the young Germans were examining their thighs in the sun. They had flown in from Hamburg two days earlier and had already been involved in a brawl at the Club Nautico disco. Now Mrs Shand had confined them to quarters, where she could literally keep her hands on them. Raising the brim of her hat, she watched them with the proprietary gaze of a madam supervising the leisure moments of her charges.

'Mrs Shand, if Frank didn't kill the Hollingers, who did? Can you think of someone with a strong enough grudge against them?'

'No one. I can't honestly think of anyone who'd want to harm them.'

'They weren't popular, though. People I've talked to complain that they were a little stand-offish.'

'That's absurd.' Mrs Shand grimaced at the silliness of this. 'He was a film producer, for heaven's sake. She was an actress. They loved Cannes and Los Angeles and all those widescreen hustlers. If they kept aloof it was because they saw Estrella de Mar becoming a little too . . .'

'Bourgeois?'

'Exactly. It's all so earnest and middle-class now. The Hollingers came here when the only other Brits were a few remittance men and a couple of burnt-out baronets. They were the *ancien régime*, they remembered Estrella de Mar before the cordon bleu classes and the . . .'

'Harold Pinter revivals?'

'Too true, I'm afraid. I don't think the Hollingers ever really got the hang of Harold Pinter. For them the arts meant the California of black-tie subscription concerts, fine art foundations and Getty money.'

'What about business rivals? Hollinger owned a lot of land around Estrella de Mar. He must have been a brake on development here.'

'No. He was resigned to what was going on. They did keep to themselves. He was happy with his coin collection and she worried about her face-lifts coming apart.'

'Someone told me they were trying to sell their stake in the Club Nautico.'

'Frank and I were about to buy them out. Remember, the club had changed. Frank brought in a younger and livelier crowd who danced to a different tune.'

'I hear it every night when I'm trying to sleep. It's certainly a lively tune, especially when played by Bobby Crawford.'

'Bobby?' Mrs Shand smiled to herself in an almost girlish way. 'Sweet boy, he's done so much for Estrella de Mar. How did we get on without him?'

'I like him. But isn't he a little . . . unpredictable?'

'That's just what Estrella de Mar needs. Before he arrived the Club Nautico was dead on its feet.'

'How did he get on with the Hollingers? I don't suppose they cared for the drug-dealers at the club.'

Mrs Shand stared at the sky, as if expecting it to retreat from her gaze. 'Are there any?'

'You haven't seen them? I'm surprised. They're sitting around the pool like Hollywood agents.'

Mrs Shand sighed deeply, and I realized that she had been holding her breath. 'You'll find drugs anywhere these days, especially along the coast. Something new and strange happens when the sea meets the land.' She pointed to the distant pueblos. 'People are so bored, and drugs stop them going mad. Sometimes Bobby is a little too tolerant, but he wants to wean people off all these tranquillizers that people like Sanger prescribe. Now those are the really dangerous drugs. Before Bobby Crawford arrived the whole town was Valiumed out of its mind.'

'I imagine business generally was rather slack?'

'Flat on its back. People didn't need anything except another bottle of pills. But they've picked up now. Charles, I'm sorry about the Hollingers. I'd known them for thirty years.'

'You were an actress?'

'Do I look like it?' Mrs Shand sat forward and patted my hand. 'I'm flattered. I was an accountant. Very young and very ruthless. I wound up Hollinger's film business – a bottomless resource sink, all those people on the payroll, buying rights and never shooting a single frame. After that he asked me to join his property company. When the building boom ended in the 1970s it was starting out here. I had a look at Estrella de Mar and thought it seemed promising.'

'So Hollinger was very close to you?'

'As close as a man ever gets to me.' She spoke matter-of-factly. 'But not in the way you mean.'

'You hadn't fallen out with him?'

'What on earth are you trying to say?' Mrs Shand took off her hat, as if clearing the decks before a fight, and stared unblinkingly at me. 'Good God, I didn't set fire to the house. Are you suggesting that?'

'Of course not. I know you didn't.' I tried to pacify her, changing tack before she could summon Sonny Gardner to her aid. 'What about Dr Sanger? I keep thinking of that scene at the funeral. Everyone there clearly disliked him, almost as if he was responsible.'

'For Bibi's pregnancy, not the fire. Sanger is the sort of psychiatrist who sleeps with his patients and thinks he's doing them a therapeutic favour. He specializes in drugged-out little things who are searching for a friendly shoulder.'

'He may not have started the fire, but could he have paid someone to do it for him? The Hollingers had effectively taken Bibi from him.'

'I don't think so. But who knows? I'm sorry, Charles, I haven't been much help.' She stood up and slipped on her beach robe. 'I'll walk you back to the house. I know you're worried about Frank. You probably feel responsible.'

'Not exactly responsible. When we were young it was my

job to feel guilty for both of us. The habit has stuck – it's not easy to throw off.'

'Then you've come to the right place.' As we passed the pool she gestured at the crowds lying on the beaches below. 'We don't take anything too seriously in Estrella de Mar. Not even . . .'

'Crime? There's a lot of it around, and I don't mean the Hollinger murders. Muggings, burglary, rapes, for a start.'

'Rape? Awful, I know. But it does keep the girls on their toes.' Mrs Shand lowered her glasses to peer at my neck. 'David Hennessy told me about the attack in Frank's apartment. How vile. It looks like a choker of rubies. Was anything stolen?'

'I don't think theft was the motive – I wasn't really hurt. It was a psychological assault, of a curious kind.'

'That sounds rather new and fashionable. One has to remember how much crime there is along this coast. Retired East End gangsters who can't get rid of the itch.'

'But they're not here. That's the odd thing about Estrella de Mar. The crime here seems to be committed by amateurs.'

'They're the worst of all – they leave such a mess to be cleared up. You can only trust the professionals to do a decent job.'

Behind us Helmut and Wolfgang had returned to the pool. They dived from the twin boards and raced each other to the shallow end. Mrs Shand beamed at them approvingly.

'Handsome boys,' I commented. 'Friends of yours?'

'Gastarbeiters. They're staying in the annexe until I find work for them.'

'Waiters, swimming coaches . . . ?'

'Let's say they have all sorts of uses.'

We left the terrace and stepped through the French doors into a long, low-ceilinged lounge. Film industry memorabilia covered the walls and mantelpiece, framed photographs of award ceremonies and command performances. On a white baby grand was a portrait of the Hollingers standing by their pool during a barbecue. Between them was a good-looking and confident young woman in a long-sleeved shirt, eyes challenging the photographer to catch her restless spirit. I had last seen her on the television screen in Frank's apartment, smiling bravely at another camera lens.

'Something of a character . . .' I pointed to the group portrait. 'Is that the Hollingers' daughter?'

'Their niece, Anne.' Mrs Shand smiled sadly to herself and touched the frame. 'She died with them in the fire. Such a beauty. She might have made it as a film actress.'

'Perhaps she did.' The chauffeur waited by the open front door, a burly Maghrebian in his forties who was clearly another bodyguard and seemed to resent me even looking at the Mercedes limousine. 'Mrs Shand, you might know – is there a film club in Estrella de Mar?'

'There are several. They're all very intellectual. I rather doubt if they'd find you up to scratch.'

'I don't suppose they would. But I'm thinking of a club that actually makes films. Did Hollinger shoot any footage here?'

'Not for years. He hated home movies. There *are* people who make films. In fact, I think Paula Hamilton is something of a camera buff.'

'Weddings and so on?'

'Possibly. You'd have to ask her. By the way, I think she's much more suited to you than to Frank.'

'Why? I hardly know her.'

'What can I say?' Mrs Shand pressed her ice-cold cheek to mine. 'Frank was awfully sweet, but I suspect that Paula needs someone with a taste for the . . . deviant?'

She smiled at me, well aware that she herself was charming, likeable and totally corrupt.

12

A Game of Tease and Chase

DEVIANCE IN ESTRELLA DE MAR was a commodity under jealous guard. Watched by the wary and suspicious chauffeur, who was logging my licence number into his electronic note-book, I freewheeled down the drive past the Mercedes. With its tinted windows, the bodywork seemed both paranoid and aggressive, like medieval German armour, and the nearby villas shared this nervous stance. Razor-glass topped almost every wall, and security cameras maintained their endless vigil over garages and front doors, as if an army of housebreakers roamed the streets after nightfall.

I returned to the Club Nautico, trying to decide on my next move. Elizabeth Shand, just conceivably, had a motive for killing the Hollingers, if only to get her hands on a piece of prime real estate, but she would have chosen a less crude weapon than arson. Besides, she clearly liked the old couple, and the five murders would certainly have been bad for business, frightening away potential property investors.

At the same time she had given me a glimpse into another Estrella de Mar, a world of imported bed-boys and other genial pleasures, and had identified Anne Hollinger for me. Sitting by the television set, I rewound the cassette of the porno-film, then played through the violent scenes again, trying to identify the other participants. How had this maverick and high-spirited young woman found herself in such a crudely exploitative movie? I froze her brave smile to camera as she sat in the tattered wedding dress, and imagined her playing the tape as she injected herself in the bathroom, trying to blot out all memory of the pale-skinned young man who had been determined to humiliate her.

The frightened eyes wept their black ink, and the lipstick skewed across her mouth like a gasp. I reeled back to the moment when the second bridesmaid entered the bedroom and the mirror-door reflected the balcony of the apartment and the sloping streets below.

Again I froze the frame and tried to sharpen the blurred image. A church spire was visible between the balcony rails, its weather-vane silhouetted against a white satellite dish on the roof of a building somewhere near the marina. Aligned together, they virtually pinpointed the apartment's location on the heights above Estrella de Mar.

I sat back and stared at the spire, for the first time unaware of the tennis machine as it fired its balls across the practice court. I realized now that it was this view across the town that I had been intended to see, and not the rape of Anne Hollinger. The police forensic team would have discovered the cassette within moments of searching the fire-gutted bedroom.

Someone had planted the cassette in the video-recorder, after learning that Paula and I were to visit the Hollinger house, confident that Cabrera would be too busy with his autopsy report to re-check the original findings. I remembered the Hollingers' chauffeur, endlessly buffing the old Bentley. Had this melancholy Andalucian become Anne's confidant and even, perhaps, her lover? His threatening stare, far from trying to make me Frank's guilty proxy, might have been an attempt to alert me to some undiscovered evidence.

At eight that evening Paula and I were meeting for dinner at the Restaurant du Cap, but I set off for the harbour an hour early, eager to search for the satellite dish. Pornographic film-makers often rented expensive apartments for the day, rather than construct stage sets that could provide evidence for the police. The exact location of the rape scene would take me no nearer to the Hollinger murders, but the loose corners of too many carpets had begun to curl under my feet. The more I nailed down, the less likely was I to trip as I moved from one darkened room to the next.

While I walked down to the harbour, past the antique shops and art galleries, I scanned the rooftops of the town. The weather-vane of the Anglican church rose above the Plaza Iglesias, without doubt the one I had glimpsed in the film. I stood on the steps of the church, a white geometrical structure that was a modest replay of Corbusier's Ronchamp Chapel, more space-age cinema than house of God. The notice-board announced forthcoming performances of Eliot's *Murder in the Cathedral*, meetings of a help-the-elderly charity, and a guided tour of a Phoenician burial site on the southern tip of the peninsula, organized by a local archaeological society.

The weather-vane pointed towards Fuengirola but there was no sign of the satellite dish. Lit by the setting sun, the western skyline of Estrella de Mar ran from the Club Nautico to the ruin of the Hollinger house. A dozen apartment blocks looked down from the high corniche, a cliff-face of mysteries. On the roof of the yacht club a white satellite dish cupped the sky, but its bowl was at least twice the diameter of the modest dish in the video.

The tapas bars and seafood restaurants along the harbour were packed with residents relaxing after their day's work at the sculpture table and potter's wheel. Far from being dismayed by the Hollinger tragedy, they seemed more animated than ever, talking noisily across their copies of the *New York Review of Books* and the arts supplements of *Le Monde* and *Libération*.

Intimidated by this cultural power-dressing, I stepped into

the boatyard beside the marina, comforted by the presence of stripped-down engines and oily sumps. The yachts and motor-cruisers sat in their trestles, revealing their elegant hulls, a geometry graced by speed. Dominating all the other craft in the yard was a fibre-glass powerboat almost forty feet long, three immense outboards at its stern like the genitalia of a giant aquatic machine.

His engine-tuning over for the day, Gunnar Andersson stood beside the craft and washed his arms in a bucket of detergent. He nodded to me, but his narrow, bearded face was as closed and self-immersed as a Gothic saint's. He ignored the evening crowds and followed a flight of martins setting off for the coast of Africa. The flesh of his cheeks and scalp was stretched across the sharp points of his skull, as if constrained by some intense internal pressure. Watching him grimace at the noisy bars, I felt that he controlled his emotions from one second to the next, fearing that if he showed the slightest anger the skin would split and reveal the shrieking bones.

I walked past him, and admired the speedboat and its sculptured prow.

'It's almost too powerful to be beautiful,' I commented. 'Does anyone need to go this fast?'

He dried his hands before replying. 'Well, it's a working ship. It has to earn its keep. The Spanish patrol boats at Ceuta and Melilla can really shift.'

'So it crosses to North Africa?' He was about to move away, but I reached out and shook his hand, forcing him to face me. 'Mr Andersson? I saw you at the service in the Protestant cemetery. I'm sorry about Bibi Jansen.'

'Thank you for coming.' He looked me up and down, and then washed his hands again in the bucket. 'Did you know Bibi?'

'I wish I had. From what everyone says, she must have been great fun.'

'When she was given a chance.' He threw the towel into his work-bag. 'If you didn't know her, why were you there?'

'In a sense I was involved in her . . . death.' Gambling on the truth, I said: 'My brother is Frank Prentice, the manager of the Club Nautico.'

I expected him to turn on me and show some of the anger he had vented at the funeral, but he took out his tobacco pouch and rolled a cigarette with his large fingers. I guessed that he was already aware of my relationship to Frank.

'Frank? I worked on the engine of his thirty-footer. If I'm right, he hasn't paid me yet.'

'He's in jail in Malaga, as you know. Give me the bill and I'll settle it.'

'Don't worry – I can wait.'

'That could be a long time. He's pleaded guilty.'

Andersson drew on the loose-packed cigarette. Shreds of burning tobacco flew from the glowing tip and sparked briefly against his beard. His eyes roved around the boatyard, avoiding my face. 'Guilty? Frank has a special sense of humour.'

'It's not a joke. This is Spain, and he could serve twenty or thirty years. You don't believe he started the fire?'

Andersson raised his cigarette and scrawled a cryptic symbol on the night air. 'Who can say? So, you're in Estrella de Mar to find out what happened?'

'I'm trying to.'

'But not getting very far?'

'To tell the truth, I've made no headway at all. I've been up to the Hollinger house, talked to people who were there. No one believes Frank started the fire, not even the police. I may have to fly in a couple of detectives.'

'From London?' Andersson seemed more interested in me. 'I wouldn't do that.'

'Why not? They might find something I've missed. I'm not a professional investigator.'

'You'd be wasting your money, Mr Prentice. People in Estrella de Mar are very discreet.' He gestured with a long arm at the villas on the hillside, secure behind their surveillance cameras. 'I've lived here for two years and I'm still not sure if the place is real . . .'

He left the boatyard and led me along the walkway between the moored yachts and cabin-cruisers. The white-hulled craft seemed almost spectral in the dusk, a fleet waiting to sail on a phantom wind. Andersson stopped at the end of the quay, where a small sloop rode at anchor. Beneath the Club Nautico pennant at the stern was its name: *Halcyon*. Police exclusion tapes looped along its rails, falling into the water where they drifted like streamers from a forgotten party.

'The *Halcyon*?' I knelt down and peered through the miniature portholes. 'So this is Frank's boat?'

'You'll find nothing on board to help you. Frank asked Mr Hennessy to sell it for him.'

Andersson stared at the craft, raking his beard with his fingers, a gloomy Norseman exiled among the plastic hulls and radar scanners. As his eyes searched the sky over the town I noticed that he was looking everywhere but at the Hollinger house. His natural aloofness shaded into some unhappy emotion that I could only glimpse around the bony corners of his face.

'Andersson, I need to ask – were you at the party?'

'For the English Queen? Yes, I drank the toast.'

'You saw Bibi Jansen on the upstairs veranda?'

'She was there. Standing with the Hollingers.'

'Did she seem well?'

'Too well.' His face was crossed by flickers of light from the dark water lapping the yachts. 'She was very fine.'

'After the toast she went to her room. Why didn't she come down to meet you and the other guests?'

'The Hollingers . . . they didn't like her mixing with too many people.'

'Too many of the wrong people? Especially the kind who might have given her acid and cocaine?'

Andersson stared at me wearily. 'Bibi was on drugs, Mr Prentice – the drugs that society approves. Sanger and the Hollingers made her into quiet little Princess Prozac.'

'Better than acid, though, for someone who's overdosed. Or the new amphetamines the chemists are cooking up with their molecular roulette.'

Andersson put a hand on my shoulder, sympathizing with my lack of insight. 'Bibi was a free spirit – her best friends were acid and cocaine. When she took acid she made us part of her dreams. Sanger and the Hollingers reached inside her head and took out the small white bird. They broke its wings, closed the cage again and said to everyone: "Bibi is happy."'

I waited as he sucked back the last of his cigarette smoke, scowling to himself as he overruled his emotions.

'You must have hated the Hollingers. Enough to kill them?'

'Mr Prentice, if I wanted to kill the Hollingers it wouldn't be because I hated them.'

'Bibi was found in the jacuzzi with Hollinger.'

'Impossible . . .'

'That they could have had sex together? You know she was pregnant? Were you the father?'

'I was *her* father. We were good friends. I never had sex with her, even when she asked me.'

'So who was the father? Sanger?'

Andersson wiped his mouth, trying to rid himself of the taste of Sanger's name. 'Mr Prentice, do psychiatrists sleep with their patients?'

'They do in Estrella de Mar.' We climbed the steps from the marina to the harbour road, where the evening crowds were already blocking the traffic. 'Andersson, something nightmarish happened up there, something no one counted on. You don't like looking at the Hollinger house, do you?'

'I don't like looking at anything, Mr Prentice. I dream in Braille.' He hoisted his work-bag on to his shoulder. 'You're a decent man, go back to London. Go home, go on your travels. There might be another attack on you. No one in Estrella de Mar wants you to be frightened . . .'

He walked away through the crowd, a gloomy gallows-tree swaying above the cheerful diners.

I waited for Paula in the bar of the Restaurant du Cap, striking another name from my cast of suspects. As I listened to Andersson there had been a hint of complicity, perhaps the same regret for having mocked the Hollingers that Paula had expressed, but I was sure that he could not have killed them. The Swede was too morose, too immersed in his grudge against the world, to be able to act decisively.

By nine-thirty Paula had not arrived, and I assumed that an emergency had kept her at the Clinic. I ate alone at my table, stretching the bouillabaisse as long as I could without attracting the Keswick sisters' curiosity. It was eleven o'clock when I left the restaurant, and the nightclubs along the quay were opening, their music booming across the marina. I paused by the boatyard, and stared at the huge powerboat on which Andersson had been working. I could imagine it outrunning the Spanish police cutters, racing across the Strait of Gibraltar with its cargo of hashish and heroin for the dealers of Estrella de Mar.

Feet rang against the metal steps that led down to the marina. A party of Arab visitors were returning to their craft in the short-term harbour beside the mole. I guessed that they were Middle Eastern tourists who had rented a summer palace at the Marbella Club. They wore full Puerto Banus fig, a dazzle in the dark of white drill, jewelled Rolexes and the plushest silks. One group of middle-aged men and young Frenchwomen boarded a cabin-cruiser tied up near the *Halcyon*. Expert with mooring lines and engine controls, they were about to set off when the younger men in the second group began to shout from the steps of the mole. They shook their fists and waved their yachting caps at a small, twin-engined speedboat that had slipped its moorings and was gliding silently through the undisturbed water.

As if unaware that he had stolen the craft, the thief stood calmly in the cockpit, thighs pressed against the helm. The beam of the Marbella lighthouse swept the sea, touching his pale arms and hair.

Within moments a chaotic sea-chase had begun. Jointly steered by two of its excited captains, the cabin-cruiser surged from its berth while the startled Frenchwomen clung to the leather banquettes. Unconcerned by the craft bearing down on him, the hijacker continued to motor towards the sea, barely leaving a wake behind him as he saluted the furious young men on the mole. At the last moment he rammed the throttle forward, expertly side-slipping into a lane of calm water between the moored yachts. Too clumsy to turn, the cabin-cruiser ploughed past and clipped the bowsprit of a venerable twelve-metre.

The thief eased back his throttle, seeing that his exit to the open sea was blocked by the cruiser. Changing course, he drove below the lattice footbridge to the central island, a maze of interlocking waterways and exits. Trying to cover every escape route, the cruiser reversed through a cloud of exhaust, then surged forward when the speedboat emerged from the darkness under its nose. Still standing at the helm, legs stylishly braced apart, the thief rolled the wheel and banked around the cruiser's bows. Free at last, the craft porpoised through the rough water towards the advancing waves.

I leaned against the harbour wall, surrounded by people who had carried their drinks from the nearby bars. Together we waited for the speedboat to disappear into one of a hundred bays along the coast, before slipping under the cover of night into a marina at Fuengirola or Benalmadena.

But the thief had still to satisfy his appetite for play. A game of tease and chase began in the open water three hundred yards from the mole. The cruiser swerved after the circling speedboat, which leapt nimbly past its pointed bows like a *torero* evading an overweight bull. Wallowing in the churned water, the cruiser's captains searched the criss-crossing wakes, their lights sweeping the confused waves. The speedboat's engines were silent, as if the thief had at last tired of his game and was about to slip into the shadows of the Estrella peninsula.

I decided to turn away when a blaze of orange fire lit up the sea, exposing a thousand wave-crests and the passengers standing on the foredeck of the cruiser. The speedboat was burning, its engines still pushing it through the water. In the moments before it sank, bows following the heavy outboards into the deep, a last explosion tore apart its fuel tank and bathed the marina and the watching crowds in a copper halo.

I looked down at my hands, which flared at me in the darkness. The harbour road was packed with cheering spectators who had stepped from the nightclubs and restaurants to enjoy the display, eyes gleaming like their summer jewellery. Arm-in-arm, a cheerful couple swayed past me into the path of a passing car. As it edged by them the man slapped its roof with his hand. Alarmed, the driver looked over her shoulder, and through the confused air I saw Paula Hamilton's anxious face.

'Paula!' I shouted. 'Wait for me . . . park by the boatyard.'

Had she come to look for me, or had I read her features into those of another driver? The car moved through the crowd, then left the harbour and joined the lower corniche road to Fuengirola. Half a mile away, below the ruins of a Moorish watch-tower, it stopped beside the breaking waves, its lights fading in the darkness.

The cabin-cruiser circled the floating debris of the speed-boat, its crew hunting the waves. I assumed that the thief would be swimming towards the rocks below the watch-tower, to a rendezvous previously arranged with the car's driver, who waited for him like a chauffeur outside a stage-door after the evening's performance.

13

A View from the High Corniche

CRIME AT ESTRELLA DE MAR had become one of the performance arts. As I drove David Hennessy from the Club Nautico to the harbour, the curving hillside above the town resembled an amphitheatre warmed by the morning sun. Residents sat on their balconies, some with binoculars, watching the Guardia Civil salvage launch drag the remains of the stolen speedboat into the shallows below the corniche road.

'Frogmen . . . ?' Hennessy pointed to the goggled black heads moving among the waves. 'The police are taking it all very seriously.'

'They're under the impression that a crime has been committed.'

'Hasn't it? Charles . . . ?'

'It was a piece of night-theatre, a water-borne spectacular to perk up the restaurant trade. A party of Middle East tourists played the clowns, with a chorus line of French good-time girls. Brutal, but great fun.'

'I'm glad to hear it.' Eyebrows raised, Hennessy tightened his seatbelt. 'And who played the villain? Or the hero, I should say?'

'I'm not sure yet. It was quite a performance – we all admired his style. Now, where exactly is Sansom's cottage?'

'In the old town above the harbour. Take the Calle Molina and I'll show you the turn-off. It's an unexpected side of Estrella de Mar.'

'Unexpected? The place is a set of Chinese boxes. You can go on opening them to infinity . . .'

Hennessy was closing Sansom's house, packing up his possessions before freighting them back to his cousins in Bristol. I was curious to see this weekend retreat, presumably the love-nest where Sansom had entertained Alice Hollinger. But I was still thinking of the speedboat thief playing his games with the cabin-cruiser. I remembered the eager eyes of the people emerging from the nightclubs along the quay, flushed by more than the copper sun of the exploding fuel tank.

We drove around the Plaza Iglesias, packed with residents drinking their morning espressos over copies of the *Herald Tribune* and the *Financial Times*. Scanning the headlines, I commented: 'The rest of the world seems a long way off. The scene last night was bizarre, I wish I'd filmed it. The whole waterfront came to life. People were sexually charged, like spectators after a bloody bull-fight.'

'Sexually charged? My dear chap, I'll take Betty down there tonight. She's obviously spent too much time with her watercolours and flower-arranging.'

'It was a show, David. Whoever stole the speedboat was putting on a performance. Someone with a taste for fire . . .'

'I dare say. But don't read too much into it. Boats are stolen all the time along the coast. Estrella de Mar is remarkably free from crime, compared to Marbella and Fuengirola.'

'That's not strictly true. In fact, there's a great deal of crime in Estrella de Mar, but of a unique kind. It seems unconnected, but I'm trying to piece it all together.'

'Well, let me know when you do. Cabrera will be glad of your help.' Hennessy guided me into the Calle Molina. 'How's the investigation going? You've heard from Frank?'

'I talked to Danvila this morning. There's a chance Frank may agree to see me.'

'Good. At last he's coming to his senses.' Hennessy was watching me obliquely, as if trying to read my thoughts through the sides of my eyes. 'Do you think he'll change his plea? If he's ready to see you . . .'

'It's too early to say. He may feel lonely, or realize how many doors are about to shut on him.'

I turned off the Calle Molina into a narrow roadway, one of the few nineteenth-century streets in Estrella de Mar, a terrace of renovated fishermen's cottages that ran behind the restaurants and bars of the Paseo Maritimo. The once modest dwellings in the cobbled street had been tastefully bijouized, the ancient walls pierced by air-conditioning vents and security alarms.

Sansom's house, painted a dove-egg blue, stood on a corner where the terrace was divided by a side-street. Lace curtains veiled the kitchen windows, but I could see lacquered beams and horse brasses, a ceramic hob and an antique stone sink with oak draining board. Beyond the inner windows lay a miniature garden like a powder-puff. Already I could sense the freedom that this intimate world would have given to Alice Hollinger after the vastness of the mansion on the hill.

'You'll come in?' Hennessy heaved himself from the car. 'There's some decent Scotch that needs to be finished.'

'Well . . . a few drinks always make the car go better. Have you found any of Alice Hollinger's things?'

'No. Why on earth should I? Have a look round. You'll find it interesting.'

While Hennessy unlocked the front door I worked the wrought-iron bell-push, eliciting a few bars of Satie from the electronic annunciator. I followed Hennessy into the sitting room, a chintzy arbour of fluffy rugs and elegant lampshades. Packing chests stood on the floor, partly filled with shoes, walking-sticks and expensive leather shaving tackle. Half a dozen suits lay on the settee, next to a pile of monogrammed silk shirts.

'I'm sending all this stuff to the cousins,' Hennessy told me. 'Not much to remember the fellow by, a few suits and ties. Decent chap – he was very formal up on the hill, but when he came here he changed into another personality, rather blithe and carefree.'

Beyond the sitting room was a dining alcove with a small blackwood table and chairs. I imagined Sansom having two lives, a formal one with the Hollingers and a second down here in this doll's-house of a cottage, furnished as a second boudoir for Alice Hollinger. Her husband's discovery of the affair might have released an anger strong enough to consume the entire mansion. The notion of Hollinger committing suicide had never occurred to me, a Wagnerian immolation that might have appealed to a film producer, he and his unfaithful wife dying with their lovers in a gigantic conflagration.

When Hennessy returned with a tray and glasses I commented: 'You say there's nothing of Alice Hollinger's here. Isn't that rather strange?'

Hennessy poured the pale malt into our glasses. 'But why, dear chap?'

'David . . .' I paced around the sitting room, trying to adjust my mind to this half-sized world. 'We have to assume that she and Sansom were having an affair. It may have been going on for years.'

'Unlikely.' Hennessy savoured the whisky's bouquet. 'In fact, wholly impossible.'

'They died in his bed together. He was gripping her shoes, obviously part of some weird fetishistic game they played. It's enough to make Krafft-Ebing sit up in his grave and whistle. If Hollinger learned of the affair he must have been devastated. Life would have had no meaning for the poor man. He toasts the Queen for the last time and then commits his version of hara-kiri. Five people die. Perhaps Frank, unwittingly, told Hollinger about the affair. He realizes he is responsible, and pleads guilty.' I looked hopefully at Hennessy. 'It might be true . . .'

'But it isn't.' Hennessy smiled judiciously into his whisky. 'Come into the kitchen. It's hard to think clearly in here. I feel like a character in the Alice books.'

He stepped into the kitchen and sat at the glass-topped table as I prowled around the dainty space with its burnished copper pans and earthenware dishes, ruched tea-towels and tissue rolls. Above the stone sink was a notice-board covered with personal miscellanea: holiday postcards from Sylt and Mykonos, pasta recipes torn from a Swedish magazine, and photographs of handsome young men in minuscule swimming thongs lounging on a diving raft or lying side by side on a shingle beach, naked as seals.

Thinking of the young Spaniards in their posing pouches, I asked: 'Was Sansom an amateur sculptor?'

'Not that I know of. Is that part of your theory?'

'These young men – they remind me of the male models in the sculpture classes here.'

'They're Swedish friends of Sansom's. Sometimes they'd visit Estrella de Mar and stay here. He'd take them for dinner at the Club. Charming youths, in their way.'

'So . . .'

Hennessy nodded sagely. 'Exactly. Roger Sansom and Alice were never lovers. Whatever was going on in that tragic bed had nothing to do with sex.'

'Idiot . . .' I stared at myself in the Venetian mirror above the pastry board. 'I was thinking of Frank.'

'Of course you were. You're sick with worry.' Hennessy stood up and handed me my drink. 'Go back to London, Charles. You can't solve this thing on your own. You're tying yourself into a mess of knots. We're all concerned that you may actually damage Frank's case. Believe me, Estrella de Mar isn't the sort of place you're used to . . .'

He shook my hand at the doorway, his soft palm the gentlest of brush-offs. Holding a set of silk ties, Hennessy watched me step into my car like a schoolmaster faced with an over-eager but naive pupil. Annoyed with myself, I set off along the narrow street, past the surveillance cameras that guarded the lacquered doorways, each lens with its own story to tell.

Hidden perspectives turned Estrella de Mar into a huge riddle. *Trompe-l'œil* corridors beckoned but led nowhere. I could sit all day spinning scenarios that proved Frank innocent, but the threads unravelled the moment they left my fingers.

Trying to find the Plaza Iglesias, I turned in and out of the narrow streets, and soon lost myself in the maze of alleys. I stopped in a small square, little more than a public courtyard, where a fountain played beside an open-air café. I was tempted to walk to the Club Nautico, and pay one of the porters to retrieve the car. A flight of worn stone steps climbed from a corner of the square to the plaza, but in my present mood I would soon transform it into an Escher staircase.

The café was untended, the owner talking to someone in the basement. Beyond the pin-tables and a television set bearing the notice, 'Corrida, 9-30 p.m.', an open door led to a backyard. I stood among the beer crates and rusting refrigerators, trying to read the contours of the streets above me. A white satellite dish was bolted to an outhouse roof, tuned to the frequency that would relay that evening's bull-fight to the café's patrons.

As I stepped past it I noticed the spire of the Anglican church rising above the Plaza Iglesias. Its weather-vane pointed to a penthouse balcony of a cream-faced apartment building on the Estrella de Mar skyline. The silver diamond trembled in the morning air, like an arrow marking a bedroom window on a holiday postcard.

I parked the Renault across the street, sat behind my newspaper and looked up at the Apartamentos Mirador, an exclusive complex built along the high corniche. Balconies freighted with ferns and flowering plants turned the cream façades into a series of hanging gardens. Heavy awnings shielded the low-ceilinged rooms, and a deep privacy layered like geological strata rose floor by floor to the sky.

A decorator's van stood outside the entrance, and workmen carried in their trestles and paints. A pick-up truck passed me and pulled in behind the van, and two men stepped from the driving cab and unloaded a jacuzzi's pump and motor unit.

I left my car and crossed the road, reaching the entrance as the men climbed the steps. A uniformed concierge emerged from the lobby, held open the doors and beckoned us through. An elevator took us to the penthouse level. Two large apartments occupied the floor, one with its door held open by a wooden trestle. I followed the workmen into the apartment, and made a pretence of checking the electrical wiring. Wide balconies surrounded the rooms, from which all furniture had been removed, and decorators were painting the walls of the split-level lounge.

Ignored by the workmen, I strolled around the apartment, already recognizing the art deco motifs, the strip lighting and porthole niches. I assumed that the apartment had been leased by the makers of the porno-film, who had now fled the scene. I stood in the hall, sniffing the scents of fresh paint, solvents and adhesive, while the men with the jacuzzi motor lowered it to a bathroom floor.

I stepped into the master bedroom, which overlooked the harbour and rooftops of Estrella de Mar, and closed the mirror-backed door behind me. A white telephone rested on the floor, its jack pulled from the socket, but otherwise the room was almost antiseptically bare, as if sterilized after the completion of the film.

With my back to the mantel, I could almost see the bed with its blue satin spread and teddy bear, and the Hollingers' niece with her wedding dress and sinister bridesmaids. I framed my fingers around my eyes, trying to place myself where the camerawoman had stood. But the perspectives of the room were elusive. The positions of windows, balcony and the mirror-door were reversed, and I guessed that the rape had been filmed within a second mirror, reversing the scene in an attempt to disguise the participants.

I unlatched the door on to the balcony and looked down at the spire of the Anglican church. Beyond it the satellite dish had moved a few feet to the right, searching the sky for its bull-fight, and the weather-vane pointed to the rear door of the café.

A woman's voice, more familiar than I wanted to admit, sounded from a nearby window. Beyond the glass-walled stairwell was the balcony of the apartment that shared the penthouse floor. Leaning over the rail, I realized that the porno-film had been shot in one of its bedrooms, the symmetrical twin of the one in which I stood, from where the weather-vane and satellite dish would be exactly aligned.

While the woman's laughter continued, I peered around the stairwell. Twenty feet from me, Paula Hamilton leaned against the rail, face raised to the sun. She wore a white surgical coat, but her hair was unpinned and floated on the wind in a bravura display. Bobby Crawford sat beside her in a deck-chair, pale thighs emerging from his dressing-gown. Without inhaling, he touched his lips with the gold tip of his cigarette and watched the smoke sail across the gleaming air, smiling at Paula as she remonstrated playfully with him.

Despite her untethered hair, Paula Hamilton was paying a professional visit to Crawford's apartment. His right forearm and the back of his hand were freshly bandaged, and a roll of gauze stood on a nearby table. He seemed tired and drawn, the tone drained from his cheeks by some fierce duel with the tennis machine. Yet his boyish face had an appealingly stoic air. As he grinned at Paula he looked down at the town below, watching every balcony and veranda, every street and car park, an earnest young pastor keeping an ever-vigilant eye on his flock.

14

A Pagan Rite

'MR PRENTICE, for reasons of its own your motor decided to overheat itself.' Inspector Cabrera gestured at the burnt-out engine compartment of the Renault. 'The Spanish sun is like a fever. It's much closer to us than it is to you in England.'

'This fire started at midnight, Inspector. I spent the evening in my brother's apartment. Still, as you say, the engine decided to ignite itself. The seats, the carpets, the four wheels, even the spare tyre, all chose the same fate. It's rare to find such unanimity.'

Cabrera stepped back to survey the gutted car. He waited as I moved restlessly around the vehicle, puzzled by my light-hearted manner. This tough-minded graduate of the police academy clearly found the British residents of the Costa del Sol well beyond the reach of even the most modern investigative techniques.

'Perhaps the cigarette lighter was partly engaged. Mr Prentice? A short circuit . . . ?'

'I don't smoke, Inspector. Mr Hennessy needn't have called you, it's only a rental car. I won't be out of pocket.'

'Naturally. They'll bring a replacement. Or you can use your brother's car in the basement garage. The forensic team have finished with it.'

'I'll think about it.' Whistling, I walked Cabrera back to his Seat. 'The manager at the rental office in Fuengirola tells me that spontaneous fires are very common along the Costa del Sol.'

'As I said.' Cabrera turned to peer at me, unsure whether I was being ironic. 'At the same time, be careful. Keep the doors and windows closed whenever the car is out of your sight.'

'I will, Inspector. You can relax – I'm sure the point has been made.'

Cabrera stopped to scan the windows of the Club Nautico. 'You think it was another warning to you?'

'Not exactly. More of an invitation. Fires are the oldest signalling system.'

'And if it was a signal, what was the message?'

'Hard to say. Something like "Come on in, the water's fine". Same as the speedboat fire the other night.'

Cabrera tapped his temple, despairing of me. 'Mr Prentice, that fire was deliberate. They found an empty gasoline can floating on the sea. There were traces of human skin on the handle. The thief must have burned himself when the fire flashed back across the waves. In the case of your car, the investigation shows nothing.'

'That doesn't surprise me. Whoever started the fire would hardly want to do your work for you.'

'You saw no one running from the car park?'

'The blaze had begun by the time I woke. Mr Hennessy was in his pyjamas – he thought I was inside the Renault.'

'I spoke with him earlier.' Cabrera put on his most sombre expression. 'He's very concerned, Mr Prentice. The danger to you, and also the atmosphere in the club.'

'Inspector, there's nothing wrong with the atmosphere. Five minutes after the fire service arrived everyone was enjoying a pool party. It lasted till dawn.' I pointed to the stream of members moving through the entrance. 'The Club Nautico is having one of its busiest days. Frank would have been impressed.'

'I spoke to Señor Danvila this morning. It's possible that your brother will see you.'

'Frank . . . ?' The name had a curious echo, as if refracted through a more rarified medium. 'How is he, Inspector?'

'He works in the prison garden, his face is not so pale now. He sends his affections, and thanks you for the parcels, the laundry and books.'

'Good. He knows I'm still trying to discover what happened at the Hollinger house?'

'Everyone knows that, Mr Prentice. You've been very busy at Estrella de Mar. It's even possible that I will re-open the investigation. Many things are unexplained . . .'

Cabrera placed his hands on the roof of the Seat and stared through the haze at the wooded slopes of the Hollinger estate. His talk of re-opening the case unsettled me. I had begun to take an almost proprietary view of the gutted mansion. Despite its tragic outcome, the fire had served its purpose for Estrella de Mar, and satisfied certain needs of my own. Part of the past had vanished in the conflagration, unhappy memories that had dispersed with the rising smoke. Nothing pointed to the identity of the arsonist, but a trail of sorts had been laid for me. I did not want Cabrera and his forensic team stumbling over my heels.

'Inspector, is there really anything to explain? Clearly, someone set fire to the house, but it might have been no more than . . . a practical joke that got out of hand.'

'A very sinister joke.' Cabrera stepped towards me, suspecting that I had been touched by the sun. 'In any case, you know the circumstances of the deaths.'

'Hollinger and Bibi Jansen in the jacuzzi? Probably innocent – with the stairs on fire and her own bedroom blazing, where else could Bibi have gone but across the hall to Hollinger's room? They may have hoped to lie under the water until the fire had passed.'

'And Mrs Hollinger in the secretary's bed?'

'*On* the bed. There was a window overhead. I can imagine them trying to escape on to the roof. He held her feet as she reached towards the window catch. It's possible, Inspector . . .'

'It's possible.' Cabrera hesitated before getting into his car, unsettled by my change of tack. 'As you say, your brother holds the key. I'll telephone when he agrees to see you.'

'Inspector . . .' I paused before committing myself. For reasons that I scarcely understood I was now in no hurry to see Frank. 'Give me a few more days. I'd like to have something solid to bring to Frank. If I can prove to him that no one else wanted to kill the Hollingers he's more likely to admit that his confession is meaningless.'

'I agree.' Cabrera started the engine, then switched off the ignition and carefully scanned the other vehicles in the car park, taking care to read their licence plates. 'It may be that we are looking in the wrong place, Mr Prentice.'

'Meaning what?'

'That outside elements are involved. The fire at the Hollinger house was untypical of Estrella de Mar. Likewise the theft of the speedboat. Compared with the rest of the Costa del Sol, there is almost no crime here. No burglaries, no car thefts, no drugs.'

'No drugs and no burglaries . . . ? Are you sure, Inspector?'

'None are reported. Crime is not a characteristic of Estrella de Mar. That's why we are happy to leave the policing to your volunteer force. Perhaps, after all, the Renault's fire was a short circuit . . .'

I watched him drive away, and repeated his last words to myself. No crime at Estrella de Mar, no drug-dealing, burglaries or car thefts? In fact, the entire resort was wired up to crime like a cable TV network. It fed itself into almost every apartment and villa, every bar and nightclub, as anyone could see from the defensive nervous system of security alarms and surveillance cameras. At the pool-side terrace below Frank's balcony half the talk was of the latest ram-raid or housebreaking incident.

At night I listened to the wailing sirens of the volunteer police patrols as they chased a car thief around the steep streets. Every morning at least one boutique-owner found her plate-glass windows lying shattered among the couture gowns. Drug-dealers haunted the bars and discos, prostitutes high-heeled the cobbled alleyways above the harbour, and the cameras of the porno-film makers probably turned in a score of bedrooms. Crimes took place in abundance, yet Cabrera knew nothing of them, since the residents of Estrella de Mar never reported them to the Spanish police. For reasons of their own they kept silent, fortifying their homes and businesses as if playing an elaborate and dangerous game.

Walking around Frank's apartment, I thought of him working in the prison garden, homesick for the Club Nautico. No doubt he was hungry for news and eager to see me, but a certain distance had opened between us. I felt too restless to spend any time in a gloomy invigilation room at the Zarzuella jail, hunting for clues to the truth among the nuances and studied vagueness of Frank's elliptical replies.

The sight of the Renault burning in the night had excited me. Roused by flames that seemed to leap across the bedroom ceiling, I ran to the balcony and saw the passenger cabin lit like a lantern, smoke swirling in the headlamps of the members' cars as they backed away to safety. One of the modern world's pagan rites was taking place, the torching of the automobile, witnessed by the young women from the disco, their sequinned dresses trembling in the flames.

When the pool party began as an excited response to the inferno, I almost changed into my swimsuit and joined the revellers. Trying to calm myself, I sipped Frank's whisky and listened to the shrieks and laughter as the sun came up over the sea, its copper rays touching the villas and apartment houses, a premonition of the last carnival blaze that would one day consume Estrella de Mar.

After lunch a replacement Citroën arrived at the Club Nautico, and the gutted wreck of its predecessor was hoisted on to the back of a breakdown truck. I signed the papers and then, out of curiosity, walked down the ramp to the basement garage. Frank's Jaguar sat in the pale light under its dust-sheet, police tapes around its fenders. A spare set of keys was in the concierge's office, but the thought of sitting behind the wheel made me uneasy. I took the service lift to the lobby, glad to leave the car to its dim underworld.

The tennis machine sounded across the lawns as the afternoon's practice sessions began. As ever, Bobby Crawford was busy with his trainees. Undeterred by his bandaged hand and arm, he moved restlessly around the courts, vaulting the net to retrieve a stray ball, skipping from one baseline to the next, cajoling and encouraging.

I thought of him sitting beside Paula on the balcony of his apartment on the morning after the speedboat chase in the harbour. I took for granted that he had set fire to the craft, not out of malice but to provide a handsome spectacle for the evening crowds, and that he or some collaborator had torched my rented Renault.

His motive, if any, seemed obscure, less an attempt to force me to leave Estrella de Mar than to integrate me into its inner life. I replayed the cassette of the porno-film shot in his apartment, still convinced that he was too committed to his fellow-residents in the resort to have taken any part in the brutal rape.

But had he murdered the Hollingers? So many witnesses had seen him at the Club Nautico's tennis courts at the time of the fire, but others could have acted for him. Someone with a taste for fire presided over the secret spaces of Estrella de Mar.

15

The Cheerleader's Cruise

THE TENNIS MACHINE had fallen silent. Soon after four o'clock the players began to leave the courts and make their way home to a late siesta. Waiting for Bobby Crawford, I sat in the Citroën outside the bar where the amateur whores patrolled the night. One by one, the cars turned through the gates of the Club Nautico, drivers happily exhausted, dreaming of the perfect backhand brought to them by this handsome evangel of the baseline.

Crawford was the last to leave. At five-fifteen the shark-like snout of his Porsche appeared at the gates. It paused as he scanned the road, then accelerated past me with a throaty burble. He had changed from his tennis gear into a leather jacket, gangster-black against his white shirt, and his blow-dried blond hair gleamed from the shower. With his dark shades, he resembled a likeable young actor in his James Dean phase, chewing a knuckle as he pondered his next film role. Behind his head the torn roof liner fluttered in the wind.

I let a few cars pass and followed him towards the Plaza Iglesias. The Porsche waited at the traffic lights, exhaust thrumming among the motor-scooters and diesel taxis. With the sun vizor lowered, I pulled in behind a bus to Fuengirola packed with British tourists clutching their souvenirs of Estrella de Mar – miniaturized busts of the Apollo Belvedere, art deco lampshades and videos of Stoppard and Rattigan productions.

Untouched by snobbery, Crawford waved to the tourists,

giving a cheerful thumbs-up to their choices. When the lights changed he pulled sharply to the right in front of the bus, barely missing the bull-bars of an oncoming truck, and set off down the Calle Molina for the old town.

For the next hour I trailed him around Estrella de Mar, along an itinerary that seemed to trace a secret map of this impulsive man's mind. He drove almost without thinking, and I guessed that he took the same route every evening when he finished his duties as the Club Nautico's tennis coach and set off to visit the outposts of a very different kingdom.

After a quick circuit of the Paseo Maritimo, he returned to the Plaza Iglesias and left the Porsche with its engine idling. He crossed the central gardens to the open-air café beside a newspaper kiosk, and joined the two brothers who spent their nights outside the doors of the Club Nautico disco. Edgy but affable, these former East End car-dealers sometimes offered me a generous discount on a new shipment of Moroccan hashish brought in by the powerful speedboat whose engines Gunnar Andersson tuned so expertly.

Leaving their iced tea, they stood up to greet Crawford with the deference of experienced NCOs towards a trusted young officer. They spoke softly as Crawford scanned his diary, ticking off entries in what seemed to be his order book. When they returned to their tea, supplies assured, Crawford signalled to a beefy Maghrebian in a dark uniform who sat at the shoe-shine stand.

This was Elizabeth Shand's chauffeur, Mahoud, who had watched me with his sour gaze while logging my licence number into his electronic notepad. After pressing a roll of pesetas into the shoe-shine boy's blackened hand, he joined Crawford in the Porsche. They circled the plaza, turned into a narrow side-street and stopped outside the Baalbeck Lebanese restaurant, a popular rendezvous and pick-up point for rich Arabs sailing down the coast from Marbella.

While Crawford waited in the Porsche the chauffeur entered the restaurant, and emerged moments later with two fair-haired women in gaudy tops, leather micro-skirts and white stilettos. They pretended to blink at the open air, as if sunlight was a phenomenon they had never experienced at first-hand. With their patent handbags they were dressed in a high-style pastiche of Pigalle streetwalkers, their garish garb incongruously assembled from the racks of Estrella de Mar's most expensive boutiques.

As the taller of the two hobbled along the narrow sidewalk I recognized under the platinum wig another of the mourners at Bibi Jansen's funeral, the English wife of a yacht-broker with offices at the marina. She was doing her best to play the whore, fleshing out her mouth and rolling her hips, and I wondered if this was all the whim of some avant-garde theatre director staging a street production of *Mahagonny* or *Irma la Douce*.

The women joined Mahoud in the back of a taxi, which sped towards the luxury apartment houses of the high corniche. Satisfied to see them off to work, Crawford stepped from the Porsche and locked its doors. He strolled past the parked cars in the side-street, right hand hidden in the folds of his jacket, testing the door latches. When the passenger door of a silver Saab opened to him he slipped into the driver's seat and reached under the steering wheel shroud.

I watched from the doorway of a tapas bar as he expertly jumped the car's ignition circuits. When the engine began to turn he pulled the Saab out of the parking lane and accelerated down the cobbled street, clipping the wing mirrors of the stationary cars.

By the time I returned to the Citroën I had lost him. I drove around the plaza, and then searched the harbour and the old town, waiting for him to reappear. I was about to give up and set off for the Club Nautico when I saw a group of tourists outside the Lyceum theatre club in the Calle Dominguez trying to calm an impatient driver. Crawford's stolen Saab was boxed into the kerb by an unattended pick-up van loaded with Egyptian costumes for a forthcoming production of *Aida*.

Before anyone could find the driver, Crawford shouted his thanks and drove forward, ramming the Saab into the space between the van and the car parked ahead of him. There was a rasp of torn metal as a wing buckled, and a headlamp shattered and fell between the wheels. The costumes danced on their hangers, a line of drunken pharaohs. Smiling to the startled tourists, Crawford reversed and then threw the Saab forward again, his arms raised as the van's crushed wing stripped the paint from his door.

No longer bothering to conceal myself, I followed Crawford when he broke free and resumed his circuit of Estrella de Mar. Part inspection tour and part criminal jaunt, his route took him through a hidden Estrella de Mar, a shadow world of backstreet bars, hard-core video-stores and fringe pharmacies. Not once did money change hands, and I assumed that this whirlwind cruise was primarily inspirational, an extension of his cheerleader's role at the Club Nautico.

Towards the end he parked again in the Plaza Iglesias, left the Saab and plunged into the crowds that overflowed the pavements outside the galleries and bookstores. Ever-smiling, his face as open as a friendly adolescent's, he seemed popular with everyone he met. Storekeepers offered him a pastis, shop assistants were happy to flirt with him, people rose from their café tables to banter and jest. As always I was struck by how generous he was, giving of himself as if drawing on a limitless source of warmth and goodwill.

Yet just as freely he stole and shoplifted. I watched him pocket an atomizer from a perfumery on the Calle Molina, then skip along the sidewalk, spraying scent at the feral cats.

He supervised a streetwalker's make-up in the Galleria Don Carlos, examining her eyeliner with the seriousness of a beauty specialist, then slipped past her into the nearby bodega and helped himself to two bottles of Fundador that he placed between the feet of the winos dozing in a nearby alley. With the deftness of a conjuror he spirited a pair of crocodile shoes from a display stand under the nose of the store's manager, and minutes later emerged from a busy jewellery shop with a small diamond on his little finger.

I assumed that he was unaware of my presence twenty yards behind him, but as we crossed the gardens of the Plaza Iglesias he waved to Sonny Gardner, who stood on the steps of the Anglican church, mobile phone to his plump lips. The sometime barman and sail-rigger nodded to me when I walked past him, and I realized that others had probably joined Crawford on his evening crime spree.

Returning to the battered Saab, Crawford waited for me to take the wheel of the Citroën and start the overheated engine. Tired of the town and its tourist crowds, he left the plaza and drove past the last of the shops towards the residential streets on the wooded slopes below the Hollinger mansion. He led me in and out of the palm-lined roads, always keeping me in sight, and I wondered if he intended to break into one of the villas.

Then, as we circled the same traffic island for the third time, he suddenly accelerated away from me, lapped the Citroën and sat on my tail before swerving off into the maze of avenues. His horn sounded a series of cheery toots that faded across the hillside, the friendliest of goodbyes.

Twenty minutes later I found the Saab outside the drive of a large, half-timbered villa two hundred yards from the gates of the Hollinger estate. Beyond the high walls and security cameras an elderly woman watched me from an upstairs window. Crawford, I decided, had caught a lift from a passing driver, and the inspirational tour of Estrella de Mar had ended for the day.

I walked over to the Saab and gazed at its battered bodywork and by-passed ignition system. Crawford's fingerprints would be all over the vehicle, but I was sure that the owner would not report the theft to the Guardia Civil. As for the volunteer police force, its main function seemed to be the preservation of the existing criminal order, rather than the tracking down of miscreants. Twice during Crawford's jaunt around Estrella de Mar the police patrol's Range Rovers had provided him with an escort and kept an eye on the stolen Saab while he shoplifted in the Plaza Iglesias.

Exhausted by the effort of chasing Crawford, I sat down on the wooden bench beside a nearby bus stop and gazed at the battered car. A few feet from me a flight of stone steps climbed the hillside towards the rocky summit above the Hollinger house. Whether or not by coincidence, Crawford had left the Saab at almost the exact spot where Frank's Jaguar had been found with its incriminating flask of ether and gasoline. It occurred to me that the arsonist had reached the lemon orchard by climbing the steps. On his return, seeing the Jaguar by the bus stop, he had seized the opportunity to implicate its owner by leaving the unused flask on its rear seat.

Consigning the Citroën to the care of the elderly woman's security cameras, I began to mount the worn limestone steps. Centuries older than Estrella de Mar, according to a local guidebook I had read, they led to an observation post constructed during the Napoleonic wars. The perimeter walls of the adjacent villas reduced their width to little more than my shoulders. Beyond the encroaching shrubbery a hang-glider turned in the cloudless sky, the pilot's vizored helmet silhouetted against the rustling canopy.

The last of the villas fell below me as I climbed the final steps to the observation platform. Sitting on the castellated wall, I caught my breath in the cool air. Stretched out beneath me were the peninsular heights of Estrella de Mar. Ten miles to the east the hotel towers of Fuengirola faced the sinking sun, their curtain walls like huge screens waiting for the evening's *son et lumière* performance. From the stone platform the ground sloped down to the blackened grove of lemon trees and then to the rear gate and the garage apartment beside the fire-swept house.

I left the platform and walked towards the orchard, searching the stony soil for any trace of the arsonist's footprints. Above my head sounded the leathery flutter of canvas. Curious to see who I was, the glider pilot hovered in the air above me, so close that his booted foot almost touched my head, his vizor masking his eyes. Too distracted to wave to him, I stepped through the charred stumps of the lemon trees, my shoes crushing the flakes of charcoal that covered the ground.

Thirty yards away the Hollingers' chauffeur stood by the gate, his back to the old Bentley in the drive. He watched me in the same fixed and half-threatening way, hands clasped across his chest. He stepped forward as I approached, his boots a few inches from a shallow pit excavated in the soil.

A tag of yellow police tape flew from a wooden stump, and I assumed that it marked the hollow where the arsonist had hidden his incendiary flagons on the night before the fire. As if out of respect, the hang-glider withdrew from the hill-crest, its canvas cracking in the air. Miguel stood at the pit's edge, the calcinated soil crumbling under his feet. Despite his aggressive stance, he was waiting for me to speak to him. Had he, conceivably, caught even the briefest glimpse of the arsonist . . . ?

'Miguel . . .' I walked up to him, a hand raised in greeting. 'I came to the house with Inspector Cabrera. I'm Frank Prentice's brother. I wanted to talk to you.'

He lowered his eyes and stared at the pit, then turned on his heel and walked back to the gate. He closed it behind him and moved quickly down the steps, shoulders hunched as he disappeared into the garage.

'Miguel . . . ?'

Irritated by the persistent hang-glider, I looked down at my feet. Two silver coins lay in the charcoal-covered soil, pieces of silver presumably intended to express the chauffeur's contempt for the family that had murdered his employers.

I knelt down and prodded the coins with my fountain pen, then realized that I was touching a pair of car keys, linked together by a small metal chain and partly buried in the earth. Without thinking, I accepted that the keys were those of the Bentley, dropped by the chauffeur as he waited for me. I wiped them and brushed away the dirt, ready to return them to Miguel. But the Bentley's engine was turning, vapour rising from the exhaust, and the keys had no doubt been dropped by a member of the police forensic team. I held them in my hand, trying to identify the make of car, but the flat chrome was unmarked. Already I suspected that the keys might belong to the arsonist, lost or forgotten by him when he retrieved the buried flasks.

The hang-glider hovered over my head, its steel guy-ropes singing in the air. The pilot's gloved hands clasped the control bar, as if reining in a winged horse. The craft banked steeply and dived across the orchard, its left wing nearly striking my face.

I crouched among the burnt-out trees as the glider circled above me, ready to make another pass if I attempted to reach the gate to the Hollinger house. Head lowered, I ran across the ashy soil, deciding to make my way down the hillside that lay beyond the outer wall of the estate. Again the glider soared forwards, riding the thermals that swept up the open slopes. The pilot seemed unaware that I was scrambling and sliding beneath him, his eyes apparently fixed on the waves rolling towards the beaches of Estrella de Mar.

Below me appeared a line of villas built among the eucalyptus trees that lay beyond the lower boundary of the Hollinger estate. The rear gardens and courtyards were protected by high walls, and from the alarmed expression of a maid watching me from a second-floor balcony I knew that none of the residents would come to my aid, let alone admit me to the shelter of their gardens.

Covered with dust and ash, I stumbled towards the rear wall of the Protestant cemetery. The thoughtless pilot had returned to the summit, circling before he set off in a steep dive towards the landing beach below him.

A stone refuse tip stood by the rear gate of the cemetery, filled with dead flowers and faded wreaths. I wiped my hands on a bouquet of cannas, trying to squeeze the last moisture on to my raw palms. Brushing the ash from my shirt, I pushed back the gate and set off through the graves.

Apart from a single visitor, the burial ground was empty. A slim man in a grey suit stood with his back to me, clasping a spray of lilies and fern that he seemed reluctant to lay on the memorial stone. When I passed the burial plot he turned and almost flinched from me, as if I had caught him at a moment of guilty thought. I recognized the mourner shunned by almost everyone at the funeral of Bibi Jansen.

'Dr Sanger . . . ? Can I help you?'

'No . . . thank you.' Sanger was feeling the face of the headstone, his gentle fingers touching the letters incised in the polished marble. The silver stone was the same colour as his hair and suit, and his eyes seemed even more melancholy than I remembered them. At last he laid the lilies against the stone and stood back, a hand on my elbow.

'Well . . . how does that seem?'

'It's a fine memorial,' I assured him. 'I'm glad everyone rallied round.'

'I ordered it myself. It was the right thing to do.' He offered me his handkerchief. 'You've cut your hand – shall I look at it for you?'

'It's nothing. I'm in a hurry. A hang-glider attacked me.'

'A hang-glider . . . ?'

He searched the sky, and followed me when I set off for the entrance. I unlatched the gates and stepped into the street, steadying myself against the roof of a parked car. I tried to read the contours of the hillside. The Citroën was at least half a mile away, parked on the slopes to the east of the Hollinger estate.

I waited for the next taxi to deliver mourners to the cemetery, then filled my lungs for the tiring walk. Fifty yards from me, outside the entrance to the Catholic cemetery, a motor-cyclist in black leathers and helmet sat astride his machine, a scarf over his face. His gauntleted hands gripped the handlebars, and I could hear the soft mutter of the machine's exhaust. The front wheel turned fractionally and seemed to point towards me.

I hesitated before stepping from the kerb. The road ran past the secluded villas, and then dipped from sight as it descended towards Estrella de Mar. Hovering in the air like an observation craft was the hang-glider, its wings placed between me and the setting sun, so that the fabric glowed like the plumage of a burning bird.

'Mr Prentice . . . ?' Dr Sanger touched my arm. His face was composed now that he had left the cemetery. He pointed to a nearby car. 'May I give you a lift? It might be safer for you . . .'

16

Criminals and Benefactors

'YOU'VE BEEN FAVOURED,' I told Sanger as we rolled up the drive towards his villa. 'Apart from New York, that's the most impressive collection of graffiti I've ever seen.'

'Let's be charitable and call it street art. But I'm afraid it has other intentions.'

Sanger stepped from his car and surveyed the garage doors. Graffiti covered every inch of the steel panels, an aerosolled display of fluorescent whorls and loops, swastikas and threatening slogans that continued across the window shutters and front door. Repeated cleanings had blurred the pigments, and the triptych of garage, windows and door resembled the self-accusing effort of a deranged Expressionist painter.

Sanger stared wanly at the display, shaking his head like the distracted curator of a gallery forced by the pressures of fashion to exhibit works for which he had little sympathy.

'I suggest you rest for a few minutes,' he told me as he unlocked the door. 'A taxi can take you back to your car. It must have been an ordeal for you . . .'

'It's kind of you, Doctor. I'm not sure if I was in any danger. I seem to have a knack for tripping over my own feet.'

'That hang-glider sounded threatening enough. And the motor-cyclist. Estrella de Mar is more dangerous than people think.'

Sanger ushered me into the hall, watching the empty street

before closing the door. With a faint sigh, a mix of relief and resignation, he stared at the bare walls, criss-crossed by the shadows of the steel grilles over the garden windows, each a dark portcullis. Our silhouettes moved across the bars, figures in a pageant of convict life.

'It reminds me of Piranesi's *Carceri* – I never thought I'd live inside those strange etchings.' Sanger turned to examine me. 'Were you in danger? Very possibly. Crawford likes to keep the pot stirred, but sometimes he goes too far.'

'I feel better than I thought. As it happens, that wasn't Crawford in the hang-glider. Or on the motor-cycle.'

'His colleagues, I dare say. Crawford has a network of sympathizers who know what he wants. I assume they were teasing you. All the same, be careful not to expose yourself, even if you are Frank's brother.'

Sanger led me into a lounge overlooking a small, walled garden almost entirely filled by a swimming pool. The long room was furnished with two armchairs and a low table. Books had once lined the walls, but now filled a collection of cardboard cartons. The air seemed motionless, as if the windows and doors to the garden were never opened.

'I can see you're moving,' I commented. 'In or out?'

'Out. I've found that this house has certain drawbacks, as well as memories of a rather painful kind. Now, sit down and try to calm yourself.' Sanger steered me from the garden door, whose handle I was trying to turn, concerned for my over-excited state. His sensitive hands raised my chin, and I could smell the faint perfume of grave lilies on his fingertips. He touched the fading bruises on my neck, and then sat in the leather chair facing me, as if ready to begin my analysis. 'Paula Hamilton told me about the attack in your brother's apartment. From what she said, the intruder decided not to kill you. Have you any idea why? You seem to have been completely at his mercy.'

'I was. I think he wanted to see how I'd react. It was a kind of initiation. Almost an invitation to . . .'

'The underworld? The real Estrella de Mar?' Sanger frowned at me, disapproving of my lack of concern for myself. 'You've unsettled a great many people since you arrived, understandably so. All these questions . . .'

'They had to be asked.' Sanger's defensive manner irritated me. 'Five people died in the Hollinger fire.'

'An horrific crime, if it was deliberate.' Sanger leaned forward, trying to smile away my brief show of testiness. 'These questions you've asked – they may not be the sort of questions that have answers in Estrella de Mar. Or not the answers you'll want to hear.'

I stood up and paced along the empty bookshelves. 'There's not much chance of that. I've had no real answers at all. I'd like to think there was some kind of conspiracy going on, but there may not have been. All the same, I must free Frank from prison.'

'Of course. His confession is so out of character. Inevitably, as the older brother you hold yourself responsible. Do sit down, and I'll bring you some mineral water.'

He excused himself, smoothing his silver hair in a mirror as he set off for the kitchen. I tried to visualize him living in this airless villa with the sedated Bibi Jansen, a curious ménage even by the standards of Estrella de Mar. There was something almost feminine about Sanger, a constant attentiveness that might have reassured the dazed drug-addict and persuaded her to invite him into her bed. I imagined him making love with all the unobtrusiveness of a ghost.

At the same time there was an evasive strain running through him that roused my suspicions. Sanger, too, had a motive for setting fire to the Hollinger house – the foetus in Bibi's womb. The discovery that he had made one of his patients pregnant would have led to him being struck from the medical register.

Yet he had clearly cared for the young woman, and had mourned her in his ambiguous way, braving the hostile crowd at the funeral and then flushing with embarrassment when I caught him alone by the headstone. Vanity and self-reproach shared the same suede glove, and despite myself I wondered if he had selected the exact shade of silver marble to match his suit and hair.

I searched for a telephone, eager to call a taxi. The excitements of chasing Crawford around Estrella de Mar, the discovery of the keys, and my duel with the hang-glider had left me ready for even more action. I walked to the garden windows and peered down at the drained pool. Someone had thrown a can of yellow paint over the wall, and a canary sunburst leaked towards the drainage vent.

'Another abstract painting,' I remarked to Sanger when he returned with the mineral water. 'I can understand why you're moving.'

'There's a time to stay and a time to leave.' He shrugged, resigned to his own rationalizations. 'I own some property in the Costasol development along the coast, a few bungalows I let out in the summer. I've decided to take one of them for myself.'

'The Residencia Costasol? It's very quiet . . .'

'Of course, practically somnambulistic. But that's what I'm looking for. The security arrangements are more advanced than anywhere else on the coast.' Sanger opened a window and listened to the evening sounds of Estrella de Mar, like an exiled political leader resigned to his heavily-guarded villa and the company of his books. 'I won't say I've been driven out, but I'm looking forward to a quieter life.'

'Will you practise there? Or are the people of the pueblos beyond psychiatric help?'

'That's a little unfair.' Sanger waited for me to return to

the armchair. 'No one would ever dare to retire if dozing in the sun was forbidden.'

I sipped the tepid water, thinking of Frank's bracing malts. 'Strictly speaking, Doctor, few of the people in the Residencia Costasol are retired. They're mostly in their forties and fifties.'

'Everything comes sooner these days. The future rushes towards us like a tennis player charging the net. People in the new professions peak in their late thirties. As it happens, I've a fair number of Costasol patients. It makes sense to move now that my practice here has dried up.'

'So the residents of Estrella de Mar are made of sturdier stuff? Few conflicts or psychic stresses?'

'Very few. They're too busy with their theatre clubs and choral societies. One needs a great deal of idle time to feel really sorry for oneself. There's something special in the air here – and I'm not thinking of your hang-glider.'

'But you do mean Bobby Crawford?'

Sanger stared at the rim of his glass, as if searching for his reflection in the crazed surface. 'Crawford, yes. He's a remarkable man, as you've seen. He has certain dangerous qualities, of which he isn't really aware. He excites people, and stirs them in ways they don't understand. But on the whole he's a force for good. He's put so much energy into Estrella de Mar, though not everyone can stand the pace. Some have to retreat to the sidelines.'

'Someone like Bibi Jansen?'

Sanger turned to stare at the patio, where a deckchair waited by the pool. Here, I guessed, the young Swede had relaxed in the sun under her psychiatrist's melancholy and wistful gaze. At the mention of her name he seemed to slip into a shallow reverie of happier times.

'Bibi . . . I was very fond of her. Before she was taken in by the Hollingers she would often ring my door-bell and ask if she could stay with me. I'd treated her for one addiction after another and always let her in. It was a chance to wean her from everything that was crippling her mind. She knew the beach bars were too much for her to take. Crawford and his friends were testing her to destruction, as if she were a Piaf or Billie Holiday with a huge talent to sustain her. In fact she was desperately vulnerable.'

'Everyone seems to have liked her – I saw that at the funeral.'

'The funeral?' Sanger re-focused his eyes, returning himself to the present. 'Not one of Andersson's better days. A sweet boy, the last of the hippies who found that he was a talented mechanic. She reminded him of his teenage years, back-packing in Nepal. He wanted Bibi to remain a child, living on the beach like a gypsy.'

'He felt she belonged there. Perhaps the world needs a few people ready to burn themselves out. By the way, Andersson thinks you were the father of her child.'

Sanger smoothed his silver hair with the back of his hand. 'So does everyone else at Estrella de Mar. I tried to protect her, but we were never lovers. Sadly, I don't think I ever touched her.'

'They say you sleep with your patients.'

'But, Mr Prentice . . .' Sanger seemed surprised by my naiveté. 'My patients are my friends. I came here six years ago when my wife died. The women I met asked me for help – they were drinking too much, addicted to sleeping pills but never getting any real sleep. Some of them had travelled to the far side of boredom. I went after them and brought them back, and tried to give their lives some meaning. For one or two, that meant a personal involvement. With others – Bibi, and the Hollingers' niece – I was no more than a guide and counsellor.'

'Anne Hollinger?' I grimaced at the memory of the gutted

177

bedroom. 'You didn't bring her back – she was a heroin addict.'

'Absolutely not.' Sanger spoke sharply, as if correcting an incompetent junior. 'She was completely clear. One of the Clinic's few successes, I can assure you.'

'Doctor, she was shooting up at the time of the fire. They found her in the bathroom with a needle in her arm.'

Sanger raised his pale hands to silence me. 'Mr Prentice, you rush to judgement. Anne Hollinger was a diabetic. What she injected into herself was not heroin, but insulin. Her death was tragedy enough without further stigmatizing her . . .'

'I'm sorry. For some reason I took it for granted. Paula Hamilton and I visited the house with Cabrera. She assumed that Anne had relapsed.'

'Dr Hamilton no longer treated her. There was a coldness between the two women, which I can't explain. Anne's diabetes was diagnosed in London six months ago.' Sanger stared bleakly at the sun setting above the miniature garden, with its drained pool like a sunken altar. 'After all she endured, she had to die with Bibi in that senseless fire. It's still hard to believe that it ever happened.'

'And even harder to believe that Frank was behind it?'

'Impossible.' Sanger spoke in measured tones, watching me for my response. 'Frank is the last person in Estrella de Mar who could have started that fire. He loved ambiguity, and sentences that end in question marks. The fire was too definite an act, it stops all further discussion of anything. I knew Frank well – we played bridge together at the Club Nautico in the early days. Tell me, did Frank steal as a child?'

I hesitated, but Sanger had slipped the question in so casually that I almost warmed to him. 'Our mother died when we were young. It left us . . . a broken family. Frank was desperately unsettled.'

'He did steal?'

'It brought us together. I'd cover up and try to take the blame. Not that it mattered – our father rarely punished us.'

'And you never stole yourself?'

'No. I think Frank was doing that for me.'

'And you envied him?'

'I still do. It gave him a kind of freedom I didn't have.'

'And now you're again assuming your child role, rescuing Frank from another of his scrapes?'

'I knew that from the start. The curious thing is that part of me suspects he may have started the Hollinger fire.'

'Of course, you envy him his "crime". No wonder you find Bobby Crawford so intriguing.'

'That's true – there's something mesmerizing about all that promiscuous energy. Crawford charms people, always sailing so close to the rocks. He graces their lives with the possibilities of being genuinely sinful and immoral. At the same time, why do they put up with him?' Too restless to sit in the chair, I stood up and paced among the cartons of books, while Sanger listened to me, constructing a series of steeples with his slender fingers. 'I followed him this afternoon – he could have been arrested a dozen times. He's a genuinely disruptive presence, running a network of drug-dealers, car thieves and prostitutes. He's likeable and enthusiastic, but why don't people send him packing? Estrella de Mar would be a paradise without him.'

Sanger collapsed his steeple, vigorously shaking his head. 'I think not. In fact, Estrella de Mar is probably a paradise because of Bobby Crawford.'

'The theatre clubs, galleries, choral societies? Crawford has nothing to do with them at all.'

'He has everything to do with them. Before Crawford arrived Estrella de Mar was just another resort on the Costa del Sol. People drifted about in a haze of vodka and Valium – I had a great many patients then, I may say. I remember the silent tennis courts at the club, a single member lying by the pool. The water's surface wasn't broken from one day to the next. You could see the dust lying on it.'

'And how did Crawford bring everything to life? He's a tennis player . . .'

'But it wasn't his cross-court backhand that revived Estrella de Mar. He made use of other talents.' Sanger stood up and walked to the window, listening to a nearby security alarm that shrilled through the evening air. 'In a sense Crawford may be the saviour of the entire Costa del Sol, and even wider world beyond that. You've been to Gibraltar? One of the last proud outposts of small-scale greed, openly dedicated to corruption. No wonder the Brussels bureaucrats are trying to close it down. Our governments are preparing for a future without work, and that includes the petty criminals. Leisure societies lie ahead of us, like those you see on this coast. People will still work – or, rather, some people will work, but only for a decade of their lives. They will retire in their late thirties, with fifty years of idleness in front of them.'

'A billion balconies facing the sun. Still, it means a final goodbye to wars and ideologies.'

'But how do you energize people, give them some sense of community? A world lying on its back is vulnerable to any cunning predator. Politics are a pastime for a professional caste and fail to excite the rest of us. Religious belief demands a vast effort of imaginative and emotional commitment, difficult to muster if you're still groggy from last night's sleeping pill. Only one thing is left which can rouse people, threaten them directly and force them to act together.'

'Crime?'

'Crime, and transgressive behaviour – by which I mean all activities that aren't necessarily illegal, but provoke us and tap our need for strong emotion, quicken the nervous system and jump the synapses deadened by leisure and inaction.' Sanger gestured at the evening sky like a planetarium lecturer pointing to the birth of a star. 'Look around you – the people of Estrella de Mar have already welcomed this.'

'And Bobby Crawford is the new Messiah?' I drank the last of Sanger's water, trying to wash the flatness out of my mouth. 'How did a small-time tennis pro discover this new truth?'

'He didn't. He tripped across it in despair. I remember how he paced those empty courts, playing endless games with his serving machine. One afternoon he left the club in disgust and spent a few hours stealing cars and shoplifting. Perhaps it was coincidence, but the very next morning two tennis lessons were booked.'

'Does one follow the other? I don't believe it. If someone burgles my house, shoots the dog and rapes the maid my reaction isn't to open an art gallery.'

'Not your first reaction, perhaps. But later, as you question events and the world around you . . . the arts and criminality have always flourished side by side.'

I followed him to the door and waited while he telephoned for a taxi. As he spoke he watched himself in the mirror, touching his eyebrows and adjusting his hair like an actor in his dressing room. Was he telling me that Bobby Crawford had started the fire at the Hollinger house, and had in some way forced Frank to be his scapegoat?

As we stood on the steps, the graffiti glowing beside us under the security lights, I said: 'One thing is missing in your scheme of things – a sense of guilt. You'd expect people here to be crippled by remorse.'

'But there is no remorse in Estrella de Mar. We've had to forgo that luxury, Mr Prentice. Here transgressive behaviour is for the public good. All feelings of guilt, however old and deep-rooted, are assuaged. Frank discovered that. And you may, too.'

'I hope I do. One last question – who killed the Hollingers? Bobby Crawford? He has a taste for fire.'

Sanger's nose was lifted to the night air. He seemed sensitive to every sound, to every squeal of brakes and blare of music. 'I doubt it. That fire was too destructive. Besides, he was very fond of Bibi and Anne Hollinger.'

'He disliked the older couple.'

'Even so.' Sanger steered me across the gravel as the taxi's headlights swept the drive. 'You won't find who was responsible by looking for motives. In Estrella de Mar, like everywhere in the future, crimes have no motives. What you should look for is someone with no apparent motive for killing the Hollingers.'

17

A Change of Heart

FRANK, UNPREDICTABLE TO the end, had decided to see me. Señor Danvila brought the good news to the Club Nautico, certain that a breakthrough of importance had taken place. He was waiting for me in the lobby as I returned from the swimming pool and seemed unsurprised when I failed to recognize him against the background of English sporting prints.

'Mr Prentice . . . ? Is there a problem?'

'No. Señor Danvila?' Taking off my sunglasses, I identified the harassed figure with his perpetually shuffled briefcases. 'Can I help you?'

'It's an urgent matter, concerning your brother. I heard this morning that he will now receive you.'

'Good . . .'

'Mr Prentice?' The lawyer followed me to the elevator and placed his hand over the call button. 'Can you understand me? You may visit your brother. He's agreed to see you.'

'That's . . . wonderful. Do you know why he's changed his mind?'

'It doesn't matter. It's important that you meet him. He may have something to tell you. Perhaps some new evidence about the case.'

'Of course. It's excellent news. He's probably had time to think everything over.'

183

'Exactly.' For all his air of a dogged but tired schoolmaster, Danvila was watching me with unexpected shrewdness. 'Mr Prentice, when you see your brother give him time to speak for himself. The visiting hour is four-thirty this afternoon. He asked you to bring Dr Hamilton.'

'That's even better. I'll call her at the Clinic. I know she's very keen to talk to him. What about the trial – will this affect it?'

'If he withdraws his confession I will petition the court in Marbella. Everything depends on your meeting this afternoon. It's necessary to be gentle, Mr Prentice.'

We arranged to rendezvous in the visitors' car park at the prison. I walked Danvila to his car, and as he stowed his briefcases in the passenger seat I took from the pocket of my towelling robe the set of keys I had found in the lemon orchard. I tested them against the door lock and, as I assumed, saw that they failed to fit. But Danvila had noticed the shift in my eyes.

'Mr Prentice, are you enjoying your stay in Estrella de Mar?'

'Not exactly. But it's a place of great charm – it even has a certain magic.'

'Magic, yes.' Danvila held the steering wheel, restraining it from any rash behaviour. 'You begin to look like your brother . . .'

I returned to Frank's apartment, trying to guess at the significance of his decision. By refusing to see me, or any of his friends and colleagues at the Club Nautico, he had drawn a line under the case, accepting the blame for the Hollingers' deaths in the way a government minister might resign after the misconduct of a subordinate. At the same time he was shielding me from any memories of the remorse we had shared after our mother's death. We had tried too hard to keep her alive, steadying her on the staircase and sweeping up the glass of the shattered whisky tumblers on the bathroom floor.

I felt a rush of affection for Frank, remembering the determined eight-year-old polishing the smeary cutlery in the kitchen drawers. Only now could I accept that this stricken, lonely woman had probably not even noticed her young sons, and had been scarcely more aware of herself, staring into the mirrors around the house as if trying to remember her own reflection.

Curiously, at Estrella de Mar any residues of remorse had almost vanished, evaporating in the benevolent sunlight like the morning mists over the swimming pools. I rang Paula's answering machine at the Clinic and arranged to lunch with her at the Club Nautico before our drive to Malaga. After my shower I stood on the balcony and watched the tennis players knocking up at the courts, as always devotedly supervised by Bobby Crawford.

Frank's tennis rackets lay in the equipment cupboard, and I was tempted to set out for the courts and challenge Crawford to a set. He would easily beat me, but I was curious to know by what margin. There would be the first stinging aces, and a high kicker aimed at my head, but then he would lower his game, losing a few points as he drew me deeper into the rivalry between us. If I deliberately fumbled my own play I might leave me with too great a lead and be tempted into one or two reckless net rushes . . .

In the car park his Porsche sat in the centre of the black-rimmed halo that the burning Renault had seared into the asphalt. Crawford always parked here, either to remind me of the blaze or in some perverse show of solidarity. Earlier that morning I had tested the lost car keys in the Porsche's door locks. Looking down at the back numbers of the *Economist*, the carton of Turkish cigarettes and the amber-lensed aviator glasses on the glove shelf, I felt a sharp sense of relief when the keys failed to match.

While I waited for Paula I packed a fresh set of clothes for Frank. Searching the wardrobe for clean shirts, I came across the lace shawl passed on to us by our grandmother. The yellowing fabric lay like a shroud among the mohair sweaters, and I remembered placing the shawl around my mother's shoulders as she sat at her dressing-table, and how the scent of her skin blended so inseparably with the tang of whisky.

Paula's BMW turned into the car park and stopped beside the Porsche. Recognizing the sports car, she pinched her nose in a show of irritation and backed away into another space. She took an orange from a hamper of fruit on the passenger seat, stepped from the car and strode briskly to the entrance. As always, I was delighted to see her. In her white trouser suit and high heels, silk scarf floating from her throat, she looked less like a doctor than one of the style-setting yacht-guests at Puerto Banus.

'Paula . . . ? Is that you?'

'It better be.' She closed the apartment door behind her and stepped on to the balcony. Lightly tossing the orange in one hand, she pointed to the circle of scorched asphalt. 'I wish they'd clear that up. Have a word with David Hennessy. Thank God you weren't inside the car.'

'I was sound asleep. It was after midnight.'

'You might have been dozing off at the wheel, or spying on a copulating couple. Some people like having sex in cars, though heaven knows why.' She lobbed the orange to me and leaned against the rail. 'So, how are you? For someone who's been attacked by hang-gliders and half-strangled to death you look remarkably well.'

'I am. I feel almost lightheaded. It's the thought of seeing Frank.'

'Of course it is.' Smiling, she walked up to me and embraced my shoulders, pressing her cheek against mine. 'We've worried ourselves sick over the poor man. At last we'll know what's been going on inside his head.'

'Let's hope so. Something must have changed his mind, though heaven knows what.'

'Does it matter?' She ran her fingers over the bruises on my neck. 'The main thing is that we're making contact. You do want to see Frank?'

'Absolutely. It's just that . . . I'm not sure what to say to him. It's so out of the blue and may not mean all that much. Cabrera will have told him about the attacks on me. I dare say Frank wants me to go back to London.'

'And you? Do you want to go back?'

'Not exactly. Estrella de Mar is a lot more interesting than I thought at first. Besides . . .'

The tennis school had broken up for lunch and the players were making their way back to the changing rooms. Crawford moved around the silent serving machine, returning the scattered balls to the hopper. He sprinted after the players, challenging them to race him back to the showers. Admiring his energy, I was about to wave to him, but Paula held my elbow.

'Charles . . .'

'What is it?'

'Control yourself. You're more concerned with Bobby Crawford than you are with your own brother.'

'That's not true.' I followed Paula into the bedroom, where she began to re-pack the case filled with Frank's clothes. 'But Crawford is interesting. He and Estrella de Mar are the same thing. I talked to Sanger the other day – he thinks we're the prototype of all the leisure communities of the future.'

'And you agree with him?'

'I may do. He's an odd man, with his taste for young girls that he tries to hide from himself. But he's very shrewd. According to him the engine that drives Estrella de Mar is crime. Crime and what Sanger calls transgressive behaviour. You're not surprised, Paula?'

She shrugged, and closed the catches of the suitcase. 'No one ever reports any crime.'

'And that's the most perfect crime of all – when the victims are either willing, or aren't aware that they are victims.'

'And Frank is one of those victims?'

'Perhaps. There's a very curious logic at work here. My guess is that Frank was aware of it.'

'You can ask him yourself this afternoon. Get changed and we'll have lunch.'

She stood by the door, waiting as I took my passport and wallet from the bureau drawer and counted out twenty 1000-peseta notes.

'What are those for? Don't tell me David Hennessy charges you for lunch?'

'Not yet. They're to soften the palm of any prison official who might be of help to Frank. I'd call them a bribe, but that sounds so ungenerous.'

'Good.' Paula nodded approvingly as she re-tied her scarf and adjusted her cleavage in the mirror. 'Don't forget your car keys.'

'They're . . . a spare set.' The keys that I had found in the orchard lay on the bureau. I had said nothing to Paula about them, deciding to wait until I had tested them against the locks of her BMW. 'Paula . . .'

'What is it? You're flitting about like a moth around a flame.' She came up to me, inspecting my pupils. 'Have you taken something?'

'Not the sort of thing you mean.' I turned to face her. 'Look, I'm not sure I can cope with Frank this afternoon.'

'Why not? Charles?'

'You go on alone. Believe me, it's not the right day. Too much has happened.'

'But he asked for you.' Paula tried to read my face. 'What on earth can I tell him? He'll be shocked when he hears that you've refused to come.'

'He won't. I know Frank. He made his decision to plead guilty and nothing will change that.'

'Something new may have cropped up. What do I say to Cabrera? You're not going to leave Estrella de Mar?'

'No.' I put my hands on her shoulders to calm her. 'Look, I want to see Frank, but not today, and not to talk about the trial. All that has slipped to the back of my mind. There are other things I have to do here.'

'Things that involve Bobby Crawford?'

'I suppose so. He's the key to everything. Getting closer to Bobby Crawford is the only way I can help Frank, not going to Zarzuella jail.'

'All right.' She relaxed, and placed her hands over mine. Her over-prompt agreement made me sense that she was following a route of her own. She was leading me through the outer corridors of a maze, guiding me to another door whenever I seemed to falter. She waited as I stared at her breasts, deliberately exposed by the low lapels of her jacket.

'Paula, you're too glamorous for those prison guards.' I moved the lapels together. 'Or is this how you keep your elderly patients going?'

'The breasts are for Frank. I wanted to cheer him up. Do you think they'll work?'

'I'm sure they will. If you're not certain you could always test them first on someone else.'

'A sort of trial run? Maybe . . . but where could I do that? The Clinic?'

'That wouldn't be ethical.'

189

'I hate being ethical. Still, it's an idea . . .'

I pushed Frank's case across the bed and sat beside it. Paula stood in front of me, hands on my shoulders, watching as I unbuttoned her jacket. I felt the mattress yield under my weight, and imagined Frank undressing this handsome young doctor, his hands between her thighs as mine were now. The regret I felt at taking advantage of Frank's absence, and having sex with his former lover on his own bed, was eased by the thought that I had begun to replace him in Estrella de Mar. I had never seen Frank make love, but I guessed that he had kissed Paula's hips and navel as I did, running my tongue around its knotted crater with its scent of oysters, as if she had come to me naked from the sea. He had raised her breasts and kissed the moist skin still bruised by the wired cups of her brassiere, he had drawn out her nipples between his lips. I pressed my cheeks to her pubis, inhaling the same heady scent that Frank had drawn through his nostrils, parting the silky labia that he had touched a hundred times.

However briefly I had known Paula, my brother's months of intimacy with her body seemed to welcome me to her, urging me on as I caressed her vulva and felt the scent glands around her anus. I kissed her knees, and then drew her to the bed, pressing my tongue to her armpits and tasting the sweet gullies with their soft underdown. Feeling not only lust but an almost fraternal affection for her, my imagined memories of her embracing Frank, I held her to my chest.

'Paula, I . . .'

She cupped her palm over my mouth. 'No . . . don't say you love me. You'll spoil it. Here, Frank liked my left nipple . . .'

She raised the breast and pressed it to my mouth, smiling at me like an intelligent eight-year-old conducting an experiment with a younger sibling. Her own pleasure was an emotion she observed from a distance, as if she and I were strangers who had agreed to an hour's practice at the nets. Yet as I lay between her legs, her knees against my shoulders, she watched me come with the first real warmth for me that I had seen her express. She pulled me into her arms and embraced me tightly, hands at first searching for Frank's bones but then happy to hold me. Taking my penis in one hand, she began to masturbate herself, eyes fixed on my still-leaking glans, forefinger parting her labia.

'Paula, let me . . .'

I tried to slip my hand below hers, but she pushed me away.

'No, I'll come more quickly on my own.'

When she came she stiffened fiercely, hand pressed against her furrow, then allowed herself to breathe. She kissed me on the mouth and nestled against me, glad to put aside the cynicism she showed to the world.

Fond of her, I ran a finger lightly along her lips and drew a sleepy smile on to her mouth, but she stopped me when I placed my hand on her pubis.

'No, not now . . .'

'Paula, why can't I stroke you?'

'Later. It's my Pandora's box. Open it and all the ills of Dr Hamilton might escape.'

'Ills . . . ? Are there any? I bet Frank didn't believe that.' I took her palm and held her fingers to my nose, inhaling the rose–damp scent of her vulva. 'For the first time I really envy him.'

'Frank's very sweet. Not as romantic as you, though.'

'Really? That amazes me – I thought he was the romantic one. What about you, Paula? Was it a good idea to become a doctor?'

'I never had much choice.' With a fingertip she gently touched the bruises on my neck. 'At fourteen I already knew that I had to be just like my aunt. I did think of becoming a nun.'

'For religious reasons?'

'No, sexual — all those masturbating sisters mind-fucking Jesus. What could be more erotic? I was such a mess when my mother left us. There were all those emotions I couldn't control, so much hate and anger. My aunt showed me the way out. She was so realistic about people, no one ever hurt or surprised her. Medicine was the best training for all that.'

'And the acid humour? Be honest, Paula, you're rather amused by most people.'

'Well . . . most people are rather odd, when you stand back and look at them. I like them, on the whole. I don't despise people.'

'What about yourself? You're pretty hard on your own feelings.'

'I'm just . . . realistic. I suppose I do have a low estimate of myself, but most of us probably should. Human beings aren't all that wonderful.'

'Not the sort of human beings you find on the Costa del Sol. Is that why you stay here?'

'Among all the alcoholics in the sun, groping each other like ancient lobsters?' Laughing, she lay against my shoulder. 'Never get a suntan, Charles, or I'll stop loving you. The people here are all right, in their way.'

I kissed her forehead. 'Your turn will come, Paula. And mine.'

'Don't say that. Last year I spent a week in the Virgin Islands — it was just like Estrella de Mar. Endless apartment blocks, satellite TV, no-questions sex. You wake up in the morning and can't remember if you fucked anyone the previous day.' She raised one knee, watching the shadows of the plastic blind wrap themselves around her thigh. 'It looks like a bar code. How much am I worth?'

'A lot, Paula. More than you think. Put a higher value on yourself. Being hyper-realistic about everything is too simple a get-out.'

'Easy to say – I spend my time with senile accountants and alcoholic airline pilots, bringing them back from the dead . . .'

'That's a rare talent. The rarest of all. Save a little for me.'

'Poor chap. Do you need resuscitating?' She rolled on to her elbows and put a hand on my forehead. 'Still warm, there's a pulse there somewhere. You seem pretty content to me, Charles. Roaming around the world without a care . . .'

'That's the problem – I ought to have more cares. All this travelling is just an excuse not to put down roots. Unhappy parents teach you a lesson that lasts a lifetime. Frank got over it somehow, but I'm still stuck in Riyadh at the age of twelve.'

'And now you're in Estrella de Mar. Perhaps it's your first real home?'

'I think it is . . . I've stopped feeling depressed here.'

She smiled like a contented child when I moved her on to her back and kissed her eyes. I began to caress her, stroking her clitoris until she parted her thighs and steered my fingers into her vagina.

'That's nice . . . don't forget my anus. Do you want to bugger me?'

She turned on to her side, forced some spit on to her fingers and pressed them between her parted buttocks. I looked down at the silky cleft, at the fine hair that covered the base of her spine. As I caressed her hips my fingers touched what seemed to be a contour line drawn across the smooth skin. A ridge of tissue curved across her hip to the small of her back, the faint trace of a long-healed surgical scar.

'Charles, leave it alone. You can't unzip me.'

'The scar's almost gone. How old were you?'

'Sixteen. My right kidney wasn't working. They resectioned the pelvis, quite a tricky piece of surgery. Frank never even noticed it.' She held my penis. 'You're going soft. Think about my bum for a minute.'

I lay back and looked down at the scar, realizing that I had

193

seen it before, in the closing moments of the porno-film. The faint crescent of hardened skin had been reflected in the mirrored bedroom door, almost certainly in Bobby Crawford's apartment. Gently stroking Paula's back, I remembered the same high rib-cage, narrow waist and broad swimmer's hips. She had held the camcorder, with the battery pack hanging from her shoulder, and filmed the bridesmaids fondling the bride in her wedding gown, and the bride's willing sex with the unknown stud. She had shared Anne Hollinger's panic as she was raped by the two men who had burst into the bedroom, but the camera had continued to turn, recording the brave smile that marked the film's end.

'Charles, are you still here? You've gone for a walk inside your head.'

'I'm here, I think . . .'

I raised myself on one elbow as I tried to smooth away the scar. In many ways the sex that had taken place between us was part of another film. I had imagined myself in Frank's role, and Paula playing his lover, as if only the pornographic image of ourselves could really bring us together and draw out the affection we felt for each other.

'Charles, if I'm going to see Frank I'll have to leave soon.'

'I know. I'll come quickly. By the way, do you know where Bobby Crawford's apartment is?'

'Why do you ask . . . ? It's on the high corniche road.'

'Have you ever been there?'

'Once or twice. I try to keep away from him. Why are we talking about Bobby Crawford?'

'I followed him there the other day. I got into the empty apartment next to his.'

'On the top floor? It's quite a view.'

'It certainly is. It's amazing what you can see there. Hold on, I'll get some cream . . .'

I opened the top drawer of the wardrobe and drew out the

lace shawl. Holding one corner, I laid the yellowing lace across Paula's waist and shoulders.

'What's this?' She peered at the ancient lace. 'It's a Victorian baby shawl . . . ?'

'Frank and I were swaddled in it. It belonged to my mother. It's just a game, Paula.'

'All right.' She looked up at me, puzzled by my calm manner. 'I'm ready for most things. What do you want me to do?'

'Nothing. Just lie there for a moment.'

I knelt across Paula and turned her on to her back, wrapping the shawl around her chest so that her nipples forced themselves through the fine mesh of this temporary bodice.

'Charles? Are you okay?'

'I'm fine. I used to wrap my mother in this shawl.'

'Your mother?' Paula winced as she eased the pressure on her breasts. 'Charles, I don't think I can play your mother.'

'I don't want you to. It looks like a wedding dress. Rather like the one you filmed.'

'Filmed?' Paula sat up, trying to free herself. 'What the hell are you up to?'

'You filmed Anne Hollinger in Crawford's apartment. I've seen the video. In fact, it's over there, I could play it for you. You filmed her in a wedding dress. And you filmed her being raped by those two men.' I held Paula's shoulders as she struggled against me. 'That was a real rape, Paula. She wasn't expecting that.'

Paula bared her teeth, fingers clawing the shawl from her breasts. I forced her thighs apart with my knees. Raising her hips from the bed, I pulled the pillow from behind her head and rammed it under her buttocks, as if preparing to rape her.

'All right!' Paula lay back as my hands held her wrists to the headboard, the tattered shawl between us. 'For God's sake, you're making a hell of a meal out of it! Yes, I *was* at Bobby Crawford's apartment.'

'I recognized the scar.' I released her arms and sat beside her, brushing the hair from her face. 'And you took the film?'

'The film took itself. I pressed the button. What does it matter? It was only a game.'

'Quite a tough one. The two men who burst in – were they part of the script?'

Paula shook her head, as if I were an obtuse patient querying the treatment she had prescribed. 'Everything was part of the game. Afterwards Anne didn't mind.'

'I know – I saw the smile. The bravest and strangest smile I've ever seen.'

Paula searched for her clothes, annoyed with herself for having been ambushed by me. 'Charles, listen to me – I wasn't expecting the rape. If I'd known I wouldn't have taken part. Where did you find the tape?'

'In the Hollingers' house. It was in Anne's VCR. Did Frank know about the film?'

'No, thank God. It was three years ago, soon after I came here. I'd always been interested in cine-photography and someone invited me to join a film club. We didn't just talk about films, we went out and made them. Elizabeth Shand put up the money. I hadn't even met Frank.'

'But you'd met Crawford.' I passed her shoes to Paula as she slipped on the jacket of her trouser suit. 'Was he the pale-skinned man who led the rape?'

'Yes. The other man was Betty Shand's chauffeur. He spends a lot of time with Crawford.'

'And the first man she had sex with?'

'Sonny Gardner – he was one of Anne's boyfriends, so that seemed all right. He nearly had a fight with Crawford afterwards.' Paula sat down and drew me on to the bed beside her. 'Believe me, Charles. I didn't know they would rape her. Crawford's so excitable, he was carried away by it all.'

'I've seen him with his tennis classes. How long had he been making the films?'

'He'd just started the club – we were going to make a series of documentaries about life in Estrella de Mar.' Paula watched me massage her bruised wrists. 'No one realized exactly what sort of documentaries he had in mind. He pointed out that sex was one of the main leisure activities here and that we ought to film it taking place, just as we filmed the theatre clubs and the *Traviata* rehearsals. Anne Hollinger liked a challenge, so she and Sonny volunteered to be first.'

I wiped the smeared mascara from Paula's cheeks. 'Even so, I'm still surprised.'

'At me? For God's sake, I was bored stiff. Working at the Clinic all day, and then sitting on the balcony and watching my tights dry. Bobby Crawford made everything seem exciting.'

'Paula, I understand. How many movies has he shot?'

'A dozen or so. That was the only one I filmed. The rape scene frightened me.'

'Why were you wearing a swimsuit – you look as if you're about to join in?'

'Charles . . . !' Exasperated with me, Paula lay back against the pillow, scarcely caring whether I approved of her or not. 'I'm a doctor here. Half the people seeing that film were my patients. Crawford had masses of copies made. Taking my clothes off was a way of disguising myself. You were the only one who wasn't fooled. You and Betty Shand – she loved the film.'

'I bet she did. You didn't help to make any others?'

'No fear. Crawford was talking about snuff movies. He and the chauffeur, Mahoud, were going to pick up some dim tourist in Fuengirola and bring her to his apartment.'

'He wouldn't have gone that far. Crawford was turning you on.'

'You're wrong!' Paula took my hands, like a serious school-girl at her first biology class who had glimpsed the realities of the living world. 'Listen to me, Charles. Bobby Crawford is dangerous. He set fire to your car, you know.'

'Possibly. This fellow Mahoud or Sonny Gardner would have carried it out. The fire wasn't what you think it was. It was a playful gesture, like some off-beat recorded voice on an answer-phone.'

'A playful gesture?' Paula turned to grimace at my neck. 'And the strangling? How playful was that? He could have killed you.'

'You think that was Crawford?'

'Don't you?' Paula shook my arm, as if trying to wake me. 'You're the one playing the dangerous games.'

'Perhaps you're right about Crawford.' I put my arm around her waist, remembering with affection how we had embraced, and thought of the hands clamped over my throat. 'I assumed it was him, part of the hazing that new recruits go through. He wants to draw me into his world. One thing puzzles me, though, and that is how he got into the apartment. Did he arrive with you?'

'No! Charles, I wouldn't have left you alone with him. He's too unpredictable.'

'But when we collided in the bedroom you said something about not playing that game any more. You took for granted it was Crawford.'

'Of course I did. I assumed he'd let himself in with a spare set of keys. He likes jumping out on people – especially women – coming up behind them and grabbing them in car parks.'

'I know. I've seen him at it. According to Elizabeth Shand, it keeps you on your toes.' I touched the almost vanished bruise on Paula's lip. 'Is that one of Crawford's little efforts?'

She lowered her jaw and revolved it in its sockets. 'He came to see me on the night of the Hollinger fire. The idea of all those terrible deaths must have excited him. I had to wrestle him off in the elevator.'

'But you picked him up from the beach after the speedboat chase? I saw you at his apartment the next day, bandaging his arm.'

'Charles . . .' Paula hid her face in her hands, and then smiled at me with an effort. 'He's a powerful figure, it's not easy to say no to him. If you've once been involved with him you find that he can draw on you whenever he wants to.'

'I understand. Could he have started the Hollinger fire?'

'He might have done. One thing leads so quickly to another – he can't control his imagination. There'll be other fires like your car and that speedboat, and more people will be killed.'

'I doubt it, Paula.' I stepped on to the balcony and gazed at the ruined mansion on its hill-top. 'Estrella de Mar is everything to him. The speedboat fire and my car were pranks. The Hollinger deaths were different – someone set out coldly to murder those people. That isn't Crawford's style. Could the Hollingers have been killed in some turf war over drugs? There are silos of cocaine and heroin sitting here.'

'But all controlled by Bobby Crawford. No other supplier gets a look in. Betty Shand and Mahoud see to it. That's why the heroin here is so pure. People thank Crawford for that – no infections, no accidental overdoses.'

'So the dealers work for Crawford? That didn't help Bibi Jansen and Anne Hollinger. They ended up in your Clinic.'

'They were addicted long before Bobby Crawford met them. But for him they'd both have died. He isn't trying to make money from drugs – Betty Shand takes all the profits. Medicinal-quality heroin and cocaine are Crawford's answer to the benzo-diazepines we doctors love so much. He once told me I was putting people under house arrest inside their own heads. For him heroin and cocaine and all these new amphetamines represent freedom, the right to be a crashed-out bar-kook like Bibi Jansen. He resents Sanger for taking her away from the beach, not for having sex with her.'

'He denies that he did.'

'Sanger can't face that side of himself.' Paula began to remake her lips in the dressing-table mirror, frowning at a still-loose canine under her bruise. 'For some people, even in Estrella de Mar, there are limits.'

She began to brush her hair with strong, efficient strokes, eyes avoiding me while she mentally prepared for her meeting with Frank. As I watched her through the mirror I had the sense that we were still inside a film, and that everything taking place between us in the bedroom had been prefigured in a master script that Paula had read. She was fond of me, and enjoyed making love, but she was steering me in a direction she had chosen.

'Frank will be sorry not to see you,' she told me as I carried the case to the door. 'What shall I tell him?'

'Say that . . . I'm meeting Bobby Crawford. There's something important he wants to discuss.'

Paula pondered the stratagem, unsure whether she approved. 'Isn't that a little devious? Frank won't mind you meeting Crawford.'

'It might trigger something if he thinks I'm trying to take his place. It's a long shot.'

'All right. But be careful, Charles. You're used to being an observer, and Bobby Crawford likes everyone to take part. You're getting too interested in him. When he sees that he'll swallow you whole.'

After a moment's reflection she leaned forward and kissed me, lightly enough not to disturb her lipstick, and long enough to leave me thinking of her for an hour after the elevator doors closed behind her.

18

Cocaine Nights

THE PORSCHE TURNED into the Calle Oporto, pausing to inspect the sunlight like a shark orientating itself above an unfamiliar sea-bed. I lay back in the Citroën's passenger seat, a copy of the *Wall Street Journal* over my chest, unnoticed among the dozing taxi-drivers who used the shadow side of the street for their after-lunch siestas. The Sanger villa stood across the road, windows shuttered, the surveillance camera fixed on the litter of cigarette packets and advertisement flyers in the drive. Pushed by the wind, they edged towards the graffiti-covered doors of the garage, as if hoping to be incorporated into this lurid collage.

Crawford moved the Porsche at walking pace down the street, and stopped to glance at the silent villa. I could see the tendons working in his neck, jaws clenched while his lips mouthed whatever harsh words he had prepared for the psychiatrist. He accelerated sharply, then braked and reversed through the open gates. He stepped on to the unswept gravel and stared at the windows, waiting for Sanger to emerge and confront him.

But the psychiatrist had abandoned the villa, resettling himself a mile down the coast in one of his bungalows at the Residencia Costasol. I had watched him leave the previous afternoon, sitting with the last of his books in a Range Rover driven by a middle-aged woman-friend. He had closed the gates before leaving, but during the night vandals had jemmied the locks on both the gates and the garage.

Crawford walked to the roller door, seized the handle and pulled it from the ground, like an installation artist rolling up a hinged metal painting. He strode across the empty garage, avoiding the oil-stains on the concrete floor, and let himself through the kitchen door into the house.

My eyes turned towards the villa's chimney. For all my belief that Crawford was innocent of the Hollinger murders, I was waiting for the first wisps of smoke to lift into the sky. Frustrated to find that Sanger had evaded him, Crawford would soon work himself into a state of tension that only a quick blaze could assuage. I started the Citroën's engine, ready to swing the car into the drive and block the Porsche's escape. Fire and flame were the signature that Crawford would write once too often across the skies of Estrella de Mar.

For ten minutes I sat behind my newspaper, almost disappointed not to see smoke billowing from the eaves. Leaving the car, I quietly closed the door and walked across the street to the villa. As I ducked into the garage I heard a shutter open on an upstairs window. I hesitated in the kitchen, listening to Crawford's feet on the floorboards above my head. He was pulling a wardrobe across the room, perhaps adding a last piece of furniture to his bonfire pile.

I stepped through the kitchen into the hall, its pale walls lit by the sunlight in the garden, once again the Piranesi antechamber where the psychiatrist had felt so at home. The vandals had continued their work inside the house, and aerosol slogans covered the walls and ceilings. On the stairs the paint was still wet, the tiled steps smeared by Crawford's trainers.

I paused on the upstairs landing, listening to the noise of scraping furniture. The bedrooms were daubed with graffiti, a riot of black and silver whorls, a demented EEG trace searching for a brain. But one room had not been vandalized, the maid's bedroom above the kitchen, where Crawford was easing a heavy Spanish dresser from the wall. Hands gripping the carved oak panels, he forced the castle of polished wood across the floor.

Lying down in the narrow space behind the dresser, he reached to some inner ledge and retrieved a schoolgirl's diary bound in pink silk. Sitting against the dresser, he held the diary to his chest, smiling with the bitter-sweet regret of a schoolboy lover.

I watched him as he untied the diary's bow and began to read its pages, fingers playing with the ribbon. He looked up at the little room, eyes lingering on the mantelpiece where a clutter of forgotten objects waited for the dustbin. A signed photograph of a punk rock group was taped to the wall, beside a family of frizzy-haired trolls, a collection of shells and beach stones and a postcard view of Malmö. Crawford stood up and leaned against the mantelpiece, running a hand across the stones, and then sat at the dressing-table below the open window.

'Come in, Charles,' he called out. 'I can hear you thinking. Don't hover out there like a ghost – there's one too many here already . . .'

'Crawford?' I stepped into the room, and squeezed past the massive dresser. 'I thought you might be . . .'

'Starting a fire? Not today, and not here.' He spoke softly, and seemed almost dreamy and lightheaded, like a child discovering a secret attic. He explored the empty drawers of the dressing-table, lips moving as he described the imaginary objects he had found. 'This was Bibi's room – think of the hundreds of times she stared into this mirror. If you look hard enough you can just see her . . .'

He began to leaf through the diary, reading the large looping script that rolled across the pink pages.

'Her moods and hopes book,' Crawford commented. 'She

started it while she was living with Sanger. She probably wrote it here. It's a pretty little room.'

I assumed that he had never visited the house, let alone the bedroom. Concerned for him, I said: 'Why don't you rent the house from Sanger? You could move in.'

'I'd like to, but why be mawkish?' Crawford closed the diary and pushed it away. A narrow servant's bed stood against the wall, stripped of everything but its mattress. He lay down, broad shoulders almost wider than the headboard. 'Not exactly comfortable, but at least they wouldn't have had sex here. So, Charles, you thought I was going to burn the place down?'

'It did occur to me.' I stared at him through the dressing-table mirror, noticing that his features were almost perfectly symmetrical, as if his face's asymmetric twin was hiding somewhere behind his eyes. 'You set fire to the speedboat and my car. Why not this place – or the Hollinger house?'

'Charles . . .' Crawford clasped his hands behind his head, deliberately revealing the surgical plaster on his forearm. He watched me in his level but friendly way, eager to help me over a minor difficulty. 'The speedboat, yes. I have to keep the troops in good heart, it's a constant worry. A spectacular fire touches something deep inside us. I'm sorry about the car; Mahoud misheard me and took off on his own. But the Hollinger house? Absolutely not, for one very good reason.'

'Bibi Jansen?'

'Not exactly, but in a way.' He left the bed and riffled through the diary, trying to restock his memories of the dead young woman. 'Let's say a very personal way . . .'

'You knew she was pregnant?'

'Of course.'

'Were you the child's father?'

Crawford paced around the room, carefully leaving a hand-print on the dusty mirror. 'Perhaps she'll see that the next time she looks out . . . Charles, it was scarcely a child. No

204

brain or nervous system, no personality. Not much more than a parcel of genetic tissue counting to a hundred. Not really a child.'

'But it felt like a child?'

He pocketed the diary, took a last look at the room and stepped past me. 'It still does.'

I followed him to the staircase, past the airless bedrooms with their graffiti and stink of paint. I accepted Crawford's word that he was not responsible for the Hollinger fire, and felt curiously relieved. For all his restless swerves and undirected energy, there was no trace of malice about him, no hint of the dark, lurking violence found in the kind of psychopath who had planned to kill the Hollingers. If anything, there was an artless strain in him, an almost earnest need to please.

'Time to go, Charles. Do you need a lift?' He noticed the Citroën across the street. 'No – you were waiting for me here. How did you know I was coming?'

'Just a guess. Sanger moved out yesterday afternoon. First the graffiti, then the . . .'

'Torch? You underestimate me, Charles. I hope I'm a force for good in Estrella de Mar. Here's an idea – we'll go for a drive along the coast. There's something I want you to see. You'll be able to write about it.'

'Crawford, I have to –'

'Come on . . . Just give me half an hour.' He took my arm and almost frog-marched me towards the Porsche. 'You need cheering up, Charles. I see a kind of lingering malaise coming over you – beach fatigue, pretty much endemic to the Costas. Fall into the clutches of Paula Hamilton and you'll be brain-dead before you can reach your next gin and tonic. Now, you drive.'

'This car? I'm not sure . . .'

'Of course! It's a puppy in wolf's clothing. It only bites out of enthusiasm. Hold the wheel like a leash and say "sit".'

I guessed that he had seen me in the Citroën when he first arrived, and that a spin at the controls of the Porsche was a gentle revenge. He watched me encouragingly as I eased myself into the driver's seat. I started the engine, missed the forward gears and propelled the car towards the garage door. I braked in a swirl of litter, hunted the gearbox again and eased the over-eager car down the drive.

'Good, good . . . you're another Schumacher, Charles. It's fun being a passenger. The world looks different, as if one's seeing it in a mirror.'

Crawford sat with his hands on the dashboard, enjoying the erratic ride, and directed me through the narrow streets to the Paseo Maritimo. Now and then his hand gripped mine as he steered the Porsche around a swerving motor-scooter, and I felt the over-developed thumb and index finger of the professional tennis player, the same combination that had left its imprint on my throat. Fingers, like keys, had a unique signature. I was sitting beside the man who had almost strangled me, and yet my anger had already given way to more confused emotions: a need for revenge, and curiosity as to his motives.

He tapped the girl's diary on his knee, amused to see that I had reined in the powerful car and declined to show off its performance. As we approached the harbour I noticed his almost childlike pleasure in everything around him. My modest driving skills, a water-skier in the bay slaloming in and out of a speedboat's wake, elderly tourists marooned on a traffic island, all prompted the same cheerful smile, as if he were seeing the world afresh at every street corner.

We drove along the lower corniche towards Marbella, past the beach bars, boutiques and crêperies. At the western limits of Estrella de Mar a mole of concrete blocks jutted into the sea. A truck loaded with fairground booths sped towards us, and Crawford seized the wheel, turning the Porsche into its path. His foot crushed mine against the accelerator, throwing the car forward as the truck's klaxon blared past us.

'Missed . . .' Crawford waved to the driver and steered the car on to the sandy verge beside the mole. 'A small errand, Charles. It won't take a moment.'

He stepped from the car, inhaling the bright spray as the waves broke among the blocks. Still dazed by our close escape, I looked down at my bruised foot. The yellow paint on the toe-cap of my shoe echoed the cleat-marks of Crawford's trainer, the same print that I had seen stamped into the scattered soil on Frank's balcony.

Shielding his eyes with the diary, Crawford gazed across the peninsula at the gutted shell of the Hollinger house.

'A year from now some hotel or casino complex will stand there. On this coast the past isn't allowed to exist . . .'

I locked the car and stood beside him. 'Why not keep the house as it is?'

'As a tribal totem? A warning to all those time-share salesmen and nightclub touts? That's not a bad idea . . .'

Buffeted by the wind, we walked to the rail at the end of the mole. Crawford glanced for a last time at the diary, smiling as he turned the pages of childish scrawl. He closed it, held it behind his head and tossed it far out into the waves, a long deep serve.

'So . . . that's done. I wanted to find the date where she mentioned the baby – now I know how old it was.' He stared at the waves rolling in from North Africa, ice-cold crests sweeping towards the shore. 'Cocaine coming in, Charles . . . thousands of lines. Out of Africa always something white and strange.'

I leaned against the rail and let the spray cool my face. The loose pages of the diary were churning in the foam beneath us, pink petals dashed among the concrete blocks.

'Wouldn't Sanger have liked the diary? He was fond of her.'

'Of course. He loved Bibi – everyone did. The whole Hollinger thing is a terrible shame. Bibi's is the one death I really regret.'

'But you kept supplying her with hard drugs – according to Paula Hamilton she was a walking Palermo lab.'

'Charles . . .' Crawford put a brotherly arm around my shoulders, but I half-expected him to hip-throw me over the rail into the seething waves. 'You have to understand Estrella de Mar. Yes, we gave her drugs – we wanted to free her from those sinister clinics up in the hills, from those men in white coats who know best. Bibi needed to soar over our heads, dreaming her amphetamine dreams, coming off the beach in the evening and leading everyone into the cocaine night.' Crawford lowered his eyes and gestured at the sea, asking the waves to witness what he was saying. 'Sanger and Alice Hollinger turned her into a lady's maid.'

'The police found her in Hollinger's jacuzzi. I don't suppose that was a film test?'

'Charles, forget Hollinger's jacuzzi.'

'I'll try – it's an image that doesn't go away. Do you know who started the fire?'

Crawford waited until the last of the diary pages had vanished in the foam. 'The fire? Well . . . I suppose I do.'

'Who, though? I need to get Frank out of Zarzuella jail and back to London.'

'He may not want to leave.' Crawford watched me, as if waiting for me to serve at a crucial tie-break. 'I could tell you who started the fire, but you're not ready yet. It's not just a matter of someone's name, but of coming to terms with Estrella de Mar.'

'I've been here long enough. I understand what's going on.'

'No – or you wouldn't be so obsessed with that jacuzzi.

Think of Estrella de Mar as an experiment. Something important may be taking place here, and I want you to be part of it.' Crawford held my arm, and led the way back to the Porsche. 'First, we'll go out for our ride. This time I'll drive, so you can take your eyes off the road. There's a lot to see . . . remember, white is the colour of silence.'

Before he started the engine I said: 'Bibi Jansen – if you made her pregnant, where did it happen? In the Hollinger house?'

'Good God, no!' Crawford seemed almost shocked. 'Even I wouldn't go that far. She visited Paula at the Clinic every Tuesday – I met her there once and we went for a drive.'

'Where exactly?'

'Into the past, Charles. Where she was happy again – just for an hour, but the longest and sweetest hour . . .'

19

The Costasol Complex

WHITE SILENCE. As we drove along the coast road, a mile to the west of Estrella de Mar, the outer-lying villas of the Residencia Costasol began to appear through the Aleppo pines that ran down to the deserted beach. The houses and apartments were set at various levels, forming a cascade of patios, terraces and swimming pools. I had visited the retirement pueblos at Calahonda and Torrenueva, but the Costasol complex was far larger than any others along the coast. Yet not a single resident was visible. No windows turned to catch the sun, and the entire development might have been empty, waiting for its first tenants to arrive and collect their keys.

Crawford pointed to the crenellated wall. 'Look at it, Charles . . . it's a fortified medieval city. This is Goldfinger's defensible space raised to an almost planetary intensity – security guards, tele-surveillance, no entrance except through the main gates, the whole complex closed to outsiders. It's a grim thought, but you're looking at the future.'

'Do the people here ever leave? They must go down to the beach.'

'No, that's the eerie thing about it all. The sea's only two hundred yards away but none of the villas looks out on to the beach. Space is totally internalized . . .'

Crawford turned off the coast road and freewheeled towards the entrance. Landscaped gardens the size of a small municipal park lay outside the Moorish gates and guardhouse. Flower-beds filled with cannas surrounded an ornamental fountain, reached by gravelled walks untouched by human feet since the day they were laid. Under an illuminated sign announcing 'The Residencia Costasol: Investment, Freedom, Security' was a road-map of the entire complex, a maze of winding avenues and culs-de-sac that emerged from their fastnesses to join the almost imperial boulevards radiating from the centre of the development.

'The map isn't really for visitors.' Crawford stopped outside the guardhouse and saluted the security man watching us from his window. 'It's there to help the residents find their way home. Sometimes they make the mistake of leaving the place for an hour or two.'

'They must go shopping. It's only a mile from Estrella de Mar.'

'But few of them ever visit the town. They might as well be on an atoll in the Maldives or in the San Fernando Valley.' Crawford drove up to the security barrier. From his breast pocket he took out a smart card embossed with the Costasol logo and fed it into the security scanner. To the guard he said: 'We'll be here for an hour – we work for Mrs Shand. Mr Prentice is your new entertainments officer.'

'Elizabeth Shand?' I repeated as the barrier fell behind us and we entered the complex. 'Don't tell me the place is one of hers. By the way, who am I supposed to be entertaining, and how?'

'Relax, Charles. I wanted to impress the security guard – the thought of being entertained always strikes terror into people. Betty buys and sells property everywhere. In fact, she's thinking of moving into here. A few of the villas are still unsold, along with empty retail units in the shopping mall. If someone could bring the place to life there's a fortune to be made – the people here are well-off.'

'I can see.' I pointed to the cars parked in the driveways.

'More Mercs and BMWs per square foot than in Düsseldorf or Bel Air. Who designed it all?'

'The main developers were a Dutch-German consortium, with a Swiss consultancy handling the . . .'

'Human systems side?'

Crawford slapped my knee, laughing cheerfully. 'You've got the jargon, Charles. I know you're going to be happy here.'

'Heaven forbid . . . happiness looks as if it might infringe the local bye-laws.'

We cruised down the north-south boulevard that ran towards the hub of the complex, a dual carriageway lined with tall palms whose parasols shaded the deserted pathways. Sprinklers turned their rainbows through the scented air, irrigating the crisply-mown grass of the central reservation. Set back within their walled gardens was a line of large villas, deep awnings over their balconies. Only the surveillance cameras moved to follow us. The dusty elephant hide of the palm trunks flickered with the reflected light of swimming pools, but there were no sounds of children playing or of anyone disturbing the almost immaculate calm.

'So many pools,' I commented. 'And no one swimming . . .'

'They're Zen surfaces, Charles. Breaking them is bad luck. These were the first houses here, built about five years ago. The final plots were filled last week. It may not look it, but the Residencia Costasol is popular.'

'Mostly British?'

'With a few Dutch and French – much the same mix as Estrella de Mar. But this is a different world. Estrella de Mar was built in the 1970s – open access, street festivals, tourists welcome. The Residencia Costasol is pure 1990s. Security rules. Everything is designed around an obsession with crime.'

'I take it there isn't any?'

'None. Absolutely nothing. An illicit thought never disturbs the peace. No tourists, no back-packers or trinket-sellers, and few visitors – the people here have learned that it's a big help to dispense with friends. Be honest, friends can be a problem – gates and front doors need to be unlocked, alarm systems disconnected, and someone else is breathing your air. Besides, they bring in uneasy memories of the outside world. The Residencia Costasol isn't unique. You see these fortified enclaves all over the planet. There are developments like this gearing up along the coast from Calahonda to Marbella and beyond.'

A car overtook us, and the woman driver turned off the boulevard into a tree-lined avenue of slightly smaller villas. Watching her, I realized that I had seen my first resident.

'And what do the people here do all day? Or all night?'

'They do nothing. That's what the Residencia Costasol was designed for.'

'But where are they? We've only seen one car so far.'

'They're here, Charles, they're here. Lying on their sun-loungers and waiting for Paula Hamilton to arrive with a new prescription. When you think of the Costasol complex think of the Sleeping Beauty . . .'

We left the boulevard and entered one of the dozens of residential avenues. Handsome villas stood behind their wrought-iron gates, terraces reaching to the swimming pools, blue kidneys of undisturbed water. Three-storey apartment houses were briefly visible beyond their drives, where groups of cars waited in the sun, so many dozing metal ruminants. Everywhere satellite dishes cupped the sky like begging bowls.

'There must be hundreds of the dishes,' I commented. 'At least they haven't given up television.'

'They're listening to the sun, Charles. Waiting for a new kind of light.'

The road climbed the shoulder of a landscaped hill. We passed an estate of terraced houses and entered the central plaza of the complex. Car parks surrounded a shopping mall lined with stores and restaurants, and I pointed with surprise to the first pedestrians we had seen, unloading their supermarket trolleys through the tail-doors of their vehicles. To the south of the plaza lay a marina filled with yachts and powerboats, moored together like a mothballed fleet. An access canal led to the open sea, passing below a cantilever bridge that carried the coast road. A handsome clubhouse presided over the marina and its boatyard, but its terrace was deserted, awnings flared over the empty tables. The nearby sports club was equally unpopular, its tennis courts dusty in the sun, the swimming pool drained and forgotten.

A supermarket stood inside the entrance to the shopping mall, next to a beauty salon with shuttered doors and windows. Crawford parked near a sports equipment store filled with exercycles and weightlifting contraptions, computerized heart monitors and respiration counters, arranged in a welcoming if steely tableau.

'Clink, clank, think . . .' I murmured. 'It looks like a family group of robot visitors.'

'Or a user-friendly torture chamber.' Crawford stepped from the car. 'Let's stroll, Charles. You need to feel the place at first-hand . . .'

He fixed his aviator glasses over his eyes and glanced around the car park, counting the surveillance cameras as if calculating the best getaway route. The silence of the Residencia Costasol already seemed to dull his reflexes, and he began to practise his forehand and cross-court drives, feet springing as he waited to return an imaginary service.

'Over here – if I'm right, there are signs of life . . .' He beckoned me towards the liquor store next to the supermarket, where a dozen customers hovered in the air-conditioned aisles and the Spanish check-out girls sat at their tills like marooned queens. The wall-to-ceiling display of wines, spirits and liqueurs was almost cathedral in its vastness, and a primitive cortical life seemed to flicker as the residents and their wives fitfully scanned the prices and vintages.

'The Residencia Costasol's cultural heart,' Crawford informed me. 'At least they still have the energy to drink . . . the elbow reflex must be the last to go.'

He stared at the silent aisles, working out his challenge to this eventless world. We left the liquor store and paused by a Thai restaurant, whose empty tables receded through a shadow world of flock wallpaper and gilded elephants. Next to it was an untenanted retail unit, a concrete vault like an abandoned segment of space-time. Crawford stepped through the litter of cigarette packets and lottery tickets, and read a faded notice announcing an over-fifties dance at the Costasol social centre.

Without waiting for me, he walked through the unit and set off across the car park to the terraced villas that lined the western side of the plaza. Gravel gardens stocked with cactus plants and pallid succulents led to the shaded terraces, where the beach furniture waited like the armatures of the human beings who would occupy them that evening.

'Charles, be discreet but look in there. You can see what we're up against . . .'

Shielding my eyes from the sunlight, I gazed into one of the darkened lounges. A three-dimensional replica of a painting by Edward Hopper was visible below the awning. The residents, two middle-aged men and a woman in her thirties, sat in the silent room, their faces lit by the trembling glow of a television screen. No expression touched their eyes, as if the dim shadows on the hessian walls around them had long become a satisfactory substitute for thought.

'They're watching TV with the sound turned down,' I told Crawford as we strolled along the terrace, past similar groups isolated in their capsules. 'What happened to them? They're like a race from some dark planet who find the light here too strong to bear.'

'They're refugees from time, Charles. Look around you – there are no clocks anywhere and almost no one wears a wristwatch.'

'Refugees? Yes . . . in some ways the place reminds me of the Third World. It's like a very up-market *favela* in Rio, or a luxury *bidonville* outside Algiers.'

'It's the *fourth* world, Charles. The one waiting to take over everything.'

We returned to the Porsche and cruised around the plaza. I watched the villas and apartment houses, hoping for the sound of a raised human voice, a too-loud stereo system, the recoil of a diving board, and realized that we were witnessing an intense inward migration. The residents of the Costasol complex, like those of the retirement pueblos along the coast, had retreated to their shaded lounges, their bunkers with a view, needing only that part of the external world that was distilled from the sky by their satellite dishes. Standing empty in the sun, the sports club and social centre, like the other amenities engineered into the complex by its Swiss consultants, resembled the props of an abandoned film production.

'Crawford, it's time to leave – let's get back to Estrella de Mar . . .'

'You've seen enough?'

'I want to hear that tennis machine of yours and the laughter of tipsy women. I want to hear Mrs Shand telling off the waiters at the Club Nautico – if she invests here she'll lose everything.'

'Maybe. Before we go we'll look in at the sports club. It's semi-derelict but it has possibilities.'

We passed the marina and turned into the forecourt of the sports club. A single car was parked by the entrance, but no one seemed to be present in the empty building. We stepped from the Porsche and strolled around the drained swimming pool, looking down at the canted floor that exposed its dusty tiles to the sun. A collection of hair-clips and wine glasses lay around the drainage vent, as if waiting for a stream to flow.

Crawford sat back in a chair by the open-air bar, watching me while I tested the spring of the diving board. Handsome and affable, he gazed at me in a generous but canny way, like a junior officer selecting a raw recruit for a sensitive mission.

'So, Charles . . .' he said when I joined him at the bar. 'I'm glad you came on the tour. You've just seen the promotional video presented to all new owners at the Residencia Costasol. Compelling stuff?'

'Absolutely. It's very, very strange. Even so, most visitors driving around wouldn't notice anything odd. Apart from this pool and those empty shops it's extremely well-maintained, there's excellent security and not a trace of graffiti anywhere – most people's idea of paradise today. What happened?'

'*Nothing* happened.' Crawford sat forward, speaking quietly as if not wanting to unsettle the silence. 'Two and a half thousand people moved in, mostly well-off and with all the time in the world to do the things they'd dreamed about in London and Manchester and Edinburgh. Time for bridge and tennis, for cordon bleu and flower-arrangement classes. Time for having little affairs and for messing about in boats, learning Spanish and playing the Tokyo stock market. They sell up and buy their dream house, move everything down to the Costa del Sol. And then what happens? The dream switches itself off. Why?'

'They're too old? Or too lazy to bother? Doing nothing may secretly be just what they wanted.'

'But that isn't what they wanted. Plot for plot, villa for villa, the Residencia Costasol is far more expensive than similar developments in Calahonda and Los Monteros. They paid a fat extra premium to have all these sports facilities and leisure clubs. Anyway, the people here are not that old. This isn't a geriatric ward. Most of them are the right side of fifty – they took early retirement, cashed in their share options or sold their partnerships, made the most of a golden handshake. The Costasol complex isn't Sunset City, Arizona.'

'I've been there. Actually, it's a lively spot. Those seventy-year-olds can get pretty frisky.'

'Frisky . . .' Wearily, Crawford pressed his palms against his forehead. He stared at the silent villas around the plaza, their shaded balconies waiting for nothing to happen. I was tempted to make another flippant remark, but I could see that he felt an almost impatient concern for the people of the Residencia. He reminded me of a young district commissioner in the days of Empire, faced with a rich but torpid tribe that inexplicably refused to leave its huts. The bandage on his arm had leaked a little blood on to his shirtsleeve, but he was clearly un-interested in himself, driven by a zeal that seemed so out of place in this land of jacuzzis and plunge-pools.

'Crawford . . .' Trying to reassure him, I said: 'Does it matter? If they want to doze their lives away with the sound turned down, let them . . .'

'No . . .' Crawford paused and then reached forward to grip my hand. 'It does matter. Charles, this is the way the world is going. You've seen the future and it doesn't work or play. The Costasols of this planet are spreading outwards. I've toured them in Florida and New Mexico. You should visit the Fon-tainebleau Sud complex outside Paris – it's a replica of this, ten times the size. The Residencia Costasol wasn't thrown together by some gimcrack developer; it was carefully planned to give people the chance of a better life. And what have they got? Brain-death . . .'

'Not brain-death, Bobby. That's Paula-speak. The Costa del Sol is the longest afternoon in the world, and they've decided to sleep through it.'

'You're right.' Crawford spoke softly, as if accepting my point. He took off his aviator glasses and stared at the harsh light reflected from the pool tiles. 'But I intend to wake them up. That's my job, Charles – why I was picked I don't know, but I stumbled on a way of saving people and bringing them back to life. I tried it at Estrella de Mar and it worked.'

'Perhaps. I'm not sure about that. But it won't work here. Estrella de Mar is a real place. It existed before you and Betty Shand arrived.'

'The Residencia Costasol is real. Too real.' Crawford doggedly recited his uncertain credo, rehearsing an argument that I guessed he had run through many times, an amalgam of alarmist best-sellers, *Economist* think-pieces and his own obsessive intuitions that he had put together on the windswept balcony of his apartment. 'Town-scapes are changing. The open-plan city belongs to the past – no more *ramblas*, no more pedestrian precincts, no more left banks and Latin quarters. We're moving into the age of security grilles and defensible space. As for living, our surveillance cameras can do that for us. People are locking their doors and switching off their nervous systems. I can free them, Charles. With your help. We can make a start here, in the Residencia Costasol.'

'Bobby . . .' I met his engaging, sea-blue eyes, fixed on me with their curious mix of threat and hope. 'There's nothing I can do. I came here to help Frank.'

'I know, and you *have* helped him. But now help me, Charles. I need someone to hold the fort for me, keep an eye on the ground and warn me if I'm going too far – the role Frank played at the Club Nautico.'

'Look . . . Bobby, I can't –'

'You can!' Crawford held my wrists and drew me towards him across the table. Behind his pleading was a strange missionary fervour that seemed to float across his mind like the malarial visions of that young district officer he so resembled, reaching out for the aid of a passing traveller. 'We may fail but it's worth trying. The Residencia Costasol is a prison, just as much as Zarzuella jail. We're building prisons all over the world and calling them luxury condos. The amazing thing is that the keys are all on the inside. I can help people to snap the locks and step out into real air again. Think, Charles – if it works you can write a book about it, a warning to the rest of the world.'

'The kind of warning that no one is keen to hear. What do you want me to do?'

'Keep an eye on this club. Betty Shand has bought out the lease – we re-open in three weeks' time. We need someone to run the place for us.'

'I'm the wrong man. You need a trained manager. I can't hire and fire staff, keep accounts and run a restaurant.'

'You'll soon learn.' Confident that he had recruited me, Crawford gestured dismissively at the bar. 'Besides, there's no restaurant and Betty will do the hiring and firing. Don't worry about the accounts – David Hennessy has all that under control. Join us, Charles. Once we get the tennis club going everything else will follow. The Residencia Costasol will come alive again.'

'After a few games of tennis? You could stage Wimbledon here and no one would notice.'

'They will, Charles. Of course, there'll be more than tennis. When they set up the Costasol complex there was one ingredient missing.'

'Work?'

'Not work, Charles. No.'

I waited as he gazed at the silent villas around the plaza and the cameras on the lamp standards that tracked the cars leaving the shopping mall. His open and eager face was touched by a determination that Frank must have found equally intriguing.

The modest sports club with its shabby courts and drained pool was a far cry from the Club Nautico, but by pretending to manage it I would draw closer to Crawford and Betty Shand, and might at last step on to the path that had led to the burning of the Hollinger mansion and Frank's absurd confession.

A yacht had entered the marina, a white-hulled sloop with furled sails, moving under its engine. Gunnar Andersson stood at the helm, his slim-shouldered figure as tall as a mizzen-mast, shirt floating from his shoulders like a strip of tattered sail. The craft seemed neglected, its hull smeared with oil, and I assumed that Andersson had sailed it through the tanker lanes from Tangier. Then I noticed the tag of yellow ribbon flying from the fore-rail, the last of the police tapes that had wrapped themselves around the craft.

'It's the *Halcyon*. Frank's sloop . . . what's it doing here?'

'That's right.' Crawford stood up and waved to Andersson, who doffed his cap in return. 'I talked to Danvila. Frank agrees the yacht will be safer in the Costasol marina – no tourists cutting off bits of rigging. Gunnar is going to work in the boatyard and start servicing all these arthritic engines. With a little luck we'll make the Costasol regatta the swankiest show on the coast. Believe me, Charles, sea air is what people need. Now, here's Elizabeth, looking more handsome every day. Bratwurst obviously agrees with her . . .'

The stretch Mercedes was turning into the car park of the sports club. Betty Shand lay back against the leather upholstery, a wide-brimmed hat screening her veiled face, a gloved hand jerking the passenger strap as if reminding the huge car of its rightful owner. The swarthy Maghrebian sat at the wheel, the two young Germans on the jump seats behind him. When the car stopped by the steps Mahoud sounded the horn, and a moment later David Hennessy and the Keswick sisters emerged from the Thai restaurant. Together they set off towards the club, bundles of property prospectuses under their arms.

A team was assembling in the central plaza of the Residencia Costasol. Crawford, Elizabeth Shand, Hennessy and the Keswick sisters were coming together, ready to discuss their plans for the complex and its residents. The manager of the Thai restaurant waved to his departing guests, little realizing that his menus would soon be changing.

'Betty Shand and the Keswicks . . .' I commented. 'The seafood's going to be good.'

'Charles? Yes, the Keswick girls are taking over the Thai place. They know what people need, always a big help. Now, have you thought about working for us?'

'All right,' I said. 'I'll stay until Frank's trial. But nothing too arduous.'

'Of course not.' Crawford leaned across the table and clasped my shoulders, smiling with unfeigned delight, and I sensed that for a few seconds I had become the most important person in his world, the one friend he had relied upon to come to his aid. As he beamed at me proudly his face seemed almost adolescent, blond hair spilling over his forehead, lips parted across immaculate white teeth. Squeezing me with his strong hands, he spoke in a rush of lightheaded words. 'I knew you would, Charles – you're the one person I need here. You've seen the world, you understand how much we have to do if we're going to help these people. By the way, a house comes with the job. I'll find you one with a tennis court, and we'll play a few games. I know you're a lot better than you let on.'

'You'll soon see. By the way, you can pay me a small salary. Living expenses, car-hire and so on. Since I'm not earning a cent any more . . .'

'Absolutely.' He sat back and gazed at me fondly as Elizabeth

Shand made her imperial way into the club. 'David Hennessy's already written out your first cheque. Believe me, Charles, we've thought of everything.'

20

A Quest for New Vices

SUNLIGHT CRAZED the broken surface of the swimming pool, as if released from the glassy depths by my dive. I swam a leisurely length, touched the tiled gutter and hoisted myself on to the diving board. The waves slapped the sides of the pool, refusing to calm themselves, and eager to applaud the next pre-breakfast swimmer in search of an appetite.

As I towelled myself, however, I guessed that another day would pass and I would remain the swimming pool's only customer, just as I would be the only visitor to the tennis courts and gymnasium. Killing time beside the open-air bar, reading the London newspapers and thinking about Frank's trial, I knew that time had died in the Residencia Costasol long before my arrival.

During my first week as 'manager' of the sports club I sat back and watched Elizabeth Shand's groundsmen re-vamp the entire premises. They cleaned and filled the pool, watered the lawns and white-inked the tennis courts, then buffed the hardwood floor of the gymnasium to a mirror-like finish, ready for the first aerobics classes.

Despite these efforts, and the expensive pool-side furniture waiting to cushion their exhausted limbs, none of the Costasol residents had put in an appearance. My hours, David Hennessy told me, ran from eleven a.m. to three p.m., but 'take as long as you want for lunch, dear boy, we can't have you going mad with boredom.'

Nevertheless, I usually drove from the Club Nautico before breakfast, curious to see if the dozing residents of the complex had been tempted to leave their balconies. Hennessy would arrive at noon, retreat to his office and return to Estrella de Mar once he had paid the waiters and ground staff. Sometimes Elizabeth Shand would visit him, arriving in her limousine with the two Germans. In a curious pantomime each would hold open a passenger door for her, while she gazed at the sports club like a predatory widow visiting an entailed property about to fall into her grasp.

Had her legendary business savvy deserted her for once? Eating my breakfast at the bar, surrounded by the silent waiters and the empty sun-loungers, I guessed that she might soon be writing off her investment and leaving for the richer pastures at Calahonda. The caravan would move on to the retirement pueblos of the coast, taking with it my last hopes of discovering the truth about the Hollinger fire.

Frank, absurdly, still maintained his guilt, and I had twice postponed my visit to Zarzuella jail, convinced against all the evidence that the Residencia Costasol might be a back door into the secret Estrella de Mar for so long closed to me. His trial had been set for 15 October, four months to the day after the tragic fire, and despite all my efforts I would be no more than a character witness. I thought constantly of Frank and our childhood years together, but found it almost impossible to face him across the hard table of a prison interview room. His plea of guilty had seemed to embrace us both, but I no longer felt the sense of shared guilt that had once united us.

Behind me a car door opened and a motor faded. I looked up from my *Financial Times* to find that a familiar BMW had pulled into the car park. Paula Hamilton sat at the wheel, peering up at the bright new awnings that flared from the windows of the sports club. She had changed at the home of one of her patients at the Residencia, and wore a yellow beach robe over her black swimsuit.

She left the car and climbed the steps towards the swimming pool. Ignoring me, she walked to the deep end, left her robe and bag on the diving board and began to fasten her hair, arms raised as she showed off the hips and breasts that I had embraced so eagerly. I had repeatedly rung her flat near the Clinic, but since visiting Frank in Zarzuella jail she kept away from me. I wanted to see her again, and do my best to ease away the strain of contempt she felt for herself, like the prickly humour that shielded her fear of showing her real emotions. But the video-cassette of Anne Hollinger's rape separated us like the memory of a crime.

She swam ten lengths, her streamlined body and clean strokes scarcely disturbing the surface of the pool. Waist-deep in the shallow end, she wiped the foam from her eyes and accepted the towel that I took from the pile beside the bar. Holding my hands, she sprang from the pool and stood dripping beside me, water sparkling at her feet. Happy to see her, I draped another towel around her shoulders.

'Paula – you're our first new member. I hope you want to join the club?'

'No. Just testing the water. It looks pure enough.'

'It's brand-new. You've christened it with your own lips. Now it knows its name.'

'I'll think about that.' She nodded approvingly at the sun-loungers and tables. 'It must be the cleanest pool on the Costa del Sol. Better than all that dissolved muck we usually swim through, under the misguided idea that it's water – detergent, sun-oil, anti-perspirant, aftershave, vaginal jelly, pee and God only knows what else. You look healthier for it, Charles.'

'I am. I swim every day, knock a few balls around with the groundsmen. I've even tried the gym machines.'

'And now you're working for Elizabeth Shand? That's really bizarre. Does she pay you well?'

'It's an honorary post. Hennessy covers my expenses. Bobby Crawford thought I might write a book about it all.'

'"Is there Death after Life? The Resurrection of the Residencia Costasol." How is our tennis pro?'

'I haven't seen him for days. The Porsche flashes by now and then. All mysterious errand stuff – speedboats, remote beaches, drug drops. I'm too square for him.'

Paula stopped to stare at me as we walked towards the diving board. 'You're getting involved. Be careful, he'll damage you if he wants to.'

'Paula, you're too hard on him. I know about the films and the dealing and the car thefts. He tried to strangle me, for reasons he probably doesn't understand. But it's all in a good cause, or so he thinks – he wants to bring people back to life. In many ways he's very naive.'

'There's nothing naive about Betty Shand.'

'Or David Hennessy. But I'm still trying to find what happened at the Hollingers'. That's why I'm playing Frank's role. Now, tell me how he is.'

'Pale, very tired. He's resigned to everything. I think the trial's already over for him. He accepts that you don't want to see him.'

'Not true. Paula, I do want to see him. But I'm not ready yet. I'll visit him when I have something to tell him. Is there any chance of him changing his plea?'

'Of course not. He thinks he's guilty.'

I drove a fist into my palm. 'That's why I can't see him! I won't collude with whatever lies he's hiding behind.'

'You're colluding with everything else here.' Paula watched me, frowning to herself as she slipped into her robe, uncertain whether the bronzed and muscular man beside her was an impostor masquerading as the soft-skinned journalist who had embraced her on Frank's bed. 'You're involved with Elizabeth Shand, Hennessy and Bobby Crawford. It's almost a conspiracy, based on this club.'

'Paula . . . this isn't Estrella de Mar. It's the Residencia Costasol. Nothing happens here. Nothing ever will.'

'Now you're being naive.' Shaking her head at my foolishness, she strolled with me to her car. She tossed her bag into the passenger seat and then pressed her cheek to mine, her hands on my chest, as if reminding herself that we had once been lovers. 'Charles, dear, a great deal is happening here, far more than you realize. Open your eyes . . .'

Almost on cue, a Spanish police car circled the central plaza. It stopped beside the marina, and one of the uniformed officers shouted to the boatyard where Andersson worked each morning on Crawford's speedboats. Often I walked down to the quay, but the morose Swede avoided me, unwilling to talk about the Hollinger fire and still nursing his memories of Bibi Jansen. During his rest periods he retreated to the *Halcyon*, which was berthed near the boatyard, and sat in the cabin, ignoring my feet on the deck above.

Hennessy was waiting in the entrance to the sports club, smiling affably under his reassuring moustache. A Hawaiian shirt covered his ample paunch, and he seemed the epitome of the shady businessman with whom the Spanish police would feel most at ease. He ushered them into his office, where a bottle of Fundador and a tray of tapas were ready to speed their investigation.

They left twenty minutes later, faces flushed and confident. Hennessy waved when they drove off, beaming the benign smile of a department-store Father Christmas. No doubt he had reassured them that he would personally see to the security of the Residencia Costasol and so free them to pursue their proper tasks of manhandling hitch-hikers, plotting against their superiors and collecting backhanders from the Fuengirola bar-owners.

'They don't seem too worried,' I commented to Hennessy. 'I thought they left us alone.'

'Spot of bother on the outer perimeter road – some sort of break-in last night. One or two people have had VCRs stolen. They will leave their patio doors open.'

'Burglaries? Isn't that unusual? I thought the Residencia Costasol was a crime-free zone.'

'I wish it were. Sadly, we're living in today's world. I've heard reports of car thefts, though heaven knows how the thieves get through the security barrier. These things happen in waves, you know. Estrella de Mar was as quiet as this when I first arrived.'

'Car thefts and burglaries?' For some reason I felt a stir of interest. The air around me had become crisper. 'What do we do, David? Start a neighbourhood watch scheme? Recruit some volunteer patrols?'

Hennessy turned his mild but steely eyes on to me, unsure whether I was being ironic. 'Do we need to go that far? Still, you may have a point.'

'Think about it, David. It might help to rouse people from this dreadful torpor.'

'Do we want them roused? They could become a nuisance, develop all sorts of odd enthusiasms. I'll mention it to Elizabeth.' He pointed to the stretch limousine moving through the gates of the sports club, its burnished carapace outshining the sun. 'How sleek she looks today, positively purring. I dare say she's bought up the last of the leases. Curious how a few robberies can be a boost to business. People get nervous, you know, and start shifting their cash around . . .'

*   *   *

So crime was coming to the Residencia Costasol. After its brief years of peace, the unending slumbers of the sun-coast were about to be disturbed. I counted the silent balconies overlooking the plaza, waiting for the first signs of morning life. It was ten o'clock, but scarcely a resident had stirred, though the first glimmers of a breakfast-television programme had begun to play across the ceilings. The Costasol complex was about to wake itself from the deep sea-bed of sleep and break the surface of a new and more bracing world. I felt surprisingly elated. If Bobby Crawford was the young district officer, then David Hennessy and Elizabeth Shand were the agents of the trading company who dogged his heels, ready to rouse the docile natives with their guns and trinkets, beads and brummagem.

This time, however, merchandise of a different kind was being delivered. From the trunk of the Mercedes the young Germans lifted a computerized cash-register. Elizabeth Shand broke off her tête-à-tête with Hennessy and beckoned me towards her. Despite the heat, her immaculate make-up was untouched by the slightest hint of perspiration. A cooler blood chilled her veins, as if her predatory mind worked best at temperatures lower than the heart's. As always, though, her lips parted generously when she greeted me, holding out the promise of an erotic encounter so strange that it might jump the species barrier.

'Charles, how good of you to be here so early! I do value keenness. These days no one wants anything to be a success, as if failure were somehow chic. I've brought something that should help to make the profits sing. Show Helmut and Wolfgang where you want it.'

'I'm not sure.' I stood back to let the Germans carry the computer into the foyer. 'Elizabeth, it's a great show of confidence in us, but don't you think it's a little premature?'

'Why, dear?' She pressed her veiled cheek to mine, her handsome body sheathed in a cascade of silks that rustled against my bare chest like the plumage of a tremulous bird. 'We must be ready when the flood comes. Besides, you won't be able to cheat me, or not quite so easily.'

'I'll happily cheat you – it sounds rather exciting. It's just that we haven't had a single recruit. Not one resident has applied to join the club.'

'They'll come. Believe me.' She waved to the Keswick sisters, who were pacing out an area of the terrace behind the bar, as if defining the margins of an open-air restaurant. 'There'll be so many new attractions that no one will be able to resist. Don't you agree, David?'

'Absolutely.' Hennessy stood by the concierge's counter, his arm around the computer, welcoming a new confederate in crime. 'I'm sure we'll be as busy as the Club Nautico.'

'You see, Charles? I'm completely confident. We may have to build out on to the car park, and lease parking space from the marina.' She turned to the docile young Germans, waiting in their tennis whites for her next command. 'Wolfgang and Helmut – I think you've already met them, Charles. I want them to help you here. They can move into the apartment upstairs. From now on they work for you.'

I shook hands with the Germans. As if embarrassed by their own musculatures, they bounced lightly on their feet, huge knees moving like bronzed piston heads, forever trying to rearrange their bodies in some less self-conscious configuration.

'Good . . . but, Elizabeth, what exactly will they do?'

'Do?' She patted my chin, pleased by my teasing. 'They will do nothing. Wolfgang and Helmut will "be". They will be themselves and become very popular. I know about these things, Charles. As it happens, Helmut is extremely good at tennis – he once beat Boris Becker. And Wolfgang is a frightfully good swimmer. He's covered enormous distances in the Baltic Sea.'

'Useful . . . getting from one side of the jacuzzi to the other is more than most people here can manage. So they could be sports coaches?'

'Exactly. I know you'll put their talents to good use. All their talents.'

'Naturally. They can help with the recruitment drive.' I accompanied her to the limousine, where Mahoud stood beside the open passenger door, heavy jowls sweating under his peaked cap. 'The club does need new members – I thought I might mail a few leaflets. Or hire a plane to fly around the Residencia every day with a banner. Free tennis lessons, aerobics classes, massage and aromatherapy, that sort of thing . . . ?'

Elizabeth Shand smiled at Hennessy, who was carrying her briefcase to the car. The underwriter seemed equally amused, frisking up the ends of his moustache, eager for them to join in the fun.

'Leaflets and banners? I don't think so.' She took her seat, settling herself in a bower of silks. When Mahoud had closed the door she reached through the window to squeeze my hand reassuringly. 'We need to wake everyone up. The people at the Residencia Costasol are desperate for new vices. Satisfy them, Charles, and you'll be a success . . .'

'Of course.' I pointed to the clock in the foyer. 'Do you want to wait? It's two-forty-five. Everything here is in deep sleep.'

'Perfect – it's the most interesting time of day. People are either dreaming or having sex. Perhaps both at the same time . . .'

As I started the engine he settled himself into the passenger seat of the Citroën, one arm trailing out of the window and the hold-all between his legs. He nodded approvingly as I fastened my seatbelt.

'Sensible, Charles. I do admire an orderly mind. It's hard to believe, but accidents happen even in the Residencia Costasol.'

'The whole place is an accident. This is where the late twentieth century ran into the buffers. Where do you want to go – the Club Nautico?'

'No, we'll stay here. Drive around, any route you like. I want to see how things are.'

We crossed the plaza and its deserted shopping mall, and then cruised past the marina and its ghost fleet of virtually mothballed yachts. I turned at random into one of the secondary residential avenues in the eastern quadrant of the complex. The detached villas stood in their silent gardens, surrounded by dwarf palms, oleanders and beds of cannas like frozen fire. Sprinklers swayed across the lawns, conjuring rainbows from the overlit air, local deities performing their dances to the sun. Now and then the sea wind threw a faint spray across the swimming pools, and their mirror surfaces clouded like troubled dreams.

'Slow down a little . . .' Crawford leaned forward, peering up at a large deco house on a corner site. A shared access road ran towards a group of three-storey apartment houses.

Awnings flared over the balconies, tethered wings that would never touch the sky. 'Stop here . . . this looks like it.'

'What's the number? For some reason people here refuse to identify themselves.'

'I forget exactly. But this feels right.' He pointed fifty yards beyond the access road, where the fronds of a huge cycad formed a pedestrian shelter. 'Park there and wait for me.'

He unzipped the hold-all and removed what seemed to be a set of golf putters wrapped in an oilcloth. He stepped from the car, face hidden behind his peaked cap and dark glasses, patted the roof and set off in a light stride towards the drive. As I freewheeled down the slope to the cycad, my eyes on the rear-view mirror, I saw him vault the side gate that led to the servants' entrance.

I waited in the car, listening to the faint hiss of sprinklers from the walls and hedges around me. Perhaps the owners of the villa were away on holiday, and a lover was waiting for him in another maid's room. I imagined them playing clock-golf on the carpet, a formal courtship like the mating dance of a bower-bird . . .

'Right, let's go.' Crawford seemed to step from the screen of vegetation around the cycad. Under one arm he carried a video-cassette recorder, cables tied around it to form a black parcel. He placed it on the rear seat and loosened his cap, keeping a careful eye on the access road. 'I'm checking it for them – a couple called Hanley. He's a retired personnel manager from Liverpool. By the way, it looks as if I've recruited two new members.'

'For the sports club? Great stuff. How did you persuade them?'

'Their television set isn't working. Something's wrong with the satellite dish. Besides, they feel that they ought to get out

236

more. Now, let's drive over to the west side of the complex. I need to make a few house calls . . .'

He adjusted the climate-control unit on the instrument panel, sending a stream of cooler air into our faces, and lay back against the head-rest, so relaxed that I could hardly believe that we had embarked on a criminal spree. He stowed the golf putters in the hold-all, deliberately allowing me to see that they were, in fact, a pair of steel jemmies. I had guessed from the moment we left the sports club that he intended to carry out a series of provocative acts, petty burglaries and nuisance raids designed to shake the Residencia Costasol out of its dozing complacency. I assumed that the crimes which the Spanish police had reported to David Hennessy were Crawford's doing, the overture to his campaign of harassment and aggravation.

Twenty minutes later we stopped by the next villa, an imposing mansion in the Moorish style with a speedboat parked in its drive. Almost certainly, the residents would be asleep in the bedrooms upstairs, and the garden and terrace were silent. A slow drip of water from a forgotten hose counted the seconds as Crawford scanned the surveillance cameras, his eyes following the cables that ran from the satellite dish on the roof to the switchbox beside the patio doors.

'Leave the engine running, Charles. We may as well do this in style . . .'

He slipped away, disappearing among the trees that flanked the drive. My hands fretted at the wheel as I waited for him to return, ready to make a quick getaway. I smiled at an elderly couple who passed me in their car, a large spaniel sitting between them, but they seemed unconcerned by the Citroën's presence. Five minutes later Crawford slipped into the passenger seat, casually brushing a few splinters of glass from his jacket.

'More television trouble?' I asked as we set off.

'It looks like it.' Crawford sat straight-faced beside me, now and then taking the wheel from my nervous hands. 'These satellite dishes are very sensitive. They need to be constantly recalibrated.'

'The owners will be grateful. Possible members?'

'Do you know, I think they are. I wouldn't be surprised if they dropped in tomorrow.' Crawford unzipped his jacket and removed an engraved silver cigarette case, which he laid beside the cassette-recorder on the rear seat. 'The husband was a Queen's Club committee member, a keen tennis player. His wife used to be something of an amateur painter.'

'Perhaps she'll take it up again?'

'I think she might . . .'

We continued to make our calls, threading our way through the quiet avenues of the Residencia Costasol like a shuttle weaving a rogue pattern across a sedate tapestry. Crawford pretended to visit the properties at random, but I took for granted that he had selected his victims after carrying out a careful survey, picking those who would send out the largest ripples of alarm. I imagined them dozing through the siesta hours as Crawford moved around the rooms below, sabotaging the satellite systems, stealing a jade horse from a coffee table, a Staffordshire figure from a mantelpiece, rifling the desk drawers as if in search of cash or jewellery, creating the illusion that a gang of skilled house-breakers had taken up residence in the Costasol complex.

While I waited in the car, expecting Inspector Cabrera and the Fuengirola flying squad to seize me on the spot, I wondered why I had allowed Crawford to inveigle me into this criminal romp. As the Citroën's engine trembled against the accelerator pedal I was tempted to drive back to the sports club and tip off Cabrera. But Crawford's arrest would put an end to any hopes of discovering the arsonist who had murdered the Hollingers. Looking up at the hundreds of impassive villas, with their security cameras and mentally embalmed owners, I was sure that Crawford's attempts to transform the complex into another Estrella de Mar would fail. The people of the Residencia had not only travelled to the far side of boredom but had decided that they liked the view. Crawford's failure might well provoke him into a desperate act that would expose his complicity in the Hollinger killings. One fire too many would burn more than his fingers.

Yet his commitment to this bizarre social experiment had a charm all its own. Frank too, I guessed, had been seduced by his gaudy vision, and like Frank I said nothing as the rear seat of the Citroën accumulated its booty. By the sixth villa, one of the older mansions on the north-south radial boulevard, I found a blanket in the trunk and held it ready for Crawford when he emerged from the shrubbery with a waisted Ming vase under one arm, a blackwood stand under the other.

He patted me reassuringly as I draped the blanket over his treasure-trove, pleasantly surprised by the way in which I had held up under pressure.

'They're tokens, Charles – I'll see they find their way back to the owners. Strictly speaking, we don't need to take anything, just convey the sense that a thief has urinated on their Persian carpets and wiped his fingers on the tapestry.'

'And tomorrow the entire Residencia Costasol will feel like a game of tennis? Or decide to take up flower-arranging and needlepoint?'

'Of course not. The inertial forces here are colossal. But one elephant fly can start a stampede if it bites a sensitive spot. You sound sceptical.'

'A little.'

'You don't think it will work?' Crawford pressed my hand to the steering wheel, steeling my resolve. 'I need you, Charles – it's difficult to do this on my own. Betty Shand and Hennessy are only interested in their cash flow. But you can see beyond that to the larger horizon. What happened in Estrella de Mar will happen here, and then move on down the coast. Think of all those pueblos coming to life again. We're freeing people, Charles, returning them to their true selves.'

Did he believe his own rhetoric? Half an hour later, as he burgled a small apartment block near the central plaza, I unzipped the hold-all and glanced through its contents. There were jemmies and wirecutters, a selection of lockpicks and perforated entry cards, jump leads and electronic immobilizers. A smaller valise contained several aerosol paint cans, two camcorders and a clutch of fresh video-cassettes. A segmented plastic snake of cocaine sachets wrapped itself around a wallet filled with drug capsules and pills in foil dispensers, packs of syrettes and ribbed condoms.

The aerosols Crawford put to immediate use. Barely bothering to step from the car, he held a can in each hand and sprayed a series of lurid patterns on the garage doors that we passed. After only two hours a lengthy trail of theft and vandalism lay behind us – damaged satellite dishes, graffiti-daubed cars, dog turds left floating in swimming pools, surveillance cameras blinded by jets of paint.

Within earshot of the owners he broke into a silver Aston Martin and freewheeled the car down the gravelled drive. I followed as he drove to a disused builder's yard on the northern perimeter road, and watched him scrape the sides of the car with a jemmy, scratching the paintwork with the care of a chef scoring a side of pork. When he stood back and lit a cigarette I waited for the fire to come. He smiled at the mutilated vehicle, the lighter still flaming in his hand, and I expected him to stuff a rag into the fuel tank.

But Crawford treated the car to a rueful salute, and calmly

smoked his cigarette when we drove off, savouring the Turkish fumes.

'I hate doing that, Charles – but sacrifices have to be made.'

'At least it's not your Aston Martin.'

'I was thinking of *our* sacrifices – it's painful medicine for both of us, but we have to swallow it . . .'

We set off along the perimeter road, where the cheaper villas and apartment houses looked out over the Malaga highway. Home-made 'For Sale' signs hung from balconies, and I assumed that the Dutch-German developers had sold the properties at a discount.

'Take that house on the right – the one with the empty pool.' Crawford pointed to a small villa with a faded awning over its patio. A drying frame exposed a selection of gaudy tops and flimsy underwear to the sun. 'I'll be back in ten minutes. They need a little arts counselling . . .'

He reached into the hold-all and removed the valise that contained the camcorders and pharmaceuticals. Waiting for him by the front door were two women in swimsuits who shared the villa. Despite the heat they wore a full maquillage of lipstick, rouge and mascara, as if ready for a session under the film lights, and greeted Crawford with the easy smiles of hostesses at a dubious bar welcoming a regular patron.

The younger of the women was in her twenties, with a pale, English complexion, bony shoulders and eyes that for ever watched the street. I recognized the older woman beside her, the platinum blonde with the over-large breasts and florid face who had played one of the bridesmaids in the porno-film. Glass in hand, she pressed a Slavic cheekbone to Crawford's lips and beckoned him into the house.

I stepped from the car and strolled towards the house, watching them through the patio windows. Together they made their way into the lounge, where a television set played to itself, blinking as the frame-hold lost its grip on an afternoon serial. Crawford opened the valise and took out one of the camcorders and a brace of cassettes. He tore a dozen sachets of cocaine from the plastic snake, which the women tucked into the cups of their swimsuits, and began to demonstrate the camcorder to them. The older woman raised the viewfinder to her eye, snapping at herself as her long fingernails scratched at the tiny push-buttons. She practised the pan and zoom, while Crawford sat on the sofa with the young Englishwoman. No one exchanged the slightest banter, as if Crawford were a salesman demonstrating a new household appliance.

When he returned to the car the women filmed him from the door, laughing over each other's shoulders.

'Film school?' I asked. 'They look like quick learners.'

'Yes . . . they've always been film buffs.' Crawford waved to them as we pulled away, grinning to himself as if genuinely fond of the women. 'They came here from Estepona to open a beauty parlour, but decided the prospects weren't good enough.'

'So now they'll go into the film business? I imagine they'll find that profitable.'

'I think so. They have an idea for a film.'

'Documentary?'

'More of a nature film, you might call it.'

'The wildlife of the Residencia Costasol.' I savoured the notion. 'Courtship rituals and mating patterns. I think they'll be a success. Who was the platinum blonde? She looks slightly Russian.'

'Raissa Livingston – widow of a Lambeth bookie. She's a tank-trap full of vodka. A great sport. She's done a little acting before, so she'll get things off to a good start.'

Crawford spoke without irony, staring at the roof of the car as if already screening the first day's rushes. He seemed content with his afternoon's work, like a neighbourhood evangelist who had unloaded his stock of biblical tracts. The burglaries and break-ins had left him calm and relaxed, his day's duty done for the benighted people of the Residencia.

When we returned to the sports club he directed me to the service entrance behind the kitchen and boiler room. Here he had parked his Porsche, safely out of sight from any police who might call at the club.

'We'll move the gear to my car.' He threw back the blanket, exposing the booty. 'I don't want Cabrera to catch you redhanded, Charles. You've got that guilty look again.'

'There's a lot of stuff here. Can you remember who owns what?'

'I don't need to. I'll stash it in the builder's yard where we left the Aston Martin and tip off the security people in the gatehouse. They'll put everything on show there and make sure the entire Residencia gets the message.'

'But what is the message? That's something I haven't quite grasped.'

'The message . . . ?' Crawford was lifting a cassette-recorder from the seat, but turned to stare at me. 'I thought you understood everything, Charles.'

'Not exactly. These break-ins, wrecking a few TV sets and painting "Fuck" on a garage door – is that going to change people's lives? If you burgled my house I'd just call the police. I wouldn't join a chess club or take up carol-singing.'

'Absolutely. You'd call the police. So would I. But suppose the police do nothing and I break in again, this time stealing something you really value. You'd start thinking about stronger locks and a security camera.'

'So?' I opened the Porsche's boot and waited as Crawford lowered the cassette-recorder into it. 'We've returned to square one. I go back to my satellite television and my long sleep of the dead.'

'No, Charles.' Crawford spoke patiently. 'You're not asleep. By now you're wide awake, more alert than you've ever been before. The break-ins are like the devout Catholic's wristlet that chafes the skin and sharpens the moral sensibility. The next burglary fills you with anger, even a self-righteous rage. The police are useless, fobbing you off with vague promises, and that generates a sense of injustice, a feeling that you're surrounded by a world without shame. Everything around you, the paintings and silverware you've taken for granted, fit into this new moral framework. You're more aware of yourself. Dormant areas of your mind that you haven't visited for years become important again. You begin to reassess yourself, as you did, Charles, when that Renault caught fire.'

'Perhaps . . . but I didn't take up t'ai chi or start a new book.'

'Wait – you may do.' Crawford pressed on, keen to convince me. 'The process takes time. The crime wave continues – someone shits in your pool, ransacks your bedroom and plays around with your wife's underwear. Now rage and anger are not enough. You're forced to rethink yourself on every level, like primitive man confronting a hostile universe behind every tree and rock. You're aware of time, chance, the resources of your own imagination. Then someone mugs the woman next door, so you team up with the outraged husband. Crime and vandalism are everywhere. You have to rise above these mindless thugs and the oafish world they inhabit. Insecurity forces you to cherish whatever moral strengths you have, just as political prisoners memorize Dostoevsky's *House of the Dead*, the dying play Bach and rediscover their faith, parents mourning a dead child do voluntary work at a hospice.'

'We realize time is finite and take nothing for granted any more?'

'Exactly.' Crawford patted my arm, happy to welcome me to his flock. 'We form watch committees, elect a local council, take pride in our neighbourhoods, join sports clubs and local history societies, rediscover the everyday world we once took for granted. We know that it's more important to be a third-rate painter than to watch a CD-ROM on the Renaissance. Together we begin to thrive, and at last find our full potential as individuals and as a community.'

'And all this is set off by crime?' I lifted the silver cigarette case from the rear seat of the Citroën. 'Why that particular trigger? Why not ... religion or some kind of political will? They've ruled the world in the past.'

'Not any longer. Politics is over, Charles, it doesn't touch the public imagination any longer. Religions emerged too early in human evolution – they set up symbols that people took literally, and they're as dead as a line of totem poles. Religions should have come later, when the human race begins to near its end. Sadly, crime is the only spur that rouses us. We're fascinated by that "other world" where everything is possible.'

'Most people would say there's more than enough crime already.'

'But not here!' Crawford gestured with the jade horse at the distant balconies beyond the alley. 'Not in the Residencia Costasol, or the retirement complexes along the coast. The future has landed, Charles, the nightmare is already being dreamed. I believe in people, and know they deserve better.'

'You'll bring them back to life – with amateur porn-films, burglary and cocaine?'

'They're just the means. People are so hung up about sex and property and self-control. I'm not talking about crime in the sense that Cabrera thinks of it. I mean anything that breaks the rules, sidesteps the social taboos.'

'You can't play tennis without observing the rules.'

'But, Charles . . .' Crawford seemed almost lightheaded as he searched for a retort. 'When your opponent cheats, think how you raise your game.'

We carried the last of the stolen property to the Porsche. I walked back to my car, ready to leave Crawford, but he opened the door and slipped into the passenger seat. The sun shone through the side windows of the Citroën, flushing his face with an almost fevered glow. He had been eager for me to hear him out, but I sensed that he no longer cared if anyone believed him. Despite myself, I felt drawn to him, this small-time healer moving like a mendicant preacher down the coasts of the dead. I knew that his ministry would almost certainly fail and lead to a cell in Zarzuella jail.

'I hope it works,' I told him. 'How did Frank feel about all this? Was it his idea?'

'No, Frank's far too moralistic. I'd thought about it for years, in fact ever since I was a child. My father was a deacon at Ely Cathedral. Unhappy man, never knew how to show affection to me or my mother. What he did like was knocking me around.'

'Nasty – did no one report him?'

'They didn't know, not even my mother. I was hyperactive and always banging into things. But I noticed it made him feel better. After a session with the strap he'd hold me tight and even love me. So I started getting up to all kinds of naughty pranks just to provoke him.'

'Painful medicine. And that gave you the idea?'

'In a way. I found that thieving and little criminal schemes could stir things up. Father knew what was going on and never tried to stop me. At the choir school he'd see me gingering up the boys before an away match, stealing from their lockers and messing up their kit. We always won by six tries to nil. The last time Father used the strap he suggested I take holy orders.'

'Did you?'

'No, but I was tempted. I wasted a couple of years at Cambridge reading anthropology, played a lot of tennis and then joined the army on a short-service commission. The regiment went out to Hong Kong, working with the Kowloon police. A totally demoralized bunch – morale was flat on the floor. They were waiting for the mainland Chinese to take over and send them all to Sinkiang. The villagers in the New Territories were just as bad, already paying cumshaw to the Chinese border guards. They'd lost all heart, letting the paddy fields drain and making a pittance out of smuggling.'

'But you put a stop to that? How, exactly?'

'I livened things up. A spot of thieving here and there, a few gallons of diesel oil in the congs where they stored their rice. Suddenly everyone was sitting up, started rebuilding the dykes and cleaning the canals.'

'And the Kowloon police?'

'Same thing. We had problems with cross-border migrants looking for the good life in Hong Kong. Instead of handing them back we roughed them up a little first. That did the trick with the local police. Believe me, there's nothing like a "war crime" to perk up the soldiery. It's a terrible thing to say, but war crimes do have their positive side. It's a pity I couldn't have stayed on longer, I might have put some backbone into the colony.'

'You had to leave?'

'After a year. The Colonel asked me to resign my commission. One of the Chinese sergeants got over-enthusiastic.'

'He didn't appreciate that he was taking part in a . . . psychological experiment?'

'I don't think he did. But it all stayed in my mind. I started playing a lot of tennis, worked at Rod Laver's club and then came here. The curious thing is that Estrella de Mar and the Residencia Costasol are rather like Kowloon.' He adjusted the rear-view mirror and stared at his reflection, nodding to himself in confirmation. 'I'll leave you, Charles. Take care.'

'Good advice.' As he opened the door I said: 'I assume it was you who tried to strangle me?'

I expected Crawford to be embarrassed, but he turned to stare at me with genuine concern, surprised by the stern note in my voice. 'Charles, that was . . . a gesture of affection. It sounds strange, but I mean it. I wanted to wake you and make you believe in yourself. It's an old interrogation technique, one of the Kowloon inspectors showed me all the pressure points. It's amazingly effective at giving people a clearer perspective on everything. You needed to be roused, Charles. Look at you now, you're almost ready to play tennis with me . . .'

He held my shoulder in a friendly grip, saluted and sprinted back to the Porsche.

Later that evening, as I stood on the balcony of Frank's apartment at the Club Nautico, I thought of Bobby Crawford and the Kowloon police. In that world of corrupt border officials and thieving villagers a young English lieutenant with a taste for violence would have fitted in like a pickpocket in a Derby Day crowd. For all his strange idealism, the Residencia Costasol would defeat him. A few bored wives might film themselves having sex with their lovers, but the attractions of t'ai chi, madrigals and volunteer committee work would soon pall. The sports club would remain deserted, leaving Elizabeth Shand to tear up her leases.

I felt the bruises on my neck, and realized that Crawford had been recruiting me when he stepped from the darkness and seized my throat. A laying-on of hands had taken place, as he appointed me to fill Frank's vacant role. By not injuring me he had made the point that the Hollinger murders were irrelevant to the real life of Estrella de Mar and the new social order sustained by his criminal regime.

*   *   *

Soon after midnight I was woken by a flash of light across the bedroom ceiling. I stepped on to the balcony and searched for the beacon of the Marbella lighthouse, assuming that an electrical discharge had destroyed the lantern. But the beam continued its soft circuit of the sky.

The flames leapt from the centre of the Costasol marina. A yacht was on fire, its mast glowing like a candlewick. Cut loose from its moorings, it drifted across the open water, a fire-ship searching the darkness for a phantom fleet. But after scarcely a minute the flames seemed to snuff themselves out, and I guessed that the yacht had sunk before Bobby Crawford could rouse the Costasol residents from a slumber even deeper than sleep. Already I suspected that the yacht was the *Halcyon*, and that Crawford had persuaded Andersson to sail the craft from its berth at Estrella de Mar, ready to signal his arrival to the peoples of his ministry.

The next morning, when I passed the marina on my way to the sports club, a police launch circled the debris-strewn water. A small crowd stood on the quay, watching a frogman dive to the submerged sloop. The usually silent yachts and cruisers had begun to stir with activity. A few owners were testing their rigging and engines, while their wives aired the cabins and buffed the brass. Only Andersson sat quietly in the boat-yard, face as bleak as ever, smoking a roll-up cigarette as he stared at the rising sails.

I left him to his vigil and drove across the plaza to the club. A car turned through the gates ahead of me and parked by the entrance. Two middle-aged couples, dressed in their crispest tennis whites, stepped nimbly from the car, rackets swinging in their hands.

'Mr Prentice? Good morning to you.' One of the husbands, a retired dentist I had seen in the wine store, strolled up to me. 'We're not members, but we'd like to join. Can you sign us up?'

'Of course.' I shook his hand and beckoned the party towards the entrance. 'You'll be glad to know that the first year's membership is entirely free.'

Bobby Crawford's first recruits were signing on for duty.

22

An End to Amnesia

THE RESIDENCIA COSTASOL had come to life. A sun-bleached cadaver of a community, lying inertly beside a thousand swimming pools, had raised itself on one elbow to taste the quickening air. Waiting for Crawford to begin his morning inspection tour, I sat in the Citroën and listened to the eager chorus of hammers nailing together the proscenium arch of the open-air theatre beside the marina. Led by Harold Lejeune, a sometime marine surveyor at Lloyd's Register of Shipping, a team of enthusiastic carpenters was putting together a credible copy of an end-of-pier playhouse.

Lejeune squatted astride the crown pole, baseball cap rakishly across his head, nails clamped in his strong teeth as he waited for the last section of the pitched gable to be hoisted into place. A furious salvo of hammerheads signalled the raising of the roof by this work-gang of former accountants, lawyers and middle-managers.

Below them, shielding their ears from the din, their wives were unrolling the bolts of silky bombazine that would form the side and rear walls of the theatre. A group of energetic daughters unloaded a stack of collapsible metal chairs from a pick-up truck beside the quay, adding them to the rows of seats that faced the stage.

The Marina Players were about to mount their first production, a performance of *The Importance of Being Earnest*, which would alternate with *Who's Afraid of Virginia Woolf?*.

Future productions included plays by Orton and Coward, all to be directed by Arnold Wynegarde, a Shaftesbury Avenue veteran, their amateur casts stiffened by several one-time stage professionals.

Green shoots of a forgotten metropolitan culture were poking through the property developer's plaster and lath. When the hammers paused briefly from their work I could hear the strains of *Giselle* from the gymnasium, where a ballet class of younger wives were practising their *fouettés* and arabesques. They would end the session bouncing in their leotards to a rock number, then lie panting by the swimming pool.

In the five weeks since Crawford had taken me on my first tour of the complex a remarkable transformation had occurred. Refurbished restaurants and boutiques had opened in the shopping mall, briskly profitable as they prospered under Elizabeth Shand's steely gaze. An impromptu arts festival had conjured itself from the air, drawing troupes of eager volunteers from the sleepy afternoons.

The Residencia Costasol had decided that it needed a facelift. A rush to activity of every kind was on, the quest for a new civic pride expressed in parties and barbecues, tea-dances and church services. Newsletters circulated on the e-mail computer screens, inviting residents to stand for a new municipal council and its projected sub-committees.

The sounds of serve and volley came from the tennis courts, where Helmut drilled his eager pupils, and there was a heavy splash in the swimming pool as Wolfgang demonstrated a jackknife and reverse swallow to his diving class. Water-skis, trampolines and exercycles were being moved by the groundsmen from forgotten storerooms under the gymnasium. Below the arched bridge of the coastal road the first yachts of the morning were setting out for the open sea. The once-silent marina echoed to the strains of capstan and hawser as hulls weakened by osmosis were drained and varnished by Andersson and his Spanish repair team.

Meanwhile, in the centre of the marina, a fire-ravaged sloop was lashed to a steel lighter, the half-submerged hulk of the *Halcyon*. Its charred mast and blackened sails presided over the waterways, urging the yachtsmen of the Residencia Costasol to reef their sails and search for the keenest winds and steepest seas.

A hand held my shoulder, then clasped my temples before I could raise my head, pinning me to the driving seat of the Citroën. I had fallen asleep in the car, and someone had slipped into the seat behind me.

'Bobby . . . !' I pushed his hand away, angered by his brutal humour. 'That's a –'

'Mean trick to play?' Crawford chuckled to himself like a child savouring a favourite joke. 'Charles, you were sound asleep. I hired you as my bodyguard.'

'I thought I was your literary adviser. You were supposed to be here at ten.'

'Pressing work. All kinds of things are happening. Tell me, what were you dreaming about?'

'Some sort of . . . fire-storm. The yachts in the marina were blazing. God knows why.'

'Strange. Did you wet the bed as a child? Never mind. How's everything at the club? It sounds busy.'

'It is. Membership's up to three hundred, with another fifty application forms in. There's already a waiting list for the courts.'

'Good, good . . .' Crawford scanned the pool, smiling at the sight of so many handsome women oiling themselves in the sun. Wolfgang was demonstrating a back-flip, whipping the board under his feet with a crack that roused everyone

253

from their seats. 'Handsome fellow – any Greek sculptor would have given his eye-teeth to stick him in a frieze. It looks great, Charles. You've done a superb job. You may not realize it, but your real ambition is to run a nightclub in Puerto Banus.'

He patted my back and gazed at the busy scene, smiling in an almost innocent way, delighted by these signs of civic renewal and at that moment wholly unconscious of the means he had used to achieve them. Despite myself, I was glad to see him. As always I felt buoyed by his evangelical zeal and his selfless commitment to the people of the Residencia. At the same time I was still sceptical about his belief that the crime wave he had launched was the engine of change. The theatre and sports clubs, like their counterparts at Estrella de Mar, flourished as a result of some small but significant shift in people's sense of themselves, a response to something no more radical than simple boredom. Crawford had seized on the coincidence to give vent to a latent strain of violence in his make-up, an almost childlike faith that he could provoke the world to rise on its toes and respond in kind. Just as he had willed the tennis machine to beat him, he now urged the Costasol complex to rally itself against the secret enemy within its walls.

Yet his affection for the residents was unfeigned. When we left the sports club and drove past the Marina Players he reached over me and sounded the Citroën's horn. He waved his baseball cap at Lejeune and his fellow-carpenters on the roof and whistled at the wives tacking up their bombazine.

'When do the tickets go on sale?' he shouted cheerily. 'Let's do a drag version – I'll play Lady Bracknell . . .' He lay back in the rear seat and clapped his hands. 'Right, Charles, we're off. Let's visit your new home. You're now a paid-up resident of the Costasol complex.'

I was watching the women in the rear mirror. Charmed,

as always, by Crawford's handsome and easy style, they waved until he was out of sight.

'They need you, Bobby. What happens when you return to Estrella de Mar?'

'They'll keep going. They've found themselves again. Charles, have more faith in people. Think about it – a month ago they were dozing in their bedrooms and watching replays of last year's Cup Final. They didn't realize it, but they were waiting for death. Now they're putting on the plays of Harold Pinter. Isn't that an advance?'

'I suppose it is.' As we passed the marina I pointed to the blackened wreck of the *Halcyon*, lashed like a corpse to the lighter. 'Frank's sloop – why not have it removed? It's an eyesore.'

'Later, Charles. One mustn't rush these things. People need constant small reminders. It keeps them on their toes. Now, look at that . . .' He pointed to the ornamental roundabout where the western boulevard entered the plaza. 'A volunteer police patrol . . .'

A jeep in freshly painted khaki camouflage was parked by the verge. A resident in his sixties stood between the head-lamps, clipboard in hand, checking the numbers of passing cars. A one-time bank manager from Surrey named Arthur Waterlow, he sported an RAF moustache and calf-length white socks that resembled the gaiters of a military policeman. Sitting erectly behind the steering wheel, radar-gun in hand, was his seventeen-year-old daughter, an intense young woman who flashed the jeep's lights at any car that exceeded the twenty miles per hour speed limit. They had called at the sports club the previous day. Pleasantly surprised by the facilities, both had applied for membership.

'Licence checks, my God . . .' Crawford saluted them solemnly from the rear seat, like a general being chauffeured into an army base. 'Charles, maybe we can offer them our computer? Build up a fresh database of all vehicles in the Residencia and their exact locations.'

'Is that wise? It smacks to me of officiousness. You'll be giving him tips next on the Kowloon interrogation technique.'

'He's a bank manager – he doesn't need any tips on interrogation. You have to understand, a community must have its busybodies, its subscription collectors and committee bores, all those people you and I run a mile from. They're the cement, or at least the grouting. They're as vital as plumbers and TV maintenance men. One obsessive with a PC and a printer, turning out a residents' association newsletter, is worth more than a dozen novelists or boutique operators. It isn't shopping, or the arts, that makes a community but that duty we all owe to each other as neighbours. Once lost, it's hard to bring back, but I think we're getting there. You can feel it, Charles.'

'I can. Believe me, I listen to them at the club. There are projects galore – a local newspaper, a citizens' advice bureau, kung fu classes, hypnotherapy, everyone seems to have an idea. There's a retired Jesuit priest who's ready to hear confessions.'

'Good. I hope he's busy. Hennessy tells me there are plans for a rival sports club.'

'There are. We're not exclusive enough for some people's taste. The Residencia Costasol may look homogeneous, but it has the class structure of Tunbridge Wells. You'll have to see Betty Shand about a big cash injection. We need six more tennis courts, new gym equipment and a paddling pool for the toddlers. Hennessy agrees.'

'Then you're both wrong.' Crawford reached across my shoulder and steered the Citroën around an erratic elderly cyclist who had taken to two wheels under the apparent impression that they were part of some folkloric heritage. 'Too many tennis courts are always a mistake. They tire people out and prevent them getting up to mischief. Likewise all those parallel bars and vaulting horses.'

'It's a sports club, Bobby.'

'There are sports and sports. What we need is a disco – and a mixed sauna. The club's evening activities are more important than the daytime ones. People need to stop thinking about their own bodies and start thinking about other people's. I want to see them coveting their neighbours' wives, and dreaming of illicit pleasures. We'll talk about this later. First, we need to get on with the job of laying down the infrastructure. There's a lot of work to be done, Charles . . . Take the next right turn and put your foot down. Let's give Waterlow's daughter something to get indignant over.'

The infrastructure, as I knew, belonged to that other and more quickening realm that lay below the surface of the Residencia Costasol, a reversed image of the amateur theatricals, cordon bleu classes and neighbourhood watch schemes. As we sped towards the perimeter road I waited for Crawford to signal a halt before setting off to vandalize a parked car or spray-paint obscenities on a garage door.

But he had moved from this phase of primary spadework to the larger strategic task of laying down his administrative network, his bureaucracy of crime. In time-honoured fashion, the three pillars of his regime were drugs, gambling and illicit sex. As our house calls revealed, he had soon recruited his team of dealers – Nigel Kendall, a retired Hammersmith vet, an unblinking man in his early forties with a silent wife perpetually dazed by Paula Hamilton's tranquillizers; Carole Morton, a predatory hairdresser from Rochdale who ran the refurbished beauty salon at the shopping mall; Susan Henry and Anthea Rose, two widows in their thirties who had already set up a small agency direct-selling exotic underwear and perfumery around the complex; Ronald Machin, a one-time police inspector who had resigned from the Met after bribery allegations; Paul and Simon Winchell, both in their late teens, sons of one of the more prominent Residencia families, who supplied the youth trade.

Under the guise of delivering the latest property brochures, Crawford slipped his manila envelopes through their letter-boxes. Opening his sales rep's suitcase while he was ringing Machin's doorbell, I found a stack of information wallets emblazoned with 'The Residencia Costasol – for Investment Opportunities and Peace of Mind', each a compact pharmaceuticals kit packed with cocaine, heroin, amphetamines, amyl nitrite and barbiturates.

His gambling syndicate ran in parallel, a still modest operation overseen by Kenneth Laumer, a retired Ladbroke's executive who already e-mailed a financial services newsletter to the Residencia's six hundred personal computers. Encouraged by Crawford, he now offered a betting service based on the Italian football leagues. He had expanded his operations by recruiting a team of Costasol widows to serve as his door-to-door numbers runners. The first roulette and blackjack evenings had been held in Laumer's converted dining room, though Crawford had intervened to ban the rigged wheel and marked cards.

Closest to Crawford's evangelical heart, since it directly involved the women of the Residencia, was illicit sex. Hand-printed cards had begun to appear in telephone kiosks around the complex, inviting volunteers with massage skills and escort agency experience to phone a number in Estrella de Mar – in fact, the Baalbeck Lebanese restaurant. Unsettled by the spate of burglaries and car thefts, a few of the Residencia's widows and divorcees began to put their talents to work on the community's behalf. Flabby musculatures were kneaded into shape, stomachs hardened after the couch-bound television years, double chins conjured away by probing fingers. As the masseuses worked at their clients' bodies in the shaded bedrooms, blood pressures soon rose, heartbeats quickened, and extra services found their way on to the credit-card bills.

'Nothing is more natural,' Crawford assured me when we neared the end of the morning rounds. 'Where sexual desire is concerned, nature already provides the infrastructure. All I'm doing is stimulating the traffic. Think how much better everyone looks.'

'You're right. Paula Hamilton will soon have to move to Marbella. Where to now?'

I waited for him to reply, but he had momentarily fallen asleep, head almost on my shoulder. As a child Frank had often slept against me while I did my homework. With his unlined face and blond eyebrows, Crawford resembled a large adolescent boy, and I imagined him playing in the precincts of Ely Cathedral, innocent and visionary eyes already gazing beyond the flat fenland to the waiting world beyond.

He woke with a grimace, surprised that he had slept. 'Charles, I'm sorry . . . I dropped off.'

'You look tired. Sleep here – I'll walk myself around the block.'

'We'll move on. One last call.' He lay back, rallying himself with an effort. 'It's been hard work – out every night, some close shaves too. If Cabrera catches me . . .'

'Bobby, relax and go back to Estrella de Mar. Everything's up and running here.'

'No . . . I can't leave them yet.' He rubbed his eyes and cheeks, forcing the blood back into his facial muscles, and then turned to face me. 'Well, Charles, you know what's going on. Are you with me?'

'I'm running the club. Or going through the motions.'

'I mean the complex as a whole. The larger scheme of things.' Crawford spoke slowly, listening to his own words. 'It's a noble project – Frank understood that.'

'I'm still not sure.' I switched off the engine and gripped

the wheel, trying to steady myself. 'I shouldn't really be here. It's difficult to see what lies in store.'

'Nothing. You've seen it all, at Estrella de Mar and now the Residencia. You haven't grasped it yet, but you're sitting in an outpost of the next century.'

'Massage parlours, gambling, and ten thousand lines of cocaine? It sounds rather old-fashioned. All you need next is rampant inflation and deficit financing.'

'Charles . . .' Crawford took my hands from the steering wheel, as if even the stationary car was too much for my confused view of the road ahead. 'A real community has created itself here. It rose spontaneously out of people's lives.'

'Then why the drugs and burglaries and whoring? Why not step back and let everyone get on with it?'

'I wish I could.' Almost despairingly, Crawford stared at the villas that surrounded us in the residential avenue. 'People are like children, they need constant stimulation. Without that the whole thing runs down. Only crime, or something close to crime, seems to stir them. They realize that they need each other, that together they're more than the sum of their parts. There has to be that constant personal threat.'

'Like Londoners in the Blitz? Wartime camaraderie?'

'Exactly. After all, war is a kind of crime. There's nothing like finding someone else's shit in your swimming pool. Before you know it you've joined the neighbourhood watch scheme and taken your old violin out of its case. Your wife starts fucking you with real pleasure for the first time in years. It works, Charles . . .'

'But it's a fierce recipe. Isn't there any other way? You could preach to them, become the Savonarola of the Costa del Sol.'

'I've tried it.' Crawford gazed glumly at himself in the rear-view mirror. 'No Messiah can compete with the siesta hour. Crime has a respectable history – Shakespeare's London,

Medici Florence. Warrens of murder, poisons and garrotting. Name me a time when civic pride and the arts both flourished and there wasn't extensive crime.'

'Ancient Athens? Mathematics, architecture and the state as political philosophy. Was the Acropolis crawling with pimps and pickpockets?'

'No, but the Greeks had slavery and pederasty.'

'And we have satellite television. If you left Estrella de Mar crime would appear spontaneously. This coast is a hotbed of petty criminals and crooked politicians.'

'But they're Spanish and Maghrebian. The Mediterranean shoreline is a foreign country to them. The real natives of the Costa del Sol are the British and French and Germans. Honest and law-abiding to the last man, woman and Rottweiler. Even the East End crooks grow honest when they settle here.' Aware of the stale sweat rising from his clothes, Crawford turned on the car's fan. 'Trust me, Charles. I need your help.'

'You've . . . got it. So far.'

'Good. I want you to keep running the club. I know you have time on your hands, and I'd like you to expand a little.'

'My kung fu is pretty rusty.'

'Not kung fu. I'd like you to start a film club.'

'Nothing easier. There's a video-rental store in the shopping mall with a good classics selection. I'll order a hundred copies of *The Battleship Potemkin.*'

Crawford closed his eyes to the thought. 'That's not the kind of club I have in mind. People have to learn to switch off their TV sets. I want a club where people make their own films, learn how to storyboard a narrative, how to handle close-ups, dollies, pans and tracking shots. Film is the way we see our world, Charles. There are two retired cameramen living here who worked on British features for years. There's also a husband and wife documentary team – they can teach film classes. I want you to be the producer, keep an overview of everything, steer funding to the right places. Betty Shand is keen to support the arts. So much is happening, and it needs to be recorded.'

I watched him expand on this luminous project, genuinely unaware that an accurate documentary about the Residencia Costasol would be the single greatest testimony against him at his trial, and send him to Zarzuella jail for the next thirty years. I thought of the porno-film he had helped to make at his apartment, and guessed that he had something similar in mind, part of that web of corruption he was spinning across the people of the complex.

'I understand . . . vaguely. What's the subject of these films?'

'Life in the Residencia. What else? There's a kind of amnesia at work here – an amnesia of self. People literally forget who they are. The camera lens needs to be their memory.'

'Well . . .' I was still doubtful, reluctant to find myself running a pornographic film company. But I needed to enter the innermost circle of the criminal syndicate controlled by Elizabeth Shand, Crawford and David Hennessy if I were to find the arsonist responsible for the Hollinger fire. 'I'll give it a go. There must be a few professional film actors living here. I'll ask around at the club.'

'Forget the professionals. They're less flexible than amateurs. In point of fact, I have someone in mind.' Crawford sat forward and switched on the wipers and window-wash, clearing the morning's accumulated debris from our view. He had recovered his energies, as if he needed to touch bottom before springing to the surface. 'She's going to be a great star, Charles. As it happens, she lives next door to the house I've found for you. We'll drive there now. I know you'll be intrigued – she's very much your sort of woman . . .'

He turned the ignition key and waited for me to move off,

smiling like the bruised and boyish visionary who had ransacked his schoolmates' lockers, leaving behind a treasure of incitement and desire.

23

Come and See

'YOUR NEW HOME, Charles. Take a look. Handsome, isn't it?'

'Very. Are you going to burgle it?'

'Only when you've settled in. You'll be happy here. I want to get you away from the Club Nautico. Sometimes one can have too many memories.'

We approached the gates of an untenanted villa in a quiet residential avenue three hundred yards to the west of the central plaza. An estate office's signpost impaled the square of yellowing grass beside the empty swimming pool. Unoccupied since its construction, the house seemed almost ghostly in its faded newness, haunted by the human occupants who had never lived in its vacant rooms but left their imprints like patches of fog on an exposed photographic film.

'It's an imposing place,' I commented as we stepped from the car. 'Why has no one lived here?'

'The owners died before they could leave England, and there was some sort of family dispute over probate. Betty Shand picked it up for a song.'

Crawford unlocked the gates and strolled along the drive ahead of me. The kidney-shaped pool resembled a sunken altar reached by the chromium ladder. Votive offerings of a dead rat, a wine bottle and a sun-bleached property brochure waited for whatever minor deity might claim them. The garden of unwatered palms and bougainvilleas was blanched by the heat. Dusty windows, through which no one had ever stared, now sealed off the unfurnished rooms.

Crawford gripped the estate office's sign and worked the post to and fro. He wrenched it from the dry soil and threw it to the ground. Climbing the tiled steps to the front door, he took a set of keys from his pocket.

'You'll be glad to know that we won't break in – it seems strange going in through the front door, almost illicit. I want you to experience the Residencia Costasol at first-hand. The mysteries of life and death hover over villas like this . . .'

He let us into the silent interior. Sunlight fell through the unshaded windows, blunted by the dust. The empty rooms lay around us, their white walls enclosing nothing, ready for dramas of boredom and ennui, the meaningless flicker of a thousand football matches. Devoid of all furniture and ornaments, the house lacked any clear function. The fitted kitchen resembled a survival station, part intensive care unit, part medical dispensary. As Crawford watched me approvingly I realized that his character-reading was all too accurate – I already felt at ease in the villa, free of the encumbrances of the past, the terminal moraine of memories that lay for ever around my feet.

'Charles, you've come home . . .' Crawford beckoned to me, urging me to stroll around the large living room. 'Enjoy the sensation – strangeness is closer to us than we like to think.'

'Perhaps it is. Empty houses have a special magic. I'm not sure if I want to live here. What about the furniture?'

'Delivered tomorrow. White-on-white drapes, chrome and black leather, absolutely you. Betty Shand's choice, not mine. Meanwhile, let's see the next floor.'

I followed him up the stairs, where the landing divided into wide corridors and an exposed concrete terrace like a side-chapel of the sun. I walked around the empty bedrooms and their mirror-walled bathrooms, trying to imagine how newly-arrived residents would respond to these motionless interiors, cut off from the world by their security systems and sensors. The outer desert of the Residencia Costasol was reflected in the inner desert of these aseptic chambers. The lighter gravity of this strange planet would numb the brain and maroon the residents in their armchairs, eyes clinging to the horizon lines of their television screens as they tried to stabilize their minds. By forcing a window or jemmying a kitchen door Crawford had broken the spell, and the clocks would begin to race again . . .

'Bobby . . . ?' Leaving the master-bedroom, and its view over the palm garden and tennis court below, I searched the corridor. The nearby bedrooms were empty, and I at first assumed that he had abandoned me to the house as part of some teasing experiment. Then I heard him moving around a small back bedroom that overlooked the kitchen courtyard.

'Charles, I'm in here. Come and see – it's rather unusual . . .'

I stepped into the unfurnished room with its miniature bathroom scarcely larger than a broom cupboard. Crawford stood by the window, peering through the slatted blades of a Venetian blind.

'The maid's room?' I asked. 'I hope she's pretty.'

'Well . . . we haven't thought of that, yet. But it does have an interesting view.'

Crawford's fingerprints were visible on the dusty vanes as he parted them for me. Beyond the kitchen courtyard lay the tennis court, its clay surface recently swept and chalked. A crisp new net hung between the posts, and a tennis machine similar to the Club Nautico's stood at the baseline, waiting for its first opponent.

But Crawford was not admiring the tennis court he had generously prepared for me. To our left, beyond the perimeter wall that followed the drive down to the avenue, was the neighbouring estate, a trio of handsome bungalows grouped like motel cabins around a shared swimming pool. For once the flat terrain of the Residencia Costasol had yielded to rising ground, a modest hill that gave the three dwellings a pleasant view over the surrounding gardens and brought the pool within clear sight of the window through which we peered.

Light trembled across the palm trunks and dappled the walls of the bungalows, reflected from the broken water. A teenaged girl stepped from the pool and stood bare-breasted on the verge, fingers squeezing the water from her nose. Her blonde hair lay across her shoulders like fraying hemp. Shouting to herself, she ran along the verge and dived noisily into the water.

'She's lovely, isn't she, Charles? Beautiful, in a damaged way. You should be able to do a lot with her.'

'Well . . .' I watched the teenager splashing in the shallow end, whooping at the rainbows lifting from her palms. 'She's certainly sweet.'

'Sweet? My God, you've moved in some tough circles. I wouldn't call her sweet.'

I watched the girl playfully slapping the water, and then realized that Crawford was gazing beyond the pool to a sun-shaded table beside the nearest bungalow. A slim, silver-haired man with a matinée idol's handsome profile stood beside the umbrella in a silk dressing-gown. He waved to the girl in the pool and raised his glass, admiring her eager but unskilled dives. Little more than thirty feet away, I could see the wistful smile on his thin lips.

'Sanger? So these are the bungalows he owns . . .'

'His Garden of Eden.' Crawford bit the grimy vane with his teeth. 'He can play God, Adam and the serpent without having to change his fig-leaf. One of the bungalows is the office where he sees his patients. The other he lets to a French-woman and her daughter – the girl in the pool. The third he shares with his latest protégée. Look under the umbrella.'

Sitting in a deckchair beneath the parasol was a young woman in a cotton nightdress of the type issued in hospital emergency wards. One arm rested on a clutch of unread paperbacks, exposing the infected puncture-holes that covered the inner surface from wrist to elbow. She fiddled with an empty medicinal glass, as if unable to focus on anything around her until she had received her next dose. Her dark hair had been shaved almost to the scalp, exposing the bony scars that ran above her temples. When she turned to stare at the pool the gold rings in her right nostril and lower lip caught the sun, briefly lighting her sallow face. Her toneless cheeks reminded me of the heroin addicts I had seen in the prison hospital in Canton, unconcerned by the death penalties they faced because they had already taken their seats in the tumbril.

Yet as I stared at this deteriorated young woman I sensed that some kind of wayward spirit was struggling to rouse itself from the deep Largactil trance into which Sanger had cast her. She seemed morose and sullen, but now and then her eyes would fix themselves on some interior image, a memory of a time when she had been alive. Then an almost louche smile quirked her lips, and she turned her head to gaze in an amused and even mischievous way at the sedate bungalows and their filtered pool, a princess in her tower searching for a chemise to wave, a prisoner of the medical profession's good intentions. Her true home was the druggies' squat and the pus-stained mattress, a realm of shared needles and absent hopes where moral judgements were never made. Against the backdrop of the Residencia Costasol, with its impeccable villas and sensible citizenry, she held out the promise of a free and unrooted world. For the first time I understood why Andersson and Crawford had so treasured Bibi Jansen.

'Interested, Charles?' Crawford asked. 'Our white lady of H.'

'Who is she?'

'Laurie Fox – she was working in a club in Fuengirola until Sanger found her. Father's a doctor at a local clinic; after his wife died in a road crash he began to share his heroin habit with Laurie. She's appeared in a couple of low-budget TV series made out here.'

'Any good?'

'The series were shit, but she looked good. Has the right kind of bones in her face.'

'And now she's with Sanger? How does he do it?'

'He has special talents, and special needs.'

The French teenager shrieked and dived. The shattered water sent a burst of light across the garden. Laurie Fox flinched and searched for Sanger's hand. He stood behind her, stroking her short-cropped hair with a silver-backed brush. Trying to soothe her, he loosened the nightdress and rubbed sun cream into her shoulders, his fingers as gentle as a lover's. She took his hand and wiped the oil away, then placed it over her breast.

The frankness of her erotic response, the unashamed way in which she used her sex, seemed to unsettle Crawford. The plastic vanes slipped from his grip and danced against the window, but he controlled himself and steadied them. His heavy breath blurred the dusty glass as he panted quietly, partly in anger and partly in admiration and sensual pleasure.

'Laurie . . .' he murmured. 'She's your star, Charles.'

'Are you sure? Can she act?'

'I hope not. We need a special kind of . . . presence. Your film club will love her.'

'I'll think about it. You have met her?'

'Of course. Betty Shand owns half the club in Fuengirola.'

'Well, maybe. She looks happy enough with Sanger.'

'No one is happy with Sanger.' Crawford rapped the glass with his fist, then stared fixedly at the psychiatrist. 'We'll get her away from him. Laurie needs a different sort of encouragement.'

'Such as . . . ?'

I waited for Crawford to reply, but he was watching Sanger like a hunter in a hide. The psychiatrist was walking towards the pool with a dry towel. As the French girl stepped from the water he draped the towel around her, gently drying her shoulders as he gazed at her growing nipples. Hidden in the towelling, his hands lingered over her breasts and bottom, then gathered her hair into a damp coil that he laid over the nape of her neck.

The small bedroom was strangely silent, as if the entire villa was waiting for our response. I realized that both Crawford and I were no longer breathing. His chest was still, and the muscles of his face seemed ready to burst through his cheeks. Usually so relaxed and amiable, he was about to drive his forehead through the glass. His fierce resentment of Sanger, his envy of the affection the psychiatrist was bestowing on the young woman, made me certain that he had come into conflict with the psychiatric profession in the past, perhaps during his last days in the army.

The French teenager returned to her bungalow, and Sanger strolled back to the pool-side table. He took Laurie Fox's hand, lifting her from the chair, and wrapped a comforting arm around her as they walked into the bungalow behind them.

Metal louvres tore and clattered against the window. Ripped from the wall by Crawford's hands, the blind lay on the floor at our feet, a trembling mass of plastic vanes. I stepped back, trying to take Crawford's arm.

'Bobby? For God's sake . . .'

'It's all right, Charles. I didn't mean to upset you . . .' Crawford calmed me with a ready smile, but his eyes moved around Sanger's compound. He was working out the sight-lines between the bungalows, and I was sure that some brutal challenge was about to be mounted.

'Bobby . . . there are other girls like Laurie Fox. Just as stoned and just as weird. Fuengirola must be full of them.'

'Charles . . . don't panic.' Crawford spoke quietly, his sense of irony returning. He flexed his shoulders like a boxer and grimaced over his torn hands, smiling at the blood. 'There's nothing like a violent reflex now and then to tune up the nervous system. For some reason, Sanger really gets to me.'

'He's just another flawed psychiatrist. Forget about him.'

'All psychiatrists are flawed – believe me, Charles, I've had to cope with the poor devils. My mother took me to one in Ely. He thought I was a budding sociopath and liked bruising myself. Father knew better. He understood that I loved him, despite that strap.'

'And what about the army psychiatrists in Hong Kong?'

'Even more amateurish.' Crawford turned to watch me in his most level way, eyes searching my face. 'For what it's worth they used even stronger terms.'

'Like "psychopathy"?'

'That sort of thing. Hopelessly muddled. They don't realize that the psychopath plays a vital role. He meets the needs of the hour, touches our graceless lives with the only magic we know.'

'And that is?'

'Charles . . . come on. I must have some professional secrets. Let's get back to the club and sign up all those eager new members.'

As I followed him to the door he turned and smiled his most winning smile at me, then clasped my face in his hands and left his bloody fingerprints on my cheeks.

24

The Psychopath as Saint

'INSPECTOR CABRERA . . . ?' I stood in the doorway of my office at the sports club, surprised to see the young policeman sitting at my desk. 'I was expecting Mr Crawford.'

'He's difficult to find. Sometimes here, sometimes there, but never in between.' Cabrera adjusted the mouse beside my computer keyboard, scanned the menu and scrolled through the membership list, his lips pursed almost in disapproval. 'The club is very popular, Mr Prentice – so many new members in so little time.'

'We've been lucky. Still, the facilities are excellent. Mrs Shand has put a lot of money into the club.'

I waited for Cabrera to rise from my chair, but he seemed content to remain behind my desk, as if curious to see everything from my perspective. He turned in the swivel chair, and gazed at the crowded tennis courts.

'Mrs Shand is a fine businesswoman,' Cabrera acknowledged. 'For years the Residencia Costasol was asleep, and now, suddenly . . . how could Mrs Shand know when it would wake?'

'Well, Inspector . . .' Cabrera's aggressive gaze unsettled me, like his youthful face with its too obvious hint of intellectual thuggery. 'Business people have a feel for this sort of thing. They can read the psychology of a particular street corner or sidewalk. Can I help you, Inspector? I'm not sure when Mr

Crawford will be back. There's no problem with work permits, I hope? Our staff are all EC nationals.'

Cabrera raised himself slightly from my chair, trying to find in its geometry some clue to my own activities. He frowned at the monotonous sound of the tennis machine. 'No one is ever sure about Mr Crawford – a tennis coach who has a machine to do his work for him. You at least remain in one place.'

'My job is here, Inspector. I still sleep at the Club Nautico, but I'm moving my things to the Residencia this afternoon. Mrs Shand has rented a villa for me – next-door to Dr Sanger, as it happens. I looked over the house yesterday afternoon.'

'Good. Then we will know where you are.' Cabrera's glance took in my smartly-cut safari suit, run up for me by an Arab tailor in Puerto Banus. 'I wanted to ask if you had heard from your brother?'

'My brother . . . ?' Something unsettled me about Cabrera's loaded use of the term. 'Do you mean Frank?'

'You have another brother in Spain? Not in Zarzuella jail.'

'Of course not.' I placed my hands on the desk, trying to steady the scene. 'I haven't had any recent messages from Frank. Mr Hennessy and Dr Hamilton visit him every week.'

'Good. Then he's not abandoned.' Cabrera was still looking me up and down, trying to identify some unstated change in my appearance and manner. 'Tell me, Mr Prentice, will you visit your brother before the trial? It's over two months away.'

'Of course, Inspector. Perhaps I'll see him a few days from now. I'm extremely busy here, as you know. I'm not just the manager of the club, but Mrs Shand's agent in general.'

'Her representative in limbo.' Cabrera stood up and let me take my chair. He looked down at the packed bar tables and then sat on my desk, a deliberate territorial intrusion that shut

273

off my view of the pool. Memories of seminars on sibling rivalry moved across his untrusting eyes. 'Still, not to see your brother since your meeting in Marbella – people might assume that you accept his guilt.'

'Not at all. I'm convinced he's innocent. I spent weeks investigating the case, and I'm certain he didn't kill the Hollingers. Remember, he refused to see me when I first came to Estrella de Mar. Besides . . .'

'There are problems between you?' Cabrera nodded sagely. 'You told me once about your mother. Certain feelings of guilt tied you together, and now you feel the bonds are looser?'

'Well put, Inspector. In a way Estrella de Mar has been a liberation from the past.'

'And the Residencia Costasol even more so? There's a different ecology here, and you feel free of constraint. Perhaps the Hollinger deaths unlocked certain doors. It's a pity you cannot thank your brother for that.'

'Well . . .' I tried to sidestep Cabrera's devious logic. 'One hesitates to say it, but these dreadful tragedies have their positive side. Since the Hollinger fire people are much more alert to what is going on, even here in the Residencia. There are neighbourhood watch schemes and security patrols.'

'Security patrols?' Cabrera seemed surprised, sensing that his monopoly of law enforcement was threatened. 'Is there much crime in the Residencia?'

'Of course . . . well, I mean, no.' I hunted for a handkerchief, glad to hide my face for even a few moments, wondering if Cabrera had been tipped off that I chauffeured Bobby Crawford around the complex. 'One or two cars have been stolen – probably borrowed, in fact, after late-night parties.'

'And burglaries, house thefts . . . ?'

'I don't think so. Have any been reported?'

'Very few. One or two in the early days, but then silence. Your arrival here had a calming effect.'

'Good. I've tried to keep an eye on things.'

'Yet my men tell me there's much evidence of burglary, damage to cars, your brother's yacht burned in a spectacular way. Why should no one report these crimes?'

'I can't say. The British are a self-reliant people, Inspector. Living in a foreign country where few of them speak the language, they prefer to solve the crime problem themselves.'

'And perhaps they enjoy it?'

'Very likely. Crime prevention does have a social role.'

'And crime, also. You spend much time with Mr Crawford – what is his position at the club?'

'He's the chief tennis coach, the same post he held at the Club Nautico.'

'Good.' Cabrera moved his arms through the air, as if scything the deep grass that grew invisibly around my desk. 'Perhaps he will give me a lesson. I have to ask him about certain matters – the burning of the speedboat at Estrella de Mar. The owners in Marbella have hired some investigators. There are other questions . . .'

'Of a criminal nature?'

'Perhaps. Mr Crawford is a man of such energy. He touches everything with his excitement and sometimes leaves his fingerprints.'

'I don't think you'll find his prints here, Inspector.' I stood up with some relief as Cabrera moved towards the door. 'Mr Crawford is not a selfish man. He would never take part in criminal activity for his own gain.'

'Completely true. He has accounts with many banks, and almost no money. But if not for his own gain, perhaps for the community's?' Cabrera stood at the door, watching me with an almost over-studied show of sympathy. 'You defend him, Mr Prentice, but think of your brother. Even if Estrella de Mar has set you free, you cannot stay here for ever. One day you will go back to London, and you may again need that guilt you shared. Visit your brother before the trial . . .'

I waited by the main gates while the security guard logged the licence number of the Citroën into his computer, and remembered my first arrival at Gibraltar and the border crossing into Spain. Whenever I left the Residencia I seemed to cross a far more tangible frontier, as if the complex constituted a private kingdom with its own currencies of mind and meaning. As I turned on to the coast road I could see the pueblos stretching along the shore towards Marbella, immobile as chalk tombs in their whiteness. By contrast the Residencia Costasol had returned to life, to a realm of aroused emotions and woken dreams.

But Cabrera had unnerved me, as if he had read the secret script that Crawford had written and was aware of the role assigned to me. I tried to calm myself by looking at the sea, at the long line of white-capped waves that rolled in from Africa. I had wilfully forgotten Frank, pushing him and his absurd confession into a side corridor of my mind. In this new and more bracing air I was free of the restraints that had hobbled me since childhood, and ready to face myself afresh without fear.

The corniche road forked, the beachward arm running to the marina of Estrella de Mar and the waterfront bars and restaurants. I turned towards the Plaza Iglesias, and climbed the steep avenue to the Club Nautico. Above me the burnt-out shell of the Hollinger mansion presided over the peninsula. A bonfire of private sub-poenas had taken place among its charred timbers, a tinder-blaze of those warrants we issue against ourselves, now never to be served and left to gather dust in their closed files.

*　　*　　*

'Paula . . . ? God, you startled me . . .'

She had been waiting in the bedroom after letting herself into the apartment with Frank's keys. She stepped on to the balcony and touched my shoulder as I leaned on the rail.

'I'm sorry. I wanted to see you before you left.' She tried to smooth the ruched sleeves of her white blouse. 'David Hennessy tells me you're moving your things to the Residencia.'

She stood beside me, one hand on my wrist, as if trying to take my pulse. Her hair stretched tightly from her forehead, tied in a severe black bow, and she had lavished mascara and lipstick on her face in a clear attempt to stiffen her morale. Through the bedroom door I could see the impress of her hips and shoulders in the silk counterpane, and guessed that she had decided to lie there for the last time, head against the pillows she had shared with Frank.

'Betty Shand's rented a house for me,' I told her. 'It saves me driving to and fro every day. Besides, Frank will soon be back here, once he's acquitted.'

Eyes lowered, she shook her head at this, like a tired doctor with a stubborn patient rationalizing away his symptoms. 'I'm glad you think he'll be acquitted. Does Señor Danvila agree with you?'

'I've no idea. Believe me, they won't convict Frank – the evidence against him is so flimsy. A bottle of ether planted in his car . . .'

'They don't need any evidence. Frank is still pleading guilty. I saw him yesterday – he sent his love. It's a pity you won't visit him. You might persuade him to change his mind.'

'Paula . . .' I turned and held her shoulders, trying to revive her. 'It won't happen. I'm sorry I haven't seen Frank. I know it looks odd – Cabrera assumes I think he's guilty.'

'Do you?'

'No. That isn't the reason. We went through too much

277

together, for years we were trapped by our childhoods. Frank keeps me locked into all those memories.'

'You're leaving the apartment so you can forget about Frank?' Paula laughed flatly to herself. 'When he starts his thirty-year sentence you'll finally be free.'

'That's unfair . . .' I stepped into the bedroom and took my cases from the sports equipment cupboard. Her back to the sunlight, Paula clasped her hands and watched me lay my suits across the bed. For once she seemed to lack confidence in herself. I wanted to embrace her, place my arm around her hips and lift her on to the bed, laying her in the scented mould she had left of herself. I still hoped to make love to her again, but the video-cassette had come between us. I had seen her almost naked as she filmed the rape scene, and she had decided never to appear naked before me again.

She waited while I emptied the wardrobe and then took over from me. She packed my shirts into the suitcases and folded my dressing-gown, smoothing the lapels as if brushing away all traces of her own skin.

'I'm sorry you're going.' She noticed her reflection in the mirror and stared expressionlessly at herself. 'In a way you've kept the place warm for Frank. Everyone seems to be leaving Estrella de Mar. Andersson is working at the Residencia boat-yard. Hennessy and Betty Shand have opened an office at the shopping mall, the Keswick sisters are running a new restaurant . . .'

'You'll have to come too, Paula.'

'My patients at the Residencia don't need me as much as they did. No more insomnia, no migraines or depression. It's Estrella de Mar all over again. Even Bobby Crawford has gone. He's sub-let his apartment for the rest of the summer. Hennessy claims that Cabrera is looking for him.'

There was an odd note of hope in her voice, emphasized by her offhand manner. Had she leaked some tidbit concerning

Crawford's activities to the Inspector, information about the burning of the speedboat and the dealers outside the Club Nautico disco?

'He's staying undercover at the Residencia. There's some small problem over . . . parking, I think. Bobby's always in such a rush, he forgets this isn't Spain in the 1960s. When I move into the house I'll be able to keep an eye on him.'

'Really? You're completely under his spell.' The combative sarcasm had returned. 'Charles, you're the last person to have any control over him.'

'Not true. Besides, I don't want to control him – he's done an amazing job. He's brought the Residencia Costasol back to life.'

'He's dangerous.'

'Only at first sight. Some of the things he does are a little wild, but they're necessary to wake people up.'

'Like shouting "fire" in a crowded theatre?' Paula stood next to the mirror, coolly appraising herself. 'He doesn't just shout "fire", he burns down the stage and the dress circle.'

'He's popular, Paula. Everyone likes him. People know he isn't out for himself – he's not making any money. He's simply a tennis pro. At first I thought he was some kind of gangster, with his fingers in a hundred criminal pies.'

'Isn't he?'

'No.' I turned towards her, trying to distract her from her mirror-image. 'The drugs, prostitution, gambling – they're means to an end.'

'Which is?'

'A living community. Everything you take for granted at Estrella de Mar. The Residencia is stirring – there'll soon be an elected council and a mayor. You can feel a real civic pride being born for the first time. Bobby Crawford created all that himself.'

'He's still dangerous.'

'Rubbish. Think of him as a glorified entertainments officer, on board a cruise liner filled with mental retardees. He steals from a cabin here, sets fire to curtains there, lets off a stink bomb in the dining room, and suddenly the patients wake up. They start taking an interest in the voyage and the next port of call.'

'Dear Charles...' Paula took my hand and drew me towards the mirror, speaking to my reflection as if more comfortable in this reversed world. 'You're obsessed with him. All that boyish charm, the fresh-faced young army officer rousing the shiftless natives.'

'What's wrong with that? It sounds a pretty fair description.'

'You've only seen the early stages, those stink bombs and apple-pie beds. How does he keep everything going once he's left the Residencia? He'll move down the coast, you know, to Calahonda and the other pueblos.'

'Will he?' I felt a curious pang at the thought of Crawford leaving. 'There's a lot to do still, he'll be here for a while. Everyone needs him – boyish charm and enthusiasm are pretty thin on the ground these days. I've watched him at work, Paula. He genuinely wants to help everyone. He's stumbled on this strange way of getting people to make the most of themselves. It's touching to see such simple faith. He's really some kind of saint.'

'He's a psychotic.'

'Not fair. He gets carried away sometimes, but there's no viciousness in the man.'

'Pure psycho.' She turned her back on the mirror and stared critically at me. 'You can't see it.'

'No. All right, perhaps there's a faint strain of something odd. He had a lousy childhood – I sympathize with him there. He's the saint as psychopath, or the psychopath as saint. Whichever way, he's doing good.'

'And when this saintly figure moves on? What then? You'll find another beach redeemer?'

'We won't need to. Crawford's unique. If and when he goes everything will keep on running.'

'Will it? How?'

'The formula works. He stumbled on the first and last truth about the leisure society, and perhaps all societies. Crime and creativity go together, and always have done. The greater the sense of crime, the greater the civic awareness and richer the civilization. Nothing else binds a community together. It's a strange paradox.'

'But, Charles . . .' Paula stopped me as I lifted the suitcases from the bed. 'When he leaves, what will happen? What holds everything together?'

I knew that Paula was trying to lead me on, guiding me through an equation that I had refused to solve. 'Self-interest, I hope. Estrella de Mar seems to be doing all right.'

'Actually, I've a few more patients with insomnia. By the way, has he started a film club?'

'That's an odd question.' I hesitated, aware that we were both looking down at the bed. 'As a matter of fact, he has. He's put me in charge. How did you guess?'

'It wasn't a guess. This is the moment for Bobby Crawford to start a film club.'

A film club? I repeated Paula's almost too-clever question as I drove back to the Residencia. But Crawford's argument still convinced me. There came a point when the waking sleeper stepped from his bed and stared at himself in the mirror, and a film club provided that role. Nonetheless, the example of Paula's pornographic movie was a warning. When I recruited my members I would make sure that they were genuine enthusiasts of the lens, eager to add to the growing self-awareness of a community. Crawford's porno-films were too divisive. What had begun as a mischievous bedroom romp had turned into a sordid exploitation of a few distressed women, Paula among them. I missed her now, but she was still picking the scab of her hostility to Crawford. His energy and optimism, his open-eyed seizing of the day, irritated her in some way.

As I drove through the gates of the Residencia I was already thinking of the first film I would supervise, perhaps even script and direct. Ideas had begun to stir, prompted by the white geometry of the Costasol complex. I visualized a *Last Year at Marienbad* for the 1990s, a study of the waking of a community by a mysterious intruder, with a hint of Pasolini's *Theorem* . . .

Eager to settle into the villa, to test the water in the pool and return the serves of the tennis machine, I accelerated round the last bend and almost struck a slim, silver-haired man standing outside my gates. Braking hard, I slewed the car across the road and came to a jolting halt a few inches from the massive trunk of the eucalyptus tree that presided over the drive.

'Dr Sanger . . . I nearly hit you.' I switched off the engine and tried to steady my hands. 'Doctor, you look exhausted . . . are you all right?'

'I think so. Mr Prentice? I'm sorry.' He leaned against the offside wing, and then stepped away from the car, one hand reaching out to the sunlight. He was clearly distracted by more than one anxiety, and I assumed that he had lost his glasses or a set of keys. He glanced up and down the road and then peered into the rear seat of the Citroën, his lips moving as he silently mouthed a name.

'Can I help you?' Anxious for him, I stepped from the car. 'Dr Sanger . . . ?'

'I'm looking for one of my patients. She may have lost herself. Did you see anyone as you drove here?'

'A young woman? No.'

'You didn't see her?' Sanger stared at my face, unsure whether to confide in me. 'Slim, with very short hair, and a gold ring in her lip, wearing a man's dressing-gown. Laurie Fox – she was staying with me during her treatment. I feel responsible for her.'

'Of course.' I searched the empty avenue. 'I'm afraid I haven't seen her. I'm sure she'll come back.'

'Perhaps. She was sitting by the pool as I prepared lunch – then she was gone. Your friend Mr Crawford was here, at your house. I see we're now to be neighbours.' Sanger gazed at the villa, his face as blanched as his silver hair. 'Crawford may have given her a lift.'

I smiled as reassuringly as I could at this troubled man, realizing for the first time the emotional appeal to women of a vulnerable psychiatrist. 'A lift? Yes, I think he might.'

'I assume so. If you see Crawford, if he telephones you, ask him to return her. I promised her father that I would help her. It's important that she take the medication I prescribed.' Sanger massaged his cheeks with one hand, trying to force the blood back into his face. 'Crawford has so many notions of his own. For him a young woman should be . . .'

'. . . free to be unhappy?'

'Exactly. But for Laurie Fox unhappiness is not a therapeutic option. I find it difficult to talk to Crawford.'

'I'd guess that he dislikes psychiatrists.'

'We've let him down. He needed our help, Mr Prentice. He still does . . .'

Murmuring to himself, Sanger turned away from me, slowly clapping his hands at the silent trees.

*　　　*　　　*

He was still wandering up and down the road as I carried my suitcases past the sparkling pool. As Elizabeth Shand had promised, a first consignment of furniture had been delivered – a black leather sofa and an elegant Eames chair, a giant television set and a double bed, mattress and linen. But the villa was still pleasingly empty, and the rooms were the white spaces of opportunity I had relished on my first visit.

After leaving my suitcases in the bedroom I strolled around the upper floor, and strayed briefly into the maid's room. From the window I watched Sanger standing on his hill and gazing bleakly at the silent swimming pool, the nightdress in his hands. No longer reflected by the calm water, the light in the compound had grown dimmer, as if its soul had slipped away across the rooftops.

The window was open, and the ash of a loosely wrapped cigarette lay on the sill. I could imagine Crawford signalling to Laurie Fox, letting the scent of cannabis drift towards this young woman entombed in her doses of Largactil. But I was no longer interested in the gloomy psychiatrist and his youthful lover. I assumed that Crawford was with her, speeding in the Porsche to one of his safe houses on the northern perimeter road, to the kind of camaraderie provided by Raissa Livingston.

I unpacked and showered, then helped myself to the tapas in the refrigerator and the Keswick sisters' courtesy bottle of champagne. Sitting on the terrace beside the pool, I looked through the selection of cards pushed through the letter slot. There were advertisements for taxi services and yacht-brokers, estate agents and investment advisers. One card, so freshly printed that its ink was damp, puffed a local mother-and-daughter massage-service – 'Dawn and Daphne, for a new sensation in massage. Deep, intimate, discreet. Will visit, 5 p.m. to 5 a.m.'

So the netherworld of the Residencia Costasol was stepping out into the sun. A mobile phone lay on the table beside me, another useful gift from Betty Shand. I guessed that Crawford had left the massage-service card, knowing that I would be intrigued. Commercial sex demanded special skills from the client as much as from the provider. Self-styled mother-and-daughter teams always made me uneasy, especially in Taipei or Seoul, where too many were real mothers and daughters. However pleasant, with 'mother' pacing the over-eager 'daughter', I often felt that I was the intermediary in an act of incest.

I pushed away the mobile phone, then raised it and dialled the number. A woman's recorded voice with a soft Lancashire accent informed me that there were vacancies that evening, and invited me to leave my telephone number. As I knew, Bobby Crawford made all things possible, assuaged all guilts and drew back the bedspread that lay over our lives and dreams.

25

Carnival Day

THE RESIDENCIA COSTASOL was celebrating itself, saluting its happy return to life. From the balcony of my office on the first floor of the sports club I watched the line of carnival floats across the plaza, bedecked with flowers and bunting, cheered on by an exuberant crowd whose voices almost drowned the selections from Gilbert and Sullivan relayed from the loudspeakers along the route. A cloud of petals and confetti hung in the air over the revellers' heads, borne aloft by the lungs of the tourists drawn into the Residencia from Estrella de Mar and the resorts along the coast.

For three days all thoughts of security had been abandoned. Intrigued by the first firework displays, the visitors had parked their cars along the beach, and soon overwhelmed the guards at the gatehouse. Martin Lindsay, the retired Life Guards colonel who was the elected mayor of the Residencia Costasol, swiftly consulted his fellow-councillors and ordered the security system to shut down its computers for the duration of the festival. The Costasol Arts Fair, scheduled to last a single afternoon, was now in its second day and showed every sign of outrunning another night.

Towed by Lindsay's Range Rover, a float passed the sports club and began its circuit of the plaza. A black silk banner bearing the legend 'The Residencia Philharmonic Players' wafted above the dozen members of the orchestra, who sat at their music stands, bows working across their violins and

286

cellos while the pianist strummed the keyboard of a white baby grand and a graceful harpist in an ivory evening gown plucked the strings of a harp decked with yellow roses. The medley of Vivaldi and Mozart struggled gamely with the cheers of the tourists raising their glasses outside the crowded cafés of the shopping mall.

Two handsome women members, still in their tennis whites, stepped from my office on to the balcony and gripped the rail, waving their rackets at another float that passed below us.

'Good God! Is that Fiona Taylor?'

'How wonderful – she's completely starkers!'

Designed by the Costasol Arts Club, the float carried a mock-up of an artist's studio. Six easels stood at one end of the tableau, artists in Victorian smocks sketching away with their charcoal and crayons. A sculptor, Teddy Taylor, an ear, nose and throat specialist from Purley, worked at his clay table, fashioning a model of his decorous blonde wife. Dressed in a flesh-coloured skinsuit, she posed like Lady Godiva on a stuffed studio horse, smiling broadly at the tourists who wolf-whistled at her.

'Bobby Crawford – he's arrived!' One of the tennis ladies began to shriek, almost knocking my vodka and tonic from the rail. 'Come on, Bobby, let's see you pose!'

A newsreel location van of a Spanish TV channel kept pace with the arts float, its cameraman filming the glamorous sitter in close-up. Bobby Crawford stood behind the cameraman, steadying his arm as the convoy of vehicles turned around the plaza. Rose petals covered his blond hair and black batik shirt, and silver confetti spotted his sweating face and forehead, but he was too happy to brush them away. Grinning broadly, he waved to the tourists, toasting them with a glass of wine handed to him by a passing spectator. When the location van brushed against the float he leapt aboard, almost falling across the easels, picked himself up and embraced the beaming Fiona Taylor.

'Take it off! Bobby, you handsome sod!'

'Off, off off! Charles, order him to strip!'

The women beside me bounded like cheerleaders on their tennis pumps, rackets whirling above my head, and Crawford good-naturedly unbuttoned his shirt and exposed his hairless chest, striking a Byronic pose for the sculptor. A news agency photographer ran beside the float, and Crawford peeled off his shirt and hurled it to the crowd. When they reached the shopping mall he leapt from the float and ran bare-chested past the café tables, pursued by a squealing posse of teenage girls in carnival hats.

Exhausted by the noise and relentless good humour, I left the tennis ladies and took refuge in my office. Yet another tableau had reached the plaza, an amateurish effort by the Olde-Tyme Dancing Club, but the elderly couples trying to waltz on the swaying platform received as big a cheer as Lady Godiva.

The Residencia Costasol was happy with itself, and for good reason. During the past two months – the legal documents from Señor Danvila on my desk reminded me that Frank's trial began the next day – the explosion of civic activity had astonished even Bobby Crawford. At dinner with Elizabeth Shand the previous evening he had laughed and shaken his head over what I termed 'a fast-forward renaissance', all too embarrassed by the genie that had sprung from the bottle.

The somnolent township with its empty shopping mall and deserted sports club had transformed itself into another Estrella de Mar, as if an infectious but benevolent virus had floated along the coast, invading the sluggish nervous system of the Residencia and galvanizing it into life. An intact and self-sufficient community had sprung into being. Half a dozen new restaurants thrived around the plaza, all but one financed by Betty Shand and managed by the Keswick sisters. Two nightclubs had opened near the marina, the Milroy for the older set and Bliss's for the younger. The town council met weekly at the Anglican church, whose Sunday congregations packed its pews. Meanwhile, the volunteer security patrols kept the sun-coast riff-raff from any access to the complex. A host of societies pursued every pastime from origami to hydrotherapy, the tango to t'ai chi. And all this, whatever my doubts, seemed to have been conjured into existence by the dedication of one man.

'Bobby, you're a new kind of Messiah,' I often told him. 'The Imam of the marina, the Zoroaster of the beach umbrella . . .'

'No, Charles – I'm a facilitator.'

'I'm still not sure that it isn't a huge coincidence, but I take off my hat to you.'

'Put it back on. They did it, not me. I was just the donkey-engine . . .'

With his unfeigned modesty, Crawford was quick to pass any credit to the people of the Residencia. As I had learned for myself, an immense reservoir of unused talent had lain dormant beneath the shaded awnings. The middle-class professionals who had dozed by their swimming pools were sometime lawyers and musicians, advertising and television executives, management consultants and local government officers. The skills base of the Residencia Costasol might not equal that of the Medicis' Florence, but it was far wider than most comparable towns in Europe or North America.

Even I had been touched by this infection of optimism and creativity. Resting by the pool in the evenings, I had sketched the outline of a book – 'Marco Polo: the World's First Tourist?' – that would be a history of tourism and its eclipse of the age of travel. After despairing of me for so many months, my

London agent was now bombarding me with faxes, urging me to provide him with a detailed synopsis. I frequently played bridge with Betty Shand and the Hennessys, reluctant though I was to leave the Residencia for Estrella de Mar and its baleful memories of the Hollinger fire, and had even been tempted to play a small part in a forthcoming production of Orton's *What the Butler Saw.*

From my office I looked down at the crowded swimming pool, at the busy restaurant and tennis courts, glad that I had played my role in bringing the Residencia back to life. Below me, Betty Shand was holding court at the open-air bar, keeping a motherly, if steely eye on a handsome young Russian, Yuri Mirikov; she had just recruited him as a special 'aerobics' coach. As she gazed at the scene around her, like a silken cobra sated after digesting a succulent goat, I could almost see the accumulating cash totals flicker past her eyes.

The Residencia was booming in every sense, an economy of cash, talent and civic pride that showed no signs of overheating. Newly refurbished yachts and power-cruisers crowded the marina, and Gunnar Andersson had recruited a full-time staff of mechanics to maintain the engines and navigation gear. The waterlogged hulk of the *Halcyon* still lay against its lighter, like the carcass of a forgotten whale lashed to the tender of a factory ship, but was scarcely visible through the forest of gleaming masts.

Members crowded the balcony outside my office, cheering on another carnival float, a presentation by the rapid response group of the Residencia's security service. Together they enacted the arrest of two car thieves who had strayed down the coast from Fuengirola, expertly pinioning and handcuffing the startled youths. Yet among all this good humour one long face remained, its severe expression unmoved by the festive air. As the thieves' fates were decided in a loudspeaker-borne crackle of walkie-talkies and mobile phones, I noticed Paula

Hamilton step on to the balcony. She wore a dark suit and white blouse, and carried her doctor's valise. Glad to see her, I waved through my office windows, though with her disapproving and hangdog look she more and more resembled a mendicant physician wandering through the kingdom of health in search of a single sick patient.

At my urging she had joined the sports club, and would often swim in the early morning, slipping into the water as the last of the night's revellers drove from the car park. She practised with Helmut at the tennis courts, trying to control her unwieldy, big-elbowed game. Once I knocked up with her, but she played in such a lacklustre way that I assumed she had joined the club for reasons of her own, perhaps keeping an eye open for any rival doctors on her turf.

She watched from the balcony as the security tableau passed the café crowds, and smiled briefly when Bobby Crawford, in a borrowed Hawaiian shirt, sprang on to the float and mimed a drunken British lager lout. Within seconds he turned the security exercise into a Keystone Kops routine, with the guards tripping over their own feet and scrabbling for the scattered mobile phones as the earpieces squawked their manic orders.

She turned away, clearly troubled by something, and noticed me watching her from my office. With a shy smile she opened the door and leaned against the glass panel.

'Paula . . . you look tired.' I offered her my chair. 'All this noise – you probably need a drink.'

'Thanks, I do. Why is other people's happiness so exhausting?'

'They've a lot to celebrate. Sit down, I'll ring for whatever you want. You do the prescribing.'

'Nothing. Just some mineral water.' She smiled brightly, showing her strong teeth, and tossed her black hair over her shoulders. She watched Crawford playing the fool, juggling with three mobile phones in a shower of petals and confetti. 'Bobby Crawford . . . he's popular, isn't he? Your saintly psychopath. Everyone adores him.'

'Don't you, Paula?'

'No.' She bit her lip, as if trying to erase the memory of a kiss. 'I don't think I do.'

'He meant a lot to you once.'

'Not now. I've seen his other sides.'

'They're well under control. I don't know why you're so obsessed by him.' I gestured to the crowds in the plaza, the hooting sirens and clouds of petals. 'Look at what he's done. Do you remember the Residencia three months ago?'

'Of course. I came here a lot.'

'Exactly. The place was filled with your patients. Not so many now, I dare say.'

'Almost none at all.' She placed her valise on my desk and sat beside it, nodding to herself. 'A few leukaemias I send back to London. Shin-splints from all this unnecessary exercise. Even a few cases of VD. But a little old-fashioned gonorrhoea wouldn't surprise you.'

'Not really.' I shrugged tolerantly. 'You'd expect it, given a bigger turnover of sexual partners. It's a disease of social contact – like flu, or golf.'

'There are other social diseases, some a lot more serious – like a taste for kiddie-porn.'

'Pretty rare in the Residencia.'

'But surprisingly contagious.' Paula treated me to her severest schoolmistressy gaze. 'People who think they're immune suddenly catch a rogue cross-infection from all the other porn they're looking at.'

'Paula . . . we've tried to keep it down. There's a problem in the Residencia – there are almost no children. People miss them, so sexual fantasies get mixed up with nostalgia. You can't blame Bobby Crawford for that.'

'I blame him for everything. And you – you're almost as responsible as Crawford. He's totally corrupted you.'

'That's absurd. I'm planning a book, thinking about guitar lessons and a stage career, playing bridge again . . .'

'All noise.' Paula picked up the computer mouse and held it tightly in her hand, as if wanting to crush it. 'When you came here you were the *homme moyen sensuel*, full of hang-ups about your mother and little guilts about those teenaged whores you fuck in Bangkok. Now you haven't a moral care in the world. You're the right-hand man of the local crime czar and you aren't even aware of it.'

'Paula . . .' I reached out and tried to rescue the mouse from her. 'I've more doubts than you realize.'

'You're deluding yourself. Believe me, you totally support him.'

'Of course I do. Look at what he's achieved. I couldn't give a damn how many sculpture classes there are, the important thing is that people are thinking again, looking hard at who they are. They're building a meaningful world for themselves, not just fitting more locks to the front door. Everywhere you look – Britain, the States, western Europe – people are sealing themselves off into crime-free enclaves. That's a mistake – a certain level of crime is part of the necessary roughage of life. Total security is a disease of deprivation.'

'Maybe.' Paula stood up and strolled around the office, shaking her head at the festive tourists. 'He leaves tomorrow, thank heavens. What are you going to do when he's gone?'

'Things will run as before.'

'Are you sure? You need him. You need that energy and wide-eyed innocence.'

'We'll live without it. Once the carousel is spinning it doesn't need all that much of a push to keep it moving.'

'So you think.' Paula stared at the distant pueblos along the coast, their white walls lit by the sun. 'Where is he going?'

'Further down the beach. Calahonda – it's a huge complex. There are something like ten thousand Brits there.'

'They've got a surprise in store. So he's moving on, bringing cordon bleu and tango classes to the benighted people of the pueblos. He'll recruit another edgy wanderer like you and, at the snap of a few Polaroids, the poor man will see the light.' She turned to face me. 'You'll be at Frank's trial tomorrow?'

'Of course I will. That's why I came here.'

'Are you sure?' She sounded sceptical. 'He needs you. You haven't been even once to the jail in Malaga. Not once in nearly four months.'

'Paula, I know . . .' I tried to avoid her eyes. 'I should have been to see him. That guilty plea threw me – I felt he was trying to involve me in whatever troubled him. I wanted to crack the Hollinger case, and then Bobby Crawford came along. I felt a load off my shoulders . . .'

But Paula was no longer listening to me. She stepped to the window as the last of the floats arrived, bearing a mock-sunset of pink roses on which was superimposed 'The End'. A boisterous party was in progress on the float, and a dozen younger residents of the Costasol complex performed a dance medley to music played by a three-piece band. Knees and elbows scissored through a few bars of the Charleston, arms whirled in a forties jitterbug, hips gyrated through the twist.

In the centre of the dancers Bobby Crawford kept time, clapping as he led the troupe through the hokey cokey and the black bottom. His Hawaiian shirt was soaked with sweat, and he seemed to be on a cocaine high, his eyes raised to the clouds of confetti and petals as if he were ready to rise from the dance floor and float away among the helium balloons.

Not all the dancers, however, would join him. Stumbling beside Crawford was the derelict and exhausted figure of Laurie Fox, barely able to lift her feet to the music. Several beats behind, she lurched into the dancers around her and then fell against Crawford's chest, mouth ajar below her unfocused eyes. Her hair had grown into a fuzzy black pelt, through which the scars were still visible like failed attempts to trepan herself. Her grimy vest was stained with blood that had run from her bruised nose, and outlined her breasts as they rolled like moony heads.

As we watched, she fell to the floor, vomited among the petals and began to hunt for the nose-ring that had escaped from her bloody nostril. Barely breaking his dance-step, Crawford lifted her on to her feet, encouraging her with an eager smile and a brief slap.

'Poor child . . .' Paula hid her face behind one hand as the other reached for the security of her medical valise. 'She's probably had nothing for weeks except tequila and amphetamines. Can't you get Crawford to help her?'

'He has. I'm not being callous, Paula. She's doing what she wants, terrible though it is. Crawling towards her own death . . .'

'What on earth does that mean? And what happens when he goes? Will he take her with him?'

'Maybe. I doubt it.'

'He's used her, letting her degrade herself to excite everyone else.'

'This isn't her best day – the festival's too much for her. They love her down at the marina. She sings in a jazz bar by the boatyard. Even Andersson's climbed out of his gloomy shell and started to forget Bibi Jansen. She's better off there than lying in some drug-induced coma at the Princess Margaret Clinic. The sad thing is, you're not the only one who doesn't understand that.'

I pointed to the float as it circled the plaza, the band working itself into a final flourish. Laurie Fox had given up and now sat on the floor among the vomit and dancing feet. Walking abreast of her through the crowd was Dr Sanger, one hand raised in an attempt to touch her shoulder. With a determination that seemed surprising in this slim and diffident man, he pushed the tourists and cameramen out of his way and kept a protective eye on the young woman, calling to her when she seemed to fall asleep. Since her departure from the bungalow he had roamed the streets and cafés of the Residencia, content to catch a glimpse of her shouting from the passenger seat of Crawford's Porsche or shrieking from his speedboat as it sped down the canal to the open sea. I often watched him pacing around his pool and compulsively washing the discarded nightdress. When the float circled the shopping mall I waited for Sanger to leap aboard, but Crawford was unaware of the psychiatrist, his head raised to the sun as he danced through the shower of petals.

'Poor man . . . I hate that.' Paula turned her back to the scene and paced around my desk. 'I'm going – you'll be at court tomorrow?'

'Of course. But we'll meet at the party tonight.'

'The party?' Paula seemed surprised. 'Where – at your villa?'

'It starts at nine. Hennessy should have phoned you. It's Bobby Crawford's farewell. We're giving him a special send-off. I'll see you there.'

'I'm not sure. A party . . . ?' Paula fiddled with her valise, as if unable to cope with the notion. 'Who will be coming?'

'Everyone. The key Costasol crowd. Betty Shand, Colonel Lindsay, most of his council, the Keswick sisters – all the leading lights. It should be quite a bash. Betty Shand's supplying everything – buffet, champagne, canapés . . .'

'And enough lines of cocaine to burn out my nasal septum?'

'I dare say. Hennessy says there'll be a special barbecue. Let's hope we don't burn the place down.'

'And Crawford will be there?'

'To begin with. Then he'll leave us to it. He has to clear out his things and get off to Calahonda.'

'So it's a hand-over ceremony . . .' Paula was nodding to herself, her lower lip clamped between her teeth. Her face was paler, as if her blood had suddenly chilled. 'He'll officially pass his Pan-pipes to you.'

'In a way. Before the party I'll play a last game of tennis with him.'

'He'll let you beat him.' She unlocked and closed the valise, then adjusted my inkstand and noticed the set of car keys that I had found in the orchard at the Hollinger house. She picked them up and weighed them in her hand. 'The keys to your kingdom – to all Bobby Crawford's secret places?'

'No, they're a spare set of car keys. I found them in the . . . changing rooms at the Club Nautico. I've tried them out on dozens of cars, but none of them match. I ought to give them to Hennessy.'

'Hang on to them – you never know when they might come in useful.' Carrying the valise, she walked to the door, then turned to stare at me before kissing my cheek. 'Enjoy the tennis match. Perhaps you should tie your hands behind your back – it's the only way you might lose . . .'

I stepped on to the balcony and watched her drive away, blaring her horn at the tourists who crowded the plaza, as if refusing to acknowledge the festival cheer. Already I looked forward to dancing with her that evening. As she had said, the party was a transfer ceremony, though in many ways I had already taken over the running of Crawford's activities at the Residencia. For weeks he had spent more and more of his time away from the complex, exploring Calahonda and testing out the possibilities of his tonic regime. The administration of his underground imperium he left to me, confident that I now accepted the importance of everything he had achieved.

Of my original doubts, all had gone except for those

concerning his treatment of Laurie Fox. He had cared for and charmed her, constantly at her side as they roamed the bars and clubs in the evening. But he made no attempt to curb her cocaine and amphetamine hunger, as if this bruised and deteriorating young woman was an exotic creature to be exhibited in all her feral glory.

I knew that he was punishing Sanger for the sins of those psychiatrists who had failed to help him when he was a child. During the film sessions at the villa, when Laurie had sex in my bed with Yuri Mirikov, Betty Shand's Russian Adonis, Crawford would sometimes remove the black shrouds from the windows, taunting Sanger as the film lights blazed over the bungalow compound. She had slept with Sanger, he seemed to say, and perhaps with her father, and now with any man whom Crawford picked out during their tour of the evening bars.

I took no part in these ugly sessions, which had grown out of the film club I founded, just as I tried not to involve myself too closely in the criminal conspiracy that underpinned the life of the Residencia – the drugs supplied by Mahoud and Sonny Gardner to the network of dealers, the massage and escort services which had recruited so many bored widows and a few adventurous wives, the 'creative' cabarets that entertained the more corrupt parties, and the muscle squad of two former British Airways executives who quietly burgled and vandalized their way across the Residencia, damaging cars and fouling swimming pools in the cause of civic virtue.

Sitting at my desk, I listened to the strains of *Iolanthe* and thought of Paula Hamilton. Once Crawford had left the Residencia the creative tension he had imposed would begin to relax. I would see more of her again, play tennis with her and perhaps share the costs of a small yacht. I imagined us sailing along the coast, secure in our private world, as the cutwater clicked and the bottles of white Burgundy cooled in our wake . . .

Spray struck the awning of the poolside bar. A sudden uproar had broken out on the terrace, the sounds of overturned furniture and angry voices, followed by a woman's hysterical cries somewhere between laughter and pain. Drawn by the clamour, tourists were crossing the car park and firing the last of their plastic streamers towards the pool. Cheering each other on, they scrambled over the waist-high perimeter fence and climbed the grass verge to the open-air bar.

I left my office and quickly made my way down to the petal-strewn terrace. The members around the pool had left their sun-loungers and were gathering up their towels and magazines. Some laughed uneasily, but most seemed dismayed, hands shielding their faces from the spray. Elizabeth Shand had retreated behind the counter of the bar, and was snapping at the waiters and urging them towards the water. She shouted to Bobby Crawford, who stood on the diving board, calmly observing the spectacle in the pool.

'Bobby, for heaven's sake, this is too much! Can't you stop them? Charles, where are you? Speak to him!'

I stepped through the tourists crowding against the tables. Laurie Fox was swimming naked in the pool, thrashing the waves with her arms while the blood streamed from her nose. Her thighs were clasped around Mirikov's waist as she tried to have sex with him in the water. Screaming at the sky, she pressed her bloodied breasts to his mouth, then turned and began to shout at the watching tourists. One hand fumbled for the Russian's crotch as the other beat the surface, dashing the bloodied water against the legs of the appalled onlookers.

Then a silver-haired man forced himself past me, drops of spray on his clenched lips. Ignoring Crawford, who stood at ease on the diving board, Sanger pushed through the hooting tourists and kicked aside the tables. Without removing his shoes, he leapt into the shallow end and waded strongly through the waist-deep water. He pulled the embarrassed Mirikov on to his back, dunking the Russian's blond head. As Laurie Fox screamed in her demented way, spitting out the blood she had sucked into her mouth, Sanger seized her around the waist. He lost his footing in the deeper water, and they rolled together in the carmine waves. Silver hair now flecked with blood, Sanger held the young woman to his chest and carried her to the shallow end.

Everyone moved away as I knelt down and lifted her from his arms. Together we laid her on the verge among the sodden petals and confetti. I took a towel from a nearby sun-lounger and draped it over her shoulders, trying to staunch the blood from her nose. Sanger sat beside her, too exhausted to take her hand, water streaming from his silk jacket. He seemed blanched and shrunken, as if emerging from a bath of formaldehyde, but his eyes were steady and unevasive as he stared across the bloodied pool at Bobby Crawford.

When he was strong enough to stand, I helped him to his feet. Still dazed, he stared at the barely conscious young woman, brusquely waving away the now silent tourists who crowded the tables.

'We'll carry her to my car,' I told him. 'I'll give you a lift home. It's best if she stays with you from now on . . .'

26

The Last Party

LEAVING THE BEDROOM door ajar, Sanger watched the sleeping young woman for a few moments before turning to me. He gestured with the kidney dish and hypodermic that he held in his hand, as if ready to offer me a sedative dose, and touched the dark stains on his jacket, reminding himself that the blood was not his own. His usually pallid cheeks and forehead were flushed with anger, and he gazed in a disoriented way at the books on his shelves, putting a past phase of his life, with its too-thoughtful dependencies, for ever behind him.

'She'll sleep for a few hours. We'll go on to the terrace. You probably need to rest.'

I expected him to change, but he was scarcely aware of his still-dripping clothes and the wet prints that his leaking shoes left on the tiled floor. He led the way to the umbrella and chairs beside the pool. Taking my seat, I noticed the upstairs windows of my villa and realized how close they were to the bungalow compound, and that he would have heard every sound during our boisterous parties.

'It's very quiet here,' I told him, and pointed to the calm surface of the pool, disturbed only by a small insect that struggled with the jelly-like meniscus clasping its wings. 'Your tenants have gone.'

'The Frenchwoman and her daughter? They flew back to Paris. In some ways the ambience wasn't suitable for the child.'

Sanger drew a hand across his eyes in an attempt to clear his mind. 'Thank you for the lift. I couldn't have carried her here.'

'I'm sorry she . . . collapsed.' I tried to think of a word that would better describe the nightmarish descent of the past weeks. Concerned for Sanger, I added: 'She shouldn't have left you. In her way she was happy here.'

'Laurie never wanted to be happy.' Sanger ran a hand through his damp hair, and then stared at the clots of blood left on his fingers. But he made no attempt to smooth the dishevelled mane that he had once tended so carefully. 'She's one of those people who flinch from the very idea of happiness – in her mind nothing could be more boring or bourgeois. I helped her a little, as I helped Bibi Jansen. Doing absolutely nothing is a kind of therapy in itself.'

'What about the nosebleed?' It occurred to me that she might be bleeding to death in her drugged sleep. 'Are you sure it's stopped?'

'I cauterized the septum. It seems that Crawford punched her – another of his Zen statements, so he said.'

'Dr Sanger . . .' I wanted to pacify this unsettled man, whose eyes were fixed on the bedroom door. 'It's hard to believe, but Bobby Crawford was fond of Laurie.'

'Of course. In his own deranged way. He wanted her to find her true self, as he would call it – like everyone else at the Residencia Costasol. I'm sorry he took against me.'

'You're one of the very few people he personally resents. You're a psychiatrist . . .'

'And not the first one he's met.' Sanger noticed the water streaming from his shoes. 'I must change – do wait here and I'll bring something to drink. As a friend of Crawford's, it's important that you hear of the decision I've made.'

*   *   *

302

He returned ten minutes later, wearing sandals and a floor-length towelling robe. He had washed the blood from his hands and hair, but the careful grooming and dilettante manner now belonged to the past.

'Thank you again for your help,' he told me, as he set a tray of brandies and soda on the table. 'Laurie is sleeping, I'm glad to say. I've been anxious about her for months. It's difficult to know what to tell her father, though the poor man is scarcely in a frame of mind to care.'

'I feel the same way,' I assured him. 'It's not something I've enjoyed seeing.'

'Of course not.' Sanger nodded to me. 'Mr Prentice, I distinguish you completely from Bobby Crawford – and from Mrs Shand and Hennessy. My position here is ambiguous. Technically I've retired, but in fact I still practise, and Laurie Fox is one of my patients. I can put up with a certain amount of harassment from Crawford, but the time has come to speak out. Crawford must be stopped – I know you agree with me.'

'I'm not sure if I do.' I played with the brandy tumbler, aware that Sanger was watching the open windows of my villa. 'Some of his methods are a little too . . . aggressive, but on the whole he's a force for good.'

'Good?' Sanger took the tumbler from my hand. 'He uses violence quite openly, against Paula Hamilton and Laurie and anyone else who stands in his way. The Residencia Costasol is awash with cut-price drugs that he force-feeds into almost every house and apartment.'

'Dr Sanger . . . to Crawford's generation cocaine and amphetamines are no more than mood-enhancers, like brandy or Scotch. The drugs he loathes are the ones you prescribe – the tranquillizers, especially. Perhaps he was sedated for a long period as a boy, or by the army psychiatrists who had him cashiered. He told me once that they tried to steal his soul. He's not a corrupt man. In many ways he's an idealist. Look at what he's achieved in the Residencia Costasol. He's done so much good.'

'Even more frightening.' Sanger lowered his eyes from my villa, satisfied that no one was observing us. 'This man is a danger to everyone he meets. He travels from place to place along the coast with his tennis racket and his message of hope, but his vision is as toxic as snake venom. All this ceaseless activity, these art festivals and town councils are a form of social Parkinsonism. The so-called renaissance everyone sings about is bought at a price. Crawford is like L-dopa. Cataleptic patients wake up and begin to dance. They laugh, cry, speak and seem to recover their real selves. But the dosage must be increased, to the point where it will kill. We know what medicine Crawford prescribes. This is a social economy based on drug-dealing, theft, pornography and escort services – from top to bottom a condominium of crime.'

'But no one thinks of it as crime. Neither the victims nor the people who take part. There's a different set of social conventions, as there is in the boxing ring or the bull-fight arena. Theft and prostitution exist here, but everyone sees them as "good works" of a new kind. No one at the Residencia Costasol has reported a single crime.'

'The most telling fact of all.' Sanger brusquely pushed away a lock of hair that tried to intrude across his field of vision. 'The ultimate crime-based society is one where everyone is criminal and no one is aware of the fact. Mr Prentice, this will change.'

'You're going to the police?' I watched Sanger's jutting jaw, an unexpected strain of pugnacity. 'If you bring in the Spanish authorities you'll destroy everything that's good here. Besides, we already have our own volunteer police force.'

'The kind of police who enforce a rule of crime. Your retired stockbrokers and accountants are remarkably adept in the role of small-town criminals. One could almost assume that their professions were designed for just such a contingency.'

'Cabrera and his detectives have been here. They've found nothing. No one has ever been charged.'

'Except for your brother.' Sanger had softened his harsh tone. 'His trial starts tomorrow. How will he plead?'

'Guilty. It's a nightmarish kind of irony. He's the one man here who's completely innocent.'

'Then Crawford should take his place.' Sanger rose to his feet, ready for me to leave, his ears listening for any sounds from the bedroom. 'Go back to London, before you join Crawford in Zarzuella jail. He's changed you, Mr Prentice. You now accept his logic without understanding where it will lead. Remind yourself of the Hollinger fire and all those tragic deaths . . .'

Hearing a murmur from the bedroom, Sanger fastened his dressing-gown and left the terrace. When I let myself through the front door he was sitting on the bed beside Laurie Fox, a hand stroking her damp hair, a father and lover waiting for this wounded child to meet him once again in her waking sleep.

Delivery vans were parked in front of my gates, and workmen unloaded the chairs and trestle tables for the party that evening. The drinks and canapés would arrive later, ordered by Elizabeth Shand from one of the Keswick sisters' restaurants in the plaza. The party would begin at nine o'clock, giving me ample time to change after an hour's tennis with Crawford, our first and last game together.

As the workmen carried the chairs to the terrace I stood in the centre of the tennis court, my hand on the barrel of the practice machine. The conversation with Sanger had unsettled me. The once venial and effeminate psychiatrist had found a second, more determined self. He was working himself up into a confrontation with Crawford, probably fearing that he would try to abduct Laurie Fox when he set off for Calahonda. With a little help from Sanger, Inspector Cabrera would soon unearth the depots of drugs and pornography, and expose the car thieving and the dubious escort services.

Life in the Costasol complex, everything that Crawford and I had worked for, would come to an end as the frightened British residents, fearful of losing their residence permits, abandoned their clubs and societies and retreated into the twilight world of satellite television. A social experiment of the most ambitious and idealistic kind would fade in the settling dust of another moribund sun-coast resort.

I started the tennis machine, and listened to the first ball as it exploded from the barrel, thinking of a harder projectile that might be fired from a different weapon . . .

David Hennessy was at his desk on the ground floor of the sports club, scanning the computer screen while Elizabeth Shand stood behind him. The accumulating totals seemed to light up the tailored business suit into which she had changed, dressing the sleek fabric with a sheen of pesetas. I realized that the Costasol festival had ended, and that the profit-taking had begun. The tourists were leaving the plaza, and the cafés around the shopping mall were almost empty, the few patrons gazing out at a sea of litter and fading petals. The tennis courts and swimming pool of the sports club were deserted, and the members had left early to prepare for the evening's private parties. Wolfgang and Helmut stood by the draining pool, watching as the Spanish groundsmen changed the water and the waiters straightened the tables.

'Charles . . . ?' Hennessy stood up to look more closely at me. He had put aside his avuncular clubroom manner and now resembled a shrewd accountant faced with an extravagant and thoughtless client. 'That was generous of you, dear chap – helping Sanger with the girl. Was he right to take her, though . . . ?'

'She is his patient. And she obviously needed help.'

'Even so. The two of you turned a bit of horse-play into a medical emergency. Not exactly good for the members, would you think?'

'Never mind. You put an end to a nasty scene.' Elizabeth Shand picked up a scab of dried blood on my shirt, grimacing with distaste as if reminded of the messy and unreliable fluid coursing through even her cool veins. 'Bobby did so much to help her, but these kindnesses are never appreciated. You took her back to Sanger's bungalow?'

'He's looking after her. She's asleep now.'

'Good. Let's hope she remains asleep and gives us all a chance to calm our nerves. I must say Sanger's dedication to that damaged child is touching. Of course, I knew her father, another of those doctors with wandering hands. I only pray that Sanger can restrain himself.'

'I don't think he will.'

'Really? I feared as much. There's something deeply unsavoury about the thought. I always suspected that psychiatry was the ultimate form of seduction.'

I joined her at the window, and looked down at the grass verge scarred and trampled by the tourists. 'I talked to him before I left – I think he may go to the police.'

'What?' Elizabeth Shand's make-up seemed about to crack. 'Report himself for professional misconduct? David, what would the General Medical Council make of that?'

'I can't imagine, Betty.' Hennessy raised his hands to the heavens. 'I don't suppose the contingency has ever arisen. Are you sure about this, Charles? If the news got out it would cause a good few problems here. The London tabloids would have a field day.'

'This has nothing to do with Laurie Fox,' I explained. 'It's Bobby Crawford he's concerned about. Sanger loathes everything we've done here. I'm fairly certain he's going to lay the whole operation out in front of Cabrera.'

'How silly of him.' Elizabeth Shand gazed calmly at Hennessy, unsurprised by what I had told her. She rested her hand on my shirt and began to pick again at the dried blood. 'That's rather worrying, Charles. Thank you for letting us know.'

'Betty, it's more than a possibility. The scene in the pool pushed him over the edge.'

'It probably did. He's a curious man, with all those difficult moods. Why the girls like him I can't imagine.'

'We do need to head him off.' Trying to sound a more urgent note, I said: 'If Sanger sees Cabrera there'll be an army of detectives here, pulling up every floorboard.'

'We don't want that.' Hennessy switched off the computer and stared at the ceiling with the distracted expression of someone faced with a difficult crossword clue. 'It's a bit of a poser. Still, the party tonight should clear things up.'

'Exactly.' Elizabeth Shand nodded vigorously. 'A good party solves all sorts of problems.'

'Shall I invite him?' I asked her. 'You could have a friendly word with him, reassure him that everything will settle down once Bobby leaves for Calahonda.'

'No . . . I think not.' She picked away the last of Laurie Fox's blood. 'In fact, make sure you don't invite him.'

'He'd enjoy the party.'

'He will, anyway. You'll see, Charles . . .'

Scarcely reassured, I left the sports club and set off across the plaza, hoping to find Crawford and persuade him to take a more combative line with Elizabeth Shand. The festival had ended, and the last tourists had left the bars and cafés and returned to their cars beside the beach. I walked across the fading petals and confetti as a few helium balloons floated in a desultory way above the litter, hunting their own shadows.

The floats that had so entertained the crowds were drawn up in the supermarket compound, where half a dozen small children romped around them. Leading them in their game of hide and seek was Bobby Crawford, still tirelessly pouring out his energy and enthusiasm. As he leapt around the abandoned tableaux, arms wreathed in the tattered bunting, pretending to search for a squealing little girl who had hidden herself under the piano, he seemed like a forlorn Peter Pan trying to stir the remnants of his never-land into a second life. His Hawaiian shirt was stained with dust and sweat, but his eyes shone as eagerly as ever, driven by that dream of a happier world that had sustained him from childhood. In a sense he had turned the Costasol residents into children, filling their lives with adult toys and inviting them out to play.

'Charles . . . ?' Delighted to see me, he held the little girl in his arms and jumped from the float, the children hunting around him. 'I've been looking for you – how is Laurie?'

'She's all right, sleeping quietly. Sanger gave her a sedative. She's better off there.'

'Of course she is.' Crawford seemed surprised that I might have thought otherwise. 'For weeks I've been telling her to go back to him. She'd burned herself out, Charles, she needed to feel angry and depressed again – Sanger's the man for that. I couldn't help her, though God knows I tried.'

'Listen, Bobby . . .' I waited for him to calm himself, but he was still watching the children, ready to join them in another game. 'I'm concerned about Sanger. I'm fairly certain that he's going to –'

'Cabrera?' Crawford waved to the children as they ran off to join their parents by the supermarket entrance. 'I'm afraid he will, Charles. I've known it for a long time. He's an unhappy psychiatrist, and the police are the only way he can get back at me.'

'Bobby . . .' Anxious for him, I tried to distract him from the little girl waving to us. 'Is Sanger the reason why you're leaving the Residencia?'

'Good God, no! My work here is done. You can run the show by yourself, Charles. It's time for me to move down the coast. There's a whole world waiting out there, filled with people who need me.' He held my shoulder and surveyed the litter-strewn scene around him, with its faded bunting and drifting balloons. 'I have to dream for them, Charles, like those Siberian shamans – during times of stress, to give the tribe some sleep, the shaman dreams their dreams for them . . .'

'But, Bobby . . . Sanger may cause trouble. If he goes to Cabrera the Spanish police will overrun the Residencia and undo everything you've achieved.'

'You're worried, Charles – don't be.' Crawford was smiling at me like an affectionate brother. 'We'll talk about it at the party. Believe me, everything will be fine. We'll play a couple of sets this evening and you can show me the new backhand you've been practising.'

'Sanger is serious – I spoke to him an hour ago.'

'The party, Charles. There's nothing to fear. Sanger won't harm us. I've dealt with psychiatrists before – they're only interested in their own flaws, and spend their lives looking for them . . .'

He waved for a last time to the children driving away in their parents' cars, and then leaned against the float behind him, tearing a handful of petals from the floral sign of 'The End'. He watched them flutter to the ground. For once he seemed tired, exhausted by the responsibilities he had borne, and numbed by the vastness of the task that lay ahead of him, the endless coasts waiting to be brought to life.

Reviving himself, he slapped my shoulder. 'Think of the

future, Charles. Imagine the Costa del Sol as another Veneto. Somewhere here a new Venice might be born.'

'Why not? You've given them every chance, Bobby.'

'The important thing is to hold them together.' Crawford took my arm as we strolled back to the sports club. 'Things may happen that will surprise you, even shock you, Charles. But it's vital that we stay together, and keep the memory alive of everything we've done. Sometimes it's necessary to go too far just to stay in the same place. Be with you in an hour – I can't wait to see that backhand . . .'

I was practising on the court when the telephone rang, but I ignored the call and concentrated on the barrage of balls from the tennis machine, returning them deep to the baseline. The telephone drilled away in the empty house, its sound magnified by the lines of gilt chairs.

'Charles . . . ?'

'What is it? Who's this?'

'Paula. I'm calling from the Club Nautico.' She seemed self-controlled but oddly strained. 'Can you come over?'

'I'm playing tennis. When exactly?'

'Now. It's important, Charles. It's vital that you be here.'

'Why? There's the party this evening. Can't it wait till then?'

'No. You must come now.' She paused and muffled the telephone, speaking to someone beside her, and then continued: 'Frank and Inspector Cabrera are here. They need to see you.'

'Frank? What is it? Is he all right?'

'Yes. But they must see you. It's about the Hollinger fire. We're in the basement garage at the Club. We'll wait for you here. And, Charles . . .'

'What is it?'

'Don't tell anyone you're coming. And bring those spare car keys. The ones I saw this morning in your office. Cabrera is very interested in them . . .'

27

An Invitation to the Underworld

THE CLUB NAUTICO had closed for the day, its awnings furled over the silent balconies, a house of secrets hoarding its memories from the sun. I left the Citroën in the car park and walked down the ramp to the basement garage. During the drive from the Residencia Costasol I had tried to prepare myself for the face-to-face meeting with Frank, all too aware of how much everything had changed between us. We had ceased to be the brothers bonded together by their unhappy mother, and in a larger sense had ceased to be brothers at all.

In my hand I held the car keys that I had found in the orchard above the Hollinger house. As I crossed the gloomy basement I watched them glitter in the trembling light of a defective neon tube. For Frank to have been released from prison on the eve of his trial, even into the custody of Inspector Cabrera, suggested that vital new evidence had emerged, contradicting his confession and incriminating the true murderer.

I stood at the bottom of the ramp, surprised to find that there were no uniformed police guarding the garage. A dozen cars were parked in the numbered bays, Frank's dusty Jaguar against a corner wall with its police stickers peeling from the windshield.

Then I noticed that the car parked next to the Jaguar was Paula Hamilton's small BMW. She watched from the driver's seat as I walked towards her, her hands gripping the steering wheel as if ready to make a quick getaway, her slim face almost jaundiced in the yellow light. A man sat beside her, head hidden behind the sun vizor. He wore a motor-cyclist's leather jacket, of a kind Frank would never have owned, perhaps lent to him from the prison stores.

'Frank . . . you're free. Thank God!'

When I reached the BMW I felt all my old affection surge back. I smiled through the insect-scored glass, ready to embrace him as the doors opened. Paula stepped from the car, face pinched in the stuttering light, her eyes avoiding me. From the passenger seat Gunnar Andersson extended his bony knees, hands clasping the roof while he lifted himself on to his feet. He buttoned the leather collar across his throat and walked around the rear of the car. He took his place behind Paula and stared sombrely at the keys in my hand, his sallow cheeks even more gaunt in the cement half-light.

'Paula – where's Frank?'

'He's not here.' Calmly, she met my eyes. 'We needed to talk to you.'

'Then where is he? In his apartment? What about Cabrera?'

'They aren't here. Frank's in Zarzuella prison, waiting for the trial tomorrow.' She tried to smile in the glare of defective neon. 'I'm sorry, Charles, but we had to get you here.'

'Why? What is all this?' I stared around me, trying to see through the windows of the parked cars, still certain that Frank was sitting in the rear seat of an unmarked police vehicle. 'This is absurd – we can talk at the party tonight.'

'No – you mustn't go to the party!' Paula held my wrist and tried to shake me, as if rousing a sedated patient. 'Charles, for heaven's sake . . . Cancel the party!'

'I can't. Why cancel it? The party's celebrating Bobby Crawford's farewell.'

'It won't be just Crawford's farewell. Can't you understand? People are going to die. There'll be a huge fire.'

'Where? At the villa? Paula, that's absurd – no one wants to harm Crawford.'

'It's not Crawford they're after. The fire will be at Sanger's bungalow. They'll kill him and anyone else there.'

I turned away from her, unsettled by her fierce gaze, still hoping that Cabrera would step through one of the nearby maintenance doors. When I stared at Andersson, waiting for him to speak out and contradict her, he began to nod slowly, lips repeating her words.

'Paula, tell me . . .' I freed my wrist from her strong grip. 'When did you hear about this fire?'

'Gunnar told me this afternoon. They all know about it. Everything's planned – that's why they've closed the Club Nautico.'

The Swede stood behind Paula, his gothic features barely visible in the greasy air. When he nodded, his head was bowed.

'That's impossible!' I drummed my fist against the windshield of Paula's car. 'I spoke to Crawford an hour ago. No one could have planned anything so quickly.'

'They've known for weeks.' Paula tried to calm my hands, holding them against her breasts. She spoke clearly, in a strained but matter-of-fact voice. 'It's all arranged – the party is just the cover. They've prepared explosives, some sort of petrol bomb set off by marine detonators. Charles, it's all true. They're taking advantage of you.'

'I can't believe it . . .' I pushed past Paula, ready to confront Andersson, but he stepped away and stared at me across the roof of Frank's car. 'Andersson – is this true?'

'Completely.' The Swede's eyes, which had retreated into their deep orbits, now emerged briefly. 'I didn't hear who the target was until this morning. They needed some help with the fusing system – Mahoud and Sonny Gardner. While Sanger was out looking for Laurie they broke into the crawl space below the bungalow and then fitted the bomb under the floorboards of Sanger's bedroom. They didn't tell me, but I think there's gasoline in the sprinkler system – within minutes everything will be ash.'

'And who's in charge of all this – Crawford?'

'No.' Reluctantly, Paula shook her head. 'He'll be miles away in Calahonda. Drinking with friends at the new tennis club.'

'But you say he planned everything?'

'Not exactly. In fact, he knows almost nothing about the details.'

'Then who does? Mahoud and Sonny Gardner didn't dream this up themselves. Who's behind it all?'

Paula wiped the smudge left by my fist on her windscreen. 'There's no single person. They're in it together – Betty Shand, Hennessy, the Keswick sisters, and most of the people you saw at Bibi Jansen's funeral.'

'But why do they want to kill Sanger? Because he's going to the police?'

'No, they didn't think of that. No one even knew until today, when you talked to Betty Shand and Hennessy.'

'Then what conceivable motive is there? Why pick Sanger as the target?'

'For the same reason they picked the Hollingers.'

Paula steadied me when I swayed against the car, suddenly dizzied by the trembling light. I realized for the first time that I was involved in a conspiracy to kill the psychiatrist. Paula squeezed my arms, trying to pump the chilled blood back to my heart.

'All right . . .' I leaned against Frank's car, and waited until my breath was even. 'You can tell me now, Paula – why were the Hollingers killed? You've always known.'

Paula stood beside me, waiting until I calmed myself. Her face was composed, but she seemed to speak from behind a mask, like a tour guide at some macabre historical site.

'Why were they killed? For the sake of Estrella de Mar and all that Crawford had done for us. To stop everything falling apart when he left. Without the Hollinger fire Estrella de Mar would have sunk back into itself and turned into just another brain-dead town on the coast.'

'But how does that explain all those deaths? Five people were murdered.'

'Charles . . .' Paula turned to Andersson, hoping that he would help her, but the Swede was staring at the instrument panel of the Jaguar. Controlling herself, she continued: 'A great crime was needed, something terrible and spectacular that would bind everyone together, seal them into a sense of guilt that would keep Estrella de Mar going for ever. It wasn't enough to remember Bobby Crawford and all the minor crimes he committed – the burglaries and drugs and sex-films. The people of Estrella de Mar had to commit a major crime themselves, something violent and dramatic, up on a hill where everyone could see it, so we'd all feel guilty for ever.'

'But why the Hollingers?'

'Because they were so visible. Anyone would have done, but they had the big house on the hill. They'd begun to cause trouble for Betty Shand, and threatened to bring in the Spanish police. So the finger pointed to them. *Tant pis.*'

'And who did start the Hollinger fire? Not Crawford?'

'No – he was playing tennis with his machine at the Club Nautico. He knew nothing about the detailed plans. I don't think he knew the Hollingers were the target.'

'Then who did? Who planned the fire?'

Paula lowered her head, trying to hide her cheeks behind the black tresses that fell from her temples. 'All of us. We all did.'

'All of you? Not the whole of Estrella de Mar?'

'No. Just the same key group – Betty Shand and the others, Hennessy, Mahoud and Sonny Gardner. Even Gunnar here.'

'Andersson? But Bibi Jansen died in the fire.' I turned accusingly towards the Swede. 'You loved her.'

Andersson stared stony-faced at the garage ramp, feet shifting, ready to race away and join the wind. He spoke tersely, as if he had already heard his words repeated a hundred times inside his echoing head. 'I did love her. I know it looks bad for me – Crawford had taken her away and made her pregnant, she went to live with the Hollingers . . . But I didn't want her to die. She should have got out by the escape stairs. But the fire was so strong.' He tore the police tape from the Jaguar's windows and crushed it in his hands.

I left him and turned to Paula. 'And what about you?'

She pressed her lips together, reluctant to let the words emerge. 'They didn't tell me what they planned – I thought it was some sort of glorified prank that would send up the Hollingers' feudal notion of how to run a party. The idea was to start a small fire in the house, let off some smoke bombs and drive them down the fire escape. At last they'd have to mingle with their guests.'

'But why the ether? It's not all that flammable, compared with petrol or kerosene.'

'Exactly. They needed a volatile liquid, and asked me to supply it. The real motive was to bind me to them, and they were right. Mahoud added petrol to the ether, and I have five deaths on my hands.' Angry with herself, she brushed the hair out of her eyes and gazed coldly at her reflection in the windscreen. 'I was a fool – I should have guessed what they were really planning. But I was under Bobby Crawford's spell. He'd created Estrella de Mar, and I believed in him. After the fire I knew people would go on killing for him, and that he had to be stopped. Still, he and Betty Shand were right – the fire and the deaths held everyone together and kept Estrella de Mar alive. Now they plan to do the same thing for the Residencia Costasol, with poor old Sanger as the sacrifice. If

Laurie Fox dies with him in his bed that makes it all the more lurid – no one will ever forget it, and the bridge parties and sculpture classes will run for ever.'

'And Frank? Where was he in all this?'

Paula wiped the dust from her hands. 'Did you bring the car keys? The ones I saw on your desk?'

'They're here.' I took them from my pocket. 'Do you want them?'

'Try the door.'

'Your BMW? I already have – weeks ago, when we first met. I've tried every car in Estrella de Mar. They don't fit.'

'Charles . . . not my car. Try the Jaguar.'

'Frank's car?' I stepped past her, wiped the grime from the lock on the driver's door and inserted the key. The socket was stiff, and I felt a surge of relief that the key failed to fit and Frank was still innocent. But when I reversed the key I heard the four-door locking mechanism unclasp itself.

I lifted the handle, opened the door and gazed into the car's musty interior, at the route maps and driving gloves on the passenger seat, and the copy of my travel guide to Calabria on the rear shelf. A sense of loss and exhaustion came over me, as if all the blood had been drained from my body in some blundered transfusion. I no longer wanted to breathe, and sat in the driving seat with my feet on the garage floor. Paula knelt beside me, a hand pressing my diaphragm, eyes watching the pulse in my neck.

'Charles – are you all right?'

'So Frank was there. He took part in the Hollinger fire, after all. Did he plan it?'

'No, but he knew something spectacular was going to happen. He accepted that Bobby Crawford was right, that once he left Estrella de Mar everything he'd done would fall apart. We needed something to remember him by. Frank thought the fire would be some kind of stunt for the Queen's birthday.

He didn't realize that the Hollingers would be trapped in the house and burn to death. Frank felt responsible, since he organized everything.'

'And you all played a part?'

'All of us. I ordered the ether from a laboratory supplier in Malaga, Betty Shand moved it around in one of her vans, the Keswick sisters stored it in their refrigerators at the Restaurant du Cap. Sonny Gardner buried the flagons in the orchard. By then Mahoud had secretly poured off most of the ether and refilled them with petrol. Frank and Mahoud dug up the flagons a few minutes before the loyal toast and carried them into the kitchen while the housekeeper was serving the canapés on the terrace. Cabrera's timetable was pretty well right.'

'But who rigged the air-conditioning system? Frank?'

'I did.' Andersson stared at his hands, trying to pick the oily flakes from his nails. He spoke in a low voice, as if afraid of being overheard. 'Frank asked me to fix the system so that it filled the house with coloured smoke. Mahoud and I drove there in the afternoon when the housekeeper was busy. I told her I was the maintenance engineer and that Mahoud was my assistant. I opened the intake manifold and showed Mahoud where to put the smoke flares.'

'And then?'

Andersson raised his long hands, exposing his wrists as if offering them to an axe. 'After the Queen's toast Frank left Mahoud in the kitchen and climbed the stairs to the fireplace. He took a small carpet from the floor, laid it on the grate and set it alight. He didn't know that Mahoud had drained the reservoir of the humidifier and filled it with gasoline. After Mahoud left he switched on the air-conditioning system to warn the Hollingers. But no smoke came out of the ventilation grilles . . .'

'So Frank wasn't aware there would be an explosion?' I let Paula help me from the driving seat. 'Even so, all this petrol and ether . . . it's insane. You must have realized the risk of the whole house going up.'

Paula pressed her fist to her cheek, searching for her old bruise. 'Yes, but we didn't let ourselves think about that. We needed a spectacle for Bobby Crawford – the Hollingers in a panic, coloured smoke coming out of their ears, perhaps a little damage to the house. The fireplace was huge – Frank said that if the flames did spread they'd take half an hour to get a hold on the staircase. By then the guests would have broken into the house and set up a human chain from the swimming pool. No one was going to die.'

'No one? Did you really believe that? So the whole thing went wrong. What happened to Frank after the explosion?'

Paula grimaced at the memory. 'He ran off when he saw what had happened. He was totally shattered by it all, he could hardly speak. He told me he'd tried to hide the unused flagons but somehow lost his car keys. Gunnar found them the next day when he was flying his hang-glider. They were all we had. We wanted to report Crawford and Betty Shand to the police but there was no evidence against them. Crawford didn't know we would set fire to the Hollinger house, and he'd taken no part in the planning. If we'd confessed to Cabrera all of us would have been charged and the one person really responsible would have escaped. Frank pleaded guilty to save us.'

'So you said nothing until I came along. It was you who fed me the porno-cassette I found in Anne Hollinger's bedroom.'

'Yes – I hoped you'd recognize Crawford and Mahoud, or at least work out where the apartment was.'

'That bit was easy. But I might never have seen the cassette in Anne Hollinger's bedroom.'

'I know. At first I was going to leave it in the Bentley and get Miguel to show you over the car. Then I saw you staring at her TV set – you were so curious to know what she'd been watching as she died.'

'That's true . . . I hate to have to say it. And the cocaine sachet in Frank's desk? Cabrera's men would have found that in seconds.'

Paula turned her back to me, still uneasy at the thought of the tape. 'I put it there when David Hennessy told me you were flying in from London. I wanted to lead you to Crawford, and make you realize there was more to Frank and Estrella de Mar than a picture-postcard resort. If you thought Crawford was involved in the fire you might have exposed his other activities. He'd have been charged with drug-dealing and car thefts and spent the next ten years in jail.'

'But instead I was drawn to him like everyone else. And the car keys?'

'The only thing left was to steer you towards Frank. If you knew he was involved in the fire it would have blown the lid off everything.'

'So you got Miguel to leave the keys in the orchard. What made you think I might go back there?'

'You never stopped looking at the house.' Paula reached out and touched my chest, smiling for the first time. 'Poor man, you were absolutely obsessed with the place. Crawford could see that too – that's why he left you by the steps to the observation platform. Even then he was preparing you for the next great fire.'

'But he didn't know the keys were waiting for me. Still, I might never have seen them. Or was that where the hang-glider came in?'

'I flew the glider.' Andersson raised his arms and gripped an imaginary control bar. 'I guided you towards the keys, then chased you down to the cemetery. Paula was waiting on the Kawasaki.'

'Paula? That was you in the menacing leather?'

'We wanted to frighten you, make you realize that Estrella de Mar was a dangerous place.' Paula took the keys from the Jaguar's door and gripped them tightly. 'We watched you chasing Crawford all over Estrella de Mar and guessed that he'd take you back to the Hollinger house. Luckily, you found the keys and began to test them on all the cars.'

'But I never tested Frank's car.' I patted the roof of the dusty Jaguar. 'I took for granted this was one car I didn't need to test. Meanwhile Frank had pleaded guilty, the Hollingers were dead, and the rest of you were locked into Crawford's insane little kingdom. Yet Bibi Jansen died in the fire – didn't he feel that was a high price to pay?'

'Of course he did.' Paula stared at me through her tears, refusing to wipe them away. 'When we killed Crawford's child we committed a crime against him – that bound us to him even more tightly.'

'And Sanger? Did he know the truth about the fire?'

'No. Apart from you he was almost the only person at the funeral who didn't. He must have guessed.'

'Even so, he never went to the police. Nor did anyone else, though most of them can't have expected that the Hollingers would die in the blaze.'

'They had their businesses to run. The Hollinger fire was good news for the cash tills. No one lay around watching television, they went out and calmed their nerves by spending money. The whole thing was a nightmare, but the right man had pleaded guilty. Technically, Frank had started the fire. Most people didn't know about Mahoud and the petrol in the air-conditioning system – that was Betty Shand's idea, along with Hennessy and Sonny Gardner. Everyone else saw it as the kind of tragic accident that happens when a party trick goes wrong. God knows, I did myself. I'd helped to murder all those people, and I almost accepted it. Charles, that's why we have to stop the party tonight.'

As she raised her arms I briefly embraced her, trying to still her shaking shoulders. I could feel her heart beating against my breastbone. All the duplicities of the past months had been shed, leaving behind this nervous young doctor.

'But how, Paula? That could be difficult. We'll have to warn Sanger. He and Laurie can leave for Marbella.'

'Sanger won't leave. He's already been driven out of Estrella de Mar. Even if he did go they'd simply pick someone else – Colonel Lindsay, Lejeune, even you, Charles. The important thing is to sacrifice someone and seal the tribe into itself. Charles, believe me – Bobby Crawford has to be stopped.'

'I know. Paula, I'll talk to him. When he sees that I know everything about the Hollingers he'll cancel the party.'

'He won't!' Exhausted, Paula turned to Andersson for support, but the Swede had moved away from us, staring at the parked cars. 'It isn't up to Crawford any more – Betty Shand and the rest of them have made their decision. He'll move on to other pueblos and other towns, bring them to life and then demand a sacrifice, and always there'll be people willing to carry it out. Listen to me, Charles – blood pays for your arts festivals and civic pride . . .'

I sat in the driver's seat of Frank's car, holding the steering wheel as Andersson raised a hand in a brief farewell salute and walked up the ramp into the late afternoon sunlight. Paula stood beside the Jaguar, watching me through the windshield as she waited for me to respond to her. But I was thinking of Frank and our childhood years together. I understood how he had fallen under Crawford's spell, accepting the irresistible logic that had revived the Club Nautico and the moribund town around it. Crime would always be rife, but Crawford had put vice and prostitution and drug-dealing to positive social ends. Estrella de Mar had rediscovered itself, but the escalator of provocation had carried him upwards to the Hollinger house and the engulfing flames.

Paula paced around the car, her confidence in me ebbing as the blood drained from her flushed cheeks. At last she gave up, dismissively throwing an arm across the gloomy air, aware that I would never rally myself to challenge Crawford. I stretched across the rear seat and took the Calabria travel guide from the window shelf, then turned to the dedication I had written to Frank on the flyleaf. Reading the warm words that I had penned three years earlier, I heard the engine of Paula's car turn beside me, its sound lost in the memories of boyhood days.

28

The Syndicates of Guilt

THE STEADY BEAT of the tennis machine rose from the court as I parked in the villa's drive, that monotonous thumping that had presided over Estrella de Mar and the Residencia Costasol since my arrival in Spain. I listened to the hiss and wheeze of the loading mechanism, followed by a faint creak as it adjusted its angle and trajectory. While driving from the Club Nautico I had thought of Crawford tirelessly returning the balls, preparing himself for his departure that evening and the tasks that lay ahead of him in Calahonda. With nothing but his battered Porsche and a collection of tennis rackets he would set off to arouse another stretch of the suncoast.

I switched off the Citroën's engine and gazed at the lines of gilt chairs and trestle tables on the terrace, trying to decide what I could safely say to Crawford. The preparations for the party would begin within an hour, when the canapés and drinks were delivered, and there would be little time for our first and last tennis match. I was sure that Crawford would let me win, part of that generosity of spirit that so charmed everyone who met him.

Before leaving the Club Nautico I had telephoned Inspector Cabrera, asking him to meet me at my villa. There I would tell him everything I had learned of the Hollinger deaths and of the arson attempt on Sanger's bungalow. Aware of my changed tone of voice, Cabrera had begun to question me, then accepted the seriousness of my call and promised to meet me as soon as he could drive from Fuengirola.

Replacing the receiver, I had looked around Frank's apartment for the last time. The silent rooms seemed airless, and all too aware that Frank would never return. They had decided to withdraw into the secret past of his evenings with Paula and his long conversations with an eager young tennis professional who had drifted down the coast and discovered, in the somnolent beach resort, an elixir that would wake the world.

I listened to the tennis machine, feeding itself from the hopper of balls. The boom of the firing mechanism was followed by each ball's impact as it crossed the net and struck the clay, but there was no sound of Crawford's return service, no rasp of his sliding feet and familiar grunting breath.

I stepped from the car and walked past the cooling Porsche. The swimming pool was smooth and undisturbed, the vacuum hose roving the surface, sucking away the leaves and insects. I followed the pathway around the house, past the garage and kitchen entrance. Through the wire screen that surrounded the tennis court I could see Crawford's towel and sports bag on the green metal table beside the net. The surface of the court was strewn with balls, each newcomer cannoning among them like the white on a crowded snooker table.

'Bobby . . . ?' I called out. 'There's just time for a quick set . . .'

The machine varied its trajectory, tilting upwards and to the right. The ball shot across the net, struck something on the baseline and ricocheted almost vertically into the air, soaring over the wire screen. I ran the few paces towards it, hand above my head, and caught the ball as it fell.

Blood spattered my arms and face. Holding the sticky ball

in my fingers, I stared at the tarry carmine. I wiped the clotting blood from my cheeks, my hands smearing the sleeves of my shirt.

'Crawford . . . ?'

I opened the wire door and stepped into the court as the tennis machine fired its last ball and fell silent. A final unreturned service, it struck the scuffed clay beside the body of a man in white shirt and shorts who lay across the baseline. Racket in hand, he rested face up in a lake of blood that leaked across the yellow clay.

Mouth gaping, as if he had died in a moment of unfeigned surprise, Bobby Crawford lay among the bloodied balls. His left hand was open, its fingers splayed fiercely at the sun, and I guessed that he had tried to catch the two bullets fired into his chest. The punctures stood out clearly in his cotton shirt, one beside his left nipple, the other below his collarbone.

A few feet from him was a small automatic pistol, its chromium barrel reflecting the cloudless sky. I dropped the stained ball in my hand, knelt down and picked up the pistol, then gazed at the murdered man. Crawford's lips were parted as they prepared to shape themselves into the first grimace of death. I could see his ice-white teeth, and the porcelain caps that he always claimed had been his most valuable investment before setting out on his career as a tennis professional. As his head struck the ground the cap of his left incisor had broken loose, and the steel peg shone in the sun, a small dagger like a concealed fang in the smile of this dangerous but likeable man.

Who had shot him? I held the pistol in my blood-soaked hand, carefully erasing the killer's fingerprints. The low-calibre weapon was a lady's handbag pistol, and I imagined Paula Hamilton carrying it inside her purse, her white hand clasping the cleated butt, letting herself into the court and walking through the service balls as Crawford waved to her. Assuming that I would never betray him, she had decided to kill

Crawford before the farewell party could embark on its lethal evening's programme.

Or had Sanger shot him, revenging himself for everything that Crawford had done to Laurie Fox? In my mind I could see the slim but determined psychiatrist striding through the stinging balls that Crawford served at him, impassive as a vicious ace struck his shoulder, the pistol held tightly in his hand, smiling for the first time when Crawford lowered his racket to plead with him . . .

Cars were pulling into the drive, led by Cabrera's Seat. The Inspector leaned from the window, as if already smelling the scent of blood on the air. Behind him Elizabeth Shand and Hennessy sat in the rear seat of the Mercedes, waiting while an uncertain Mahoud pulled the limousine on to the grass verge. None of them was dressed for the party, and had called at the villa to supervise the storage of the drinks and canapés. Two delivery vans were parked in the road, and men in white overalls unloaded trays of glasses and bales of tablecloths. Sanger stepped past them, head raised as he tried to see beyond Cabrera's car, one hand holding his silver hair. Whoever had shot Crawford – Paula Hamilton, Sanger or Andersson – had known that the tennis machine would disguise the pistol's sounds, and had slipped away less than a minute before my arrival.

Cabrera reached the wire door and stepped into the tennis court. He walked through the scattered balls and halted by the net, watching me with his pensive, seminar gaze. I knelt beside the body, the pistol in my hand, covered with Crawford's blood. Cabrera raised his hands to calm me, aware from my face and posture that I was ready to defend the dead man.

Did he already know, as he walked towards me, that I would take responsibility for the death? Crawford's mission would endure, and the festivals of the Residencia Costasol would continue to fill the sky with their petals and balloons, as the syndicates of guilt sustained their dream.

P.S.

Ideas,
interviews
& features ...

Snapshot: A Ballard short story

About the author

Read on

The Man Who Walked on the Moon
by J.G. Ballard

I, too, was once an astronaut. As you see me sitting here, in this modest café with its distant glimpse of Copacabana Beach, you probably assume that I am a man of few achievements. The shabby briefcase between my worn heels, the stained suit with its frayed cuffs, the unsavoury hands ready to seize the first offer of a free drink, the whole air of failure. . . no doubt you think that I am a minor clerk who has missed promotion once too often, and that I amount to nothing, a person of no past and less future.

For many years I believed this myself. I had been abandoned by the authorities, who were glad to see me exiled to another continent, reduced to begging from the American tourists. I suffered from acute amnesia, and certain domestic problems with my wife and my mother. They now share my small apartment at Ipanema, while I am forced to live in a room above the projection booth of the Luxor Cinema, my thoughts drowned by the sound-tracks of science-fiction films.

So many tragic events leave me unsure of myself. Nonetheless, my confidence is returning, and a sense of my true history and worth. Chapters of my life are still hidden from me, and seem as jumbled as the film extracts which the projectionists screen each morning as they focus their cameras. I have still forgotten my years of training, and my mind bars from me any memory of the actual space-flights. But I am certain that I was once an astronaut.

Years ago, before I went into space, I followed many professions – freelance journalist, translator, on one occasion even a war correspondent sent to a small war, which unfortunately was never declared. I was in and out of newspaper offices all day, hoping for that one assignment that would match my talents.

Sadly, all this effort failed to get me to the top, and after ten years I found myself displaced by a younger generation. A certain reticence in my character, a sharpness of manner, set me off from my fellow journalists. Even the editors would laugh at me behind my back. I was given trivial assignments – film reviewing, or writing reports on office-equipment fairs. When the circulation wars began, in a doomed response to the onward sweep of television, the editors openly took exception to my waspish style. I became a part-time translator, and taught for an hour each day at a language school, but my income plummeted. My mother, whom I had supported for many years, was forced to leave her home and join my wife and myself in our apartment at Ipanema.

At first my wife resented this, but soon she and my mother teamed up against me. They became impatient with the hours I spent delaying my unhappy visits to the single newspaper office that still held out hope – my journey to work was a transit between one door slammed on my heels and another slammed in my face.

My last friend at the newspaper commiserated with me, as I stood forlornly in the lobby. 'For heaven's sake, find a human interest story! Something tender and affecting, that's what they want upstairs – life isn't an avant-garde movie!'

Pondering this sensible advice, I wandered into the crowded streets. I dreaded the thought of returning home without an assignment. The two women had taken to opening the apartment door together. They would stare at me accusingly, almost barring me from my own home.

Around me were the million faces of the city. People strode past, so occupied with their own lives that they almost pushed me from the pavement. A million human interest stories, of a banal and pointless kind, an encyclopaedia of mediocrity . . . Giving up, I left Copacabana Avenue and took refuge among the tables of a small café in a side-street.

It was there that I met the American astronaut, and began my own career in space.

The café terrace was almost deserted, as the office workers returned to their desks after lunch. Behind me, in the shade of the canvas awning, a fair-haired man in a threadbare tropical suit sat beside an empty glass. Guarding my coffee from the flies, I gazed at the small segment of sea visible beyond Copacabana Beach. Slowed by their midday meals, groups of American and European tourists strolled down from the hotels, waving away the jewellery salesmen and lottery touts. Perhaps I would visit Paris or New York, make a new life for myself as a literary critic . . .

A tartan shirt blocked my view of the sea and its narrow dream of escape. An elderly American, camera slung from his heavy neck, leaned across the table, his grey-haired wife in a loose floral dress beside him.

3

The Man Who Walked on the Moon (*continued*)

'Are you the astronaut?' the woman asked in a friendly but sly way, as if about to broach an indiscretion. 'The hotel said you would be at this café . . .'

'An astronaut?'

'Yes, the astronaut Commander Scranton . . . ?'

'No, I regret that I'm not an astronaut.' Then it occurred to me that this provincial couple, probably a dentist and his wife from the corn-belt, might benefit from a well-informed courier. Perhaps they imagined that their cruise ship had berthed at Miami? I stood up, managing a gallant smile. 'Of course, I'm a qualified translator. If you –'

'No, no . . .' Dismissing me with a wave, they moved through the empty tables. 'We came to see Mr Scranton.'

Baffled by this bizarre exchange, I watched them approach the man in the tropical suit. A nondescript fellow in his late forties, he had thinning blond hair and a strong-jawed American face from which all confidence had long been drained. He stared in a resigned way at his hands, which waited beside his empty glass, as if unable to explain to them that little refreshment would reach them that day. He was clearly undernourished, perhaps an ex-seaman who had jumped ship, one of thousands of down-and-outs trying to live by their wits on some of the hardest pavements in the world.

However, he looked up sharply enough as the elderly couple approached him. When they repeated their question about the astronaut he beckoned them to a seat. To my surprise, the waiter was summoned, and drinks were brought to the table. The husband unpacked his camera, while a relaxed conversation took place between his wife and this seedy figure.

'Dear, don't forget Mr Scranton . . .'

'Oh, please forgive me.'

The husband removed several bank-notes from his wallet. His wife passed them across the table to Scranton, who then stood up. Photographs were taken, first of Scranton standing next to the smiling wife, then of the husband grinning broadly beside the gaunt American. The source of all this good humour eluded me, as it did Scranton, whose eyes stared gravely at the street with a degree of respect due to the surface of the moon. But already a second group of tourists had walked down from Copacabana Beach, and I heard more laughter when one called out:

'There's the astronaut . . . !'

Quite mystified, I watched a further round of photographs being taken. The couples stood on either side of the American, grinning away as if he were a camel driver posing for pennies against a backdrop of the pyramids.

I ordered a small brandy from the waiter. He had ignored all this, pocketing his tips with a straight face.

'This fellow . . . ?' I asked. 'Who is he? An astronaut?'

'Of course . . .' The waiter flicked a bottle-top into the air and treated the sky to a knowing sneer. 'Who else but the man in the moon?'

The tourists had gone, strolling past the leatherware and jewellery stores. Alone now after his brief fame, the American sat among the empty glasses, counting the money he had collected.

The man in the moon?

Then I remembered the newspaper headline, and the exposé I had read two years earlier of this impoverished American who claimed to have been an astronaut, and told his story to the tourists for the price of a drink. At first almost everyone believed him, and he had become a popular figure in the hotel lobbies along Copacabana Beach. Apparently he had flown on one of the Apollo missions from Cape Kennedy in the 1970s, and his long-jawed face and stoical pilot's eyes seemed vaguely familiar from the magazine photographs. He was properly reticent, but if pressed with a tourist dollar could talk convincingly about the early lunar flights. In its way it was deeply moving to sit at a café table with a man who had walked on the moon . . .

Then an over-curious reporter exploded the whole pretence. No man named Scranton had ever flown in space, and the American authorities confirmed that his photograph was not that of any past or present astronaut. In fact he was a failed crop-duster from Florida who had lost his pilot's licence and whose knowledge of the Apollo flights had been mugged up from newspapers and television programmes.

Surprisingly, Scranton's career had not ended there and then, but moved on to a second tragi-comical phase. Far from consigning him to oblivion, the exposure brought him a genuine small celebrity. Banished from the grand hotels of Copacabana, he hung about the cheaper cafés in the side-streets, still claiming to have been an astronaut, ignoring those who derided him from their car windows. The dignified way in which he maintained his fraud tapped a certain good-humoured tolerance, much like the affection felt in the United States for those eccentric old men who falsely claimed to their deaths that they were veterans of the American Civil War.

So Scranton stayed on, willing to talk for a few dollars about his journey to the moon, quoting the same tired phrases that failed to convince the youngest schoolboy. Soon no one bothered to question him closely, and his chief function was to be photographed beside parties of visitors, an amusing oddity of the tourist trail.

But perhaps the American was more devious than he appeared, with his shabby suit and hangdog gaze? As I sat there, guarding the brandy I could barely afford, I resented Scranton's bogus celebrity, and the tourist revenue it brought him. For years I, too, had maintained a charade – the mask of good humour that I presented to my colleagues in the newspaper world – but it had brought me nothing. Scranton at least was left alone for most of his time, something I craved more than any celebrity. Comparing our situations, there was plainly a strong element of injustice – the notorious British criminal who made a comfortable living being photographed by the tourists in the more expensive Copacabana restaurants had at least robbed one of Her Majesty's mail-trains.

At the same time, was this the human-interest story that would help me to remake my career? Could I provide a final ironic twist by revealing that, thanks to his exposure, the bogus astronaut was now doubly successful?

During the next days I visited the café promptly at noon. Notebook at the ready, I kept a careful watch for Scranton. He usually appeared in the early afternoon, as soon as the clerks and secretaries had finished their coffee. In that brief lull, when the shadows crossed from one side of the street to the other, Scranton would materialise, as if from a trapdoor in the pavement. He was always alone, walking straight-backed in his faded suit, but with the uncertainty of someone who suspects that he is keeping an appointment on the wrong day. He would slip into his place under the café awning, order a glass of beer from the sceptical waiter and then gaze across the street at the vistas of an invisible space.

It soon became clear that Scranton's celebrity was as threadbare as his shirt cuffs. Few tourists visited him, and often a whole afternoon passed without a single customer. Then the waiter would scrape the chairs around Scranton's table, trying to distract him from his reveries of an imaginary moon. Indeed, on the fourth day, within a few minutes of Scranton's arrival, the waiter slapped the table-top with his towel, already cancelling the afternoon's performance.

'Away, away . . . it's impossible!' He seized the newspaper that Scranton had found on a nearby chair. 'No more stories about the moon . . .'

Scranton stood up, head bowed beneath the awning. He seemed resigned to this abuse. 'All right . . . I can take my trade down the street.'

To forestall this, I left my seat and moved through the empty tables.

'Mr Scranton? Perhaps we can speak? I'd like to buy you a drink.'

'By all means.' Scranton beckoned me to a chair. Ready for business, he sat upright, and with a conscious effort managed to bring the focus of his gaze from infinity to a distance of fifty feet away. He was poorly nourished, and his perfunctory shave revealed an almost tubercular pallor. Yet there was a certain resolute quality about this vagrant figure that I had not expected. Sitting beside him, I was aware of an intense and almost wilful isolation, not just in this foreign city, but in the world at large.

I showed him my card. 'I'm writing a book of criticism on the science-fiction cinema. It would be interesting to hear your opinions. You are Commander Scranton, the Apollo astronaut?'

'That is correct.'

'Good. I wondered how you viewed the science-fiction film . . . how convincing you found the presentation of outer space, the lunar surface and so on . . .'

Scranton stared bleakly at the table-top. A faint smile exposed his yellowing teeth, and I assumed that he had seen through my little ruse.

'I'll be happy to set you straight,' he told me. 'But I make a small charge.'

'Of course.' I searched in my pockets. 'Your professional expertise, naturally . . .'

I placed some coins on the table, intending to hunt for a modest bank-note. Scranton selected three of the coins, enough to pay for a loaf of bread, and pushed the rest towards me.

'Science-fiction films –? They're good. Very accurate. On the whole I'd say they do an excellent job.'

'That's encouraging to hear. These Hollywood epics are not usually noted for their realism.'

The Man Who Walked on the Moon (*continued*)

'Well . . . you have to understand that the Apollo teams brought back a lot of film footage.'

'I'm sure.' I tried to keep the amusement out of my voice. 'The studios must have been grateful to you. After all, you could describe the actual moon-walks.'

Scranton nodded sagely. 'I acted as consultant to one of the Hollywood majors. All in all, you can take it from me that those pictures are pretty realistic.'

'Fascinating . . . coming from you that has authority. As a matter of interest, what was being on the moon literally like?'

For the first time Scranton seemed to notice me. Had he glimpsed some shared strain in our characters? This care-worn American had all the refinement of an unemployed car mechanic, and yet he seemed almost tempted to befriend me.

'Being on the moon?' His tired gaze inspected the narrow street of cheap jewellery stores, with its office messengers and lottery touts, the off-duty taxi-drivers leaning against their cars. 'It was just like being here.'

'So . . .' I put away my notebook. Any further subterfuge was unnecessary. I had treated our meeting as a joke, but Scranton was sincere, and anyway utterly indifferent to my opinion of him. The tourists and passing policemen, the middle-aged women sitting at a nearby table, together barely existed for him. They were no more than shadows on the screen of his mind, through which he could see the horizons of an almost planetary emptiness.

For the first time I was in the presence of someone who had nothing – even less than the beggars of Rio, for they at least were linked to the material world by their longings for it. Scranton embodied the absolute loneliness of the human being in space and time, a situation which in many ways I shared. Even the act of convincing himself that he was a former astronaut only emphasised his isolation.

'A remarkable story,' I commented. 'One can't help wondering if we were right to leave this planet. I'm reminded of the question posed by the Chilean painter Matta – "Why must we fear a disaster in space in order to understand our own times?" It's a pity you didn't bring back any mementoes of your moon-walks.'

Scranton's shoulders straightened. I could see him counting the coins on the table. 'I do have certain materials . . .'

I nearly laughed. 'What? A piece of lunar rock? Some moon dust?'

'Various photographic materials.'

'Photographs?' Was it possible that Scranton had told the truth, and that he had indeed been an astronaut? If I could prove that the whole notion of his imposture was an error, an oversight by the journalist who had investigated the case, I would have the makings of a front-page scoop . . . 'Could I see them? – perhaps I could use them in my book . . .?'

'Well. . .' Scranton felt for the coins in his pocket. He looked hungry, and obviously thought only of spending them on a loaf of bread.

'Of course,' I added, 'I'll provide an extra fee. As for my book, the publishers might well pay many hundreds of dollars.'

'Hundreds . . .' Scranton seemed impressed. He shook his head, as if amused by the ways of the world. I expected him to be shy of revealing where he lived, but he stood up and gestured me to finish my drink. 'I'm staying a few minutes' walk from here.'

He waited among the tables, staring across the street. Seeing the passers-by through his eyes, I was aware that they had begun to seem almost transparent, shadow players created by a frolic of the sun.

We soon arrived at Scranton's modest room behind the Luxor Cinema, a small theatre off Copacabana Avenue that had seen better days. Two former storerooms and an office above the projection booth had been let as apartments, which we reached after climbing a dank emergency stairway.

Exhausted by the effort, Scranton swayed against the door. He wiped the spit from his mouth onto the lapel of his jacket, and ushered me into the room. 'Make yourself comfortable . . .'

A dusty light fell across the narrow bed, reflected in the cold-water tap of a greasy handbasin supported from the wall by its waste-pipe. Sheets of newspaper were wrapped around a pillow, stained with sweat and some unsavoury mucus, perhaps after an attack of malarial or tubercular fever.

Eager to leave this infectious den, I drew out my wallet. 'The photographs . . .?'

Scranton sat on the bed, staring at the yellowing wall behind me as if he had forgotten that I was there. Once again I was aware of his ability to isolate himself from the surrounding world, a talent I envied him, if little else.

'Sure . . . they're over here.' He stood up and went to the suitcase that lay on a card table behind the door. Taking the money from me, he opened the lid and lifted out a bundle of magazines. Among them were loose pages torn from *Life* and *Newsweek*, and special supplements of the Rio newspapers devoted to the Apollo space-flights and the moon landings. The familiar images of Armstrong and the lunar module, the space-walks and splashdowns had been endlessly thumbed. The captions were marked with coloured pencil, as if Scranton had spent hours memorising these photographs brought back from the tideways of space.

I moved the magazines to one side, hoping to find some documentary evidence of Scranton's own involvement in the space-flights, perhaps a close-up photograph taken by a fellow astronaut.

'Is this it? There's nothing else?'

'That's it.' Scranton gestured encouragingly. 'They're good pictures. Pretty well what it was like.'

'I suppose that's true. I had hoped . . .'

I peered at Scranton, expecting some small show of embarrassment. These faded pages, far from being the mementoes of a real astronaut, were obviously the prompt cards of an impostor. However, there was not the slightest doubt that Scranton was sincere.

I stood in the street below the portico of the Luxor Cinema, whose garish posters, advertising some science-fiction spectacular, seemed as inflamed as the mind of the American. Despite all that I had suspected, I felt an intense disappointment. I had deluded myself, thinking that Scranton would rescue my career. Now I was left with nothing but an empty notebook and the tram journey back to the crowded apartment in Ipanema. I dreaded the prospect of seeing my wife and my mother at the door, their eyes screwed to the same accusing focus.

Nonetheless, as I walked down Copacabana Avenue to the tram-stop, I felt a curious sense of release. The noisy pavements, the arrogant pickpockets plucking at my clothes, the traffic that aggravated the slightest tendency to migraines, all seemed to have receded, as if a small distance had opened between myself and the congested world. My meeting with Scranton, my brief involvement with this marooned man, allowed me to see everything in a more detached way. The businessmen with their briefcases, the afternoon tarts swinging their shiny handbags, the salesmen with their sheets of lottery tickets, almost deferred to me. Time and space had altered their perspectives, and the city was yielding to me. As I crossed the road to the tram-stop several minutes seemed to pass. But I was not run over.

This sense of a loosening air persisted as I rode back to Ipanema. My fellow passengers, who would usually have irritated me with their cheap scent and vulgar clothes, their look of bored animals in a menagerie, now scarcely intruded into my vision. I gazed down corridors of light that ran between them like the aisles of an open-air cathedral.

'You've found a story,' my wife announced within a second of opening the door.

'They've commissioned an article,' my mother confirmed. 'I knew they would.'

They stepped back and watched me as I made a leisurely tour of the cramped apartment. My changed demeanour clearly impressed them. They pestered me with questions, but even their presence was less bothersome. The universe, thanks to Scranton's example, had loosened its grip. Sitting at the dinner table, I silenced them with a raised finger.

'I am about to embark on a new career . . .'

From then on I became ever more involved with Scranton. I had not intended to see the American again, but the germ of his loneliness had entered my blood. Within two days I returned to the café in the side-street, but the tables were deserted. I watched as two parties of tourists stopped to ask for 'the astronaut'. I then questioned the waiter, suspecting that he had banished the poor man. But, no, the American would be back the next day, he had been ill, or perhaps had secretly gone to the moon on business.

In fact, it was three days before Scranton at last appeared. Materialising from the afternoon heat, he entered the café and sat under the awning. At first he failed to notice that I was there, but Scranton's mere presence was enough to satisfy me. The crowds and traffic, which had begun once again to close around me, halted their clamour and withdrew. On the noisy street were imposed the silences of a lunar landscape.

However, it was all too clear that Scranton had been ill. His face was sallow with fever, and the effort of sitting in his chair soon tired him. When the first American tourists stopped at his table he barely rose from his seat, and while the photographs were taken he held tightly to the awning above his head.

By the next afternoon his fever had subsided, but he was so strained and ill-kempt that the waiter at first refused to admit him to the café. A trio of Californian spinsters who approached his table were clearly unsure that this decaying figure was indeed the bogus astronaut, and would have left had I not ushered them back to Scranton.

'Yes, this is Commander Scranton, the famous astronaut. I am his associate – do let me hold your camera . . .'

I waited impatiently for them to leave, and sat down at Scranton's table. Ill the American might be, but I needed him. After ordering a brandy, I helped Scranton to hold the glass. As I pressed the spinsters' bank-note into his pocket I could feel that his suit was soaked with sweat.

'I'll walk you back to your room. Don't thank me, it's in my direction.'

'Well, I could use an arm.' Scranton stared at the street, as if its few yards encompassed a Grand Canyon of space. 'It's getting to be a long way.'

'A long way! Scranton, I understand that . . .'

It took us half an hour to cover the few hundred yards to the Luxor Cinema. But already time was becoming an elastic dimension, and from then on most of my waking hours were spent with Scranton. Each morning I would visit the shabby room behind the cinema, bringing a paper bag of sweet-cakes and a flask of tea I had prepared in the apartment under my wife's suspicious gaze. Often the American had little idea who I was, but this no longer worried me. He lay in his narrow bed, letting me raise his head as I changed the sheets of newspaper that covered his pillow. When he spoke, his voice was too weak to be heard above the sound-tracks of the science-fiction films that boomed through the crumbling walls.

Even in this moribund state, Scranton's example was a powerful tonic, and when I left him in the evening I would walk the crowded streets without any fear. Sometimes my former colleagues called to me from the steps of the newspaper office, but I was barely aware of them, as if they were planetary visitors hailing me from the edge of a remote crater.

Looking back on these exhilarating days, I regret only that I never called a doctor to see Scranton. Frequently, though, the American would recover his strength, and after I had shaved him we would go down into the street. I relished these outings with Scranton. Arm in arm, we moved through the afternoon crowds, which seemed to part around us. Our fellow pedestrians had become remote and fleeting figures, little more than tricks of the sun. Sometimes, I could no longer see their faces. It was then that I observed the world through Scranton's eyes, and knew what it was to be an astronaut.

Needless to say, the rest of my life had collapsed at my feet. Having given up my work as a translator, I soon ran out of money, and was forced to borrow from my mother. At my wife's instigation, the features editor of the newspaper called me to his office, and made it plain that as an immense concession (in fact he had always been intrigued by my wife) he would let me review a science-fiction film at the Luxor. Before walking out, I told him that I was already too familiar with the film, and my one hope was to see it banned from the city forever.

So ended my connection with the newspaper. Soon after, the two women evicted me from my apartment. I was happy to leave them, taking with me only the reclining sun-chair on which my wife passed most of her days in preparation for her new career as a model. The sun-chair became my bed when I moved into Scranton's room.

By then the decline in Scranton's health forced me to be with him constantly. Far from being an object of charity, Scranton was now my only source of income. Our needs for several days could be met by a single session with the American tourists. I did my best to care for Scranton, but during his final illness I was too immersed in that sense of an emptying world even to notice the young doctor whose alarmed presence filled the tiny room. By a last irony, towards the end even Scranton himself seemed barely visible to me. As he died I was reading the mucus-stained headlines on his pillow.

After Scranton's death I remained in his room at the Luxor. Despite the fame he had once enjoyed, his burial at the Protestant cemetery was attended only by myself, but in a sense this was just, as he and I were the only real inhabitants of the city. Later I went through the few possessions in his suitcase, and found a faded pilot's log-book. Its pages confirmed that Scranton had worked as a pilot for a crop-spraying company in Florida throughout the years of the Apollo programme.

Nonetheless, Scranton had travelled in space. He had known the loneliness of separation from all other human beings, he had gazed at the

13

The Man Who Walked on the Moon *(continued)*

empty perspectives that I myself had seen. Curiously, the pages torn from the news magazines seemed more real than the pilot's log-book. The photographs of Armstrong and his fellow astronauts were really of Scranton and myself as we walked together on the moon of this world.

I reflected on this as I sat at the small café in the side-street. As a gesture to Scranton's memory, I had chosen his chair below the awning. I thought of the planetary landscapes that Scranton had taught me to see, those empty vistas devoid of human beings. Already I was aware of a previous career, which my wife and the pressures of everyday life had hidden from me. There were the years of training for a great voyage, and a coastline similar to that of Cape Kennedy receding below me . . .

My reverie was interrupted by a pair of American tourists. A middle-aged man and his daughter, who held the family camera to her chin, approached the table.

'Excuse me,' the man asked with an over-ready smile. 'Are you the . . . the astronaut? We were told by the hotel that you might be here . . .'

I stared at them without rancour, treating them to a glimpse of those eyes that had seen the void. I, too, had walked on the moon.

'Please sit down,' I told them casually. 'Yes, I am the astronaut.'

1985 ∎

An Investigative Spirit

Travis Elborough talks to J.G. Ballard

IN SEVERAL OF **your novels you have used a small community, the residents of a luxury housing development or a high-rise block for example, as a microcosm with which to explore the fragility of civil society. Do you think that your preoccupation with social regression, de-evolution even, stems from your childhood experiences in the internment camp when you saw, first hand, how easily the veneer of civilization could slip away?**

Yes, I think it does; although anyone who has experienced a war first hand knows that it completely overturns every conventional idea of what makes up day-to-day reality. You never feel quite the same again. It's like walking away from a plane crash; the world changes for you forever. The experience of spending nearly three years in a camp, especially as an early teenage boy, taking a keen interest in the behaviour of adults around him, including his own parents, and seeing them stripped of all the garments of authority that protect adults generally in their dealings with children, to see them stripped of any kind of defence, often losing heart a bit, being humiliated and frightened – and we all felt the war was going to go on forever and heaven knows what might happen in the final stages – all of that was a remarkable education. It was unique, and it gave me a tremendous insight into what makes up human behaviour.

You've written that the landscape of even your first novel, *The Drowned World*, a ▶

> 6 Anyone who has experienced a war first hand knows that it completely overturns every conventional idea of what makes up day-to-day reality. It's like walking away from a plane crash. 9

15

LIFE
at a Glance

BORN
Shanghai, China, 1930

EDUCATED
Cathedral School,
Shanghai

The Leys School,
Cambridge

King's College,
Cambridge

FAMILY
Married Helen Mathews,
1956. One son, two
daughters

An Investigative Spirit *(continued)*

◄ futuristic portrait of a flooded twenty-first-century London, was clearly informed by your memories of Shanghai. I wondered if you could say a little about how, after having possibly explored it obliquely in your works of science fiction, you came to write so directly about your childhood experiences in *Empire of the Sun*?

I had always planned to write about my experiences of the Second World War, Shanghai under the Japanese and the camp. I knew that it was such an important event, and not just for me. But when I came to England in 1946 I had to face the huge problem of adjusting to life here. England in those days was a very, very strange place. There was an elaborate class system that I'd never come across in Shanghai. England . . . it was a terribly shabby place, you know, locked into the past and absolutely exhausted by the war. It was only on a technicality that we could be said to have won the war; in many ways we'd lost it. Financially we were desperate. I had to cope with all this. By 1949 the Communists had taken over China and I knew I would never go back. So there seemed no point in keeping those memories alive, I felt I had to come to terms with life in England. This is, after all, where I was educated. I got married and began my career as a writer.

England interested me. It seemed to be a sort of disaster area. It was a subject and a disaster in its own right. I was interested in change, which I could see was coming in a big way, everything from supermarkets to jet travel, television and the consumer society.

I remember thinking, my God, these things will bring change to England and reveal the strange psychology of these tormented people.

So I began writing science fiction, although most readers of science fiction did not consider me to be a science fiction writer. They saw me as an interloper, a sort of virus that had got into the cell of science fiction, entered its nucleus and destroyed it. But all this while I could see bits of my China past floating up and I knew I was going to write it up at some point.

You studied medicine and have stated that you believe that the contemporary novelist should be like a scientist. Do you ever regret not qualifying as a doctor?
I was very interested in medicine. The experience of dissecting cadavers for two years was a very important one for me, for all sorts of reasons. I do think that novelists should be like scientists, dissecting the cadaver . . . I would like to have become a doctor, but the urge to write was too great. I knew from friends of mine who were a year or two ahead of me that once you actually joined a London hospital or became a junior doctor the pressures of work were too great. I'd never have any time to write, and the urge to write was just too strong.

Do you think there is a moral purpose to your fiction?
I am not sure about that. I see myself more as a kind of investigator, a scout who is ▶

TOP TEN
BOOKS

Moby-Dick
Herman Melville

The Loved One
Evelyn Waugh

The Big Sleep
Raymond Chandler

Alice's Adventures in Wonderland
Lewis Carroll

The Trial
Franz Kafka

The Tempest
William Shakespeare

Catch-22
Joseph Heller

Our Man in Havana
Graham Greene

1984
George Orwell

Brave New World
Aldous Huxley

◄ sent on ahead to see if the water is drinkable or not.

As a scout or investigator you've been uncannily prescient, famously predicting Reagan's presidency in *The Atrocity Exhibition*, and I noticed that one commentator made reference to *The Drowned World* in the aftermath of the New Orleans disaster. Have you ever worried that you might be *too* prescient? An investigator and a sort of early warning system, let's put it like that. I suppose one of the things I took from my wartime experiences was that reality was a stage set. The reality that you took for granted – the comfortable day-to-day life, school, the home where one lives, the familiar street and all the rest of it, the trips to the swimming pool and the cinema – was just a stage set. They could be dismantled overnight, which they literally were when the Japanese occupied Shanghai and turned our lives upside down. I think that experience left me with a very sceptical eye, which I've turned onto something even as settled as English suburbia where I now live. Nothing is as secure as we like to think it is. One doesn't just have to think of Hurricane Katrina and New Orleans – this applies to everything. A large part of my fiction tries to analyse what is going on around us, and whether we are much different people from the civilized human beings we imagine ourselves to be. I think it's true of all my fiction. I think that investigative spirit forms all my novels really. ■

A Writing Life

When do you write?
Morning and early afternoon.

Where do you write?
In my sitting room.

Why do you write?
The great mystery.

Pen or computer?
Pen, then type myself.

Silence or music?
Silence.

How do you start a book?
I usually write a detailed synopsis.

And finish?
With a large full stop.

**Do you have any writing rituals or
superstitions?**
No.

Have You Read?
A selection of J.G. Ballard's other books

The Complete Short Stories, Volumes I and II
For over four decades, J.G. Ballard has been
one of Britain's most celebrated novelists, but
from the beginning he has been equally
admired for his distinctive and highly
influential short stories, the first of which –
'Prima Belladonna' and 'Escapement' –
appeared in print in 1956. Arranged in order
of publication and presented in two volumes,
The Complete Short Stories provides an
unprecedented opportunity to review the
career of one of Britain's greatest writers.

....

The Atrocity Exhibition
The irrational, all-pervading violence of the
modern world is the subject of this
extraordinary tour de force. The central
character's dreams are haunted by images of
John F. Kennedy and Marilyn Monroe, dead
astronauts and car-crash victims as he traverses
the screaming wastes of nervous breakdown.
Seeking his sanity, he casts himself in a number
of roles: H-bomber pilot, presidential assassin,
crash victim, psychopath. Finally, through the
black, perverse magic of violence he transcends
his psychic turmoil to find the key to a bizarre
new sexuality.

....

High-Rise
Within the walls of an elegant forty-storey
tower block, the affluent tenants are hell-bent
on an orgy of destruction. Cocktail parties
degenerate into marauding attacks on 'enemy'
floors and the once-luxurious amenities

become an arena for technological mayhem. In this classic visionary tale, human society slips into violent reverse as the inhabitants of the high-rise, driven by primal urges, recreate a world ruled by the laws of the jungle.

The Day of Creation

In parched Port-la-Nouvelle in central Africa Dr Mallory watches his clinic fail as constant warfare between a ragged band of guerrillas and the local chief of police causes the tribal residents to flee. In this drought-plagued and poverty-ridden country he dreams of discovering a third Nile to make the Sahara bloom. During his search an ancient tree stump is accidentally uprooted and water wells up, spreading until it becomes an enormous river. Naming it after himself, Mallory becomes obsessed with his creation, but almost as soon as he has discovered it he resolves to destroy it. With the once arid land now abounding in birds and beasts, he forges upriver in an old car ferry, clashing with hostile factions in a dangerous quest to find the source of his own creation.

Super-Cannes

Paul Sinclair and his bright young wife Jane drive down to the south of France in his vintage Jaguar so that she can take up a post as doctor to the new community of Eden-Olympia, just above Cannes. According to its resident psychologist, Wilder Penrose, the community is 'a huge experiment in how to ▶

Have You Read? *(continued)*

◄ hothouse the future . . . an ideas laboratory for the new millennium'. But Paul finds what he sees mystifying and unsettling, and when he learns that he and his wife have been housed in a villa whose previous occupant had been driven to massacre notable executives on a horrific shooting spree, he begins to look under the surface. For all the dawn-to-dusk hard work, for all its productivity and profits, Eden-Olympia is the venue for games of the most serious sort. So Paul joins in . . .

Millennium People

When a bomb goes off at Heathrow it looks like just another random act of violence to psychologist David Markham. But then he discovers that his ex-wife Laura is among the victims. Acting on police suspicions, he starts to investigate London's fringe protest movements, falling in with a shadowy group based in the comfortable Thameside estate of Chelsea Marina. Led by a charismatic doctor, the group aims to rouse the docile middle classes to anger and violence, to free them from both the self-imposed burdens of civic responsibility and the trappings of a consumer society. Soon Markham is swept up in a campaign that spirals rapidly out of control. Every certainty in his life is questioned as the cornerstones of middle England become targets and growing panic grips the capital.

Kingdom Come

When the father of Richard Pearson, unemployed advertising executive and life-long rebel, is fatally wounded as a deranged mental patient opens fire on a crowd of shoppers at the Metro-Centre, Richard suspects that there is more to his father's death than meets the eye – especially when the main suspect is released without charge thanks to the dubious testimony of self-styled pillars of the community, including Julia Goodwin, the doctor who treated his father on his deathbed. Determined to unravel the mystery, Richard soon realises that the Metro-Centre, with its round-the-clock cable channel and sports clubs, lies at the very heart of his father's death. Consumerism rules the lives of everyone in the motorway towns and feeds the cravings of this bored community with its desperate need for something new, whatever the cost . . . ∎

If You Loved This,
You Might Like . . .

Lord of the Flies
William Golding

Dead Babies
Martin Amis

The Maze of Death
Philip K. Dick

The Book of Dave
Will Self

Fahrenheit 451
Ray Bradbury

Find Out More

SURF:

www.jgballard.com
A comprehensive website of all things Ballard, including links to interviews, reviews and much more.

www.ballardian.com
Alongside current and archival news about J. G. Ballard, this site hosts a forum for discussion of the author's work.

J. G. BALLARD

The Drowned World

'Britain's number one living novelist'

JOHN SUTHERLAND, Sunday Times

Fluctuations in solar radiation have caused the icecaps to melt and the seas to rise. Nature is on the rampage. London has been transformed into a primeval swamp, and within its submerged landscape giant lizards, dragonflies and insects compete for dominance. Human fertility is in decline and buildings sink beneath waters infested with decaying matter. Into this wasteland a group of intrepid scientists venture to record the flora and fauna of this new Triassic Age. Soon ghostly voices haunt their waking and nightmares permeate their sleep . . .

'One of the brightest stars in post-war fiction. This tale of strange and terrible adventure in a world of steaming jungles has an oppressive power reminiscent of Conrad'   KINGSLEY AMIS

'Powerful and beautifully clear . . . Ballard's potent symbols of beauty and dismay inundate the reader's mind'   BRIAN ALDISS

ISBN: 0-00-722183-5

J. G. BALLARD

Rushing to Paradise

'Pure Ballard. I read it with rapt fascination . . . wonderful'

WILLIAM BOYD

Veteran campaigner Dr Barbara Rafferty's obsessive crusade to save the albatross on the Pacific atoll of Saint-Esprit gains international support when millions of TV viewers witness the shooting of her young acolyte Neil Dempsey. Soon Dr Barbara turns the deserted island into a sanctuary – a remote paradise home for Neil, an odd team of eco-enthusiasts and a growing collection of the world's endangered species. As the extraordinary story unfolds it soon becomes clear that some species are more in danger than others . . .

'Ballard is a magician of the contemporary scene and a literary saboteur. *Rushing to Paradise* is a Wellsian drama of extremity and isolation . . . a parable about the ratlike behaviour of marooned human beings. No one else writes with such enchanted clarity or strange power'   *Guardian*

'A subversive version of *Lord of the Flies* . . . Ballard's relentless intelligence and wildly irreverent, absurdist humour collaborate in creating comically satiric sequences. A body blow to the pretensions of our century'   *Irish Times*

'A satisfyingly bizarre mixture of fantasy and fact . . . a dystopian vision of a paradise island overrun by a band of environmentalists'   *Sunday Times*

'*Robinson Crusoe* in reverse. Teasing and sardonic . . . Ballard at his best'   *Independent on Sunday*

ISBN: 0-00-654814-8

J. G. BALLARD

The Drought

'The world's mutated panoramas are densely realised and portrayed with livid beauty, full of wonder and anxiety...All we know for certain is that the novels Ballard will write could not be written, could not even be guessed at, by anyone else'

MARTIN AMIS, *Observer*

Water, man's most precious commodity, is a luxury of the past. Radioactive waste from years of industrial dumping has caused the sea to form a protective skin strong enough to devastate the Earth it once sustained. And while the remorseless sun beats down on the dying land, civilisation itself begins to crack. Violence erupts and insanity reigns as the remnants of mankind struggle for survival in a worldwide desert of despair...Remarkable for its prescience and the originality of its vision, *The Drought* is a work of major importance from the writer widely acclaimed as Britain's No 1 living novelist.

'At a time when we live with constant warnings of a world destroyed by global warming, it is easy to forget that writers such as Ballard were exploring the fear of global blight nearly forty years ago'

The Times

'Weird, grotesque, magnificently gothic' *Sunday Times*

'Full of haunting landscapes, phantasmagoria and disaster that clangs on the mind. An impressive novel at any level. Its surrealist flourishes only heighten the dreamlike atmosphere' *Guardian*

ISBN: 0-586-08996-9

J. G. BALLARD

The Crystal World

'Something magical and not to be missed'   *Guardian*

Through a 'leaking' of time, the west African jungle starts to crystallize. Trees metamorphose into enormous jewels. Crocodiles encased in second glittering skins lurch down the river. Pythons with huge blind gemstone eyes rear in heraldic poses. Most people flee the area in terror, afraid to face what they cannot understand. But some, dazzled and strangely entranced, remain to drift through this dreamworld forest: a doctor in pursuit of his ex-mistress, an enigmatic Jesuit wielding a crystal cross and a tribe of lepers searching for Paradise . . . In this tour de force of the imagination, the acclaimed author of *Crash*, *Empire of the Sun* and *Cocaine Nights* transports the reader into one of his most unforgettable landscapes.

'Beautifully rendered . . . Ballard the poet in full ecstatic blast'
ANTHONY BURGESS

'Brilliantly imagined . . . as a human adventure in a suddenly alien and frightening environment, the book is convincing and powerful'
New Statesman

'A haunting vision of diseased beauty . . . Ballard sustains it with extraordinary intensity'   *Observer*

'Ballard transports us once more into his own mystical, glittering and poetic universe'   *Sunday Telegraph*

ISBN: 0-586-02419-0